The Chosen One's Assistant

By: Kimber Grey

GrayWhisper Graphics Productions
http://www.KimberGrey.com

This is a work of fiction. Names, characters, places and incidents either are the product of the author's imagination or are used fictionally, and any resemblance to actual persons, living or dead, business establishments, events, or locales is entirely coincidental.

"The Chosen One's Assistant"

All rights reserved
Copyright © 2023 Kimber Grey
This book may not be reproduced in whole or in part in any form without permission.

ISBN: **9798851108464**
EAN-13: **978- 9798851108464**

Dedication

For: Mikey*. You know who you are.
(And you know what you did)

*see: *About the Bard*

Also by Kimber Grey

Defying Chaos Books

Rise of Faiden (Series)
1. Kingdoms Lost
2. Fallen Heroes
3. History Forgotten
4. The Gathering
5. Hope and Sacrifice*
6. The High Kingdom*
6.5. Visions Shared*

Time's Up (Novella)

Deathbringer's Apprentice (Novella)

Other Books

Seeking Destiny

Blood in the Sand (Novella)

Singular Irregularity (Anthology)

A Whisper of Grey (Anthology)

*Coming Soon

Campaign Chapters

1. It Was the Best of Days, It Was the Worst of Days
2. Call Me Tiberius
3. There Was a Man Called The Chosen One, and He Almost Deserved It
4. The Stranger Came Early in the Morning, One Drunken Night
5. It Was a Dark and Stormy Night
6. It Was the Shadow of the Waxing Sun
7. Far Out in the Uncharted Backwaters of the Gorod River
8. In My Newer and More Vulnerable Days, The Chosen One Gave Me Some Advice
9. In the Town They Tell the Story of the Great Sickness
10. The Sun Shone, Having No Alternative, on The Chosen One
11. It Is Truth Universally Acknowledged, That a Single Man in Possession of Good Fortune, Must Be in Want of a Slave
12. All Children, Except One, Grow Up
13. I Have Never Begun a Day with More Misgiving
14. The Cold Passed Reluctantly from the Earth, and the Retiring Fogs Revealed a Frightened Town
15. He Was a Portly Man Who Stood Alone on a Well in Vevesk
16. They Say When Trouble Comes Close Ranks, and So the Villagers Did
17. The Towers of Skalah Aspired Above the Morning Mist
18. Somewhere in Opolchia, in a Place Whose Name I Don't Care to Remember
19. In a Hole in the Ground There Lived a Monster
20. This Is the Saddest Prayer I Have Ever Heard

A Note from the Author

Rise of Faiden

About the Author

About the Bard

1. It Was the Best of Days, It Was the Worst of Days

His was the face known everywhere—The Knight of All Kingdoms, The Immortal Hero of Men, The Bearer of Gods' Blessings... *The Chosen One*. The first time I saw him, it was the worst day of my life, and perhaps not coincidentally, the day I became his assistant.

I had spent the preceding week traveling from one trades-house to another, futilely attempting to acquire gainful employment as a scribe, translator, or even a wizard's assistant. I'd been laboring as a scribe for years in Noblan, from where the Gorod River sprung in south-west Opolchia. My now-former employer had acquired a scribe who was slightly more fluent in two languages, but more importantly, belonged to the Wizards' Guild as a gray-sash. My own status in the same guild had ended a few years back when the master wizard I served accidentally turned himself into a sparrow and flew away. The blame fell to the lowly, ungifted white-sash who had prepared some of the components for the transmigration spell. Me.

It was a series of regrettable circumstances, much like those I just described, that found me homeless, guildless, unbathed, unshorn, and on Market Street selling the last of my spare clothing to afford supper after two days of fasting—or as some prefer to call it, starving. I tucked the procured copper coins and silver pennies into a coin pouch in my girdle bag and slipped a now-empty shoulder bag over my arm. As soon as I had stretched one copper to purchase a misshapen loaf of bread, I found a quiet place just off of the main way to devoir the entire parcel. I was both reveling in and regretting my overfull belly, when a shadow blotted out the warm sun.

Journeyman Allen Writ and two brutes from the Scriveners' Guild towered ominously over me. A quick glance around for help offered little hope as the few nearby townsfolk openly watched, eager for the violence that was about to ensue. Too late to hide my alarm, I vainly attempted to flash them a friendly smile.

"Allen, and um, well... Allen," I fumbled, unable to put names to the goons. "Good to see you. Did the guild reconsider my application—"

"You know why we're here," the lanky, middle-aged journeyman grumbled. "Let's just get this over with." He jerked his head toward the man to his left. "Get him."

"I—hey!" Before I could maneuver myself into a better position from which to flee, the brutes surged forward and grappled my arms behind my back. "Wait! Stop!" I heard snickering from an onlooker and glared at the old woman. "Enjoying the show?" I snapped at her, but my anger melted into gut-churning fear when I realized they were dragging me toward a dark alcove between two buildings. "By Anetrael! Don't do this! We've corresponded! We—"

"Don't shame yourself, Anetrael is watching," Allen cut in, his expression grim in spite of the leering grins on the brutes' faces. "You've been hawking scribe trade all around town for weeks and trying to undercut guild prices."

"Hey, no one took me up—"

"Doesn't matter," he growled. "You know the price of crossing a guild."

As the shadow of the buildings engulfed me, I frantically sawed back and forth against my abductors. "Let me go!"

Allen pressed a hand against my sternum, and the three men slammed my back against the wall, further wrenching my arms as the air rushed from my lungs. "This'll be over quick," Allen promised, a hint of empathy in his voice. "You've got beautiful penmanship, and I've always kind of liked you... so we're not going to break your hand. *This* time."

A fist exploded across my jaw from the brute on my left, followed by another blow from the brute on my right. I reeled to the ground, and many boots pummeled by ribs and stomach until I vomited out my hard-purchased supper. As I lay gasping and blinking back tears of pain and embarrassment, all three men opened their trousers and urinated on me. As promised, it was over in a handful of horrible moments, and Allen and the brutes left me sobbing on the ground.

Several townsfolk were jeering and excitedly recounting the display as I rolled away from the worst of the mess in the dirt and collapsed quietly in the darkest shade of the alcove. No one helped or bothered me in the hours I lay there drifting in and out of consciousness.

The shifting sun baking into the skin of my boots roused me, and I awoke with a groan of disgust and misery. I tried to roll away from the stink searing my nostrils, but the smell only grew more powerful with movement, and I realized the reek was coming from me. The onlookers had dispersed some time before, so the occasional glances I earned as I struggled painfully to my feet were ones of curiosity rather than malicious amusement.

Holding my aching ribs and angry, empty-again stomach, I shuffled toward the more civilized side of town. My feet carried me to a familiar tavern, The Hare and the Cat. I hesitated in the open door by the shrine to Jaya, goddess of sleep and jesters, until Goldie saw me from behind the bar. She was a tough, fair, older woman who had inherited the inn from her third husband. She slid an ale across the counter to one of her regulars and peered at me under the flat of her hand, a frown hardening her features. "No beggars," she shooed. "Come back at first light for scraps."

"I'm not a beggar, Goldie," I mumbled through swollen lips.

She gasped and jerked the skirt of her blue gown around to hasten her movement to the door. "Gods! Who did this to you? Were you robbed?" She seized my chin, and not gently, turned my face right then left.

"No." I winced. "Allen and some guild brutes."

She tsk-tsk me and shook her head. "You got off easy. Allen is a good fellow."

"Doesn't seem like it at the moment," I lamented. "Goldie, if you don't mind, I'd like to have a bowl of pottage. I'll eat it out here on the stoop. I know I smell awful. I have coin for it."

She planted her fists on her hips. "Have you seen a surgeon?"

"That, I do *not* have coin for."

She tsk-tsk again and pulled a wooden token from a girdle pouch. "Go to the bathhouse, and I'll give you a bowl on the house."

I hesitated a long moment, staring at the chip, my stomach twisting in shame at the prospect of accepting charity even so meager as a bath and a meal. I thought about my split lip and various scrapes, all soiled, and sighed with resignation.

She jerked the coin back just as I was reaching for it. "If you *promise* not to tell anyone I did this. I don't need any heat from the guild." She eyed me critically. She had been a scribe with her second husband, and had inherited his guild reputation and a small treasury in books. "And promise me you'll not continue trading as a scribe unsolicited."

I nodded somberly to both demands and accepted the bath token.

Everywhere a boot had struck, muscles refused to function and threatened to locked up. It took me far longer than it should have to reach the public bathhouse, and I was panting and sweating from pain and effort when I got there.

The bath keeper frowned at me when I held up the token. I was certain I didn't look much like his usual customers, otherwise known as *the employed*. "You cannot wear your clothing into the bath," he grumbled at me, his lip curling in disgust. "It's for washing bodies, not... rags." He examined the proffered token with much more scrutiny than was necessary before scratching my name into his ledger.

"Can I leave my clothes in your care to be taken to a washhouse while I bathe?" I asked. I was not looking forward to undressing in the street, but I had few options, since I'd just sold my spare clothing that morning to purchase bread I'd held in my stomach for scarcely five minutes.

The following negotiation, which would stagger even the most frugal of barterers with its complexity and inane nature, took longer than either deed that followed and cost me one of my silver pennies in addition to the laundering service. I suppose I couldn't blame the man for not wanting to take hold of the soiled garments, and certainly didn't begrudge him for not wanting to see me as the gods made me. In spite of his obvious contempt, I espied a measure of pity when he saw the fresh painting of bruises on my torso, and he refrained from further complaint.

Goldie must have known the warm soak and vigorous scrubbing would ache terribly but also help. I felt considerably better when I headed back to the inn smelling of bath oils and laundry lavender.

The Hare and the Cat was the finest of the three tavern-inns in Noblan with better ale, food, and lodging. It sat near the easterly gate on Crownway Avenue, the main thoroughfare of the city, and was often frequented by traveling nobility and rich merchants. When I came onto Crownway from a second street, there was an unexpected pack of people so dense I couldn't push through them to cross to the inn. With a raucous cheer, they parted from the center of the road, pushing me back into an alley.

That was when I saw The Chosen One for the first time. His was the name known everywhere, held in esteem above that of kings. Wherever written, it was capitalized, whenever spoken it was uttered with reverence often reserved for gods and miracles.

The Chosen One's Assistant

Every man, woman, and youngling has seen his face emblazoned on tapestries, inked on countless manuscripts, or gleaming on the front of a Gold Chosen. I'd beheld many of the heavy gold coins when keeping records of earnings for the master wizard who flew away. A sixty-silver denomination piece of currency was not often traded on the street, but nearly every person had seen one at least once, since it was the only coin that was universally traded in all of the kingdoms throughout the entire world.

The Chosen One sat astride a tall, white, destrier warhorse, and both he and the mount were dressed in glistening armor emblazoned with his colors, gold and royal blue. The man was broad and excessively muscular, just as he appeared in all of the gold-tipped illustrations I'd always thought were an idealized exaggeration of the most admired man in the world. He proudly wore an impossibly expensive tyrian-purple cloak and had a mane of long, pale curls that fell to the middle of his back. His strong jaw, richly tanned skin, and bright blue eyes were distinctive and unmistakable. His was certainly the face on the illustrious coins, and he glowed like liquid gold beneath the adoration of the crowd.

A tall, lean man followed behind The Chosen One, leading a pair of sumpter horses who pulled a canvas-covered wagon. He wore simple brown and gray trousers and tunic, but bore the bright blue and gold tabard of The Chosen One, which sported the great warrior's golden features over a field of royal blue. I likely wouldn't have noticed the second man had he not seemed to be the only person in sight who was not impressed by his master. He walked with his head bowed, a book open in his free hand, reading as he followed quietly behind The Chosen One.

A shower of glittering gold tokens arched over the crowd, and I flinched as one struck my forehead with a smart thump. Suddenly the crowd was alive, pushing, cheering, writhing like a pack of wild dogs. I backed further into the alley and another wave of shining objects arched across my vision. This time I saw from where they'd come. The Chosen One was pulling coins from a girdle bag and throwing them out into the crowd. The pack of bodies seemed to expand and undulate as everyone fought to catch the coins or retrieve them from the cobbles and dirt.

I was thrown backwards by a pair of brawling youths and landed on my side with a cry of pain from the still-fresh bruises across my body. I wriggled further from the fight and rolled to my knees, crawling quickly away from the surging mob. A flash of gold caught my eye, and I seized it up, tucking it into the neck of my tunic. I looked back, but no one had seen the coin or my recovery of it. I quickly glanced around the dirt, and when I could see no other metallic flashes, I fled the main street. I could hear the excitement, anger, and fear escalating as the crowd descended into true chaos in the wake of The Chosen One.

Only when I was two blocks away did I retrieve the heavy coin from the belly of my belted tunic. It was a Gold Chosen. I stared at the waves of hair and grinning features of the hero for a long moment. I couldn't believe my fortune, and it could not have come on a more needed day. Eager to avoid the urgency that was soon to follow in my wake, I was the first from the crowd to reach the nearest money-changer. For a copper, he changed the single coin into one penndoz, thirty-five silver pennies, eighteen half pennies, and fifteen coppers. I couldn't remember the last time I'd had so much coin to spend. I carefully distributed the wealth throughout my girdle bag, pouches, and boots.

When I returned to The Hare and the Cat, the crowd had dispersed save a few desperate peasants still looking for coins. The inn was packed with merry, boisterous travelers and townsfolk, trading in stories about The Chosen One while a few musicians tried their hand at some heroic ballads featuring the same. I gingerly pushed my way up to the corner of the bar and looked out at the flushed faces around me.

"You look better," Goldie shouted over the din. "I'll get your pottage."

I grinned over at her. "Actually, I'd like a room and your finest meal for the night."

She hesitated suspiciously, and then shook her head, tossing me a warm smile. "You caught a coin. Good for you." She patted my hand. "You should eat the pottage and spend the coin on a surgeon. I'm out of rooms, but I can give you a spot in the common room for a half-penny. Or if you want to stay in the carriage house, again, there's still a few spots left for a copper."

"I've had a night and could use the rare fare. I'll take the best meal you have left and the common room, Goldie." I squeezed her hand to show my appreciation for her concern. Such kindness was not common, and she was a rare woman to show it after a hard life of learning three trades with three dead husbands and no surviving children to inherit any of it.

She nodded. "Well, everyone here is rich tonight. I'm out of the veal and scallops, but I'll make sure you get the partridge, for three and a half."

I slid four silver across the counter and shook my head when she moved to give change. With an appreciative smile, I caught a tankard of the best ale in the house and found a place at a table in the back of the room. I watched the merriment of the lucky as they spent their spontaneous wealth. Goldie eventually brought me a plate of richly seasoned partridge, seared pearl onions and vegetables, marbled rye bread with a dollop of creamed butter, and another tankard. I savored the rare, fine feast as the room slowly settled. Hours overcame the enthusiasm of the hardworking townsfolk. They eventually calmed and went home, travelers retired to their rooms, and Goldie began mopping the floor as one remaining musician strummed the few wakeful patrons into a hazy state.

Goldie stopped by my table and quietly whispered. "The Chosen One's assistant just informed me he won't be in need of his second room. So, if you still want it, I held it for you."

I smiled up at her. "You are too good for this world, Goldie, thank you. I'll take it. That's seven more silver, if I'm right?"

"Nah. He wouldn't let me refund him, so it's paid for. You've two meals tomorrow to make up what you've already paid."

I knew she was talking about the silver, since ale and common meals were provided with a room, and I had essentially upgraded to a fine meal. "I will take you up on that. My luck has certainly covered the full spectrum today."

She nodded. "You still look like you need a surgeon."

"Nothing that won't mend with time."

She smiled. "And rest. You should go up soon, room 20. Mind you don't wake The Chosen One in 21."

"Thank you, again, Goldie."

I lingered a little while longer to finish my ale. When I was the last patron in the tavern, and the musician passed my table on his way to the entertainers' room, I handed him two copper and thanked him for staying up so late. Goldie had already barred the door to the common room and entrance and retired to her quarters, leaving instructions to pour myself one more if I wanted it.

I slid the empty tankard back and forth between my hands and considered retrieving a final pour to take to bed with me. I had had a hard day, but a lucky one, my first bit of luck in months. I didn't want to wake up guildless, homeless, *and* worthless from hangover the following morning, but a good buzz was just a few swallows away. It had been some time since I'd been able to indulge, and another cup would not cost me but a day that I likely should spend resting anyway. Decision made, I rose and meandered behind the bar to retrieve my last draft and contemplate my future.

I could get by for some time sleeping in stables and outbuildings for a copper a day. I could probably eat and live off of the Gold Chosen's remains for nearly two months, more if I went hungry more often than not and slept in the open when the weather would permit. After this day, the Scriveners' Guild certainly was not going to allow me entry of merit. I would have been considered a master with my written fluency in three languages, one of them being the wizards' tongue. I was passable in two more languages, and could manage written translations of a sixth with tools and a codex. Qualifications or not, I had irrevocably offended the guild, and by proxy, likely every other guilded trade house in Noblan.

I could not avoid the inevitable. I needed to travel to another town and hope my reputation did not precede me. With the coin I possessed, I could book steerage down the Gorod River and apply at the guilds in Artueteva, Riga, or Rshavin. At least I had bathed recently, and I could spare some copper to visit a barber before each round of applications. For the first time in months, I had a plan for my future. It was bleak, but not without hope.

A patron from the inn came down the stairs as I was topping off my mug, and I watched him place a trades-needed letter on the open work board near the door. Over the last few months, I'd followed every lead on that board, but to no avail. I was too old to apprentice, and the guilds controlled most of the trades. No one would hire someone with no guild affiliation or reputation, and applying to anything in Noblan was now hopeless. My path around the bar took me alongside him as we both headed up the stairs. I was intimidated by his towering height, so naturally, striking up a conversation with the stranger was the best method to alleviate an awkward, silent walk. "What trade are you calling for," I asked as amiably as my still-mangled mouth could muster.

"The Chosen One's Assistant," he replied, wearily.

I jerked to a halt and realized I recognized the man as the herald behind The Chosen One earlier that day. I took fresh stock of him; he was toweringly tall, apathetic, and lean to the point of seeming frail. "Did you say... ?"

"Yeah," he sighed out, turning at the top of the stairs to look down at me. "Must be willing to travel. Must know how to use navigation equipment. Must know at least three languages, and one of them must be wizards' tongue," he droned as if he'd practiced the same a dozen times. He yawned into the back of his hand. "Must read and write said languages..."

"I can do all of that," I exclaimed, louder than I should have, given the hour. "And I was recently a white-sash to a master wizard!"

The man seemed to come awake at my words. He stared at me for a long moment, undoubtedly wondering how someone of my appearance could have such training. Then he headed back down the stairs. "Pour me an ale."

"I don't actually..." I watched him descend and bit my tongue. He must have thought I was a barkeep because he'd seen me pouring myself a drink. "All right," I answered. I slipped around behind the bar and made a show of wiping down a glass for him. While I did, I tucked a penny under a napkin behind the bar. I had seen him drinking all night, and I knew he'd already paid, but it didn't feel right to pour him another on the house without Goldie. I slid him the tankard and stayed behind the bar, sipping from my own.

This was an expensive gamble, a whole silver penny, but if I looked employed at a tavern that proudly displayed the guild sigil, it would explain why I hadn't acquired a Scriveners' Guild membership. To my knowledge, The Chosen One had not been on the Gorod River in several decades, so neither he nor his herald would have heard of me. If I was truly lucky, they would hire me without looking too closely at the references I intended to fabricate.

"Does The Chosen One have many assistants?"

The herald shook his head, a wry smirk turning up the corner of his mouth. "Only one."

"And he needs to be a scribe and know how to travel?"

The herald nodded. "What else can you do?"

I hesitated, not sure what he was looking for. "Um, I've traveled quite a bit more than most, considering I was never a journeyman. I'm excellent with numbers. I am known for my penmanship as a—"

"Can you read a map?"

"Um, yes. I'm quite good, actually. One of my instructors was a mapmaker and he—"

"You were a white-sash. Did you have to mix healing poultices and tonics? Low grade, of course."

"Yes, often. I was responsible for most of the component preparation, since I was the highest skill level of the master's white-sashes, and quite a bit of the minute casting."

"So you have some magic, but not enough to move up to gray?"

I frowned, but pushed back my chagrin at the astute observation and hid a flush behind the tankard of ale. "I made up for it by aggressively learning all of the mixing, muddling, and crafting I could. I can flawlessly replicate a diagram, and I can—"

He held up his hand and took a long draught. Then he stared at me for several uncomfortable moments. "You're from Epsosia."

"Yes, that's right!" I chuckled quietly. "From Petria. Most can't distinguish my accent from that of southern Opolchia."

"We travel a lot."

"I imagine," I laughed, but he didn't. I hid my discomfort once more behind the tankard.

"It's hard work. And varied. You would be responsible for all of his needs. There are very detailed and extensive accounts of your duties."

"Of course, but... it would be an *honor* to work for him. Really." I surprised myself with the adoration in my tone. "Everyone has heard the songs, the stories. I've even transcribed many accounts of his great deeds. Dragons, evil wizards, ghouls, undead, hauntings!" I shook my head. "A true honor."

He nodded somberly throughout my monologue and finished his ail. "I can't give you specific details of your duties until you take a binding oath to not disclose anything I tell you about the position."

"Oh, yes. Of course." I realized I sounded too eager, desperate even, but I didn't care. This was indeed the pinnacle of my luck that night. I needed a trade, and one had placed itself at my feet. I would be a fool not to jump at it.

He frowned. "Tentatively, you're hired. I need to prepare the binding before we can continue. I also need to prepare the transition of the Tiberius Blessing. Do you live in the inn?"

"I will be here all day and night," I answered, hoping he didn't notice I omitted the word 'working' from that declaration.

"Tomorrow at high noon will be best, so meet me in room 21 at eleven."

"Wait..." I sputtered as he rose from the barstool.

"Is something wrong?" A trace of tired irritation in his voice gave me pause.

"No, I just... that's *his* room."

The herald laughed softly and shook his head, as if I had said something he'd heard too often. "I have work to do," he explained patiently. "White-sash labor, and some of it must be done in his presence." He fixed me with a level stare. "I will be sleeping on the floor."

It took me a moment in my exhaustion and ale addled brain to realize what he *thought* I'd meant when I registered surprise that he was sleeping in the room of The Chosen One. "Oh! No," I quickly sputtered. "I didn't mean *that*, that you and he... I only meant..." I sighed and chuckled at my own awkwardness. "I'm going to *his* room. I'm going to... to *meet* him? Tomorrow morning?"

The herald smiled and relaxed a little, weary wrinkles appearing at the corners of his eyes once more. "I remember when I was as eager as you, not so very long ago." He strummed his fingers on the bar in a lighthearted fashion that seemed unlike his character thus far. "He will be at the local lord's manor. There is a feast and a ball in his honor for slaying an undead bevy of cursed beavers that had swarmed upstream. He will be away until late, if he returns tomorrow night at all."

"He doesn't need his herald?"

The man smiled and then chuckled, but I didn't understand the joke. "I am *not* his herald," he insisted. "And he will not be expecting me to assist him tomorrow."

"Wait," I said when he started toward the stairs. "We haven't introduced ourselves. I am—"

"No need for that," he quietly cut in, waving dismissively at my confused frown. "Tomorrow, you will understand." He yawned into the back of his hand again. "Today, I am exhausted from a two-year campaign that has finally come to an end." He smiled again in a self-amused way, and started up the stairs. "Will you do me the kindness of taking down my trades-needed poster?"

He didn't wait for my response, his voice drifting down from the dark corridor above. I stared where he'd gone long after I heard the quiet open and close of the door at the end of the hall. I could not believe my fortune. If this *not*-a-herald was really qualified to hire me as The Chosen One's assistant, my troubles would be over! I imagined the duty paid well, but even if it didn't, it would take me out of this city, and it would certainly repair my reputation. "Questers' Guild," I whispered to myself. I wondered if, like wizards, becoming the assistant to a hero granted me membership.

I eagerly tore down the parchment that began: *Seeking Trades: Assistant to Grandmaster Hero.*

2. Call Me Tiberius

I awoke to a knock on my door, and moaned miserably into consciousness. Everything ached, and my face felt like raw, tenderized meat. The knock sounded again, and Goldie's voice called past the wood frame. "I was told to wake you by ten."

I jerked alert and tripped over the covers in my haste to cross the small room. Grimacing from newly awakened pain, I jerked open the door. "Who? Was it, um, the herald of—"

Her gaze flashed over my underpinnings, her brows rising in surprise as her lips turned up in a decidedly unladylike smirk. Without preamble, she shoved a plate crowded with porridge, two boiled eggs, a thick slice of ham, and bread into my hands. "Tiberius," she answered. "He said to tell you he expects you promptly at eleven." After I took the plate, she pinched my chin and again roughly examined my face. "I still say you should see the surgeon. From the looks of the rest of you, there might be damage that time will worsen rather than heal."

I gingerly pulled back and managed as much of a smile as my swollen lips could manage. "He'll just say I'll live," I mumbled. "And offer to bleed me."

She shook her head. "Salves, poultices—"

"Which I can ill afford." I nodded my appreciation for her concern, and she turned abruptly to stride down the hall toward the tavern. I sighed wearily and brought my breakfast into the room. My stomach howled in hunger and knotted in pain simultaneously. I was so excited and anxious about my meeting in an hour, I could barely enjoy the sumptuous meal.

I used the water basin and towel to scrub my face and hands, though the treatment awakened a few unmanly tears. When I stripped out of my undergarments to scour my body as well, I gasped at the horrendous array of violet and sickeningly yellow bruises all over my stomach and chest. I hesitated in uncertainty. What if I did meet The Chosen One today? What if I still looked like the fool I felt? I considered visiting the surgeon or the apothecary. Both might have a salve to take down the swelling on my face to make me more presentable. "No time," I mumbled. "Be prompt."

I redressed, scraped the last of the porridge from the bowl with the heel of the bread, and took several deep breaths. Today my fortunes changed. Today I wasn't vagrant; I was traveling with the man known in every kingdom. I wasn't guildless; I was in the employ of a hero who was honored as a grandmaster and founder in every Questers' Guild in every city in every kingdom *throughout the world*. I would be clothed, fed, sleep in security, and travel in safety. There was even a fair chance that I would be treated with deference and respect wherever I went.

"Don't ruin this," I told myself as I walked the very short distance down the hall to the room of The Chosen One. I straightened my tunic and knocked in a fashion I imagined was confident, though decided immediately afterwards sounded overly eager.

"Come in," the not-a-herald called through the door.

The room was clearly the most spacious and finest in the inn. There was a large bed, a desk with two chairs pulled up to it, and a table with a basin and a large brass mirror. A bed had been made on the floor and clearly slept in. All around the room, boxes and trunks filled the walls and corners, some open with fine garments spilling out, others secured with locks. One very large trunk near the bed was sealed with magic that even my limited skill could detect from across the room.

The not-a-herald waved me over to the desk where he sat surrounded by a small fortune in books and scrolls. I made the terrible mistake of glancing toward the mirror as I passed. I gasped at my swollen and discolored jaw, lips, and eyes. I was not an overly attractive man, not particularly tall, and my hair and eyes were as unremarkably brown as they could be... but I had never considered myself to look grotesque until just then.

The man looked up, frowning at my delay, then he glanced toward the mirror. "Oh, yes. Not to worry." He gestured to the chair next to him again, and returned to his work. He was scrawling into the last few pages of leather-bound tome. When I drew closer, I saw the language he was using was wizards' tongue. As he was writing, the ink disappeared, and only by watching the pen could I read the words. I noticed his pen did not have an inkhorn or well, and wondered if it somehow contained the ink within it. Not wanting to appear as though I was prying, I glanced toward the many scrolls. I wanted to read them. I was immensely curious about what manner of correspondences I might be writing or receiving. And what did the expensive and elaborately bound books contain?

The not-a-herald lifted a small, corked vial from where it had rested somewhere amongst the rolls of parchment. "For your face," he mumbled without looking up. He held it in my direction until I took it from him. "Typical activation," he said.

I stared at the murky, opalescent liquid in the vial. My fingers tingled, and I immediately knew what it was. A healing tonic. I glanced back at the not-a-herald, but he offered no further instructions. Perhaps this was a test to see if I knew basic support magic. I did.

I walked to the mirror and carefully uncorked the bottle. If it was meant to be imbibed, it would smell strongly of herbs and mint. If it was meant to be applied, it would smell more like earth and sediments. When I unstopped the glass, however, the substance was odorless. My stomach dropped. I glanced back to the man, but he continued to ignore me, his pen never pausing in its labors. I scoured my mind for some piece of information that would help me identify the "typical activation" cant for this particular healing tonic. My previous master had been older and set in his ways, relying on the same methods over and over. I had occupied my mind by reading whatever he left unguarded, thus a majority of my education came from my own intellectual avarice rather than his direct guidance.

Opalescent, I thought to myself. Shellfish, perhaps. In such cases, it would be applied. I could think of no other thing it could be. Some minerals also had the same moving-mirror type appearance, but they were also applied. I hesitated longer, not wishing to waste the expensive tonic, but also not wishing to fail the test.

The not-a-herald set down the pen and turned to look at me. "Never encountered that particular elixir before?"

I frowned, wanting desperately to imply that I had, but magic was tricky and dangerous. If the wrong cant was used, it could become caustic or toxic. "My previous master preferred salves," I explained, instead. "I did quite a lot of independent study, but knowledge without an example to learn from can tend to limit one." Even to my ears, it sounded like a lame excuse. "I've never actually seen many of the elixirs I've read about," I confessed.

He nodded his understanding. "Elixirs are more potent."

"But salves are more stable," I countered quietly, hearing my old master's words issue from my lips.

"And if your master was on in years, he might have clung to tradition over innovation." He withdrew a two-inch thick burgundy tome from the bottom of the stack of books. "The answer is in here, and that is all of the assistance I intend to give." He turned his back and took up his pen once more. "If you cannot work that little bit of magic with your skills and this knowledge, then you should leave."

I let out a relieved breath. "Thank you!" I sat beside him in the second chair and opened the tome. Luckily there was an index. It was all in wizards' tongue, but it was my second language, and I had used it more in the past decade than my first. I found the section on healing, and thumbed to elixirs. Though one of the first magic workings described the liquid as being of a pearl-like appearance, I skimmed all of the other items in the section. The second to the last one described the contents as mostly transparent with an opal-rainbow coloration. No odor. I smiled, having found it in only a few moments, and read the instructions. "Oh," I said. "Interesting."

The not-a-herald looked up at me, then down at the page my book was turned to. A flash of approval crossed his features before he returned to his work. Though I was confident enough to not require confirmation, I felt a small swell of pride at his reaction. I returned to the mirror and uncorked the vial. I went over the cant several times in my head, not wanting to mispronounce any of the few words. Activating a working took magic, often not very much, but sometimes quite a bit, and tomes never seemed to give an indication of which it would be. I hoped this one didn't pull so much from me it revealed the weakness that had kept me from earning color in my sash, but I needed to take the chance. I called on the subtle stirring of power within me that responded to the vial tingling in my fingers, and exhaled that energy, while delivering the cant.

Saying words of power took training and practice. It sometimes took a white-sash years to learn how to recognize what magic felt like within himself and how to expel it with breath. During my brief apprenticeship, it had only taken me weeks. My last master had said I was incredibly adept, but suffered the misfortune of having nearly nothing to speak of by way of power or the ability to channel it. I could activate workings, use bespelled items, cast very minor spells, and assist wizards, but I would never be anything more. I was permanently demoted to a wizard's assistant; my sash would never contain color. I squared my shoulders and met the mirror's eye, shoving that life-long shame from my head.

Today I would wear blue and gold.

My activation was flawless in spite of how anxious I felt and my awareness that the not-a-herald was certainly paying close attention to everything I did. The elixir began to boil in the glass and erupted into great plumes of white mist. I held the vial under my chin and let the tingling mist pour over my features. It was cool, then cold, then biting. I hissed, but waited till the tingling abated indicating it had completed its work. When I drew the vial away, my face was damp, but unmarred. I stared in shock at the effectiveness of the working. The apple of my cheek had been cut, and my lip had been split. Not even a scar remained.

Mist was still pouring up from the vial, so I glanced down at my tunic. I hated to waste the working, and I was still in a great deal of discomfort. I didn't read enough of the description to know if it would be effective through clothing, so I quickly worked at the buckle on my belt. I glanced at the not-a-herald, but he was still pretending to be uninterested in what I was doing. I slid the belt to the floor and held my tunic out, letting the mist drift up under my garments. I felt the tingle and then the sharp pain of the working. When only a damp coolness remained across my stomach and chest I withdrew the vial. Only a thin tendril of mist drifted up from a small amount of liquid in the bottom of the glass, and I held it up to my arm that bore scrapes from when I had fallen to the street a few times the previous day. It immediately eased some of the ache in them. The mist snuffed out before it had quite finished the job, but the scrapes were much improved.

As I corked the bottle, I realized in the absence of my pain how damaged I had truly been. Perhaps the brutes had cracked a rib or two. Only in health did I realize how badly they had actually beaten me. Even my mind had been muddled, and now I was thinking quite clearly. I looked at my reflection, frowning at the dusting of gray in my thin, dark beard and barely-kempt hair. I had aged ten years in the last two, and my features had grown gaunt and weary. Why was I only then realizing just how much the struggle of the previous years had worn on me?

"Introspection is a side effect," not-a-herald said. "Don't spend too much time in the mirror. You'll want to jump from a precipice by the end of the hour."

I blinked in surprise and abandoned my reflection. I returned to the seat provided and offered back the vial. "That was... thank you."

He looked up at me for the first time since giving me the burgundy book and smiled. "You look a sight better, and you can work an activation cant and read wizards' tongue with near flawless pronunciation. All good." He slid an astrolabe over to me. "What time is it?"

I laughed softly and went to the window. The shutters were already open, and I leaned out to catch the sun. After a frustrating few moments trying to contort my body to line the alidade up with the sun, I gave up and positioned the alidade, latitude plate, rete, and rule where they would be had I made the measurement. It was close to 11:30 in the morning, so I maneuvered it to show a little before that, since I'd been early in the first place. I returned the astrolabe to not-a-herald, and he frowned down at it, then up at me.

"Well, I suppose you must know how to use the tool to fabricate the measurement," he commented, setting it aside.

I flushed a little with chagrin, though I wasn't sure how he could tell I hadn't done the actual measurement. He unrolled a parchment, revealing a map. "What is our current location?"

I looked down at the circular diagram meant to vaguely resemble the landmass of Opolchia, but was really only a series of lines depicting distances between cities. "This is a last century map," I complained. "Very inaccurate. And Noblan doesn't even appear on it." I received no response, so I examined it a while longer. "Well, here is the port city Gorod, so the river that also does not appear on this map runs mostly east-west, so Noblan would be near here." I set the map down and poked a finger down on the approximate location inward from the crudely drawn coast.

He took the parchment away and handed me another map, this one had latitude and longitude lines and actually resembled the shape of the landmass of the country. I immediately pointed to Noblan, which was not depicted, but was located at the tip of the Gorod River. "Here."

"Plot a course to Krichev."

I pretended to study the map, though I already knew the answer because I had taken the journey to Opolchia's capitol a few times before with the master wizard. "I believe I would... ferry to Gorod. Then I would charter a boat to Aunon and take the main trade road to Druragunum, across the narrowest arm of northern Opolchia. Then it would be best to charter a craft across Opolchia Lake to Krichev."

He pursed his lips. "By sea? A much greater distance than by land."

I laughed, but when he didn't I cleared my throat and stifled it. "Nearly forty leagues across unsettled Opolchia? You do have a cart, I notice."

"There are roads."

"Not from here to there. Even if you were to contact local guilds to acquire trade maps depicting roads in the area at every city along the way, there are valleys, gorges, high, rolling hills... the dirt ruts are not well grooved," I argued, circling back to my first and most important observation. "You have a heavy cart."

"You didn't mention thieves and brigands," he observed.

I laughed again. "Or trolls on every bridge, or merchant-controlled roads. But, you travel with *The Chosen One*."

He nodded and smiled. "You may have very similar arguments to this one when plotting courses in the future; I wanted to be sure you could be insistent."

I watched him for a moment, not sure what he was implying. "Would *I* be planning the path of The Chosen One?"

He sat back in his chair and scrutinized me for an uncomfortable long time. Finally, he said, "I think you're smart, and I think you have the skills this position requires. You ambitiously educate yourself. You are clearly stubborn, and can function injured."

I blinked in alarm at his last comment. "You think I might become injured?"

He ignored my anxiety. "I can tell you no more until you take the oath of silence. It is a binding oath, so I don't do this lightly. After you do, however, you are only moments away from being worthy of the Tiberius blessing. Which means... I would not offer to tell you more if I was not already willing to give you the position." He paused in thought, and the gravity of what he was saying sunk into my chest like a stone. "After we begin, you have only to say that you wish to be The Chosen One's assistant, and the position is yours. You will have to sign a contract that will enlist your services for no less than two years, and this contract will also be magically binding."

I shook my head in amazement. "So much binding and secrecy, why?"

"To protect The Chosen One and his legacy." His response was quick, almost rehearsed.

I looked down at my hand on the desk and contemplated what I knew thus far. I wasn't sure I wanted to be magically bound in any way, but this seemed to be the greatest trade I could ever aspire to be. I gave him a skeptical glance. "Wait. You know nothing about me except what I have told you. I could be lying."

"You aren't," he stated simply.

"How do you know?" I demanded.

He smirked and tapped the astrolabe. "It is also bespelled. It detects deception."

I looked down at the device. I had held it in my hand and not felt the tingle of magic. I reached out to touch it again. "My skin is a lovely shade of tyrian purple." I felt an odd, somewhat unpleasant twinge, and not-a-herald smiled. I picked up the instrument and stared in awe at it, the tingle of magical energy now unmistakable. "Amazing! So subtle!" I glanced over at him. "This was in your pocket!"

He nodded. "Always. It only alerts someone within a few inches of a lie. It becomes a little confused if a deception is occurring but a direct lie was not told."

I laughed. "Wait, but when I was moving the dials..."

"I had momentarily deactivated it. There is a combination of turns that will activate and deactivate it. Instructions are contained in the burgundy tome."

"I didn't see you turn any dials when I gave it back."

He nodded his head. "It was only just eleven, and you had set the device for eleven-twenty or so."

I sighed and shook my head. "I couldn't catch the sun, not at the right angle to—"

"I know. I was testing your resourcefulness," he explained, a self-satisfied glint in his eye. "Your deception was very convincing."

"You still don't know me or what life I am from. I could be a murderer—"

"Are you," he asked, pointedly lifting the astrolabe.

I laughed. "No. I have an aversion to violence."

He nodded. "You will need to learn to stomach it. The Chosen One is called upon to kill all manner of things in the process of all manner of violent acts. In fact, at times, he revels in it." He slid the device back into his pocket. "I have excellent intuition. I know all I need to know."

"How much does it pay?" I asked the question before I thought better of it, but it grated a little that he was offering me bonded service without discussion of what I would gain in my two years of servitude.

"Well, it would get you away from the Scrivener's Guild, for one," he stated, looking at me askance.

So, he did know some things about me. "You asked around, I assume."

"This morning," he confirmed. "And a little last night when I saw you in the corner. You looked like trouble, but Miss Goldie assured me you were a good soul."

I smiled faintly and nodded. "She's the best this town has to offer."

"And three men have partaken," he mused with a chuckle. Then he gave me a measuring glance, perhaps at the fond smile on my face. "She's a little old for you, but—"

"Hey!" I glowered, not sure why I was so quick to take offence. Then I shrugged. "You know, I don't mind that you would imply such. She may be older, but she's a good mind, and I never thought about children." I sighed. "Not that I thought much about marriage, either."

"Good," he replied. "Because you will want to remain unwed while bonded. You cannot have a traveling companion, and you will often not see the same town for a year or more."

"Does The Chosen One not have a home?"

"Certainly," not-a-herald said. "Wherever he lays his head is home." He gestured to the many trunks and boxes. "He travels with all he cares to own, save what he has in various banks at every major port town. He's been gifted land in most kingdoms, and I dare say most are tended by vassals he's never met."

I frowned. "To live so sparse but have such a grand life, devoting yourself to so many in need!"

He laughed, and again I didn't understand the joke.

"I am quite sincere," I insisted. "He travels ceaselessly, defending the helpless, saving the hopeless from all the horrible magical beings that mortal men could never hope to—" He laughed again, and I bit my lip to keep from demanding he stop. His mirth was making light of the great impact his master had on the lives of the weak and hopeless.

"When you travel with him, you will see that he does not live a 'sparse' life," not-a-herald said at length. "He travels and lives like a king most nights."

"As he should," I stubbornly retorted.

He nodded and sighed. "Yes, well, he certainly deserves an assistant as insistently loyal as you."

I hesitated before saying, "You never answered my question."

"About the pay? Oh, yes. One percent. Net, not gross."

I frowned. "Of what?"

"Hoards, rescued treasure, fees, payments, ransoms, goods, bribes, endorsements, et cetera..."

"Bribes and endorsements?"

He smiled at me. "Basically anything worth any value coming into his possession is assessed, expenses and conversion fees are paid, and you receive one percent of the remaining."

I tried to imagine how much coin that could possibly be, then I remembered The Chosen One throwing fistfuls of Gold Chosen into the crowd. "I want the trade," I said, possibly too quickly.

Not-a-herald laughed. "First the oath of silence." He opened a large trunk that sat on the floor beside the desk and withdrew a thickly rolled parchment. "You are free to read this if you like," he stated, holding it out to me. "Half of the scroll is a binding working with indications of what misfortune should befall you should you reveal any of the secrets I am about to tell you, anything The Chosen One tells you in confidence, or that you learn in the Tomes of Tiberius." His hand gestured toward one of the closed trunks. "The next half of the scroll is detailing what is considered 'in confidence' and what is considered 'private,' and thus protected by this oath. Basically, if it is not common knowledge, do not divulge anything you learn about The Chosen One, his deeds, or operations."

I frowned. "Punishments?"

"There are various 'warnings,' jolts of electricity, that sort of thing. But they lead up to and can include death."

I gasped and shoved the scroll away from me. "Fate binding! No! Definitely not!"

He chuckled and shook his head as if I were being silly and unrolled the lower part of the scroll to read aloud. "Should you reveal information about The Chosen One, including weaknesses, sources of strength or power, locations or times of vulnerability, et cetera... with the *direct intent* of causing or enabling another to cause him harm, and should he, as a result of such harm, become a state of deceased that cannot be reversed by healing or true resurrection, then the following punishments shall be levied against you: After a delay of sufficient time, i.e. twelve to twenty days depending on location of The Chosen One at the time of his death, for you to acquire assistance with healing and resurrection, your fate shall be equaled to his." He fixed me with a pointed look. "If you *intentionally* arrange for his death using information you learn about him from me, him, or the Tomes of Tiberius, then this contract will exact the highest punishment, resulting in your death as well."

    I stared dubiously at the scroll. "That is the only fate clause?"

    He nodded, somberly. "The service is a *minimum* of two years. If you dislike The Chosen One so much that you would consider having him killed, just wait out your service and move far away from him. And if an ogre comes to your town, be somewhere else when The Chosen arrives to slay it."

    I sighed. "And the contract warns me if it thinks I will breech it?"

    "Oh, yes," he chuckled. "You *will* know."

    I frowned at his insistence, but this binding was necessary to procure the position, so I grudgingly nodded. "You said I could read it?"

    He handed it back without a word, his eyes still glittering with mirth.

    I started to reroll the scroll from the bottom to the top, skimming backwards as I did. When I reached the top, I paid more attention to the wizards' tongue than I did the Opolchian that followed. I wanted to understand the working that would have the power to kill me. It was complex, nuanced, and powered by a wizard whose name I did not recognize. "Who is this?" I asked, pointing to the worlds *Grandmaster Wizard Mayson.*

He glanced at the name and shook his head. "He maintains The Chosen One's contracts. That is all I can tell you until you sign this scroll."

I skimmed the rest of the contract and ascertained that, through all of the flowery language, it was exactly as not-a-herald had said. The most intimidating paragraph was the one he had read to me. "This takes a special quill?" Most binding contracts had their own quill, one that used blood or some other token of the signees.

Not-a-herald opened the trunk again and withdrew a thick, blue, leather-bound tome. The spine was impressed with a grouping of five horizontal lines and a second grouping of four. The cover bore hand-span tall vertical lines, also grouped by five and four. Tiberius pulled a feather quill from between the spine and the headband. It was two hand-spans tall, and the tip of the fletching was painted with small gold symbols used in wizard workings.

"This will sting, don't be surprised," he warned.

"I've signed a bonded contract before," I responded.

"Yes. As a white-sash," he agreed, clearly knowing apprenticeship to a wizard required bonding. "It is a shame about what happened to your previous master."

I frowned up at him. "In spite of my reputation, it was *not* my fault. I don't make mistakes when it comes to magic. It's too dangerous to be foolish with it."

He smiled broadly. "You're telling the truth. I was hoping I would have an answer to that question before the day was out."

For a moment, I was confused. Then, I remembered the astrolabe of deception. "Yes. Well, you're the only one who has ever believed me."

"Surprising that the Wizards' Guild didn't do a truth spell."

"There was no point in it," I grumbled. "It wouldn't matter to them that *I* believed I was not to blame. The alternative was that a master wizard was at fault. That was unacceptable to them and would not regain their loss."

He shook his head. "Your acceptance of the unchangeable will serve you well."

I cast him a suspicious frown and took up the quill. I had already noticed he occasionally alluded to an unsavory aspect to the position I would be filling, but I couldn't imagine anything more tedious or menial than the scribe trade or assistant trade I'd been doing for over a decade since I was expelled from the Wizards' Guild. I was skilled enough to be the lowest tier on the highest coveted guilds in the world, but not gifted enough to be accepted into any of them. How could this two years of service possibly be worse?

I put the pen to the bottom of the parchment and felt a sharp prick in my thumb. I resisted the urge to drop it as the warm, red ink flowed down the shaft to the nub, and I quickly scrawled my full name. When I set the pen down, it was clean. I waited, and then said, "I don't feel the working."

"I have to sign before it is binding." He took up the pen and signed in large, flourishing letters, simply: *Tiberius*. The magic came over me, so powerful that it filled all of my senses for several uncomfortable moments. I felt giddy, blind, deaf, and awash with almost painful tingling. A bitter taste filled my mouth, and my heart pounded in my chest, sending my lungs heaving to catch up. Finally, it abated, leaving me weary. I felt the same, but somehow different.

After my heart had calmed, I smiled weakly at him. "So, Tiberius *is* your name."

"Not for long," he answered, cryptically. "What questions do you have?"

I shook my head, trying to clear it after the overwhelming experience of the binding. "What will I be doing? Specifically? I mean, besides navigation and activation cants?"

He lifted the tome for me to see. "This is the ninth Tome of Tiberius. You will catalog The Chosen One's great deeds in here, as well as his not-so-great deeds. Essentially, it's a diary. Every assistant takes up where the last left off. When the tome is full, a new one will appear in your trunk." He kicked the trunk beside him with his toe. "The first Tome of Tiberius," he said as he pulled an identical blue leather tome from the trunk, this one with only one hash on the spine and cover. "Will have all of your tasks, great and small, explained in detail. Consider this your primer for being the assistant to the busiest hero in the world."

I held my hand out for it, but instead he riffled through the pages and stopped at an apparently random location.

"Laundry," he read. "Tiberius will be responsible for ensuring The Chosen One has clean and brightly dyed livery, banners, clothing, and dress for himself, his horses, his transport, and his assistant or assistants." He looked up at me. "And then it goes into detail about each garment, how to ensure the aforementioned task is completed appropriately, and so on... in *exhaustive* detail."

"That does not seem so terrible. So, I will ensure the domestic tasks are completed?"

"Exactly," he answered rifling to another page. "Tiberius will be responsible for the prompt and efficient treatment of The Chosen One's ailments, wounds, or physical discomfitures. Et cetera... The entire book is thus."

"Well," I said, not sure why his tone had turned sour. "I suppose I am grateful that there is a detailed guide of my duties."

He nodded. "Did you have more questions?"

"Um, when did you say I would start? Do I need to get any affairs in order? Will I be apprenticing with someone? Is there some sort of transfer of duties ritual or procedure I would need to do?" I paused, realizing I was rambling some in my growing excitement.

"Today, if you wish," he answered. "My understanding is you have no affairs, and only what you carry for possessions. You will be responsible for reading and learning from the Tomes of Tiberius in your own time; you will *not* have an apprenticeship period, as your duties will be complete and start immediately. There *is* a ritual to transfer those duties to you; it begins with you saying aloud that you wish to take the position. Afterwards you will swear an oath of fealty, duty, and silence, and sign the last page of the first Tome of Tiberius to initiate the binding that will begin your two years of service."

My heart was pounding with excitement as he rattled off the answers to my many hurried questions. I was an oath and a signature away from more wealth and honor than I had ever had. He could have said I would be mucking stables naked while the townsfolk threw stones at me for two years, and I would have signed. "I do. I want the trade. I'm ready."

He smiled and slid the blue tome with one marking on it toward me. "Place both hands on the book, accepting your role as his new assistant and the keeper of these tomes," he instructed. "Repeat after me."

I did as he instructed and repeated word for word every phrase. It was in wizards' tongue, and I noticed that his pronunciation wasn't perfect. Mine was.

"I accept the responsibility of The Chosen One's assistant for no less than two years—I will protect him from harm and dishonor—I will do all within my power and endurance to give him aid—in any manner I am capable—to ensure his success in every campaign—I will keep his confidences and protect his secrets—I will respect and honor his and my duty—I will follow the conduct dictated in the first Tome of Tiberius—I accept the blessings extended to me by wizards and gods as a result of this oath—I accept the name and duties of Tiberius.*"*

He took the tome from me to open it to the last page, and I frowned in confusion. "Blessings of gods?" I asked.

"Yes, the Blessing of Tiberius," he said, as if that answered my question. "It is extended to you until you complete your service, and a less powerful version of it protects you after... provided you procure the services of an acceptable replacement." He turned the book toward me, and I looked at the last page. *Tiberius* was signed six times in different hands, one from a man who was clearly writing with his left.

"What is this blessing," I asked as I accepted from him the same quill we'd used to sign the contract.

"Longevity, resilience, resistance to pestilence, deep rest, healing, and bolstering your natural gift of magic," he responded.

I stared at him in shock. Such a magnificent gift, given by the gods no less, would have been worth a thousand bindings, countless menial jobs. "My natural gift?"

His smile broadened. "Exactly what it sounds. Yours is so subdued, I doubt it would elevate your magic to a point where you could attain anything higher than a second or third level sash."

"But, I would never be a white-sash again," I concluded. "I could... I could be a wizard."

He laughed and nodded, his expression one of understanding and genuine empathy.

"Did you make that elixir I used earlier?"

He shook his head. "No, no. I did not even have *your* gift when I began. Most of the items of that sort you will procure from wizards. There are instructions in the tome."

I looked down at the names on the paper. "Longevity... healing... Which gods?" I perhaps should have thought to ask sooner. It would not do to be under the thumb of Trion, god of darkness and strife.

"Skalah, primarily. But also Anetrael, Butev, and Dindrel," he answered.

I nodded thoughtfully. Skalah, king of the gods, made sense. He was god of the sun, joy, misery, and wealth. He was also expected to be involved if three other gods teamed up. Anetrael, god of diplomacy and shame, oversaw contracts and was often associated with his cousin Butev, beautiful goddess of the forge and justice, and Dindrel, a favorite of wizards, the god of prophecies, rivers, and magic. I could understand why each would want to be part of a blessing that protected The Chosen One, the warrior who was gifted great power and immortality by the gods to protect mankind.

"So, I will have to answer to four gods if I fail in my duty or break my oath," I observed.

He nodded somberly. "And all four will aid you to ensure your success."

I lowered the quill to the book, felt a sharp prick, and watched red fill the shaft.

He quickly said, "Sign: *Tiberius*."

"But my name is—"

"*Tiberius*," he insisted. "As long as you are his assistant, you are accepting that name as your own. You will sign all documents thus and answer to previous documents signed by past assistants of that same designation."

"Wait," I said. "I have to answer to contracts *you* made?"

"And those before us, yes. Just as I do and did." He smiled. "Because he will be The Chosen One for hundreds of years, but his assistants come and go. You will notice many pages of signatures before this one." He gestured to the book. "Continuity must be maintained on contracts and correspondences that will out-endure your service. Thus, *you* are Tiberius."

"That is what you meant when you said it would not be your name for long."

He nodded. "When you take the oath and sign, I return to being Ethan." He rose from his seat and walked to the window, looking down at the busy street below. "Like before, but with much better prospects," he mumbled. I watched him for a moment, struck again by his height, easily a head taller than me. His very lean frame only made him seem more toweringly tall. He looked tired, but his eyes were shining like they hadn't been the first few times I'd seen him. Was this job so very hard, so trying?

I was wary, but for the blessing alone, for the wealth alone, for the escape from Noblan alone... I signed, *Tiberius*. "Well, Ethan, gods' speed to you in all—" A more powerful working than I had ever before experienced or witnessed slammed into me, overwhelming every sense simultaneously, and hurtling me savagely into darkness.

3. There Was a Man Called The Chosen One, and He Almost Deserved It

My head was pounding when I had enough sense to realize I still had one. I groaned and writhed a little on the hard wood beneath me. Something clattered to the ground at my side, and I absently groped for it with one hand as I pressed my other palm to my forehead. I groaned again in misery as all of my limbs and appendages came awake with tingling pain. Spells and workings had been cast on me before, but nothing like this. Every part of me felt foreign and ablaze. Finally, my clumsy fingers found the glass vial that had been resting upon my sternum. It tingled with active power against my already oversensitive skin.

A note was wrapped around it, and I rolled away from the window to shield my aching eyes from the blinding light of the late afternoon sun. I struggled to get my fingers to work and eventually freed the small scroll from the vial.

> *Dear Tiberius,*
> *Congratulations. Drink this vial; no cant needed. It is already activated. You will find a list of tasks you need to complete today on the desk when you are more in sorts. Please be sure to complete the list before night fall, such duties do not lend well to fading light. After that, stay in the inn, in the room if possible, and read the first tome. Fear not, The Chosen One will know you.*

Gratefully and Sincerely,
Ethan

  I glowered at the note. I could not believe that he had left me there, alone and with no further instructions. He didn't even intend to introduce me. Luckily, I was too miserable to be afraid. It was an ordeal to get my limbs to obey enough to wriggle into a seated position, albeit deeply slumped and leaning against a table leg. I took my time uncorking the vial with my near-useless fingers, desperately hoping I didn't spill it. I didn't hesitate to drink the elixir, knocking it back in one swig. It could have been poison, and I would have welcomed the change from my current state.

  If I had not already been about as uncomfortable as I could be, the working would have been really unpleasant. As it was, after the first few moments, I felt so much better that I hardly noticed. The pinpricks nearly vanished from my hands and feet, and my arms and legs were still sluggish but more responsive. I waited a little longer, because I could feel the magic wasn't complete. As I did, my senses cleared up quite a lot, and the pounding in my head subsided to a dull ache.

  I was surprised that an elixir could mitigate the side effects of another working when it should have compounded it. I decided I would have to find the potion in the red book to sate my curiosity when I had time. For now, I wanted to complete the task list Tiberius—*Ethan*—had left for me, so I could spend the rest of the day reading the first Tome of Tiberius.

  In spite of the major working still wreaking havoc on my body, I was having trouble believing that I was now in the employ of The Chosen One. I was, in fact, his travel companion. It seemed unreal, and I thought maybe Jaya had ensorcelled me within a fever dream. "Dream or no," I reminded myself. "I have work to do before..."

I swallowed the anxious knot that rose from my chest into my throat. The Chosen One. I was going to meet him. I was going to actually *talk* to him come nightfall. That thought alone vaulted me to my feet, and I dropped heavily into the chair the previous Tiberius had occupied. A strange surreal feeling passed over me, and for a moment I imagined if I looked in a mirror, I would bear the face of tall, gaunt Ethan. I shook my head and picked up his pen, turning it in my fingers.

"And like that, I am him," I mumbled. "Like that, the work he was doing..." I looked at the ninth Tome of Tiberius. "Is now my work." It felt like I was beginning in the middle of a very important conversation, or perhaps a ritual prayer, only someone else had started it.

There was, indeed a letter written on several sheets of paper.

Dear Tiberius,

This note was written to you with the pen you see on the desk. This pen has an endless supply of enchanted ink that only you and The Chosen One will be able to perceive. Any attempt to reveal the ink through means of magic or alchemy will result in it bleeding to ruin all legible text. Do not lose the pen. Acquiring another one is difficult.

I snorted. I had no inkling how I would acquire something I had never seen before.

> *I have already resupplied the wagon, and paid all the dues for this venture, including the inn and housing the wagon and team for another night. You will keep a ledger and control of all of The Chosen One's traveling money. There is a violet box inside your trunk with a ledger book and coin to supply your campaigns. There is a signet for Tiberius inside the box for signing documents and identifying you to money-changers. There is a list in the back of the ledger of all of the banks The Chosen One uses. For further instructions, please source chapter 3 of the tome.*
>
> *Your tasks for today revolve around chapter 7, repairing and maintaining the reputation of The Chosen One. When he has aggrieved someone, you are responsible for making amends and procuring their forgiveness, and more importantly, their discretion. This is one reason why The Chosen One will account all of his deeds to you, and you will record them in the most recent tome. Be sure to record when amends have been made; it is the only reliable method to track these things.*
>
> *Find on the desk a shoulder bag. Within it are discretionary binding scrolls and a list of names with addresses. Locate each offended party, offer your most sincere apologies, and give them a Gold Chosen.*

I stared at the words. A Gold Chosen for being offended?

> *If they refuse to sign a scroll, offer them another Gold Chosen, then one of the purses*

inside the bag if they sign. It usually does not take more than one purse, but keep increasing the incentive until they agree. Eventually, they all agree. Use some sense, for these expenses cut into your profits. This will give you a reasonable expectation of what your next two years of service will be like. Enjoy.

Sincerely,
Ethan

P.S.
That was the first time I have signed my own name in two years.

P.P.S.
Expect to find many more letters of this nature throughout the exploration of your duties. I have been preparing to transfer this blessing for over a month in anticipation of my impending two-year anniversary date.

I slid the shoulder bag toward me and looked inside. There were two large compartments and many smaller pockets all around the outside, like a money-changer's bag. One compartment contained half a dozen scrolls, all sealed with a flourishing 'T' inside a shield with a sword and a feather crossed behind it. "The seal of Tiberius?" I went to the trunk and opened it. It was full of books, scrolls, scrivener's supplies, and smaller boxes. Some of the books were covered with wood, some bound in leather. Everything looked like master craftsmanship, and every item I touched tingled. It would take some adjustment to become accustomed to encountering so many bespelled items and workings.

The violet box was a hand-span tall, two hand-spans deep, and three hand-spans wide. It was so heavy, I grunted and wheezed through my teeth as I strained to lift it. It also tingled as I carried it, cradled close to my chest to distribute the weight, and set it on the desk. There was a complex latch which clicked when I touched it. I felt surprisingly strong magic—undoubtedly bespelled to allow Tiberius, and no other, entry—which subsided when I lifted the lid. I gaped at the rows of neatly arranged Gold Chosen. A small note was folded and rested on top of the treasure.

> *Dear Tiberius,*
> *The Chosen One will permit you to carry and use only his coins. If you have any coin in your possession of lesser value than a Chosen, immediately give it to charity. For the next two years, you may not retain any coins but his. You must become accustomed to buying in bulk and offering to "Keep the remainder, with The Chosen One's blessings upon your trade and family."*
>
> *Sincerely,*
> *Tiberius*

I read the note several times. Pay in no coin but a Chosen? No wonder he was revered. I thought again about him throwing fists of gold coins into the crowd and wondered if he always did that. Then I wondered if that was also an expense that cut into my profits, or if it came from his "funds." I shook my head and decided I would need to read chapter 3 at the earliest possible convenience. "Keep the remainder, with The Chosen One's blessings upon your trade and family," I practiced as I located the ring in a small pouch resting on top of the coins. "Keep the remainder, with The Chosen One's blessings upon your trade and family." Unsurprisingly, it tingled when I took it from the pouch and tried it on. At first it was too small, but it changed size to fit. "Wow." Powerful working. "Keep the remainder, with The Chosen One's blessings upon your trade and family."

The signet was definitely the source of the T stamped into the wax on the scrolls. I decided to wear it while completing my errands, since contracts would be signed. I checked the bag again, and noticed the binding quill was inside and that all but one pocket contained a small, fine-leather, coin pouch emblazoned with The Chosen One's seal. When I lifted one of the small pouches, it clinked with multiple coins inside. The largest felt as though it contained thirty loose Gold Chosen. I felt my heart quicken. In this bag alone there was a fortune. If I wanted, I could take it and the violet box and flee the city, never to be troubled by poverty again. A sharp jolt of energy cut through me, and I dropped the bag with a groan.

I thought of Ethan's words, that there would be "warnings." The oath to honor The Chosen One undoubtedly included not robbing him and running away. Duly noted.

All the same, carrying this much coin was madness. Not even a moneychanger carried a quantity of Gold Chosen on his person. It was inviting robbery. The thought turned my stomach. I would have to in the very least appear less anxious than I felt. And I would need to make each party seem as if their compensation was the only one in the bag.

"Okay," I thought aloud. "I should have the coin and scroll in hand before approaching." I nodded at the idea and shouldered the bag. The sooner this task was completed, the sooner I could return the sum of unprecedented wealth to the room.

I paused at the door and looked down at my clothes. They were simple and clean, but they bore permanent stains. The blue and green hues of my wool tunic and trousers had clearly faded. Plus, in spite of the laundering and lingering aroma of lavender oil, there was still a faint odor of urine.

Ethan had been tall and lean, so his trousers would not fit well, if at all, but perhaps he left a tunic behind, or a tabard. A small wooden trunk next to the wall where Ethan had slept contained simple gray and brown garments. Simple, but freshly dyed and in good condition. The tunic was long, but fit comfortably enough. The trousers were even longer and uncomfortably snug, so I kept my own. A majority of the stains were covered by the rich, brown tunic that reached past my knees. I opted not to wear the tabard I found folded inside of the box. Ethan had only worn it when he was parading through town with The Chosen One.

I shouldered the bag again, and headed out the door. "This will be awkward," I mumbled as I came down the stairs and saw Goldie.

She looked up at me and smiled. "Tiberius," she greeted. "Care for a brandy?"

I frowned and approached the bar. The few patrons there glanced at me, then away. "Did he talk to you already?"

"The Chosen One? Oh, no. He's been out since you came down this morning." She cocked her head to the side and frowned at me. "Are you feeling all right? You must be stooping; you seemed to be standing much taller with sunrise." She lifted a dark bottle from behind the bar and filled a squat glass. "Have a brandy."

I stared at her, trying to decide if she was playing along for the customers, jesting with me, or genuinely thought I was Ethan. I had known Goldie for years. She could not possibly mistake me for that lanky man. I took the brandy offered and sipped, distractedly reaching toward my girdle bag.

"Oh, no," she quickly said, waving my hand away from my belt. "You're more than paid up."

I downed the last of the glass and set it on the counter, mumbling an uncomfortable thanks before I rushed out the door. The brandy had been excellent, the best in the house, I was certain. Even if she was playing along, she would have given me my usual, wouldn't she have? Did she *really* think I was Ethan? Perhaps it was one of the effects of the Tiberius Blessing. People wouldn't recognize me; they would recognize the working.

"Oh," I said, feeling considerably more comfortable. "Of course. So when I deal with those who've had arrangements with the last Tiberius, they'll think I am him." I nodded and smiled to myself, grateful that I had found a reasonable explanation for Goldie's strange behavior. This would certainly make running into anyone I knew less awkward. I realized with a grin that Allen would not recognize me, and considered visiting him as Tiberius to watch him fall over himself trying to impress The Chosen One's assistant.

By the time I reached the nearest address, a solidly built gray stone structure on Stonecutter Lane, I was glowing with joy at the good fortune that had found me. Wealth, anonymity, respect. I was an important man.

I straightened my tunic and knocked soundly on the door. When it opened, I smiled at the middle-aged man who'd appeared. He was muscular, bent from years of toil, and his features were stained white with dust. I was surprised to see the master of the house home at midday. Most of the men and women on this street worked in the quarry or a large shop near the same until sundown. "Good afternoon, mister. I am—"

"I know who you are," he snapped, glowering. He rose as much to his full height as he could and jutted his chin toward me, his eyes sharp with sudden rage. I backed away from his anger, thinking he might strike me. "You have some nerve coming here to my home after... after..." He set his jaw again, though there was a tremble in it, and moisture gathered around his eyes. "Go back to your *Chosen One*," he spat, spittle spraying from his lips. He moved to close the door, and I quickly held up a hand to stop him.

"Wait! Mister!" I cried, shaken by the man's anger and grief. I couldn't imagine what The Chosen One might have said or done to hurt him so. Even without knowing the circumstances of the grievance, I pitied him and regretted the duty I was there to fulfill.

"Masoner is the name," he snapped. "If you even *bothered* to remember!"

"Mister Masoner," I said, affecting a slight bow at the waist. "I've come to offer my most sincere apologies in the name of The Chosen One." I offered him the gold coin I held in my right hand. "And this token as compensation for the—"

"You've come to *pay* me!" He snapped, going rigid with fury. "If you were any other man... belonged to *any other man* than the great and honorable *Chosen One*," he raged, his cheeks going scarlet as tears streaked down his face. "My Ellie come into season this year! She had suitors! She was going to get away from mason work, maybe be a tailor's wife! Now what? What dowry entices a man to take spoiled goods?"

I stared in shock at the man's tirade, mortified by his accusation. The Chosen One had lain with a woman with suitors? He had taken her chastity? "I—"

"And a coin will give back what he plucked from her?" He snatched the coin from my hand and moved to close the door again.

"Wait!" I shoved my foot in the door and grimaced when the heavy wood rebounded from my toes. "Mister Masoner, please." I waited until his hardened gaze returned to mine. "I truly do offer my sincere apologies," I said, my stomach twisting in sympathy for this man and the situation in which the family found itself. "And I would like to help with her dowry. Certainly, your fair Ellie would make a fine wife to any tailor." I reached into my shoulder bag and withdrew a pouch, opting to bypass the second coin, wishing to genuinely set the account right. "I have more than just a token to offer," I explained, holding the pouch up for him to see. It clinked loudly, and I realized by the weight and feel of it that it contained four Gold Chosen, a common grouping for high-level purchases. "A Gold King for her dowry, and my shame, I offer as compensation for your grief."

His eyes fixed on the small bag, not in greed as I might have expected from any other man, but in calculation. With this coin and the one he already possessed, he could greatly improve their means, perhaps repair his daughter's soiled reputation. He could relocate. Or, he could bribe a suitor to overlook her impurity.

"I only ask for an agreement in writ for your family to maintain your discretion."

His eyes hardened again, but he didn't close the door. One does not simply turn down a Gold King; four Gold Chosen could feed a family and secure housing for a year or more. "In writ?"

I nodded offering the scroll and quill I held in my left hand. "Sign your agreement, and you have ours that your good name will not be besmirched by us in same."

He jerked the scroll from my fingers, and the quill fell to the ground. I quickly retrieved the feather while he broke the seal. He could read some, but I doubted he understood the flowery language I was certain the contract was written in. "And who should I say deflowered her if not your master," he snapped, glaring at me over the top of the paper. "Some vagrant? A married traveling merchant?"

"Or another eager youth," I supplied. "Any but The Chosen One," I instructed as gently as I could while I held the quill out to him.

He jerked the feather from me, and I flinched at the mistreatment of the exceptionally expensive tool. "It is binding, so the feather will feel like a needle prick."

He flinched, but quickly signed his illegible name on the bottom line in red. The scroll and quill he shoved into my chest just before he seized the small pouch and slammed the door in my face. I jumped back, but not fast enough to keep my toes from being pummeled by the door.

I hopped on one leg, cursing quietly and holding the boot of my abused toes in one hand. As soon as I was able to force weight onto my injured foot, I hobbled down the road and away from the stonecutter's house. A sick weight settled into my stomach as I thought of the five remaining scrolls for which to procure signatures, from likely equally furious men and women. My only fortune in this endeavor was that The Chosen One's status elevated him to a level of untouchable, which trickled down to his vassal. No man would dare issue true threats against me or The Chosen One for fear of punishment — including stocks, imprisonment, and death by the hand of a god. Just as one would not threaten or insult their lord to one of his messengers, for their own safety and that of their family.

It was a relief, but the thought of it also sickened me.

When I returned to the inn, I walked right past the bar, wordlessly taking the brandy Goldie held out, and ascended the stairs with no preamble. I was so soul weary and eager to shed myself of that shameful bag of bribes, that I did not think to knock on the door to The Chosen One's room before I opened it. Only after I saw the many trunks and boxes did I realize how brazen and foolish I had been. What if The Chosen One had been there and with some hapless husband's wife, or his daughter... or *both*? I shuddered and dropped the shoulder bag on the desk and downed the brandy in one swallow. I choked on the load of liquor, but kept it back.

I dropped to the chair at the desk and picked up the ninth Tome of Tiberius. I skimmed the last few pages written by Ethan. He was accounting the deeds The Chosen One had shared with him that required amends: two deflowered maidens, a romp with *two* women—both married—and accidently having a drunken kiss and grope with a very fair looking young man. I felt soiled beyond the ability of scrubbing to cleanse. Did Tiberius have to do this in every town? Was there a standard discretionary contract I could simply spend several nights copying for occasions such as this? Did I need to carry some on me for on-the-spot apologies?

My head dropped to the desk, and rather than weep, I let myself drift into sleep.

4. The Stranger Came Early in the Morning, One Drunken Night

The door banged open, and I nearly crashed to the floor from the chair, I was so abruptly jarred from sleep. The room was dark as pitch, and the sounds of grunting and moaning came from the open passage. My first half-asleep thought was the room had been invaded by a dying man or perhaps an incompetent robber. I slinked quietly as I could to the floor, and tried to drift toward the wall. I banged my head on a trunk, and finally reached the stage of awake where I truly remembered where I was.

A woman giggled, and a man grunted out a heady, drunken laugh. "Tiberius? Light that lantern so I may see these accursed knots!" The man's voice was deep, rich with a mixture of accents, and slurred from drink. "Or by the gods, help me with them!"

I flushed hot with shame and groped for the lantern. My fingers hesitated on the lighting flint and steel. A thought flitted through my mind as I fumbled with the mechanism; if I did manage to light the wick with the spark, he would see my face and know I wasn't Ethan.

The grunting and moaning escalated to a fevered pitch. "Never mind, Tiberius," he grumbled as the two intermingled figures groped their way to the bed. "I'll manage. Out!"

"The other room is sold—"

"Common room, stable, street... I don't care! Out!" His booming voice seemed to shake the very walls.

I rushed from the room in embarrassed panic, tripping over Ethan's bedroll, and ran down the stairs two at a time. It was the first time I'd ever spoken to The Chosen One, and I prayed to any god that might listen he didn't remember the encounter come morning. I stood at the foot of the steps, panting and swallowing back shame. After gathering my wits, I cracked the door to the common sleeping room and looked across the sea of snoring men. It was dimly lit by a few wall sconces with guttering oil lamps and was so packed with bodies I doubted I could find room to stretch out, let alone an empty cot or roll to claim. There was even a man sleeping against the exit leading to the side alley. I closed and latched the door, looking about the empty tavern for some place more comfortable than a hardwood floor.

    I made my way shakily to a stool and hoped Goldie didn't mind me resting my head upon the bar for a few hours. It took several more minutes for my heart to calm to a regular rhythm. Thankfully, after the day I'd had, I was still too exhausted to dwell for long over the embarrassing introduction. Lulled by the deep snoring of the pack of people in the other room, sleep crept quickly over me.

    The loud bang of heavy glass on wood beside my ear awoke me with a start. Goldie was smirking at me from behind the bar. "Ousted you?" She slid the tankard of ale a little nearer to my nose. "Some breakfast?"
    "Please," I groaned, blearily.

"Porridge isn't done yet, but I have cold pottage."

"Whatever," I mumbled, looking around. Morning light was only then spilling through the open door. I was the only patron, and the common room had just been opened, a few men drifting out into the street to begin their day. "Um, earlier, did a young lady... or an older lady, perhaps..."

She grinned. "A working woman left not ten minutes ago, looking ill-rested but content."

"A working woman? You're sure?"

She smiled. "One sees them around." She ladled out some pottage from the large iron pot hanging over a freshly stoked fire. "You're in luck; it's still a little warm." She slid the bowl and an iron spoon over to me.

"Thank you," I mumbled, quietly eating and drinking my ale while she prepared the tavern for business. In short order, she provided a half loaf of sourdough bread with a healthy dollop of creamed butter. The simple pottage was quite good; Goldie had a way with seasoning that made the dish taste like more than whatever she managed to throw in the pot every day to keep it going. "I never asked," I mumbled between bites. "Did married life suit you well?"

She looked over at me and raised a brow. "Curious question for someone I barely know." She shrugged. "Every time," she answered with a smile. "I loved all three of my husbands, and they me. And every one was a new life and a new adventure."

I smiled at her wistful but happy expression. "Would you marry again?"

She nodded. "Oh, sure! If I met a man who made me happy as they did. I'd have to trust him, which I would if I planned to marry him, because he gains control of all I now have."

I laughed quietly. "I doubt any man could control you. But I see your meaning."

"And I wouldn't mind learning another trade," she added with a twinkle in her eye.

We both laughed. I finished my meal as patrons of the inn drifted into the tavern for food and drink. I wasted as much of the morning as I could, hoping The Chosen One would at least be dressed when I went upstairs to introduce myself by light of day.

"Goldie," I said at last, when the hero had neither called for me nor come down. "I will take a brandy."

She filled a squat cup and slid it over to me. I down the liquor and dropped the glass onto the wood forcefully enough to draw the attention of several men around me. "I'm heading up," I declared to no one in particular.

"Oh, good," Goldie said, placing a tray in front of me. It was nearly identical to the meal I'd been served the morning before: porridge, bread, eggs, and wine.

I sighed and took the tray up with me. I tried to think of all of the ways I could explain to The Chosen One I wasn't a servant. Or rather, that I was *his* servant, or his assistant, or anything other than a worker at the inn. The tray was heavy, and I had to prop it against my hip to free up a hand and knock.

"Come," The Chosen One's deep voice boomed.

I worked the latch and repositioned the platter in both hands as I toed the door open and then closed behind me. The Chosen One sat propped up in his bed, thankfully covered by blankets, as he was clearly naked beneath. His fine clothes were thrown in every direction all over the room, and he grinned at me as if proud of his night's work. "Tiberius! I was wondering where you had gone to!"

I hesitated, and wondered if, like Goldie, he thought I was Ethan. "Um, you told me to leave last night."

"Oh, yes, the... um, *lady*." He chuckled to himself as if he had just made a funny jest. "She was lovely, wasn't she?"

"Oh, yes," I lied, remembering very little of her actual features. "Fair beyond compare. Where would you like—"

"You!" he suddenly said, freezing me in place with a stare. He squinted hard at me. "You're new." A look of disappointment shadowed his brows, and his shoulders sank. I didn't blame him. I had been ill prepared to fill the role, and I didn't believe Ethan had spared time to even say goodbye. The Chosen One gestured to his lap. "Put it there."

I did as instructed, and he gestured to his bright blue tunic on the floor.

"Have my clothes pressed by the time I'm done," he mumbled somewhat dourly. "We need to be off by noon."

"Pressed?" I gathered up his tunic, then located his under tunic, and trousers. They reeked of alcohol and other more unsavory things. I found his underpinnings flopped over the back of a chair, his standard embroidered across the back. I blinked in surprise at his miniature grin glowing up at me from the seat of his undergarment before shaking off my unease and adding it to the bundle in my arms.

"Do it yourself or send it out; I don't care. Just get on it. You still need to pack. It would be nice if you read some of that book you foolishly left open on the table over there." He nodded to the Tome of Tiberius. "Go on!"

I jumped at the bark in his tone, shouldered the bag of shame, and rushed out the door to the washhouse. Along the way, I tried to imagine what the interaction would be like, offering the women at the laundry a Gold Chosen to clean and press one set of clothing and undergarments. The moment I walked in, the woman at a table by the door smiled and held her arms out for my bundle. "Tiberius! We'll have them sent back to the inn."

I opened my mouth, prepared to explain the large over-payment, then smiled and nodded. Of course. Ethan had already paid with a Gold Chosen, so we already had credit at this establishment. How convenient. "Excellent," I said. "As soon as possible. We are leaving early."

"Oh? I'm sorry to hear you're leaving. Safe journey to The Chosen One and to you. I'll have one of my girls run it over straight away."

On my way back to the inn, I traveled wide to visit a temple of Skalah. I thought as king of the gods and the ruling force of the blessings I and The Chosen One received, he was the right god to thank for my recent fortune. I once frequently visited the temple of Dindrel, patron of wizards, but the last two years I had been a patron at the temple of Anetrael, as were most scribes. It was strange to come into Skalah's house; it was so different from the others. There were many windows of bright gold and yellow glass in the shape of sunbursts. Just inside the door were mounds of food, left as offerings to the sun god who fueled their crops and also the god of merriment and feasts.

It seemed appropriate that, bearing the blessings of such a god, The Chosen One would drink, feast, and be merry himself. I walked to the altar and knelt to the stones. "Great god of laughter and sadness, thank you for your blessing and my good fortune." There was an offering plate full of copper and silver coins in front of the altar, and I leaned forward to leave the remainder of my Gold Chosen from the day before, a fist-full of assorted coins.

I took a moment to quietly recount the many things in the past few days for which I was grateful, including Allen not breaking my hand two days prior.

When I returned to the inn, I stopped in the carriage house to check on the wagon. I tried to estimate which trunks fit in the arrangement of open spaces. As I looked through the supplies, I was happy to find a note from Ethan, signing as Tiberius, with the inventory of what he normally kept stocked on their journeys. It was a full list of supplies, gear, tack, and armor. I was stunned when I read it. It was as though he carried an entire household with him wherever he went.

My next stop was to check on The Chosen One's horses. I was expecting three to be stabled, but discovered there were actually nine: a destrier, four sumpters, two coursers, and two palfreys. It was a full Gold Chosen a night to keep and fodder the horses and hold the cart under guard. The hot-blooded destrier snorted angrily in his stable, kicking at the back wood when I passed. The sumpters, labor animals by breeding, were content to rest and feed for the few days they'd been given. The coursers were leaner and faster than the destrier, but almost as hot blooded. I'd only seen a few in my time, as they were usually campaign animals or jousting beasts. The Chosen One probably kept them as flee animals, based on what he battled, since they would be faster and more sure-footed than the destrier. I was not surprised that he had a palfrey to ride. They were comfortable for long journeys, much more so than the warhorses. I wasn't sure why he had two, since Ethan had been walking, unless he kept one as a spare when his tired. That explained the two spare sumpters as well, to pull the cart if the lead horses tired or came up lame.

I wondered if he'd arrived in Noblan just returned from battle. Perhaps that was why he rode into town in full armor and colors, astride the destrier. Having now met him, a part of me suspected the display might have been entirely for show. Ethan's disinterest at the time would support the latter theory. I hadn't seen the additional six horses before I'd been knocked down, so they must have been tied off to the back of the wagon, guided by a lead. I asked the stable hands the horses' names, but they only knew how to call the warhorses, to help them better handle the beasts. I wondered if the work animals even had names, deciding I would issue them if they had none. I would check the ninth Tome of Tiberius to be sure.

I returned to the room and knocked, entering at the direction of The Chosen One... who stood in front of the mirror wearing nothing but his Chosen underwear and the tyrian purple cloak wrapped around his shoulders. His chest was puffed out, and his enormous, muscular limbs flexed this way and that as he posed himself in dramatic battle postures with his famous great sword. Every inch of visible skin was hairless and glistening. He had worked up a sweat admiring himself, and I could still smell the liquor on him.

"Um..." I mumbled, wondering if I should return at a more convenient—and less embarrassing—time. Much to my chagrin, he didn't stop flexing on my account.

"Go ahead and pack," he grunted as he clenched his stomach to make all of his tightly bound abdomen muscles pop. "I'll wait for the pressed clothes." He turned to the side and threw the cloak over his shoulder so he could admire his hips and backside, casting daring glances at his tiny embroidered face on the seat of his underpinnings through the polished brass.

    I was certain my own face was scarlet as I skirted past him to gather up everything and return the items to the trunks that seemed the most appropriate. The entire time I worked, he didn't break from his posturing, and I wondered if it was a form of exercise for him, or if it merely exercised his ego. My work was hastened by embarrassment, and when I was done, I silently took up the first Tome of Tiberius. I turned my back, ignoring his grunting and wheezing, and flipped to chapter 3, skimming for the most pertinent pieces of information. I needed to know how to handle The Chosen One's finances.

    I quickly learned it was my duty to draw up contracts when The Chosen One agreed to take a deal, enforce the contracts, and collect the fees. It was my duty to arrange for appraisers, auctioneers, and moneychangers to convert any "spoils" of The Chosen One's labors—those that he did not keep for his personal collection—to coin. It was my duty to ensure there was sufficient coin for The Chosen One to live whatever lifestyle he chose and to fund any campaign. Incidentals incurred as a direct result of a campaign—such as bribing furious husbands—came from funds before they were deposited into a bank and Tiberius' percentage was calculated. There was a list of "lifestyle" actions that came from the bank and were not considered incidentals; "donations and women" were on that list. Thus, I assumed him throwing coins into the crowd was not an incidental, either, but came from The Chosen One's own bank holdings.

"You need to plot a course for Vevesk," The Chosen One said between poses. "They have vampire stoats."

"What," I asked, slightly startled by the break in silence. "What is a stoat?"

"I think they said it was like a long rat." He glanced over at me. "Find out. And find out how to kill it."

I stared at him until his self-admiration embarrassed me enough to look away. "You don't know how to kill them?"

"I assume I cut them up enough, they'll die," he quipped. "You need to figure out how it happened so I can stop it. Evil wizard, ancient curse, typical vampirism, that sort of thing."

"*I* have to learn what caused this outbreak of blood-sucking long rats?" I asked, incredulously. Surely he was jesting. That was *his* job.

"Chapter 2," he said, stripping off the cloak so he could better admire his shoulders.

I grimaced and turned to the second chapter in the Tome of Tiberius. This detailed how I was to conduct necessary research for a campaign and successfully translate it to The Chosen One, for him to then implement that knowledge to complete his feats of heroism. I sighed deeply. "There is no university here to hold historical works, and many of the larger temples do not have any books in them at all. I will need to visit the Wizards' Guild, the Questers' Guild, and the Scriveners' Guild," I explained.

"Go quickly," he ordered without sympathy. "We leave soon."

I gritted my teeth and rose from my chair, throwing Tiberius' quill and a stack of paper sheets into my shoulder bag. It was all but impossible to do the kind of research this would require in only a handful of hours. So, I ran. I ran to the guildhall, where all the town's guilds would have an office and representatives. To my surprise, I only had to break my stride a few times to catch my breath. Ethan had not been jesting when he said increased stamina was part of the blessing. When I reached the guildhall, I walked slowly to calm my pounding heart. I quickly found a representative for the Questers' Guild, a single young man standing near the door, wearing a tabard with a sword and shield livery emblazoned on it. I thought this guild might know of a local legend about vampirism. Or stoats.

"Good day," I said to gain the man's attention. "I need to speak with—"

"Tiberius!" the youth exclaimed with a high pitched squeal, and I jerked in surprise. "*The* Tiberius! Oh! The Chosen One requires our guild? Please, what do you need? Anything!"

"I... need to speak with your record keeper. I have—"

"I will get him," the boy interjected, running out the door at a full sprint.

I watched him run for a moment, impressed by his speed, then found a representative of the Scriveners' Guild. Another youth near the door stood at the ready, his tabard bearing a quill and scroll. "Good day," I said, but I was prepared for the wide rounding of his eyes and quickly spoke up. "I need to speak with your records keeper." I held a hand up when he started for the door. "I am short on time, I need any records he may have on vampirism or a rat-like creature called a stoat."

"Oh, a stoat is like a weasel," the boy offered.

I laughed. "Well, that's helpful. Can you please tell your man what I require and that I will wait here for the records?"

He bobbed his head and ran out the door with only slightly less eagerness than the apprentice quester had.

I found the representative of the Wizards' Guild, a young woman wearing a white sash and a blank tabard of white wool. She was seated on the ground near the door, reading from a large, wood-bound tome. I smiled when I approached, remembering well the days I had kept vigil at the guildhall in just such a fashion, a book in my lap and no expectation that any day could be better than that. The Wizards' Guild was one of the few where a woman could train just as a man, regardless of her marital status. After all, a magical gift was a magical gift. "Good day," I said to her.

She looked up at me and shielded her eyes. "Good day, mister," she responded. "How may I help you?"

It amused me that she didn't recognize me, or rather, the Tiberius Blessing. She must not have seen The Chosen One ride into town, though he'd passed right by the guildhall. "I need to speak with your records keeper. I need information on vampirism and a weasel-like creature called a stoat."

She closed the book and rose to her feet. "Yes, mister. Who may I say is requesting him? Or shall I take you to his office?"

"I will wait here for the records, thank you. You may say Tiberius, assistant to The Chosen One, has asked for his assistance."

Her eyes grew wide, and her mouth dropped open. She looked as if to speak, but tucked the book under her arm and ran from the guildhall instead.

I could really become accustomed to being treated as a man with such a high reputation, the personal assistant of the revered Chosen One. If only it was not such an unsavory job behind closed doors. Still, even if I was responsible for any amount of menial tasks and enduring his beauty routines, it was well worth the cost.

While I waited, I had a message sent to the dock, requesting a charter boat be held for The Chosen One that would accommodate nine horses and a large wagon. I hadn't had a chance to run a route by my master, but as the river was the only choice that made sense, I thought he would approve. Or be convinced. The quester apprentice returned first, flushed, breathless, and sweating. "He... invited you... to dine... and wine... his house..."

I held up a hand to stop him. "You left before I could finish," I explained somewhat apologetically. "My time in town is very limited. I need information on vampirism and a weasel called a stoat. If he would be so kind as to check his records for either one, I would appreciate it. I must wait here until I hear back from the other guilds from which I have requested assistance."

The boy deflated a little, nodded and gave an exhausted huff. Then he ran through the door with quite a bit less vigor than the first time. I felt sorry for him, but he had interrupted me twice, and a lord would cuff him for eagerness like that. Best that he learn this way that he should be patient and listen.

The scrivener apprentice returned next, followed by Master Scribe Hinale. I knew the bent old man, and though he was not the record keeper, he worked in records and was an acceptable substitute. He bore a cloth shoulder sack that clearly contained a book in one side and a few scrolls in the other. He nodded deeply to me out of respect—thankfully he didn't recognize *me*—and held out the sack. "We do not have any records on stoats, though I can tell you they are a small weasel not unlike a ferret."

I took the offering and nodded my thanks. "May I have your leave to study these at my leisure? I will ensure that they are returned to your guild in short order."

He nodded his head. "Of course, Tiberius. We are honored that The Chosen One should ask for our assistance. May I inquire about the need for such items?"

I withdrew a Gold Chosen from my girdle bag and handed it over to the old man. "I am not at liberty to discuss the matter, but this should compensate your guild for the use of these materials."

He looked surprised at the generous fee and nodded. "Of course. If you need anything else?"

I looked down at the apprentice. "Can you read and write, boy?"

He nodded. "Four languages."

"Impressive. Wizards' tongue?"

The boy nodded again, and I looked to the older scribe. "May I use this apprentice for the afternoon?"

He nodded. "You may use me as well."

I thought about his offer. "Will you copy these scrolls for me and have the duplicates sent to The Hare and the Cat? Cotton paper is fine. I do not require vellum."

He nodded again and took the shoulder sack from me. He withdrew the one book and handed it to the apprentice to keep. "I will have our staff complete them and have them to you within two hours."

"I and The Chosen One offer our thanks."

My interchanges with the other two guilds went much the same, except the quester apprentice could not read, which was not altogether surprising. I set the two apprentices down in the corner of the nearest tavern and tasked them with finding references in their materials to the information I was seeking, and I compiled notes based on what they read aloud to me.

The findings were sparse, but verified what I had already suspected. Vampirism in wildlife was most often a side effect of rising undead. Most evil wizards didn't *intend* to create undead or vampire squirrels or fish, it was usually an accidental overflow when they did their initial spells on the intended targets. Content that we had scoured the remaining books and scrolls to the best of our abilities, I sent the apprentices back to their guilds with the borrowed records, stowing my notes in my bag.

When I returned to the inn, The Chosen One was dancing with two women to a lively ballad in the tavern. He was resplendent in his bright royal blue and gold tunic and trousers, his pale-honey curls cascading over the rich fabric. I even thought he might have been glowing faintly, as though the sun were shining on only him. I sighed half in reverence, half in frustration and went up to the room. All of the trunks were gone. I frowned and returned to the tavern. I patiently waited for the song to end, but The Chosen One flipped the minstrel a gold coin, and the music started once again.

With a groan of frustration, I went to the carriage house to check on the wagon and was surprised to see all of our luggage had been loaded on... including Tiberius' trunk which contained a treasury in gold. I looked toward the carriage house doors to see only one lean, young man guarding the entrance. I shook my head and returned to the inn, flagging down Goldie. "Were there some scrolls delivered here?"

She nodded and smiled. "I had them sent up to your room."

I wanted to shout with frustration. The Chosen One could have shoved them into any of the half a dozen trunks and boxes that had been in the room.

The song ended with a high, lingering note. The Chosen One kissed both girls heartily before releasing them, and they wandered out into the tavern flushed and breathless. He came over to the bar and flagged Goldie, who was already pouring him a tankard of mead. He grinned down at me. "Ready to go?"

"The scrolls, did you read them?"

He wrinkled his nose. "Tiberius work. I put them in your trunk. Let's go." He lifted the tankard to Goldie in toast, and in one long, impressive display, drank the entire glass. He belched loudly, earning a cheer from the tavern, and slammed the glass down. He waved boisterously at the room's patrons, letting out a wordless, masculine cry, which was echoed resoundingly.

Disgusted, I walked out the door without looking to see if he was following. To my surprise, he came up behind me and threw a huge, muscled arm around my shoulders. It was then that I realized how much taller than me he was, not as much as Ethan, but close.

"You know the way?" he asked, belching again.

I took a steadying breath to keep the irritation and discomfort from my voice. "We will charter a river boat the forty leagues west to Rshavin, then take the main trade route north for twenty leagues to Vevesk."

"Hmm," he grumbled. "Two or three days on the water."

I nodded and resisted the conversational urge to look up at him. My efforts would only have been rewarded with a face full of golden hair and armpit. "And three days on the main road, maybe four."

He sighed and stopped outside the carriage house. "Well, all right." He crossed his arms and looked out at the busy thoroughfare, and I hesitated for long moment before I realized he was waiting for *me* to get his horse and have the wagon hitched.

"Oh, yes." I started toward the carriage house. "Which mount would you like?"

"Fellowyn," he answered.

I stopped short. That was not any of the names I knew. "Um... which one is that?"

He rolled his eyes dramatically. "The palfrey with white socks."

"Boy," I shouted when I came into the carriage house. Two stable hands quickly appeared from wherever they had been laboring in the stalls. "Boys," I amended. "Prepare The Chosen One's horse, the palfrey with white socks, and hitch his wagon." I pointed to the two nearest sumpters. "Those ones for the wagon. Lead the others from the back."

They rushed to do as I asked, laboring quickly, and the stolid stable marshal came out to meet me. "Tiberius," he greeted in his gruff way. "Taking your leave?"

I nodded. "The Chosen One is needed."

He watched the boys work, a trained eye tracking their progress. "That destrier has spirit. I had best ready him; he's likely to kill the lads." I didn't argue. I wanted as little to do with the blood-thirsty battle mount as possible. I was not looking forward to being in close quarters with the fierce beast on the river boat.

The marshal led the sumpters and wagon from the carriage house, handing the reins over to me. Then he helped the paid hands hitch the other horses to the back with long leads. Last, he guided Fellowyn to The Chosen One and held the palfrey steady while the hero mounted with one quick, practiced motion.

The Chosen One looked over at me, his brow twisting in displeasure. "Where is your...?" He looked to the back of the wagon. "Topher is yours, you foolish man! Why isn't he saddled?"

I opened my mouth, and then set my jaw to keep from saying something I might regret. Finally, I was able to calmly ask. "And... which one is Topher?"

Topher, as it turned out, was the black with gray palfrey. I had taken him to be The Chosen One's spare, but he apparently belonged to Tiberius. I hooked the lead of the sumpters across my saddle, and our modest procession made its way to the river dock on the other side of town. Everywhere we went, villagers stopped to cheer and clap as The Chosen One rode. He kept a full horse length ahead of me, waving and shouting to the crowd as if he was the only hero in the world.

The dockmaster was awaiting us when we led the horses out onto Riverway. He waved men over to take the leads of our mounts and to unhitch the horses from the back of the wagon. I was grateful once more that I was not the one to contend with the destrier, who showed his displeasure by shouldering a man off the dock and into the water. The river men roared with laughter, and The Chosen One strode up to the wild beast. To my and every observer's wonder, the animal mellowed for the great hero, and bowed its head in submissive kinship to him.

"I know, boy," The Chosen One rumbled to the animal. "I hate ships, too. You'll have nothing but oats for the next few nights." He led the animal up the platform and onto the ship himself as we all watched in amazement at the beast's docile behavior.

"Ensorcelled," one man muttered, but he quickly looked busy when he caught my disapproving gaze.

Once the cart was on, the horses were unhitched and picketed along the deck with just enough room to shift as needed with the sway of the boat. The captain bowed to The Chosen One. "You may take my quarters for the duration of this journey," he offered.

As there was only one cabin, I thought this was particularly generous. The Chosen One nodded. "That will do, Captain Swails. Tiberius, arrange the quarters for our use."

I wasn't sure what he meant, entirely. I wondered if he remembered that this was my second day, and I had no inkling what preparations he might prefer. There were only eight deckhands, and they all looked busy securing the wagon and unmooring the boat. I waited till there appeared to be a transition between unmooring and moving, and requested two of them help me lift the heavier of the trunks from the wagon. They were clearly irritated, but made quick work of the labor and then took their places in rowing seats. The rowers maneuvered the boat out into the main current of the river before the large, square sail was unfurled.

When the wind caught, my stomach lurched, and the sudden rocking of the ship nearly pitched me from my feet.

"I have important matters," The Chosen One declared, and quickly cloistered himself in the cabin. I had meant to find the first Tome of Tiberius to continue my studies, but decided to lean over the railing and empty my stomach into the river. Repeatedly. For the following three hours.

I knew from previous experience the sickness would pass once my stomach had been well empty for a long while. Trusting the worst of it had eased, I tentatively moved to the cabin, ignoring the grins and quiet jesting of the crew. I decided to forego formality—it seemed relatively pointless after watching the hero flex strenuously in his undergarments that morning—and entered the captain's quarters without knocking. The Chosen One was sprawled on the bed with one arm across his face and the other on his chest with his fist to his mouth.

"Are you sick as well," I asked, miserably.

"Yes," he grumbled.

His voice was strangely slurred, or perhaps muffled, and I cast a glance at him while I rifled through the trunk of Tiberius. He was sucking his thumb. I stared, dumbfounded, blinking to be sure my eyes had adjusted properly to the gloom of the cabin. "Do you... require some sort of medicine?"

"Yes. *Finally*," he replied, unmistakably around the thumb in his mouth. "There is something," he instructed, vaguely.

I shook my head and dug around in the trunk in search of a ledger or inventory. Of course, there was one. Ethan had been a good, albeit absent, instructor thus far. The entire bottom of the trunk was compartments containing elixirs, tonics, poultices, and salves. There was a salve for sea sickness, and I located it in the trunk. When I lifted the lid, it smelled strongly of peppermint.

"That's it," The Chosen One mumbled around his thumb, apparently recognizing the aroma. "He always puts it on my chest." His pathetic tone stirred me to pity, and I wondered if he had vomited. Then I wondered *where* he had vomited. There was a port window by his bed, but it looked a little small for his broad head.

The cabin was tight, so rather than rise in the rocking ship, I slid along the floor until I was next to the bed. "You will have to stop... um, move your arm."

Rather than take his thumb out of his mouth, he simply lifted his elbow from his chest and arched his back to allow me access to his clothing.

Wonderful, I thought to myself. I had to unfasten his wide girdle belt, and since he was lying on the tunic, slide my arm under it and up his body until I could reach his chest with my salve-slathered fingers. In spite of my irritation, I refused to compromise my effectiveness and went over the activation cant a few times in my mind to ensure I would have flawless pronunciation and cadence. The working required physical contact with the salve, so I held my hand to his chest for several uncomfortable moments while I prepared.

"Your hands are soft," he mumbled.

I flushed and hissed out power, quickly muttering the cant and jerking my fingers back the moment I felt the working take hold. I recovered from the uncomfortable compliment quickly, and grimaced at my own overreaction. "Well, I was not expecting to be rubbing your chest today. But, thank you. I suppose."

He shifted enough to peer at me under his arm, his eyes glittering with amusement. Though he had done nothing but disappoint me since we'd met, it did feel a little gratifying to earn his smile when he was clearly unwell. He *was* a great and noble hero, even if he was an ass. The sweet scent of the salve filled the cabin, and by way of contact on my fingers, my own nausea completely abated in a matter of minutes. I was immediately irritated that he could have told me about the salve hours ago and spared both of us suffering and embarrassment. Though, I suspected I was the only one who felt the latter.

A few minutes later, he rose and fastened his belt. I watched him adjust his clothes and wondered how he would do his morning flexes without a mirror. I smiled at the jest in my head, and imagined him posing for his reflection in the water. When I looked back at him, The Chosen One was adjusting his hair. Not combing it or styling it... adjusting its *placement on his head*.

For a moment, I didn't understand what I was seeing, and a surreal feeling of vertigo passed over me before I realized his glorious blond curls... were a *wig*. A wig! The blond locks for which he was known, that bards sang about, that emblazoned Tiberius' tabard, that waved on the Gold Chosen, countless illustrations, tapestries, and paintings. A *wig*!

He glowered over at me. "Don't just stare, help me with it. The humidity has it loosened up."

I rose to do as he asked, but couldn't bring myself to touch the fake hair or the glistening, bald scalp underneath. I gaped in amazement, and he shoved me back, hard. "A dragon burned off my hair a long while ago," he snapped as I stumbled and nearly fell over a trunk. "It never grew back." I blinked and forced myself to look away as he continued moving the hair around on his head. Finally he seemed satisfied with his ghostly reflection in the porthole glass, and glowered at me again for good measure.

"Don't forget to make the bed," he snapped. Then he squared his shoulders and strode out onto the deck like the indomitable hero he was. "How fares our journey," he called to the captain as if he hadn't just been sick for hours. I heard him make a jest of my 'sea legs,' and the crew laughed heartily. I gritted my teeth and carefully packed away the supplies I'd disturbed.

Somewhere in the distance, thunder rumbled. I checked the salve to be sure we had enough to make it through a storm, and then I located the first Tome of Tiberius. I had a lot to learn, and it appeared as though The Chosen One had no intention of making it easier on me. I quickly dressed his bed—the captain's bed—and thought to lay a blanket out for myself on the floor. Come time to sleep, it would be too dark to do it properly.

I went out onto the deck to use the last few hours of daylight and wedged myself somewhere secure to read. No one bothered me, and I was grateful for the few moments of peace. I remembered Ethan walking behind The Chosen One, reading as he led the horses, and I thought of the girl reading in the guildhall. Perhaps the most solace I would find over the next two years was moments like that, alone with a book in spite of the constantly moving life of The Chosen One. I smiled, content at that thought, and opened to Chapter 1: *Care for The Chosen One*. The first article was about mixing bespelled wrinkle cream, and I smirked.

5. It Was a Dark and Stormy Night

After only an hour of study, the light faded suddenly. I looked up toward the rapidly darkening sky and the ominous clouds that rushed in from ahead of us to the west. Lightning flashed in them, and a cold headwind slammed against me, riffling the pages of the book in my lap. I turned my face away from the gust, toward the shore, and movement caught my eye. I peered closely, thinking at first it was a deer I saw running alongside the craft.

Then his face turned toward me. It was a man with tawny brown skin and long, red hair. His body and limbs were long, lean, and muscular. He ran through the thick woods with the speed and confidence of an animal knowledgeable of its surroundings. His eyes fixed on me, but his speed didn't check in the slightest as he quickly outdistanced the riverboat. A lance of inexplicable fear cut through my gut. Lightning struck on the other side of the bank, and the light flashed eerily across the man's eyes, as if illuminating them from within. His path veered abruptly away, and he disappeared into the brush. I caught a flash of a bright blue sash, and he was gone.

My heart was pounding as if I'd just seen a predator charging the boat, and I stared into the trees, unblinking, looking for him. I felt The Chosen One come up beside me. He seemed somehow charged with energy, more than the working I had put on him an hour or so earlier. "He's ahead of the ship," I said.

"Who," he asked, his tone not alarmed in the least.

"The man." I forced my eyes away from the trees to look up at the towering warrior beside me. "You didn't see him?"

He laughed and shook his head. "No man could outdistance this craft in brush that thick. It was a deer."

"That's what I thought," I said, looking back at the forest. But it had *not* been a deer; every part of me that was a wizard knew it. The man had been a bad omen, no mistake, and my still-pounding heart was a testament to the magnitude of the threat he represented.

I put the tome back into the trunk and secured it just before the rain started. It buffeted and rocked the boat, lurching my stomach in spite of the sea sickness working. The captain shouted curtly to his men as they bundled the sail and maneuvered the craft to the wide part of the river, dropping an anchor off the side and wrapping the rope with fabric to lessen chaffing.

"We're stopping?" The Chosen One shouted over the rumble of the storm to the captain, who responded with a wide-eyed, emphatic nod.

"This storm rose up too fast to find a vegetation hole. We cannot make out the bank and hazards of the water. We have to drop anchor for the night and wait it out." He nodded to the cabin. "Bed down, this could be a rough one. Pray to your gods we don't slip anchor! I hear they listen to you." He grasped the hero's shoulder with a bracing grip, then spun away to shout more commands at a few deckhands who had slowed.

I waited until The Chosen One went into the cabin and followed him in. A part of me felt as though I needed to be near him, to protect him if need be. Deep down, however, I suspected it was *me* who wished to be near *him* for protection. "This storm is ill fated," I told him.

"Ominous," he jested, stripping off his soaked tunic and trousers.

"I am serious. The man I saw—"

"The *deer* you saw," he corrected.

"The *man* I saw," I insisted. "He was an ill omen."

"You really don't care for seafaring, do you?" He grinned over at me.

"That's not... are you *glowing*?" I had always thought he seemed to radiate a living energy in his posture and movements, but in the small, dim cabin, he did appear to be nearly fully lit.

His grin broadened. "*Blessing of Light* from Skalah. If the sun is up and his dominion is strong, my very presence can combat the dark."

I stared in awe. "You... shine with the sun?"

He nodded. "You don't see it as much when we're outside and the sun is shining, but during storms, you *sure notice*." He laughed. "I'm grateful, because I always have a light during the day, regardless of whatever dark hole I find myself in. That's why I prefer to slay during the day."

I nodded, sobered by his flippant use of the word *slay*. "And it helps you tell time."

He laughed deeply, and the merry sound actually lightened the weight in my chest a little. For a moment, I had forgotten that I traveled with The Chosen One. No man—or *deer*—in the woods could challenge the grandmaster hero who bore the blessings of gods.

"Night will fall soon," he reminded me. "Light the wick so you can read by."

I shook my head. "The boat is pitching. The last thing we need is a fire in this cabin."

"There's a light spell," he offered, nodding to the trunk. "Somewhere."

"Oh." That actually *was* useful, and I wondered if maybe he was starting to like me more. I was at least becoming accustomed to him. He certainly did not lack for confidence, and in some circumstances, it was a comfort. Such as when a strange man with glowing eyes took an unwholesome interest in the small vessel we were trapped upon. I withdrew the burgundy tome and tried to read in the dim light of the cabin.

"Sit next to me," he offered, making room for me on the edge of the bed.

I laughed quietly and took the offered spot. He did shine just bright enough to read by, and he held his hand over the text, illuminating it further. The order and index of the book was very efficient, and it didn't take me long to locate the spell.

"Oh," I said. "This is actually quite simple. Even I can cast this." I smiled up at him. "Thank you."

He nodded. "Try it," he urged.

I studied the spell for a few moments longer.

"Try it," he urged again, an edge to his voice.

"I will," I insisted. "Magic can be very dangerous if one is not precise. I've seen terrible fates befall all color of sash due to mispronunciation." I went over the words a few more times in my head. This was more than a simple incantation, it utilized a diagram in the book to shape the magic. When I was sure I had the accent and cadence correct, I called on my power and spoke the words with my hand pressed to the diagram.

The creation of the spell took a lot from me, more than half of what I had left, and I shivered at the sudden absence of it, an unnatural cold stealing over me. The feeling would pass in a moment, but it was an early warning that I had used too much magic over the previous few days. I hadn't realized how low my power had become, and I was suddenly worried that I might need it for an important working or spell for The Chosen One and not have it to call upon.

"It is good it takes so little effort to maintain this," I said. "I have so little power left, I wouldn't be able to keep it lit for long, otherwise."

"How long?" he asked.

I shrugged. "Hours, I think. I will be fine."

He nodded. "Get off of my bed."

I set my jaw at his rudeness and moved to my own improvised bedroll.

I stowed the burgundy tome and withdrew the first Tome of Tiberius, turning to where I had left off. He lay down and watched me as I read. The boat pitched back and forth, and occasionally we could hear Swails or the crewmen shouting. After a long time, the hero's voice sounded quietly from the other side of the small room.

"Read to me."

I looked up. "Read to you? What?"

"I don't know."

I looked down at the tome, deciding he might find Tiberius' duties boring. "I have the book on cursed—"

"No!"

I jumped at his sudden vehemence. "All right. Let me look in the trunk."

"Never mind. Tell me a story."

I looked over at him, his eyes shining in the scant light of my magic. The sun must have set, because his glow was gone. I thought perhaps he looked afraid, but it was surely just the dim light playing across his features. "Okay. Um..." I thought for a moment, then decided to tell him a story from my hometown. It was about a fisherman who loved the sea more than anything. So much so, that he wanted to marry it. It was a funny and sad story full of hyperbole that was really a satire of a man loving a woman so far above his station that he would die if he tried to pursue her.

I intentionally talked slowly and quietly, pacing new sentences to ebb and flow with the rocking of the ship. Before the tale was done, he was snoring loud enough to drown out the thunder. With his stolid personality gone, I felt the unease creep upon me again, and I knew I could not bring myself to turn out the light and bed down. My only hope was to exhaust myself into slumber. I read until my eyes would not stay open, and only then did I snuff the illumination spell and collapse into sleep.

The Chosen One shook me awake. The rocking of the ship had nearly stopped, and water lapped softly against the hull. Men snored on the deck outside, and the room was dark as pitch. "Tiberius! Tiberius," he hissed, his voice bordering on frantic.

"What," I whispered back, his alarm awakening my own. "What's wrong?"

"The light went out," he said.

"I know. I put it out. Do you need it?"

"Yes," he urged.

"Really? It will take most if not all of my power to make that spell..." I hesitated, my mind struggling to function with the abrupt awakening. "And I cannot see the diagram in the dark."

"You *have* to," he urged, shaking me again. "*Now!*"

"What's happened? Are you hurt?" My heart skittered at the fear in his tone, and my stomach lurched as I tried to imagine what could have so frightened *The Chosen One.*

"Just do it!" The volume of his voice had not risen, but his intensity had, and with each word, flecks of spittle were spattering across my face.

"I can't do it in the dark," I snapped, my own voice sharp with fear and frustration. He was still holding my arm from where he'd shaken me awake. A long silence followed, and he didn't release me. My panic began to calm when I realized the men on the deck were sleeping peacefully, and the only sounds from the forest beyond the waters were expected. "I can't do it in the dark," I repeated, wondering if perhaps The Chosen One had been shaken by a nightmare. Spending what little strength I had left when there was no real danger was foolishness I could not abide. "I don't have the diagram memorized. I don't think I have the power for it, at any rate."

"Maybe a lantern? Or a candle?"

I shook my head. "With this much water in the air? I couldn't get a wick to light, even if I knew where these things were in the dark."

"But..."

"Why do you need it?" I insisted again. He seemed less panicked than before, and I was beginning to suspect my nightmare theory was correct. "Are you hurt? Did you hear something? Should I wake the captain?"

"No," he hissed quickly. "Don't wake anyone."

He was still holding my arm. "Then what is it? Why do you need the light?"

A stillness followed, and my flesh under his tight grip became clammy as I waited for some form of answer from him. Perhaps he didn't have a reason to need it, but only *wanted* the light. If he didn't wish to rouse Swails, was he embarrassed by his reasons? Or perhaps he simply didn't wish to besmirch his reputation?

"Will... will you come lay with me in the bed?"

Another long—this time *exceptionally* awkward—silence followed as I tried to imagine what he had just asked of me. "What?"

"Come lay with me. Please?" His tone was so meek, so humble, it didn't seem like him at all. I placed a hand over his to see if he felt feverish, but his hands were cold.

"You want me to lay with you?" I clarified, stiffly.

"Yes."

"In the bed?"

"Yes."

"*Why?*"

Another long silence, and he still held my arm, though his fingers had loosened a little.

"Why?" I insisted, again.

"Because... I can't sleep. It's... it's too dark." His voice was so quiet and subdued that a child might have spoken the words. I had not imagined fear in his eyes earlier that night when the *light of blessing* had faded; he was certainly afraid. I wasn't sure what had upset him, but his fear made me afraid... and suddenly I didn't want to be alone in the dark, either.

"All right," I said, surprising the both of us.

"Really?" His tone actually perked up with excitement.

"Yes. Just for tonight," I insisted. I would not have agreed if the face of the eerie man with the blue sash wasn't stuck behind my eyes, leering ominously at me from the trees of my imagination.

The Chosen One practically dragged me into the bed, and I realized too late that he was only in his underpinnings. I started to protest, but a muscular arm wrapped around my middle and pulled me hard against his chest. For a long minute, I was too embarrassed to even breathe, let alone say anything. A moment later, his snoring behind my head assured me that at least *his* fears had ebbed. I contemplated crawling back to my place on the floor, but I was exhausted, and a quiet anxiety that had lived in my chest since the beginning of the storm had only become more insistent.

Instead of extricating myself from the muscular arms, I surrendered to the comfort of The Chosen One's closeness, and closed my eyes. I could still see the flash of blue fabric in my memory, and the dread that lingered was a cold snake coiled in my gut. In the back of my mind as sleep stole over me was a dark, foreboding thought:

The lightning-eyed man is ahead of the boat.

6. It Was the Shadow of the Waxing Sun

The sun didn't rise the following day. Or rather, if it did, it struggled unsuccessfully to pierce the thick, black clouds that filled the sky. The captain and crew lit lanterns and raised anchor. They were reluctant, but The Chosen One insisted that he did not wish to be stuck on the river for longer than was necessary, and we'd lost enough time to the storm.

Neither The Chosen One nor I mentioned the awkward night, and I was very grateful for that. All the same, he seemed more subdued, and lingered near me all day, except when he went to the picket line to stroke the horses. I used the sea sickness salve on him, and thus myself, and we stayed on deck in the unearthly dim world of the not-quite-day. His glow seemed to have lessened with his indomitable will, and his lackluster mood worried me. The crew shared sea rations amongst themselves, and I found bread and travel rations to feed the two of us. In all, it was a slow, haunting, dreary day.

"What's your name," I asked him sometime after noon.

"Hmm?" He was bundled in a navy blue riding cloak, watching the shore with heavily lidded eyes. "You know who I am," he finally answered.

"I know what they call you," I agreed. "But, what's your name? What do I call you when you wake me up at three in the morning?"

He looked over at me and frowned, not pleased that I had mentioned his morning of weakness. "The Chosen One."

"In public, yes. In front of anyone, sure. But in *private*?"

"Tiberius calls me The Chosen One, or sometimes just Chosen," he insisted, sharply.

I sighed. "But in private, you don't have to call me Tiberius. You could—"

"Enough!" He vaulted abruptly to his feet, coming awake with fury. All of the deckhands stood up to attention and peered our way. "When next you ask me a question, be sure to ask *only once*, and then *listen* for the answer!" He stormed into the cabin and slammed the door.

I shook my head and looked back at the seamen, who were now grinning or openly laughing at the very public rebuke. I was not surprised, and returned my attention to the scroll I had been reading. Given the already dour mood, I had decided to spend the day learning about necromancy and its connection to vampirism. My reading choice inevitably made the dreary voyage even less pleasant, and soon I found myself wanting the comfort of company. I joined The Chosen One in the cabin in spite of the seething glare he cast me.

"*Tiberius*," he greeted, curtly.

"Chosen," I returned with a flat frown.

He did not seem inclined to apologize for the scene on the deck, and I did not feel that my inquiry warranted one, either. Thus, we sat in uncomfortable silence for the remainder of midday, him sulking, me reading by his dim glow and the muted haze that drifted through the porthole.

Raised voices and a commotion on deck roused us from our stubborn standoff. The Chosen One cast off his blankets, straightened his tunic, and wordlessly strode out the door. I quickly followed but tripped awkwardly on my bedroll and stumbled down to one knee on the deck. Before I'd recovered my feet, The Chosen was standing at the prow of the boat beside the captain, surrounded by pointing and murmuring crewmen who leaned across the rail to get a better look at something in the river ahead.

My heart skipped a beat, thinking of the not-a-deer, but I pushed it back and reprimanded myself for the premature hysteria. Though I was never comfortable amidst a pack of people or exerting any kind of forcefulness, I didn't hesitate to shoulder through the strong seamen to the side of The Chosen. I peered through the murk of overcast late-day, and eventually spotted what everyone else had, another river barge. It was deeply imbedded in the reeds of the riverbank, and no crewmen could be seen moving around on deck.

"She's in fair condition," Swails was saying, peering through a glass at the distant ship. "Sails intact, hull unmarred."

The Chosen grunted and held out his hand. With an unhappy frown, the captain handed over his spyglass. "Hmm," The Chosen mumbled, peering through the instrument for a long moment. "Ah!" He straightened and shoved the glass into the captain's chest. "Draw up near but not close enough to board."

The captain gave the hero a dark look. "To what purpose?" He was obviously not enjoying being told what to do on his own vessel, and he clearly didn't know better than to argue with a man who carried the blessings of several gods.

"To *my* purpose," The Chosen One growled, standing his full height. A pulsing throb of energy filled the air, and his glow redoubled. Everyone, including Swails and me, stepped away from him, our eyes wide with awe at the naked power of the great hero. "Something sinister has befouled that ship, and *I* have been chosen by the gods to confront it," he boomed, his gaze tracking across the crew. Every man who met his eyes looked away. "You all have the great honor of assisting me in my calling on this day." He met the captain's eyes, and to the seaman's credit, he didn't turn away. "Now, draw alongside so I may aid those men."

After a tense moment, where the captain and The Chosen stared each other down, the former gestured to the crew, and the ship burst into movement and action. Swails spun away to issue a few commands, but his men were well familiar with the vessel, and were already correcting the barge into a new course.

The purposeful actions of the crew left me and The Chosen alone at the prow of the ship for a few minutes, and I decided one of us needed to break the silent stalemate. "What did you see?"

The Chosen stared down at me, apparently contemplating whether he intended to forgive my previous impertinence. Finally, he let out a breath and stiffness eased from his posture as his gaze tracked back to the barge we were slowly closing upon. "An otherwise hale ship in distress. The rest is gods-given intuition."

I pursed my lips and wondered if the intuition he spoke of was divine, experiential, or imagination. At any rate, I found myself surprisingly encouraged by The Chosen One firmly following it when he believed innocent were in trouble. In spite of all of his undesirable qualities and braggart nature, he was still a true hero. I smiled and nodded. Even if everything else he was and did grated my nerves to the fraying point, if I could remember that one redeeming quality, perhaps I could survive the next two years with my sanity intact.

As we drew near, the foul smell of decay assailed my nose, and I swallowed back a retch. Once closer, I could make out the forms of motionless men sprawled across the deck as if they'd fallen where they stood. One man's body was tangled in rigging, clearly having fallen from the mast, his blind eyes staring emptily at the sky.

Men had gathered around us again, and quiet whispers filled the air, no one daring to truly break the deathly still of the dead crew just a few dozen feet away.

"Pestilence," the captain muttered, shaking his head. "We will draw no nearer. I will not risk the crew." He cast a challenging look to The Chosen One. "I am honor-bound to protect these men."

The Chosen nodded and turned to me. "Tiberius, you can swim." It was more a demand that I knew the skill, rather than a question.

"Yes, but I—" Without any warning, he lifted and shoved me over the rail and into the cold, dark water. I felt the impact of his entry before I reached the surface. I came up sputtering and choking out vain refusals to get any nearer to the plague-wracked ship. The Chosen One seized the back of my tunic in one massive fist, and side-stroked across the water to the other barge, dragging me along like a sullen child.

Fast as lightning, he snaked a muscled arm around my torso, and one-handed, he pulled himself and me up the side of the barge and climbed the outside of the railing. The feat was nothing short of spectacular. He braced himself on the top rung, flung me onto the deck, and vaulted over the railing to land beside me. The reek was unbearable, and I glanced around to see a rotting corpse not five feet from my face. I frantically clambered backwards until my shoulders struck the railing. Then I spun to vomit over the side, my stomach wrenching in revulsion and fear.

The Chosen ignored my misery, walking from one corpse to another, looking down at them as if their pasty skin and glazed eyes weren't horrible to behold. "These men have been dead less than a day, but they look decayed as if many days have passed."

I swallowed back another bout of nausea and glanced over at the bodies. "How... how can you tell?"

"Very little scavenger work, here. Some birds and vermin, mostly." He stopped to examine the man in the rigging. "Not nearly enough flies and bugs. This is not what corpses this decayed should look like." He wrinkled his nose. "And they all died suddenly."

"How—"

"They would have cast the sick overboard," he explained. "To save the rest of the crew. I've seen it done. Or abandon him on land with some rations if they were merciful and he was well-liked."

I turned to vomit again, and The Chosen One let out a deep, long-suffering sigh. "Is this how it will always be, Tiberius?" he bemoaned. "Pull yourself together, man, and make yourself of use!"

I glowered at him, wiped my mouth on my sleeve, and pulled myself up the railing. Frustrated as

I was with his beratement, he wasn't wrong. I was supposed to be assisting him, though at the moment I wasn't sure what help I could lend. I wasn't a physician, and I certainly wasn't an undertaker. I had absolutely no experience with the dead, and had always been happy to maintain that virginal status. I turned toward the river, gulped as much mostly-fresh air as I could, and cupped the mint-smelling fingers of my left hand over my nose and mouth.

With a single, bolstering nod to myself, I turned and strode further onto the deck to come up beside The Chosen One. His lips spread into a deep, proud grin and he clapped my back in a harsh manner that I'm certain he imagined was bracing. My irritation ebbed, and I found myself oddly comforted by his approval. "So, how can Tiberius serve The Chosen One in this circumstance?" I asked. I looked down at the translucent-skinned corpse and swallowed back another surge of nausea. "And... uh, can we catch—"

"No, no," he assured me. "We're immune to nearly all disease, natural and unnatural." He glanced over at me. "My, but you are green. Never seen a dead man before?"

"Um... from a distance. A *good* distance," I confessed through cupped fingers.

"You'll get used to it," he said with an assuring smile that did not make me at all comfortable with the prospect, and strode to the cabin. "For now, just look. Use your intuition, your knowledge. You must have some, or the blessing wouldn't have taken hold. I'm looking for a source, a cause—" A quiet moan issued from inside the cabin, and The Chosen One paused, his hand on the latch.

"Hm," he mumbled, drawing a large dagger before swinging the door wide, his eyes bright with battle fury. A radiant buckler of light blazed to life across the forearm of his off hand, and he surged through the door with a fierce growl.

Foolishly, I rushed after, sliding to a stop just inside the door as he spun on his heel to take in the entire room. His own glow and that of his mystical shield filled the small chamber with warm, intense light. Nothing moved, and his shoulders sagged in disappointment when no threat waited to greet him.

The cabin was almost identical to the one in which we stayed, and a lone figure lay sprawled face-down on the floor beside the bed, issuing another semi-conscious moan at the sudden commotion. The Chosen One sheathed the dagger and the buckler winked out of existence as he crouched to pull the hair back from the man's face. The seaman's skin was sickly pale and glistening with sweat. The hero jerked his head toward me in a "come hither" gesture, and the two of us lifted the man back onto the bed. My skin crawled as we muscled his sweat-damp body in position, and I heard myself praying quietly to Sca to keep The Chosen One and me strong and safe from disease. It seemed in my life I was only inclined to pray in instances of dire need, and this certainly seemed one.

All of the manhandling jarred the sick sailor as conscious as he was likely to become in his feverish and dehydrated state. His glazed eyes fixed upon The Chosen One, and tears welled in them. "Merciful Skalah," he croaked. "Come to take me from the arms of Trion?" He sagged against the bedding. "I am prepared."

The Chosen nodded somberly and placed a hand across the man's brow. "Give yourself to the mercy of the gods, young man?"

"I do," he whispered.

"Even should your fate be death?" I was shocked at the softness in the hero's voice.

"I do. I am prepared," the captain whispered, every muscle going limp.

My stomach turned in horrible sympathy for the seafarer. The only mercy in this moment was that he wouldn't die alone, surrounded by the corpses of what must have been his crew.

"Then be it Jaya or Sca who claim your next breath, be in peace," The Chosen One whispered, closing his eyes. "Sca, your blessings are not given lightly, nor have I any claim to them, but I ask for your strength to heal this man that I may stop this dire, mystical plague that has befallen these men." His words were quiet, humble, and I stared for a moment at his bowed features, amazed that he could set aside his enormous pride for the sake of a stranger.

Moved by his gesture of humility, I knelt beside him and bent until my head nearly touched the floor. "Great Sca, I am nobody, not even a good servant, but I also ask humbly for your mercy and pity to help this man." The air changed, becoming lighter and cooler, as if carried down from a high, mountain peak. A few notes hung on the air like a distant windchime, and the man on the bed let out a deep gasp.

"I thank you this day for your mercy," The Chosen One said, lifting his head to peer down at the man who was taking long, full breaths like one who was surfacing from a deep dive underwater.

I stood and peered down at him, my mouth agape. Though I'd whispered the prayer in earnest, I never truly expected the god to answer. As I watched, the cheeks of the stranger flushed red and his eyes sharpened. "How... ?" I muttered.

The Chosen grinned broadly at the man. "Good fortune to you, my good man," he said to the seaman.

"You find yourself in the company of The Chosen One and that of merciful and kind Sca, who has healed you this day! What is your name?" I only chaffed a little that he hadn't bothered to mention me, but I was not about to complain that Sca warranted more mention than an assistant to a hero.

"M-marlo," the man rasped as he stared unblinking at The Chosen.

"What befell your crew?"

Marlo shook his head. "N-nothing. I don't..." His brow abruptly furrowed. "My crew?"

The great hero nodded. "You alone survive a magical pestilence. Do you know from where it came?"

Marlo sat up, wavering, and stared at the deck through the cabin door at the dead men outside. "Oh gods," he whispered.

The Chosen One held the man steady with one broad hand and shook his shoulder. "Certainly you saw something that was not right before you fell ill," he insisted.

Marlo shook his head, his eyes flashing to The Chosen once more. "I... there was." He swallowed, apparently gathering his thoughts, because when he spoke again, his voice was more sure. "There was a man. In the trees," he answered. "He was no normal man."

I jerked, the fear from the night before crawling up my spine. "The man in the woods," I hissed, leaning toward the captain. "Was he dark skinned and red haired with a blue sash?"

Marlo nodded, fear sealing over his features. "And the storm lived in his eyes!"

"Merciful gods!" The Chosen One cursed, turning to tower abruptly over me as he seized the front of my tunic in both hands. "You said nothing of this blue sash!"

I started in surprised fear at his anger, and then my cheeks flushed and I set my jaw in defiance. "You said it was a *deer*, remember?"

He shook me hard enough to set my teeth rattling. "A blue sash? You idiot! That was no deer, that was Trion *himself*!"

My stomach dropped out as his words sank in, and he shoved me away. I staggered back a few steps to lean against the bulkhead. A god. I had seen *a god*? My whole body began shuddering, as I became acutely aware of how small and weak I was. Cold, wet, and mortal on a ship of dead men. Trion, the god of darkness, strife, and pestilence. I looked out at the corpses, and I could suddenly no longer maintain the composure I'd cobbled together, yet I was too afraid to leave the safety of the cabin. I turned to the corner and heaved until my already-empty stomach cramped.

The Chosen One hissed in disdain and turned back to the seaman. "Can you walk? Swim?"

The man's eyes did not turn away from his dead crew as he nodded gravely. "If I must."

"You must." The Chosen helped the man to his feet, then again seized the back of my tunic and dragged me after.

"Hey!" I protested, clawing at the collar of my hopelessly disheveled garments to keep them from choking the life from me. "I can walk—" Without stopping, he threw me over the side of the ship, and I crashed into the cold water once more. This time, I didn't wait for The Chosen One to grab me; I swam for all I was worth toward the waiting vessel and away from the ship of death. Water sprayed my back from the hero and the seaman diving into my wake.

I was clearly the weaker swimmer, and was third to reach our chartered barge. I came up alongside in time to hear the captain and The Chosen One arguing.

"I'll not let that plague carrier aboard!" Swails shouted.

The Chosen vaulted over the top rail, and the sounds of swords hissing from scabbards filled the air as I treaded water and tried desperately to see what was happening over my head. Marlo and I traded concerned glances, but we stayed silent and listened.

"T'was a mystical plague that benevolent Sca himself has healed!" The Chosen One bellowed. "If you deny this man passage, you deem yourself more worthy to decide his fate than a *god*!" The great hero's booming voice became almost painful to hear. I thought I saw tiny ripples skittering away from the hull of the ship with every word.

"You think to command me and my men on my own ship!" Swails' voice took on a dark tone, and I could hear the history of violence in it.

I hissed at the escalation and looked toward Marlo. "Give me a hand up?"

He sucked in a breath, made a basket of his hands, and dipped his arms below the surface. I tucked a tow into his fingers and between the two of us, we shouldered me high enough to reach the lowest rung of the railing.

"You think you and nine men have any hope of defeating The Chosen One in battle?" the hero bellowed. He stood unarmed while surrounded by a half-circle of uncertain but unyielding seamen.

"Captain!" I shouted as I clumsily dragged myself and fifty pounds of wet clothing over the rail. "Please hear me out," I pleaded, stepping up beside The Chosen One. "I saw with my own eyes the power of Sca. I felt it; I heard the music on the wind." I nodded toward the side of the boat where Marlo was still treading water just out of site. "He was at death's door, on his final breath, and the gods *chose* to spare him through their servant," I gestured to The Chosen One who stood with stubborn set jaw. "It is possible this same mystical malady will find your own crew, regardless. If you turned this man away, you would have defied the will of the gods; think you Sca will show you the same kindness of mercy and healing when you left Captain Marlo to drown or die in the wilderness?"

    I saw sword tips drifting down as crewmen exchanged wavering glances. They would never dare mutiny and they feared pestilence, but I was getting through to them. "Captain Marlo was spared, perhaps even so that he could lend aid in finding a cure for this malady. Have any of you loved ones you wish to protect from this plague?"

    Swails listened, though his eyes remained fixed on The Chosen One. At long length, he gave the slightest shake of his head. With relieved sighs, men sheathed swords and moved tentatively back. "None of my men will touch him, and he is not to sleep in my quarters," the captain ordered. "Keep him far from us." He took a step forward, and his eyes narrowed. "You and he will be leaving *my* ship when next we dock."

    The Chosen One scoffed. "I will hear you recant that last when you've cooled enough to realize it is not wise to defy Anetrael in my presence," he replied as if they were having a simple difference of opinion. "A contract we have for services that you *will* honor, Captain." In spite of the dark glare of the seaman, the hero turned to me. "Fetch my bow and arrows."

    I hesitated, not sure why he would need them if the dispute was resolved, but ran to the cabin nonetheless, my boots squishing wetly with each step. I flipped open his weapons chest and retrieved the quiver, then jogged around to the wagon where I'd seen the longbow stowed the morning before. When I returned with both, The Chosen One fixed me with a frown.

"Know you not how to string a bow?"

My cheeks flamed, and I glared up at him, but quickly set about the task, leveraging the bow arm between my legs. I strained with all my strength to bend the wood and hook the second end of the string into position. He jerked the bow from my hands before my foot was fully free, and I nearly fell on my ass when the bow arm caught my heel. Only then did I realize he was not just being rude; he was actually angry with me. I shook my head and made my way to the side of the vessel to help Marlo onto the barge.

As I did, the Chosen bellowed a loud phrase that sounded more like an incantation than a prayer, and the arrow he'd nocked hummed with power, the point bursting into scarlet flame. He loosed the arrow at the plague-infested vessel, and it flew in a flawless arc to imbed in the rigging at the base of the mainsail. With mystical ferocity, the deck caught fire, and before it was fully out of sight of our barge, the cursed ship listed heavily and sank beneath the water.

Beside me, Marlo shivered and whispered prayers for his men.

7. Far Out in the Uncharted Backwaters of the Gorod River

The Chosen One silently moved to the cabin, the heavy gaze of all the crewmen watching him disappear into their captain's quarters. When I entered to retrieve dry clothes for the man we'd saved—the one The Chosen had promptly forgotten about—the hero ignored me and stripped out of his own sodden attire.

I handed the bundle over to Captain Marlo, who somberly thanked me and immediately stripped to change into the dry clothes. He was apparently too overwrought by the day's events to care much about exposing his nudity to the gods and everyone. I handed him one of my blankets, and he shouldered into it, stubbornly trying conceal his chattering teeth.

"Are you hungry," I asked. Marlo jerked his head *no* as he sank to the deck, and seemed intent upon staying out of the way and away from the crewmen.

I sighed and readied myself for the uncomfortable conversation that was about to follow, but as I turned to walk away, Marlo caught the still dripping cuff of my trousers. I glanced back, to see if he'd changed his mind about food. "The gods brought The Chosen One to me," he muttered, nodding his thanks. "Will you tell him I am forever in his debt?"

I sighed again, this time releasing the tension I'd been holding onto. "They brought him to me as well," I confessed. "I will tell him. I am sorry for the terrible events that cost your crew their lives and you your vessel."

He looked out at the water, a shadow haunting his gaze. "That I survived the wrath of the god of strife is a miracle I will not squander, regardless of my grief." He closed his eyes against the tears that threatened to fall. "My life and all my deeds belong to Sca, now."

His brave words bolstered me against the wrath of The Chosen One I went to face. I strode into the cabin to find the hero standing with his fists firmly planted on his hips, wet curls clinging to his face and chest, and not an inch of fabric covering his muscular frame. "Clean my clothes, and polish the muck from my boots," he demanded.

I closed the door and faced him, lifting my chin against his unabashed nudity. "First tell me why you are so angry with me."

His glower darkened. "*Never* speak over me!" He growled. "You do *not* speak for me, ever!"

"Point to fact," I responded, resolving to maintain my calm. "According to the first Tome of Tiberius, I *often* speak for you."

"Not while in my presence!"

"Well, actually, there are quite a few instances—"

"You know my meaning!" he bellowed, the glass in the lantern rattling at his booming voice.

"Had I not intervened, I suspect you would have fought the entire crew."

"I had no fear! I was in the right!"

I nodded. "So was Swails."

He growled, scooped up his pillow and hurtled it at me with all his considerable strength. I tried not to flinch, but it plopped hard against my face and knocked me partially around. I staggered a step back and nearly shouted back before I remembered him and the captain fighting only moments before. The Chosen One would not yield to force. He wasn't built for it.

I squared my shoulders and faced him, deciding to take a different tactic. "I have read countless accounts of your many great deeds, but today I actually *witnessed* a miracle."

He snorted at the obvious attempt at flattery.

"More than that," I continued. "I saw what you're truly made of. You didn't hesitate to board that vessel, to help a diseased and dying man, to humble yourself to *earn* that miracle." I shook my head, genuine in my accounting and the impression it had made upon me. "When I told Tiberius that I would be honored to serve you, I didn't realize what this servitude would be like. Today, I saw The Chosen One, *truly* saw him. I was humbled and impressed." His gaze flicked away from me at the sincerity in my tone. "I remain honored to serve you, in any way possible, even if it earns your ire by preventing you from accidently slaughtering a crew that we *need* to row this boat through the shallows."

His anger flashed again, his eyes glittering with unspoken rebuke. But it remained unspoken. I nodded deeply. "I'm sorry I overspoke you," I lied.

The Chosen crossed his arms and turned away from me, glowering out the porthole. "Don't do it again," he grumbled.

"I won't," I lied again. I withdrew clean, dry clothes for him and placed them on his bed before I stripped out of my own wet garments. "Captain Marlo wishes to express his gratitude that the gods brought you to him, and wanted me to tell you he is forever in your debt."

The Chosen One grunted. "Of course he is."

"I would also like to say a few words if you will hear them, about a way to earn the good favor of Swails again."

"*He* needs to earn *my* good favor," he snapped.

I held back the sigh that struggled to wrest from my chest. "You are a man bound by duty and honor, sworn to protect the innocent from evil and darkness," I said.

"I don't need you to remind me of that."

"Of course," I responded patiently. "Our captain is a man also bound by duty and honor, but his is to protect his crew. He witnessed another vessel whose crew was lost, and he was willing to face the fearsome and mighty Chosen One to protect his men, even if it meant enduring the wrath of the gods." His movement stilled in the process of pulling his trousers over his underpinnings, and I turned to face him. "It was likely one of the most terrifying and defining moments of his life, to stand before certain death in an effort to protect his men from what had felled Marlo's."

The Chosen One shook his head and turned his back to me. "I don't need your advice on how to earn Swails' favor," he grumbled and yanked the wig off of his head.

I was so startled by the movement that my breath stuck in my chest and a half-choked cough of breath burst through my nostrils.

The Chosen One spun and glared at me, throwing the sodden mass of tousled curls against my chest, his glistening scalp still dripping. "Silence your impudent guffaw and fetch the dry one from my chest!"

It took all of my strength to look away, and even more self-control to carefully tame the mass of wet curls into a more manageable bundle. I silently set it aside and out of sight of the door to be dealt with when I had more time. I searched his chest and found a second wig, carefully wrapped in a fine netting, the curls set into tight spirals around curlers. I was certain the eyes would bulge from my head in my effort not to explode with incredulous laughter, but somehow I managed to unwind all of the curlers without uttering a sound.

When I was done, The Chosen One was fully dressed. He gestured to a wooden tube sealed with a wide cork lid. I retrieved it, and saw there was a cant scribed into the top. "Put that on," he grumbled. "But be sure to close the container before you activate it, or you'll ruin the entire container of glue." He sat cross-legged on the bed and turned his back to me.

"Oh," I said, finally comprehending. I grit my teeth and resolved myself to the task, then slathered a generous coating of the glue all over his bald scalp. It tingled with so much power my fingers nearly went numb. No wonder the last one had not come free even when he was swimming through the water. "Magic first, or wig," I asked, carefully corking the container and silently reading the cant once more.

"*Hair* first," he ordered. "Do not call it that again."

I nodded and was glad he could not see my grimacing smirk. Of course it was not to be called a "wig." I washed my hands with a water scuttlebutt to keep from getting any glue in The Chosen One's *hair*, and maneuvered it carefully onto his head. He stood and went to the porthole, using his reflection to subtly adjust it. After several agonizingly-long moments, he held it down with both hands and gave me a pointed look.

This working was simple and did not take much power from me. It must have also had some illusionary magic, because after the power left me, even I could no longer tell it was not his true hair.

The Chosen quickly finished straightening his appearance, pulled a spare set of boots from his trunk, and stomped into them. He was out the door a moment later, and I could finally let out the breath and hysterical laughter I'd been holding back.

I checked on Marlo several times over the next hour, but he seemed equal parts irreverent and distant. I brought him another blanket and food, though he insisted he needed neither, and sat beside him to pass the time and read from the first tome. At some point the raucous laughter of The Chosen One and the crew drew my attention, and I craned my neck around to watch him. He had somehow gathered a majority of the deckhands and the captain into a bawdy story about women and a massive, enchanted serpent—the latter of which I was certain was a blatant metaphor for his manhood—and no sign of their previous disagreement remained.
"Unbelievable," I muttered. "He could charm the feathers from a peacock."

We reached the port-town of Riga just before nightfall, and every member of the crew was grateful to see Captain Marlo depart. As a very public show of generosity and support, The Chosen One gave the seafarer a pouch with a Gold King in it to find his way and to start his life anew.

The crew began unloading scheduled deliveries and taking on expected freight, and The Chosen One disappeared into the cabin once more. He still had not spared a moment to discuss the day's events with me, and after several minutes of frustrated mulling, I followed. "What about the man in the woods?" I demanded behind the closed door. "We need to talk about what it could mean. Was he actually T—"

"Don't say his name if you can help it," the hero snapped as if he were speaking to an ignorant child. Then to my surprise, he flashed me a broad grin. "He and I go way back! A bit of a rivalry, I suppose. Not to worry."

My mouth dropped open as he stripped down to his underpinnings and began riffling around in his clothes trunk, tossing garments this way and that as they were assessed and dismissed. "W—He..." I shook my head, trying to get my fear-addled brain to function. "Not to *worry*?" I shouted, finding my voice at last. The sudden shrill tone startled even me, and The Chosen One jerked. "You have a rivalry with *a god*, and I am *'not to worry'*?"

He turned to level a stare at me. "Breathe before you faint," he grumbled. He made his way to the bed with an armload of silk and linen finery. "A long while back, I had to slay someone that belonged to him. I don't think he's quite gotten over it. Gods tend to hold grudges for a long time."

I don't think my jaw could have gapped farther without unhinging from my skull. "You... you—"

"She was a dragon," he explained absently. "She developed a taste for virgin flesh and lost her ability to change back into human form." He shrugged as if he were explaining simple math. "She was a monster." He met my gaze, clearly to determine if I was following. "Huh, you're a strange pallor," he noted. "You should sit."

"You killed one of *his*, and you yet *live*?"

He nodded. "She was a monster. It *is* what I do. I have and had *four* gods," he held up four fingers to illustrate, "backing me in this endeavor, one of whom is their king." He sighed, pulling fitted leather trousers over his muscular legs with more than one grunt of effort. "It cost me, though," he grumbled unhappily.

"What?" I asked. "What great loss did you suffer, backed by half the pantheon of—"

He leveled me with another dark stare. "It cost my hair," he answered blandly. "In fact, every hair on my person save my nose, eyebrows, and lashes." He stood and began fumbling with the buttons at his long cuffs. "Burned all my skin to ash," he recounted. "Nothing remained but sinew and the sword."

My teeth clapped shut, and I frowned down at the wood floor. "I've read this story."

"Yeah," he drawled. "One of my greatest deeds." He shook his head. "When they resurrected me, I was naked as a newborn. They said my hair would grow back." He scowled at his cuff. "It never did."

I looked up at him, then shook my head and stepped forward to help with the tiny abalone buttons. "As I recall, you saved a princess. I thought it was exaggerated."

He shook his head. "No. Not in the least. *Under-*exaggerated more like. Had to kill that beast with no skin. Hardest slay of my life."

My fingers faltered at that thought. I couldn't even begin to imagine how much that must have hurt. I'd earned blisters before, mixing potions. I shuddered. "After that, and you *still* could wield the sword?"

He shrugged. "It's how this sort of thing works. You have to be willing to pay the price. The greater the deed, the reward, the monster... the greater the cost."

Then I realized what he was doing. "Hey! Why are you dressing up?"

A broad grin split his features again, and he clapped my shoulder. "Me and the men are going carousing and drinking! I'd invite you, but you've got reading to do." He nodded to the piles of books and scrolls, then wriggled his feet into his finer leather boots. "Mind you, keep it near the wagon and the horses, since you'll be the only one on guard."

I gaped at him, a cold chill running through my gut. "What if T—" I slapped a hand over my mouth for a second, almost uttering the forbidden name. "What if *he* comes back? I'll be here alone!"

He laughed. "Just vomit into the river. You're good at that. I shall smell it and come charging to your rescue!"

Without any further explanation or apology, he burst through the door. He let out a rowdy, masculine cry that was mirrored by the crew, and they all dropped down onto the dock, laughing and sharing ungentlemanly jokes.

I stared after him for a long while, a nauseating mixture of frustration, anger, and fear turning my guts. I decided to settle on anger, since it was the most manageable of the three, and gathered up my supplies. Apparently Trion was just a nuisance, and we had undead stoats to slay in a handful of days. I lit the lantern and made my way with the bundle of reading and notes to sit with the horses. At the very least, they would warn me of trouble. As I spread the book out in my lap and arranged the scrolls all around me, I thought about The Chosen One slaying the dragon. In the stories, they never mentioned the beast belonged to Trion. I wondered why it had been omitted from the telling of the great deed, and decided there must be more to the story. I would have to inquire again when the hero was in an agreeable mood.

The lightning-eye man crept into my memory, and I shuddered. A new layer of misgiving had been added to the next two years; it would take some time to reconcile with the newfound knowledge of the rivalry. Though it was a moot question, I wondered, would I have taken on this duty had I known The Chosen One and Trion were quietly at war?

8. In My Newer and More Vulnerable Days, The Chosen One Gave Me Some Advice

"Good morning, Tiberius!" The Chosen One shouted only a few inches from my face.

I came awake with a cry and a wild flail that sent several scrolls spiraling out onto the deck. The heady laughter of the crew surrounded us, and I realized with no small amount of disorientation that we were sailing once more down the river. Somehow I had slept through the cast off. Then the abruptly disrupted slumber overcame my surprise adrenaline, and I slumped wearily against the cabin wall. I glowered up at the hero, whose eyes glittered through roguishly disheveled hair. His glowing grin was deeply seasoned with pride for the previous night's conquests.

"Come, come," he said with a laugh, toeing the Tome of Tiberius closed with his boot as he stood. "We've been on our way for half an hour. Rise and make yourself useful!"

I glowered at him again, and woodenly gathered together my studies and supplies. I wasn't sure at what hour I had succumbed to sleep, but I had not been in a comfortable position, and every joint ached and was stiff from cold. I crawled to the scrolls that had rolled away, and one chuckling deckhand lightly kicked a parchment within my reach. I mumbled a thanks as he passed. When all of my affairs were in arms, the hero tucked his meaty hands under my armpits and lifted me to my feet.

I grunted a quiet argument, but leaned heavily against his chest for a moment while my legs unbent and came to life. More chuckling surrounded me as The Chosen One nudged me toward the cabin like a man putting a child to bed. "I'm fine," I grumbled. "I'll manage." But he followed me into the cabin nonetheless.

He stopped inside the door and looked around, his grin instantly disappearing. "Tiberius!" he rebuked, drawing my half-interested attention. "What did you do all night?"

I raised my brows, looked down at the armload I was carefully depositing into my trunk, and back at him as if that should explain it.

He shook his head and gestured to his rumpled bed, then to the cloak that had fallen to the floor.

"You said to watch the horses and wagon," I mumbled, turning my back to him as I organized the supplies into their stowing compartments.

"And my clothes from yesterday," he snapped, pushing the still damp garments around with his toe. "Foul and wet, *still*. And my boots!" He turned one over and water ran out. "Did you do *any* of the tasks for which you are meant?"

Anger finally seeped into my exhausted brain, and I spun, a retort on my lips... in time to receive an armload of clean but unfolded clothing that he had thrown all over the cabin the night before while preparing for his evening outing. "At least fold these!"

He stormed out, slamming the door in his wake while I stared after him in numb and impotent anger.

It took me over an hour to finish the chores he'd left me with. I had no way to clean the damp garments without suffering the embarrassment of looking like a maid to the crew, so I hung them about the cabin to dry. At least I would be able to pack them away by midday to be laundered at our next stop. I could understand his complaint there, at least. His clothes and mine from the day before reeked of river water and mildew with an undercurrent of decay. I would stow them in the trunk with crafting components to help their odor until they could be properly washed.

When I was finished, I took my notes from the night before, a handful of maps, and the Ninth Tome of Tiberius out to the deck to work. The crew had become quiet and subdued as the night's events and sobriety caught up to them. The Chosen and Swails lingered near the prow, talking comfortably, no lingering signs of discord. For that, I was grateful. Fewer people to bribe into silence. I would simply have to trust The Chosen One had not bedded anyone who required discretionary coin, as he had not disclosed his deeds to me.

After a time, the hero came to stand over me, leaning against the cabin wall as he gazed out into the passing forest. "So, what *did* you do last night?"

I snorted. "My job," I grumbled.

He raised a brow and frowned down at me. "Part of it, at any rate," he corrected.

I sighed and decided to relent before the unstoppable river of his stubborn pride. "I'm sorry about the clothes," I conceded. There was, after all, an *entire* chapter in the first tome dedicated to the subject. "I'll try harder." He seemed to accept the apology and gave a magnanimous nod. "I spent the night reading about various kinds of undead, of which vampires are one."

He grunted his agreement.

"I also read about the local wildlife." That earned an impatient look, but he refrained from telling me to get to the point. "I was reading Eth—Tiberius' notes from—"

"Don't do that," he interrupted.

"What?"

"Refer to yourself, any *version* of yourself, in the second person."

"I think you mean the third person," I corrected.

He shot me a sharp look, and I raised my hands in surrender. "Very well," I conceded. I had a feeling I would be doing a lot of that over the next two years. Ethan's comment about the virtue of being able to accept the unchangeable came to the forefront of my mind, and I smirked. He was certainly right about that one. "I was reading *my* notes on your previous campaign, the bevy of undead beavers."

"Yeah," he wrinkled his nose. "Not a fun one. I was hip deep in mud hacking at those abominations for hours." He shook his head. "That lord *owed* me that feast." He nodded firmly. Then his lips turned up in a lascivious smirk. "And those three maidens."

I cleared my throat, and he frowned at me for disrupting what was clearly a pleasing train of thought. "Eth—*I* noted that they had to have come from downstream, since the wellspring of the Gorod River was clearly not their native home. In fact, *I* noted that evidence of the damage caused by the undead beasts could be witnessed as far downstream as Rshavin."

"So?" he grumbled, crossing his arms and casting me a bored look.

"So," I continued, biting back a snide comment. "We aim to strike north at Rshavin toward Vevesk, along a major tributary to the Gorod." He stared at me flatly, and I sighed, connecting the dots for him. "Which has *vampire stoats*." He still did not seem to be following. "Both are caused by a backwash or an overflow of necromancy, both could be traced back to the same area. Necromancy is notorious for poisoning waters and wildlife that rely on that water... *beavers live in the water.*"

Finally his brows went up in realization. "Ah! The two are clearly connected," he supplied as if the idea had come from him. "Yes. So perhaps the source of the necromancy causing all of this trouble is somewhere between the two," he surmised.

I shook my head. "Not necessarily."

He glowered at me for countering his rash assumption, but listened to what I had to say. I was so shocked that he didn't take his idea and stubbornly run with it, that I hesitated a moment to gather my thoughts back together. "Well?" he snapped. "What else?"

I growled; that did the trick. "Vevesk rests on the banks of a small lake. From there a tributary runs to and spills into the Gorod River at Rshavin."

He pursed his lips, clearly not following me.

"The beavers may have come from Vevesk Lake or anywhere along the tributary."

"That's what I just said!"

I held up a hand. "Yes. But stoats are not water animals." I unrolled a map and pointed to Vevesk

Lake. "They live just north of the lake, in the unsettled, forested region at the base of this mountain outcropping. The farthest south they are normally seen are in this area and the north-most farms, where they pilfer grain from the fields."

The Chosen grunted and nodded, an odd look of acceptance and approval crossing his features for the barest flash of a moment. Then he stood tall and looked across the prow, striking what I would consider an intentionally heroic pose. "Then somewhere at the base of those mountains an evil necromancer is poisoning the land and the waters with his dark deeds." He lifted his chin. "And I, The Chosen One of the Gods, have been called upon to stop him."

As if in response, lighting flashed ominously in the distance, and a fierce headwind buffeted the boat.

"This captain is skilled," The Chosen One said as he entered the cabin, stripping his sodden cloak from his back. I had been busy recounting the great hero's deeds over the previous few days into the ninth tome by lantern light. Having lost the good daylight to a sudden storm not unlike the one we'd weathered the first night, I decided to risk the glass-ensconced flame. The comforting smell of mint drifted up from my fingers and eased another wave of nausea as the cabin pitched hard to starboard. The lantern danced drunkenly from its hook, and I looked up to give The Chosen One my attention. He was being amiable, and I wanted to reward that behavior.

"Oh?" I returned his wane smile.

"He says he wishes to be rid of us, so he's facing off the storm," he commented, disregarding me as he stripped out of his clothes. I returned to writing when he moved to removed his underpinnings. "He's using the wind well, short-sailing when needed, and keeping his oarsmen at the ready for the shallows. And he knows this river well." Something like praise and respect came to his voice, and I noted with a smile that he and Swails had certainly made up well. I even thought perhaps The Chosen One had decided to like him, after all.

"Well, when I sent the missive in Noblan, I asked for the most skilled barge captain to be had, and the lad knew exactly who to contract."

He nodded and seized my cloak to towel off with. I opened my mouth to protest, but gritted my teeth and resumed writing, which I had to stop again when he chucked my now-damp cloak into my lap. I let out a frustrated huff and stood to hang it to dry while the hero began dressing. I thought next time I might leave drying linens on The Chosen One's bed when he was out in the rain, and figured his using my garments for the task was his way of reminding me of his perceived lapse in my duties. Even if it was rude and frustrating, at least it was a form of communication that I was beginning to understand. Getting angry would solve none of my problems.

"Swails heard news in the last port that Rshavin has been pulling up entire nets of dying and rotting fish." He looked pointedly at me. "Rotten to the gills, but thrashing like live hauls."

I sighed. "Undead fish. Great." I reached for my notes, certain I'd seen the like before in some of the records from Noblan. "They're not for eating."

"No," he emphatically agreed. "Besides being foul, it could sicken the eater." He wrinkled his nose.

"Necromancy can spread like that. People will catch ill, die, perhaps rise again if the fish contained enough of it."

"And some people might not know the fish are contaminated if they're not rotten," I remarked. "Very dangerous."

"The river must be purged of the poison," he announced gravely.

I looked up, surprised by his proactive comment. When I saw the duty-bound determination in his eyes, I realized why he was being so direct. He knew this task, understood it. "What do you need me to do?"

He nodded his approval, dropping down to recline lazily on his bed. "There's instructions in that book for arranging a gathering. The whole town. We'll reach Rshavin a few hours after sunset. Leave me a lit lamp, go into town with your money bag, and do what must be done."

I didn't bother to argue that the late hours of the night in a storm were a poor time to be waking up the important people I would need to talk to. He wouldn't care, and I would have to do it, anyway. At least I knew the chapter he was referring to. It was one of the last sections about arranging for his fanfare when arriving in town, something I'd witnessed the first time I saw him. "How large of a gathering?"

"Every man, woman, and child who can speak words." He looked over at me, his expression grave. "The whole town will die if we don't. I've seen it before." He grimaced. "Ugly business, that."

I gritted my teeth, fighting a wave of nausea brought on by something other than seasickness. I thought of The Chosen One's mockery of my weakness on the plagued barge, and anger helped me fight back the sudden surge of horror and swallow back the bile that rose in my throat.

"You should get all that done in time to arrange my fanfare," he said, his voice slurring as the rocking ship finished lulling him to sleep.

"What—" I meant to argue the constraints of time and circumstance and the appropriateness of a dramatic entrance in a situation as dire as this one... but it was futile, and sleeping he was at least *less* rude. I let out a slow, patient breath, and pulled out a fresh sheet of paper. I had a lot of letters to write and a lot of planning to do if I was to pull this off in the hours before sunrise.

The Chosen One awoke from his nap irritable, and I left him to his grumblings. When he rose to head out of the cabin, I abruptly stood. "Um... you're out of dry underthings."

He glowered at me. "There's another trunk on the wagon."

I stepped forward before he could open the door all the way. "I am *not* getting a trunk off the wagon in this storm." Fury blazed in his eyes, and for a moment, I thought he might strike me in his rage. In spite of the tremor that ran through me, I lifted my chin. "I am certain my binding would be warning me right now if this refusal to do as you say was unreasonable."

He continued to glare murder at me, his breath huffing out of his nostrils in thick puffs. "Move," he growled.

"Of course. So long as you understand those clothes will not be replaced with dry ones until the end of the storm." I stepped out of his way. "Leaving you to wallow in wet things or naked for the remainder of the evening."

At that, he hesitated, staring out at the torrential rain. With a grunt, he shut the door and dropped back down onto the bed, groaning as he draped an arm across his face.

"Oh," I muttered, recognizing the posture. "Of course." I went to the trunk with tonics and pulled out the motion-sickness salve. "You don't want anyone to see you sick," I realized aloud.

"I am incapable of feeling embarrassed," he grumbled through the crook of his elbow. Then, as if to prove it, he slid his thumb into his mouth and began sucking it. I was only just able to choke back a snort, and went about renewing the seasickness working. That I hadn't felt particularly unwell meant I had finally acclimated to the movement of the ship. Naturally, just in time for the leg of our journey that was to take place on land.

"I was thinking—"

"Never a good sign," he slurred around his thumb.

I suppressed a glower. "Given the state of the town, perhaps fanfare is... well, inappropriate."

That got his attention. He lowered his arm to stare at me with an expression that was completely unreadable.

"There may be many ill," I continued, finding his intense scrutiny unnerving. "And even if they're not, they've been pulling unprofitable hauls from the river... for days... so..." I finally succumbed to the pressure of his gaze, and leaned away from him. "So maybe we shouldn't," I mumbled.

He sat up, his eyes narrowing. "You think the parade is for my *pride*," he observed. "To stroke my ego. To have the lowly peasants fall at my feet."

"Um..." I meant to say *no*, but he was right. I did more or less think that was the purpose of the affair. Especially this one.

He sucked in a deep breath and pushed to his feet. I jerked back, not sure what to expect, but nothing good. Instead, he strode past me, out the door, and into the rain without his cloak.

"What," I whispered to the still-open door. "What just happened?" Numbly, I rose and closed the door. Had I just hurt his feelings? I felt a little sick at that thought. Was I wrong about the parade? Was it not for the reasons the last several Tiberiuses had suspected? I shook my head and followed him out into the storm. He was standing near the prow, watching white water crash and course around the hull. I came up beside him and stared until he glanced aside to meet my gaze. "I'm sorry," I said. "Explain it to me." He looked away, and I put a hand on his shoulder. He quickly jerked away, and I flinched. "Please."

He glared down at me. "You are all the same," he snapped. "Just do your job and don't ask questions. In two years, you can hang it up, and someone else will be standing there asking the same damn things!" He turned abruptly and stormed back to the cabin.

I shook my head and glanced at the wagon, sheltered under a canvas and bolted down for the ride. It would be all but impossible to get a trunk out of that. That meant he was going to be naked for the rest of the night. I shook my head and followed him. He had taken no time in stripping off his clothes, which sat in a soaking heap near the door. He was laying on his back, sucking his thumb. When I entered, he turned his backside to me, not bothering to cover up. In spite of myself, I chuffed a short chuckle. "Fitting," I mumbled.

He grunted an affirmative, and I began wringing out his clothes and hanging them to dry. At this point, the space looked more like a launderer's shop than a cabin. "He should have said goodbye," I agreed. He grunted another affirmative. "And it wouldn't have killed him to stay on a few days to help us *both* out." When I was done, I turned to face him, or rather, his ass. "This situation is nothing like anything I've ever known. There's a really steep learning curve, and we're going to be facing off against a world-class necromancer in a few days. I'm scared out of my brain most of the time I'm awake, and I can't even *begin* to fathom how to do this job properly."

I let out a frustrated breath. "But I'm *trying*," I insisted. "And I *will* get better. I know it has to be even harder for you to have to break in a new Tiberius every few years, especially when they leave you in a lurch. How about I promise not to do that, and you maybe meet me halfway these first few weeks?"

He rolled onto his back and eyed me. "No more laughing," he muttered around the thumb, which earned a barely concealed smirk from me and subsequent glare from him.

"I can't promise that," I somberly replied. "But I can promise to keep trying to understand you and this service, which should cut back on that quite a bit."

He sat up and half-heartedly dragged the blanket across his lap.

I laughed softly and nodded. "Thank you for that."

"They're sick," he said, taking the thumb from his mouth. "They're dying, afraid, and they're helpless."

I realized after a moment that he was talking about Rshavin. "Yeah," I agreed. "Probably. Yes."

"Miracles require faith," he said. "Faith can be bolstered. It can be revived. It can be encouraged."

My eyebrows went up. "Oh, gods! *That's* why the parade! Raising moral, lifting spirits and faith so you can—"

"So I can do my job," he muttered. "So I can convince a bunch of sick, helpless, dying people that I *can* do my job, so that I can *do* my job."

I laughed and shook my head, looking away. "I feel like an idiot."

"You are," he agreed. I bit my lip to keep from answering. "But you're trying. That's more than a lot of them do."

I nodded and met his gaze. "I am," I agreed.

"If you don't want to look at my ass the rest of the night, get my underthings dry," he grumbled, though there was an amused glint in his eyes.

I just nodded and sat back amidst my half-circle of notes, books, and scrolls. "There is something I wanted to ask."

He rolled his eyes, flopped onto his back, and plopped his thumb back into his mouth. Thankfully, he pulled the blanket across his middle.

"Did Eth—um, did *I* mention the damage path of the beavers?"

"No," he slurred.

"What about the evidence of where the necromancy might be originating from?"

"No, why?"

"Well," I said, flipping through the ninth tome. "*I* left notes for me—*new* me—to follow, but *past* me never wrote about mentioning them to you."

He grunted "Until a few days ago, Tiberius was only concerned with *one thing*."

"Don't do that," I gently rebuked.

He turned to squint at me. "Do what?"

"Talk about me in the third person."

He laughed, a touch of irony in it. "Well, until a few days ago all *you* could do is count down the minutes until *you* could go your merry way."

"Ah," I said, following his bitter reasoning. "And following up on the source of the undead beavers..."

"A job for Tiberius, to be sure," he answered. "But not until *after* your two-year anniversary."

I shook my head again. "The men on Marlo's boat," I muttered. "However many people at Rshavin or Vevesk, or any of the surrounding towns..."

He shrugged. "For all he knew it was local."

"No," I countered. "He knew it was bigger. He *chose* to wait, to let the next *Tiberius* connect the dots. He left me notes, crumbs to follow. He's why those people died."

"You can't think like that," the hero said, a sad smile twisting his lips around his thumb. "There's *always* something bigger." He dropped his arm and stood up. "There's always another monster, and one behind him, and one behind *him*. Once we get to Vevesk, there could be another town and another."

I nodded. "Still—"

"Don't start that," he cut in, wearily. "Once you start blaming people, you'll start blaming *you*." He cut the air sharply. "The *necromancer* is to blame. Once we kill him, *or her*, we'll feast, be merry, and kill the next monster." He flopped back on the bed. "Keep it simple."

"Easier said than done," I responded, but decided to try and let it go. I would likely understand Ethan's motives better after I had two years under my belt.

"And try to get your fear under control," he mumbled. "Can't have you taking a break at some really important time to puke over the side of your horse."

I glowered, but he wasn't wrong. "I don't know how, but I'm trying." I looked toward the side of the boat, as if I could see the lightning-eyed man watching me through the trees. "I've never... this is all..."

"You've got to have faith in me, too." He turned his head to watch me. "Miracles take faith, and those are the source of my strength. *Tiberius* needs to have faith in The Chosen One, even when no one else does. It's how I keep you safe, so you can keep me safe."

I chuffed and nodded. It made a crazy amount of sense, and hearing wise words from him made it feel as though the world were upside down. At length I just sighed and pushed the books aside to lay down. "Will you wake me when we make port? I'm going to try and sleep an hour or so. I want to be fresh for the running."

He watched me for a moment, then nodded and sat up. "Fine. But remember, this is not going to be a common thing. *You* watch over *me*." He crossed his arms and looked out the porthole.

"You want something to read," I asked. "To pass the time?"

"Shut up and go to sleep," he grumbled.

9. In the Town They Tell the Story of the Great Sickness

I had been to Rshavin several times, and it had always struck me as a city full of life, diversity, and revelry. It was at the crossroads of a small waterway which brought rich grain down from the high hills and a river thick with trade from the coast as well as from inland. It was also nestled in a prime location for seafaring and fishing, being far enough inland that the salt didn't mix with the water, but having deep enough waters to allow the larger freight and fishing vessels in from the sea. Even at night, the city was always bustling, always busy, and full of foreigners eager to spend coin after a long time at sea. Except tonight.

The coast reeked of rot and spoiled fish, and no late-night fishermen or trappers moved through the sea of bobbing ships at the marina. I was standing near the starboard side when our barge came to a rest at its slip. Captain Swails fixed me with a dark frown as the crew secured us. "We are unloading, but not taking on goods," he quietly advised me. "See to it you're back in time. I want away from here by sunrise."

I nodded somberly. "Thank you for bearing us this far."

He grimaced and walked away, mumbling something about a cursed voyage.

I slipped through the vast marina and down an eerily quiet thoroughfare to the local guildhall, my bag of coins and correspondences clutched close as if it might protect me from peril due to its sheer value and importance. Once I was surrounded by buildings where Trion couldn't spy upon me from the trees, my heart calmed some. I still felt a great unease, and by the time I reached the hall, I understood why. This road was well lit, lamps every twenty or thirty paces, but it was normally full of bobbing lanterns, open shutters with light spilling out, and the sounds of merriment and debauchery around every corner and through every door. Instead, every passage was barred, every shutter closed, and only the distant throb of subdued music from a large tavern down the road could be heard.

The guildhall was also barred closed, but when I knocked, the iron speakeasy cracked open and a youth spoke through the small gate. "Closed till daylight, sir."

"In the past it was not so," I remarked, glancing warily up and down the street.

"I'm certain you've heard of our ill fortunes of late, sir," the boy answered. "I'm instructed to let no one enter—"

I held up the bag I carried that bore the seal of The Chosen One, and then lifted my hand that he might see the seal of Tiberius. "If you do not recognize these, you should not be the lad guarding this door."

His eyes widened, and the tiny iron door slammed shut. For a long moment, I fidgeted with the seal, wondering if I should have been less forceful. Just as I was about to knock again, the door opened, and a sleepy, barrel-chested man blocked my passage. "What's this about? Questers' Guild business?"

I let out a relieved breath and nodded. "Grandmaster business," I corrected, showing him the seal on the bag. "Official business of The Chosen One."

He came awake with a snort of startled breath. "Tiberius!" He jerked the door open and leaned over to slap the boy on the back of the head. "Learn your betters, lad. This here is The Chosen One's personal vassal."

I stepped in, giving the boy an apologetic look for the treatment. "The street was dark," I allowed.

"Not nearly enough as an excuse," the man grumbled. He latched the door behind him. "We are in sore need of your grandmaster hero this night, that is for sure and certain!" He turned back to me, clapped a hand on my back, and led me into the main hall. "Boy," he barked over his shoulder. "Go wake all the runners." When the youth rushed out of sight to presumably do just that, the man turned to me and cast me an amiable if weary smile. "The messengers for the other guilds will be along shortly, I'm Master Quester Barome, at your service."

I shook his thick hand and nodded. "You will have to forgive me; I haven't the time for pleasantries. I have much work and only a handful of hours to do it in if this town is to be saved."

He came to a quick stop and fixed me with a dark and intense stare. "It is as bad as all that, then?"

I nodded gravely. "We will need a gathering place large enough for everyone well enough to walk and stand, and I will need a stage constructed that all may see *him*." I adjusted the bag on my shoulder. "I have instructions for city officials, and heads of all of the major guilds."

He nodded again. "I'll set you up in my office." He gestured down a hall where lamps were just flaring to life. "I will send for everyone you require, and I will send message to the lord, himself."

He showed me into a dark but serviceable space and quickly made ready writing supplies and several lanterns. "Oh," I said, as I was settling. "And I will need someone who is capable of arranging festivities on short notice."

"Festivities?" His eyebrows shot up, a confused frown turning down his features.

"Um, yes. Someone who will have connections with local musicians, performers, dancers, actors, and the like." I nodded firmly, as if the request was not as absurd as it sounded, and settled myself in his chair. "Quickly," I reminded him. "The candle burns low."

As his steps receded down the hall, I quickly deposited the many letters I'd prepared onto the desk and began organizing them by guild. There were quite a few conversations that needed to happen in a short period of time, and the finite details of what I required of any one person could not be explained twice.

"I was certain she was lying," a sultry voice broke the silence, and my gaze jerked up in surprise. A voluptuous woman attired in fine garments intended to dramatically accentuate her assets stood just inside the doorway, one gloved hand lifted to tap a folded lace fan against her almost-bare bosom. I am a little ashamed to say it took me more than one attempt to meet her green eyes, and when I did, they sparkled with amused mischief. "Surely Tiberius would not walk right past *my* house without stopping to say greeting."

I cleared my throat and shifted uncomfortably. I was not accustomed to exceedingly attractive women speaking to me in an openly alluring tone. In spite of the seriousness of my evening's duties, my entire body reminded me that I had been involuntarily celibate since becoming outcast and destitute. The woman shifted, lifting her free hand to her hip, breaking whatever spell I was under. I shook my head, hastily pulling my eyes away. "I... um, I've important business," I muttered, forcibly returning my attention to the letters. I still had several to write, and I had yet to acquire a map to plan the parade. "I apologize if I offended—"

Her laugh was equal parts harsh and enticing. "You talk like a stranger passing through on business." She stepped into the room, glancing around. "My study is quite a bit more... accommodating." She pressed her hands to the desk and leaned toward me, blatantly angling her corseted torso into better view. "And you said you quite cared for my quills and ink."

I sat quickly back and wrested my gaze up to her face. "I..." I had no idea what to say to her. She thought I was Ethan, or perhaps some other Tiberius... or perhaps *several* other Tiberiuses. The thought turned my stomach a little. "Oh," I whispered. This was clearly the behavior of a lover. "Oh, gods." I had never anticipated having to deal with this sort of identity confusion. Concealing that I did not remember or recognize someone during business deals would be a little awkward, but I was sure I could manage. How could I have any kind of conversation with this woman without revealing that I didn't know her name or anything about our previous relationship?

With a flash of insight, I realized I could simply divert her attention away from her intentions and our supposed history. "Listen," I said. "I did not mean insult, but I am certain you are aware of what is happening in this town."

She pursed her lips and twisted to rest her hip on the desk, partially sitting while she fanned herself. The strong scent of lilac filled the air, and I held back a sneeze. "Yes," she sighed out. "So The Chosen One is still on the ship and you've come in under the cover of night to prepare his arrival?"

My eyebrows went up, and I frowned. How much had Ethan told her? "Uh... yes." I nodded. "I only have a few hours and quite a bit of planning if we are to help Rshavin."

She crossed her arms, an unconscious movement that made her seem somehow small and fragile. I realized she had dropped the temptress façade and was showing me her fear, and I felt both relieved and even more awkward than before. She was demonstrating vulnerability to a man she thought she knew. "The girls are scared," she confessed. "People are sick, some dying. There's a lot of talk about rotten fish and maddened animals. No one is saying, but they think the city has been cursed."

I picked up on a clue about her identity. "What are your girls saying?" Perhaps I could learn who she was as well as acquire some useful observations from a local.

"Oh, that some of their regulars are acting strange, looking... *wrong*. A kind of sick we've not seen. They're afraid to take the coin." She looked down at me. "And people are staying home, either because they're scared or because they're hauls have been spoiled and they haven't the coin to spare."

That was when I realized she wasn't talking about her children. *Regulars*. "Oh," I looked down at the scrolls. "Have any of your girls gotten sick?"

"A few. But I'm not stupid. We've gone to our stockroom for food and our rain-trap for water till all this settles." She stood and began to pace, her hips swaying in a practiced saunter. "So this is something for the Great Hero?" She walked around the desk and it was all I could do to keep from flinching when she brushed my hair back away from my face. She leaned down and kissed my temple, and the scents of woodsmoke, ale, and perfume washed over me. "Me and my girls are at your disposal."

I cleared my throat and nodded, grateful that the desk concealed my lap. "I was actually going to contact you tonight about that very subject." It was only a partial lie. I had intended to contact the most prestigious brothel, but if this woman knew Tiberius, I assumed she either ran or owned the business I needed to employ. "How much would the, um, *disposal* of your house cost?"

"Down to business so quickly?" She nodded, all docile pretense gone as she assumed the role of businesswoman. "The usual. A Gold King upfront, and I'll bill you later for any extras." She leaned down and winked at me. "And *our* usual arrangement still stands."

My stomach churned a little when I thought about Ethan taking her up on that offer perhaps two weeks prior. "Alas," I covered. "I have no time for diversions." She sighed in acceptance and paced away from me. "How many women do you have?"

"Tonight? Twenty-eight." She cast a smirk over her shoulder at me. "And four fair young men."

I cleared my throat again and quickly busied myself uncorking the ink and preparing a fresh sheet of parchment. "I would like to employ anyone who is not otherwise disposed or has other arrangements," I said. "To wear their finest clothes and line the streets of the thoroughfare nearest your house."

She smiled. "And to throw down flower petals from the windows and balconies?"

I looked up, surprised by the embellishment. But it told me her establishment was on the main road. "Can you acquire them at this late hour?"

"Of course. My sister still owns the flower shop by the river, and much of her supplies come by ship, free of whatever has wilted the fare of the shops that trade only local grown blossoms."

I laughed quietly to cover my surprise. "I forgot. Lucky her stock is so cultured."

She crossed the floor and held out a hand, expectantly.

"Oh, yes, the King." I withdrew one of the little pouches from the bag of shame and lowered it into her palm. She hefted it once and then tucked it down the front of her corset. I quickly glanced down at my work to hide my flush. "I would appreciate if you could send someone to the dock to keep him company until I return."

Her smile turned up again. "I know just the girl. I hope you're not expecting him to be well rested for the morning's events?"

I laughed softly and shook my head. "No, from my experience, this is better." Thinking of his good spirits the first morning we met reawakened my embarrassment, but I shook it off and wet the tip of a quill in the ink well. "The Chosen One in good spirits come morning can only do us and Rshavin a favor in this dark hour."

The next several hours were an intense and exceptionally validating series of encounters. I had spent my entire life being the least of every party to whom I belonged. A white-sash, a lowly assistant, a translator, copy-scribe, and worse. Though I considered myself intelligent to an above-average degree and singularly self-motivated, I had never been impressive to anyone. I had never been a leader, a superior, or had opinions that would be considered valuable.

As *Tiberius*, great men and women listened to my thoughts, valued my concerns, and agreed to my demands with a level of deference reserved for a minor lord, in the least. I met with guild leaders, merchants, business owners, and officials, and every one of them shook my hand with respect. When I spoke to performers and workers of a lower class, they looked up to me, though only a few days prior they might have spat at my feet.

I walked back to the ship in the dwindling dark, exhausted and drunk on the authority this new title had bestowed upon me. The streets were coming alive before the pre-dawn, earlier than most other days, awakening with hope and excitement that I had helped create. A young crier ran past me, bellowing his news up to the rooftops, "The Chosen One comes! He comes to save us! Wake up! Rise and Rejoice!"

In the distance, I could just make out the sounds of rushed and determined construction as half a dozen guilds worked together to erect a stage for The Chosen One just north of town in a large clearing beside the river, a space maintained for tourneys. Performers were setting up to entertain the gathering crowd until the Hero of Men could arrive. In the darkest hour this town had ever seen, a spectacle to rival all others was about to occur. I had put these events in motion. My words—and *his* coins—had roused dozens if not hundreds of skilled men and women to action. I couldn't imagine why any Tiberius would ever give this up.

Once aboard the barge, I rapped briskly on the cabin door and called through it, "Miss, it is time you were away."

A feminine giggle responded and The Chosen One's voice boomed irritably. "Tiberius! I will flay you alive!"

Drowsy chuckling rose up from a few dark mounds on the deck, and I sighed, knocking again. "Please be dressed when I enter."

There was a good amount of muttering, girlish giggling, and movement, and I prayed that he was getting dressed and not merely ignoring me. Thankfully, a fair if somewhat tousled young woman emerged a few minutes later, hastily combing her dark hair into a manageable state with her fingers. She was flushed and grinning, and dropped a quick kiss on my cheek when she slipped past me toward the dock. I nodded and let out a sigh in her wake.

"Come in already, now that you've ruined my fun!" The Chosen One bellowed, followed by another round of more alert laughter from the crew.

"And he asked *me* not to laugh," I mumbled. Thankfully, when I entered he was already fastening the many tiny buckles on a pair of exquisitely tooled and gold-gilt trousers of fine white leather. My eyebrows climbed, and my mouth dropped open when I took in the state of the room. Nearly every open inch of floor was covered in trunks and varied detritus from those trunks, scattered every which way. Clothing, books, cooking supplies, all unloaded without the slightest care.

The Chosen One glared over at me when he'd finished his task. "We have less than an hour to sunrise, and you never had the crew bring in my trunk of armor!" He snorted out a puff of frustration and snapped up a white silk shirt from where it was draped over my trunk. "Am I to ride into town naked?" He snarled. "Hurry up, already, and get on with those boots and greaves!"

I blinked in dumfounded and fruitless anger at the chaos I would somehow have to tame before we could ride gloriously into town. I wasn't even sure at this point where Tiberius' tabard was in all that mess. He plucked up a piece of detritus from the floor and chucked it at me.

"Tiberius! Stop gawking and get my boots!"

I shook myself out of the void left by my suddenly departed elation, and caught what appeared to be a tankard. I threw it back at him, and he knocked it aside easily, a flash of startled indignation on his face. "Are you a *child*?" I hissed as quietly as I could through my fury. "You travel with your belongings *everywhere*! Do you not know where your damned things are! Do you not know the difference between the trunk containing plates and the one that holds your armor?"

His mouth dropped open and his eyes went round with shock. "How *dare*—"

"Stuff it!" I snarled. "You can't possibly be this stupid." I jerked a hand demonstratively around at the ruined quarters.

He moved faster than I thought possible, and before I realized what was happening, a thick arm was pressed against my throat, pinning me to the wall. His face, flushed with rage, was only an inch from mine as the bar of his other arm pressed against my chest, deflating the air from my lungs with a strangled huff. "Tiberius does *not* talk to me like that!" He snarled. "He makes my bed, and cleans my clothes, and does what *I* tell him to do!"

I clawed at his wrist, twisting to get air into my throat, panic rushing in instead. I felt my feet kicking and realized he'd lifted me off of the floor. I choked out a few garbled syllables that might have resembled a plea.

"Tiberius serves *my* needs!" He continued as my vision started to go black. "He does *not* call me names or laugh at me. And he does *not* have a say in anything unless *I* say so!"

Just as I was starting to lose track of my limbs, he released me, and I crumpled to the floor croaking and gasping for breath. The Chosen One shoved me onto my back and jerked a white leather boot out from under my hip. Without another word, he retrieved the other from a few feet away and stalked over to the bed to sit and jerk them onto his feet.

I sucked in breath and cleared my throat a few times just to be sure it still worked through the grating pain. Fear subsided quickly, replaced by my own fury. When I spoke, my voice came out in a rasp. "Actually," I snapped. "I speak to you however I damn well please." When I rose shakily to my feet, his eyes fixed on me as his lip curled up into a snarl. "As it turns out, there's nothing in that tome or in my contract that says I can't tell you you're being an *enormous ass*," I growled through the pain. "No jolts of electricity to warn me not to tell you *this*," I pointed around at the emptied trunks. "Is unacceptable. And *this*," I gestured emphatically to my throat. "Is *unacceptable*!"

He jerked to his feet, and I staggered back a step but managed to raise my chin in stubborn defiance. "Look, I *know* what my duty is, but it's been *four days*!" I let out a huff and a mirthless laugh. "And already there has been plague, undead fish, and a feud with the *god of strife*!" I dropped onto the lid of a trunk and rubbed my throbbing throat. "And now... The Chosen One nearly choking me to death," I mumbled as my fury deflated into a sickening and resolved dread. I planted my elbows on my knees and buried my face in my hands. "Gods, I don't know if I'll survive this." I shook my head. "Maybe this whole mess wasn't much better than being beaten and pissed on in the gutter by guild trash."

A long silence followed where I assumed he stood glaring and waiting for my apology. I didn't intend to give it. I honestly didn't know how we were going to work together if I was under constant threat from every direction. Until that moment, in spite of our differences, The Chosen One had been a stalwart hero who would stand between me and the truly horrific things we'd seen. If he was also something to be feared, I didn't know how I could endure.

"Hand me that," The Chosen One said at last, his voice quiet and somehow demure. I looked up to see him pointing at a half-cylinder-shaped piece of armor. His anger was also gone, and he actually looked sad, perhaps regretful.

I sighed and scooped up the armor, standing up to hold it out to him. He shook his head and pointed at his leg. "It's a greave," he explained. "It goes on my left."

I knelt and positioned it over his shin, fastening the straps behind the knee and ankle. When he pointed to the matching piece, I retrieved it and secured the right greave to his other shin. Over the next several minutes, he pointed out pieces of armor, told me what they were called and where on his body they went. Though I still felt defeated and hopeless, it was a little refreshing for him to actually take the time to help me understand what I should be doing. The hauberk mail was difficult to get over his head without ruining his wig, but some absurd maneuvering on both of our parts eventually got it into place.

When he was fully dressed save the elaborate gold and silver helm which he tucked under his arm, he sat on the bed and silently watched me hastily tuck supplies back into trunks and chests. I would have to re-organize everything later, but perhaps that would work out for the best. I would at least become more familiar with the supplies I would be using consistently for the next two years. While I packed, I located what I would need for the morning's fanfare, Tiberius' finest clothing and tabard. I sat back and stared at the slacks which were still too long and too tight in the waist and *other* places. I hadn't thought to have clothing prepared for myself. I would have to ride into town in stained, off-color trousers and a ridiculously over-long tunic.

"Fantastic," I mumbled, bowing my head and letting my heavy eyelids drift closed for a moment. I just wanted to sleep, to pretend that I wasn't always at least a little aware that a literal god would plague me to death if he got the chance.

"I'm sorry," The Chosen One said.

I looked up, frowning. "What?"

He pointed to my neck. "I'm sorry." He huffed and looked down at his feet, or rather, his broad breastplate. "You're right. That was wrong."

I nodded in agreement, but I was too tired and defeated to offer up any sarcasm.

"I just can't..." He shook his head. "The other ones. They didn't talk like you. They didn't—"

"I know," I mumbled. "I shouldn't have said that—"

"No," he cut in, looking up to meet my gaze. There was something odd in his expression, something intent. "It..." he sighed and looked away again. "It usually takes them longer."

"Longer?"

"Yes. Longer to hate me," he muttered. "Longer to forget who I am. *What* I am."

I chuffed a short laugh and shook my head. "I don't *hate* you," I insisted. "I just..." I shrugged. "I'm into really unfamiliar territory in every respect, and everything is moving so quickly." I looked up at him, setting my jaw in deference I genuinely felt. "And I really don't think I'm going to forget *what* you are." I laughed and gestured to his gleaming armor. "You talk about the anger of a god as if it were an inconvenience. You literally climbed up the side of a barge while carrying me." I laughed again. "You *healed* a dying man right in front of me."

"It wasn't me, it was—"

"I know, Sca," I said. "But he heard your call and answered."

He nodded as if we were discussing the price of eggs and not the actual, tangible favor of a god.

"All of the legends, all of the tales of your great deeds," I said. "They're true. You *actually are* the greatest hero the world has ever known. You truly fight the most powerful and terrifying things that prey upon people."

He nodded again, his brows going up as pride started to show on his face.

"Even if you talk to me like I'm an ignorant slave and throw your things like a child." That earned a frown from him. "You still slay dragons when you're burned so badly you had to be resurrected. You still jump into a river and board a ship of disease-dead men to look for survivors. You still talk about protecting the innocent people of this world as if there were no other recourse to consider." I sighed. "You're still the greatest man I will ever meet."

His face broke into a wide grin and he nodded. "Aye," he agreed. "I am."

I laughed and let out a huff, standing up to change into my unimpressive ensemble.

He watched me, a sneer crawling up his lips. "*That* is what you're wearing?"

10. The Sun Shone, Having No Alternative, on The Chosen One

I managed to get all of the many displaced items back into trunks and boxes, dress myself, and help The Chosen One style his hair before the sun broke the horizon. With some curt and overbearing instruction, I was able to prepare his destrier, whom I learned was named Braknik—with a rolled "r"—for riding while the hero kept the fierce beast calm. There was some debate about whether there was time to dress the monstrous horse in his armor, which, of course, I lost. By the time I was saddling Topher, I was sweating and irritated again. We kept our activities to the far side of the cabin, concealing The Chosen One from the crowd that had gathered at the docks.

"When?" he grunted, stroking Braknik's nose and slipping him a small handful of oats.

"The music should start the moment the sunlight breaks over the trees."

He grunted, glanced toward the east, and moved up beside the warhorse. "You can mount without help." It was a statement of expectation rather than a concerned question.

"I'll manage."

The fluted instruments started so loudly, Topher danced to the side, nearly knocking me over into the water. Only a fistful of reins and mane saved me from a morning swim. The Chosen One let out a rich belly-laugh and vaulted into the saddle. "See you on dry land," he chortled, shouting his mount into motion. Before I'd recovered enough to attempt the saddle, I heard Braknik's hooves strike down on the dock and a cheer explode from the awaiting crowd.

I growled and pulled myself hand-over-hand onto the still-anxious horse and tapped a heel to his flank to get her moving. When I rounded the cabin, The Chosen One was headed down the thoroughfare, a throng of city folk surrounding him. I followed as close as I could with the pack of people not willing to part even for a mounted party, and watched his golden waves dance this way and that as he called out to the people who adored him. He cut aside to ride close to the brothel I'd employed and reached a hand out to help a red-haired maiden climb onto the saddle with him.

The onlookers went mad with adulation, and The Chosen One draped the woman across his lap, kissing her heartily while flower petals snowed down, decorating his shining visage. Braknik moved forward, snorting and stomping, parting the crowd with sheer fierce authority. After only a block or so, the hero lowered the flushed maiden to the ground and took up the reins again. His parade through town didn't lessen in intensity the entire route, and all of Rshavin emptied onto the tourney grounds where a small stage awaited, draped in gold and blue swaths of fabric. I nodded my head in appreciation of that final touch and managed to saddle up closer to him in the open.

He led the cheering mob across the field and dismounted directly onto the stage without the slightest hint of strain in spite of his full plate and mail. I pushed forward to take up Braknik's reins, pulling back just before his snapping teeth could close around my wrist, and led the beast to the side of the stage.

"Good people of Rshavin," The Chosen One shouted, and his voice carried across the great expanse of moving bodies. "Hear me, noble men and women of this beautiful city!"

I flinched at the unimaginable volume of his plea and realized there was no possible way he could be heard over the crowd, and yet he was. So loud was his voice, that people directly in front of him staggered back and covered their ears.

"Be still for a moment, good people," he called, and the cheering quieted to a buzzing murmur of whispered voices. "I come bearing the good will and blessings of the gods, here to your fine, hard-working city. I have come to heal the sickness that has befallen your people and your businesses." The noise of the crowd grew again as whispers became open discussion of what everyone knew but had been too afraid to acknowledge. When the grandmaster hero spoke again, my teeth rattled with the intensity of his booming declaration. "I have come to *heal* your river!"

Then, the last thing I could have ever expected occurred; he puffed out his chest and bellowed out the first ringing chords of a grand ballad to Sca. Apparently everyone else was as stunned as me, for they stood in rapt silence as The Chosen One's clear baritone filled the entire expanse. It was a well-known song, and before he had reached the chorus, a man not far from the front of the stage joined in. The Chosen One's eyes glittered with approval as he met the man's gaze, and as if they had only been awaiting permission, thousands of voices rang out in tune—some out of tune—with the great Hero of Men.

I found myself caught up in the rapture, and my own less-than-stageworthy performance joined the synchronized cacophony. Unbelievably, over all the rest, the Chosen could still be heard. I was certain every man, woman, and child could pick out his mighty and achingly comforting voice. Not an eye in all the field was dry when we were done singing out our praise to the god of healing and strength.

As the Chosen came to a stop, I heard the sobbing of women and men alike as they revealed the fear and despair they had been holding at bay. He allowed only a breath for all of us to start drifting free of the spell his adoration had cast before he opened his lungs and started anew. This time, it was a bawdy, vigor-filled shanty exalting Caera, goddess of lust in all forms and of the sea. His eyes shone with fierce glee as he drew the crowd once again into a chorus of rapturous worship.

At the end of that song, he went on to the next, and the next after. He gave us neither reprieve nor disappointment as he thanked each god in turn with a song that befit their great gifts to the world and to the strength of The Chosen One. Butev, goddess of the forge and the bounty of the deep earth; Dindrel, god of prophecy and the wind; Jaya, goddess of sleep and the afterlife; Anetrael, god of contracts and diplomacy. I was perhaps the only one who noticed the omission of one god, Trion, as The Chosen One stepped to the very front of the stage to offer up a song in what was clearly the pinnacle of his performance. The last ballad was in honor of Skalah, ruler of the gods, the deity of joy, misery, honor, and all living things under the dominion of the sun.

That was when I saw him—the lightning-eyed man. He stood at the outskirts of the crowd just inside the shadow of the surrounding forest, his blue cloak rippling in the wind. Just as before, choking terror rose up in me as he lifted a deeply-tanned hand to his bare chest and clenched it into a fist. A cold wind whipped through the crowd, throwing hats up and into the poisoned river. The sky darkened with storm clouds that crept in abruptly, blotting out the sun. A few stinging drops of icy rain cut through the revelry, and voices, my own included, faltered.

Lightning and booming thunder rent the air and song turned to fear and the frantic conversation of townsfolk moving to cover. I found myself shrinking back into my own cloak as the clouds released a merciless downpour upon the startled onlookers. The pack of people turned into dangerous, churning movement, accentuated by another crack of too-close thunder and blinding lightning. Nearly breathless with a sudden terror for myself and for the panicking crowd, I turned to peer up at The Chosen One.

He stood at the precipice of the stage, his voice quieted as he stared unblinking at the god of strife and pestilence, his radiating glow of the Blessing of Light dwindling. Cold clutched at me when I saw him drenched, standing alone, his protection wavering. My whole body went quivering and weak, and I shrank back, unconsciously backing Topher and Braknik further behind the scaffolding that supported the stage.

Then, like a clear bell in the back of my head, I remembered his words in the cabin. The Chosen One needed me; he needed *Tiberius* to believe in him. I tried to swallow the lump in my throat—unsuccessfully—and nudged my mount forward. I dared not look to the frightening figure in the woods, but kept my eyes on The Chosen One as I urged the anxious horses to the front of the stage. The great hero jerked his eyes away from the blue-robed figure and turned down to meet my gaze as if shaking off a distant thought. I nodded once to him, bravely I hoped, though my teeth were chattering from more than just the saturating chill.

His face broke into a broad grin, and his glow redoubled. He looked out across the crowd, taking in the scene for only a moment before his bellowing voice cut through the howling wind. "Stop!" Like children caught in mischief, everyone froze in mid-step, their eyes snapping back to the hero. He stood broad and proud, his gold ringlets clinging to his face and shoulders, shining like the sun beamed only upon him. "Since when does water turn you from the king of the gods? Since when does a mere storm silence the sun?"

He threw his arms out. "Storm rage if you must, but Skalah shall *not* be denied his tribute! And when all is done, his light shall strike through your dark waters!" He started the great god's ballad from the beginning, and slowly, the crowd joined in. I stared in awe as people drew together, huddling to stay warm against the wind while they lifted quavering but genuine voices to the god of passion and life. Though they looked miserable, the fear dissipated, and doubts subsided. It was the combined will of a people who had been beaten down but not broken, a town desperate for healing but not without hope.

Sunlight abruptly cut through the clouds, casting a brilliant ray upon The Chosen One. Topher danced a step away, as if the golden glow of the Hero of Gods' Blessings might burn him, and Braknik's eyes flashed wide and white. The rain choked back, and sunlight spread out, washing over the upturned faces of the worshipers. My skin tingled as I was awash in the illumination, and a weight I hadn't realized was there lifted away. I sucked in a full, clean breath, and a deep warmth replaced the weary dread that had wrapped my bones. The final chorus of the ballad rang out triumphantly from a grateful and invigorated town. I looked out over the sea of grinning faces, and saw the cloaked man was gone. The sun had shifted in the sky and now shone brightly into the trees where he had stood. With a shudder of memory, the dread his gaze had inspired in me drifted to the back of my mind.

  The Chosen One lifted his fist and bellowed out a fierce cry of defiance, and the town replied with a deafening roar. Topher danced, and I laughed in spite of my tired, achy, sodden body. I didn't need to see the proof, I simply knew. He had driven the pestilence from Rshavin. We all knew it. Twice more he rallied a roar of victory from the onlookers, then the hero turned his broad grin to me, though his voice carried across to everyone listening. "Now, we drink! We eat! We make merry!" A muddied cheer of agreement, laughter, and rising conversation filled the tourney grounds.

  Tables were produced from I'm not sure where, and food materialized from what must have been the kitchens of any home within easy jogging distance. The Chosen One watched the preparations with a broad grin from his high vantage and crossed his arms, appearing as a golden statue watching over the revelry. One table was borne clear to the stage and piled high with food, and the Chosen One dropped down to the ground in one easy movement. He took a seat at the head of the table as several women pushed forward with dry linens to towel him off.

  I had only made preparations for the gathering, and stared in awe as the city pulled together an impromptu festival. Everyone had been inspired to abandon their labors and duties in favor of adding what they could to the merriment, be it food, supplies, or entertainment. A hand laid across my knee, and I jerked alert, nearly slipping from the saddle. Bright emerald eyes glittered up at me in amusement, and the brothel mistress inclined her head in invitation toward the Chosen's table.

"You're shivering," she said. "Come, dine on hot ale, and I shall warm you."

I shuddered again and felt my face flush, but it would be utterly absurd and suspect for me to refuse the invitation of food and company. I slid, rather clumsily, from Topher, and the mistress' surprisingly strong arms steadied me. "My, but you *are* weathered," she cooed. "You've had a few days of strife and a long night, I'm sure." She tucked her wrist in my elbow and slid the reins from my hands. Before I could object, she handed the reins off to a handsome young boy who was standing at the ready beside her. "Put both mounts in my stables, and be careful of the war beast lest he trample you," she instructed as she led me over to the main table.

"Tiberius!" The Chosen One shouted, lifting a turkey leg in my direction like a salutation. "I see Alina found you! Come, dine, and loosen that spine of yours!" Raucous laughter erupted from the men and women at the table with him, and I flushed again as I sat down, this time in aggravated embarrassment at the jeering. Already tightly-packed diners shifted to free up a chair and two women moved to the hero's lap. No sooner had I settled my weight, then a portly woman was pushing a heavily laden plate, piled high with every manner of food on the table, into my hands. She wiped her fingers on her sodden apron and started loading up another plate for the brothel mistress, who unabashedly slid onto my lap.

My whole body went stiff with surprise and—to be completely honest—something far more base and instinctual. Her heat radiated into me almost immediately, and I found myself unable to decide what to do with my hands except awkwardly hold the plate a few inches above the table top. The mistress laughed and guided the plate down to rest, then forked a gravy-bathed potato wedge. Without any preamble, she fed it to me and wiped away a drip of gravy from my chin with her thumb.

The Chosen One bellowed in laughter. "Look at him! You'd think he was a virgin!" The crowd joined in, and I clenched my jaw, glaring down at my hands on the table.

"I would prefer to feed myself," I growled quietly, barely audible to even me.

Alina leaned away, drawing my gaze, her eyebrows raised in surprise and a hint of offense. I imagine she did not often get spurned, and being the head of a house of women, she was likely considered quite the status symbol to take to bed. My eyes tracked to The Chosen One, who was lancing me with a disapproving glower. In spite of my embarrassment and shame, I felt a slight thrill of challenge at the warning in his expression. Here, in front of all of these onlookers, I was a direct example of what should be expected of The Chosen One and a man in his company. Maybe, cloaked by anonymity, bathed in the approval of a lascivious crowd, I could overcome my timidity.

I seized the cup of my neighbor, which contained some dark amber liquor, and downed it with a choking gulp of liquid fire. I hooked an arm around the brothel mistress' waist, pulled her close, and kissed her with all the vigor and shamelessness I could muster. A deafening cheer erupted all around us, The Chosen One's voice ringing above them all. When I drew away, I was heady and breathless from both drink and warm company, and Alina was panting until her bosom threatened to burst from its satin cage. The hero lifted his glass to me, and we all roared like animals and drank till we needed air.

 The evening sped up at that point, alternating rapidly between bawdy jokes, courageous tales, and fair maidens holding us all steady while we spun apart. At some point, an acting troupe mounted the stage and began enacting impromptu retellings of some of The Chosen One's greatest and better known deeds. I knew every one to the detail, and found myself correcting their performance in drunken and prideful slurs to Alina. When they had neared to the part of the legend where The Hero of Men slayed the dragon and freed and enslaved princess, The Chosen One vaulted onto stage, took up the wooden sword, and dispatched the foul beast with a few quick, artful strokes. The two poor actors under the green wool blanket yipped in pain and danced away in perhaps genuine fear. The hind-end of the beast toppled from the stage and dragged his partner, clawing all the while, after him.

 Everyone cheered, the hero bowed, and I laughed till I was sick. The Chosen One scooped up the mock princess and bore her off the stage, smothering her with heroic kisses. She wrapped her arms around his neck and portrayed the over-joyous and grateful damsel in what was decidedly a very un-princess-like performance. The two of them took The Chosen One's seat again, and the actor scooped up the Chosen's mug and shouted, "my hero!" She downed the entire stein in one long draught as the on-looking men banged on the table in a rambunctious crescendo that nearly toppled all the other cups. The Chosen kissed his hard-earned maiden again and laughed merrily, his eyes shining and his cheeks flushed from drink and arousal.

The night went on in much the same manner. The merriment took to the streets, visiting one shop and another. Though it was long past closing, doors were opened for the grandmaster hero and every bounty of sweet, drink, and finery was offered to him in gratitude. I tossed a Gold Chosen here and there whenever I noticed him accepting their wares, and slurred out my practiced reply when they tried to refuse it. "With Chosen's blessing... and all that."

I don't know at what point we were separated, but I fell back and looked up at a curtain-draped ceiling as it spun around me. Alina's hair spilled over me, ticking my chest, and I realized with a start that I had been disrobed. I tried to mutter some form of protest, citing duties, The Chosen One's needs, and a weak apology for my long abstinence and inebriation that would likely weaken my performance. Alina laughed and silenced my sputtering with her warm lips. The room spun faster, and I surrendered to the inevitable. For once, I let myself indulge in what my arrogant brain felt was below me. And for once, I reveled in every moment of it.

Gods bless The Chosen One.

11. It Is Truth Universally Acknowledged, That a Single Man in Possession of Good Fortune, Must Be in Want of a Slave

I will never understand how I could be so overwrought after a night of drinking that I yearned for either a bed or death, yet The Chosen One could be as merry and belligerent as the night I met him. I imagined it was yet another blessing, perhaps the gift of Repercussion-free Drunken Debauchery, undoubtedly gifted by Caera and Sca. Clearly it was one of the blessings that did not pass down to Tiberius. The Chosen One was kind enough to say our goodbyes and have a slightly-less miserable stable master arrange our cart to a satisfactory state. He was entirely too pleased with my inappropriate behavior the night before to be frustrated by my lack of usefulness the following morning. He magnanimously declared that I could simply, "repack our affairs when you are better rested and in better health."

As we struck north from Rshavin on the main road toward Vevesk, I began another leg of our journey bent over, emptying my stomach into the landscape. The Chosen filled our first few hours of slow trudgery with bawdy ballads in his own honor, raising his voice on occasion to sound over my miserable retching. He neither slowed his pace, nor seemed to concern himself with my health. Nearing noon, when he deemed it time for lunch, He pulled off into a timely-positioned grass glade with clear signs of previous encampment. "I'll have some of that roast beast the innkeep was kind enough to stow in our bags," he asserted as he marched into the trees to see to his needs.

I grunted an irritable affirmative. My stomach was in no state to consume food, but naturally, I was to prepare his. In truth, it didn't really seem that unfair; I was essentially his body-man. There was an entire tome about how I was to see to his necessities down to the minute detail. Cooking was undoubtedly in there somewhere. I found the beast in a carefully wrapped mason bowl settled in the nooks of the cart and let out a relieved breath when I saw none of the gravy had drizzled out. There were large chunks of potato and stewed vegetables nestled around it, and I was grateful that very little prep would be required, since the smell of the food was already turning my stomach. I located dining utensils after only a moderate amount of riffling, and decided I would need to be certain road rations and cooking supplies were easily accessible when I re-packed the cart that night.

The Chosen One returned in short order and lowered himself to a stump that had clearly been intended for use as a seat. I only gritted my teeth a little when he cleared his throat expectantly and awaited me to serve him. He seized the bowl with a ravenous growl, forked a potato into his mouth, and immediately spat it out onto the ground with a scowl. "This is cold!"

I quickly stepped back to avoid the regurgitated food and glowered back. "Of course it's cold! Do you expect me to spend an hour building a fire and heating it up?"

He vaulted to his feet and thrust the bowl back into my hands, sloshing gravy across my tunic. "Yes!" He bellowed that one word with such intensity a handful of birds took flight from a bush nearby. I would have shot back a retort, but his booming voice stabbed through my confounded brain like a barbed lance. Instead, I turned away to fight down a wave of nauseating pain. He stormed away to his mount while I battled my temper and wiped gravy from my shirt with leaves. I heard his sword ring free of its scabbard and spun, momentarily—and admittedly irrationally—afraid he was coming after me. He proceeded to take up a fighting position, going quickly through a series of practiced blocks and parries, and I flushed with embarrassment. Luckily, he was ignoring me with the stolid determination of a child, so I doubt he noticed my start.

Aggravated silence filled the next thirty minutes as I gathered the supplies and wood needed and worked up some cooking embers. I dropped the masonware onto the hot coals, not caring if some ash fell in, and made my way to the cart. I surveyed the mess that was our supplies and tried to file away some mental notes on how to re-pack the lighter materials so I wouldn't need to shift any of the heavier chests. When we bedded down in an inn for more than one harried and drunken night, I would have to have all of the chests brought to our rooms to re-organize them. I had no idea how Ethan had kept them in order with the hero scattering their contents on a near-daily basis.

I realized with a groan that he must have just learned to anticipate the stubborn warrior's needs and had everything on hand before it could be asked for. Armor, clothes, food, personal grooming supplies... I would need to learn when he would expect them and have them at the ready. If I could keep the hulking man-child out of the trunks, I could keep them in a useful and efficient state of organization. Luckily, I had a feeling The Chosen One was accustomed to a routine, likely born of Tiberus' need to remain sane, and it would probably be borne out through all the many entries of the previous assistants' journals. "Reading in the saddle, then," I mumbled to myself. I would start with the most recent journal, since it would have Ethan's routine.

"For the love of the gods, Tiberius," the hero bellowed, jerking me from my thoughts. "It's burning!"

I huffed out an expletive and rushed to the food. I burned my hand a few times before I wised up and used a few unburnt sticks to leverage the cookware out of the fire and onto a flat stone near the pit.

"You need to get better at this," he grumbled, glowering down at the bubbling, blackened mess. He shook his head in disgust and went to his saddle bag, pulling out rations and wandering to the far end of the clearing to munch in sullen silence.

I swallowed back an unexpected lump of shame at his quiet disappointment and dropped to my rump in the dirt. He was rude, belligerent, demanding, and insulting... but he *was* a grandmaster hero, and his greatness certainly deserved a higher caliber of service than I was offering him at that moment.

"I'm sorry," I replied genuinely, drawing his dour frown. "You're right; I'm not accustomed to a lot of the duties that Tiberius is responsible for. You deserve better, and I will keep trying to improve." I gave him an entreating smile. "Please remember that this is still just my sixth day, and much of our time has been spent in urgent action."

He made a sour face but nodded. "Read faster," he grumbled. "We're coming up to it, and Tiberius needs to be on the ready."

I nodded. "Then, for a few days, can you give me a little more leniency? Maybe tell me what you expect instead of shouting it?"

He nodded absently, then his eyes took on a sharpness. "I eat well for *every* meal," he stated. "Even on the road." He shook the trail rations at me, then lifted his arms to flex his impressive biceps. "This physique requires meat, hearty vegetables, and in ready supply." He stuffed a dried fig in his cheek, grumbling around it. "I'm likely going into battle in a few days and dried berries is not good enough." He started pacing, his dismissal of the conversation evident.

A knot filled my stomach at his words, *going into battle in a few days*. I stared down at the burnt stew, my heart suddenly racing at the thought. Everything until now had swayed violently back and forth between extreme irritation and terror, and at no time had I likely been in any real danger. But in a few days...

I set my jaw against the thought, deciding I'd let it rest for now to revisit later. I hurried to the trunks and pulled out a clean wooden bowl and a few fresh ingredients that would need to be eaten in the next few days. I carefully separated the unburnt fare from the rest, being sure to take only the potatoes and meat that had not been resting on the bottom or in the gravy. I poured in some crème and added a heavy dash of rich seasoning. After tasting it, I decided it was not likely to be the best he'd had, but it was surprisingly not terrible.

When I held out the bowl, the hero eyed me skeptically, but came over to retrieve it. He sniffed, then sampled, then dropped down on his stump. "Fine," he grumbled. "Don't leave the food on the fire again."

I nodded, holding my tongue against the snarky retort that came to mind, and given that I was not likely to find any food palatable at the moment, choked down the burnt part of the meal. Using the last of our crème would only serve to ruin the perishable item when it might prove handy later. Amazed that my stomach kept down the bitter fare, I went about cleaning up our mess. Deciding I rather liked the masonware, I scoured it with dirt and ash, wiped it clean with grass, and stowed it with the other cookware. While I doused the fire and readied us to move on, The Chosen took up his fabled sword again.

I found myself staring at the silver blade, struck for a moment by its beauty as it glistened in the sun. In my mind, the steel was swathed in mystery and inspiration from all the legends it carried, and it glowed with an imagined halo born of my own reverence. When he had finished his exercises, he returned the blade to its scabbard on the saddle and wiped his shining brow with a sleeve. He cast a broad grin at my moon-eyed stare, and I quickly looked away. We mounted up in silence and took to the road, the tension of our previous argument apparently resolved.

We rode in silence for a while as I struggled in vain to read Ethan's tidy script through the burning of tired eyes and a pounding brain. When the hero pulled off the road after only an hour of riding, I quickly scanned ahead to see if there was trouble.

Nothing seemed amiss, so I frowned over at his back as he dismounted. "Is something wrong?"

"Get down," he mumbled, walking over to the wagon.

I sighed, dropping the book into a saddle-bag, and slid woodenly from the high perch. I groaned and stretched stiff muscles not aided by a night of drinking followed by a day of dehydration and vomiting. The Chosen One watched me with a surprising amount of tolerance. When I joined him alongside the cart, he banged his hand on the trunk containing a majority of Tiberus' books. I obligingly climbed into the cart, untied the necessary straps, and opened it. "What am I looking for?"

"The book of magic," he answered, his tone bored as if *I* were the one inconveniencing *him*.

"Um, there's more than one," I replied.

"Oh?" He quirked a brow and shrugged. I was just starting to wonder how he could not know that Tiberius carried a small library when The Chosen One harrumphed and said. "The one with healing salves and whatnot in it."

I carefully withdrew the burgundy tome and closed the trunk, sitting on the lid and settling the heavy book in my lap. "What do you need? Are you ill?"

"No," he grumbled. "But you clearly are. Green as earwax, your face all twisted up."

I started to snap back in chagrin, but stopped myself short. Was he actually worried about me? Was he showing concern, even stopping on his journey to insist I take medicine? "I... um, I'm just a little overwrought from too much drink."

He nodded impatiently. "There's something in there for that," he groused. "Somewhere near the middle. I think he, uh, Tiberius even kept a vial or two." He turned away to lean against the cart. "In case of need."

I nodded and turned toward the middle of the book and found the tonic section. I leafed forward until I found a list of contents and skimmed it. There was indeed a day-after remedy for drinking. I found the correct page, identified its glyph moniker, and roamed the cart in search of the trunk containing spell components and workings. It was half-buried, and it took some significant effort to free it up enough to open the lid. There were actually six remedies inside, and I wondered how often Ethan resorted to liquor to resolve his now apparent distaste for The Chosen One's company.

I reviewed the book, practiced the cant in my head a few times, then activated the vial. It took very little effort, and I was grateful it hadn't robbed too much energy from me. With a potential battle looming, I would need to be very frugal with my magic to ensure I could better support the hero's efforts. I downed the vial and quickly secured the luggage as I felt the working take hold. Before I could tighten the final buckle, my stomach twisted, and I lunged for the cart wall, just barely keeping from vomiting partially-digested charcoal all over our supplies. The Chosen's bark of laughter spoke of his foreknowledge of the tonic's side effects. I glared at him between retching, but was too occupied with my sudden illness to properly respond. With a heady rush, the nausea ebbed and my head cleared. Other than the sour taste on my tongue, I felt completely refreshed. I finished tightening the last buckle and dropped down next to the still-chuckling hero. "Why didn't you warn me?" I snapped.

He clapped me on the back. "If I had, would you have gone through all that effort to take it?" He gestured toward the wagon.

"I..." My anger deflated. "No," I confessed.

He nodded and tossed a water skin toward me. I clumsily caught it and took a swig, swishing and spitting before I took a long draught. "Thank you," I grudgingly offered.

He nodded magnanimously and vaulted back into the saddle. We took to the road again, silence stretching between us for several minutes. I started to reach for the Tome of Tiberius stowed in my bag when The Chosen One spoke up, his eyes fixed on the road and a lazy smirk alighting his features.

"I couldn't help but notice you knew all of my ballads."

I blinked in surprise and tried to follow his thinking. "Oh, at the feast."

He nodded.

"Yeah, I suppose," I mumbled, looking away to hide a slight flush. "That's natural. I was in the Wizards' Guild and very nearly the Scriveners' Guild."

He nodded, pursing his lips. "True." He chuckled. "A good cover, but not good enough. Some of those songs were not common to these parts. I was surprised to hear them. I suppose some of the performers were from the south."

I sighed and nodded. "Yes. I'm from Petria, Epsosia."

He grinned. "And you knew all the legends, too."

I frowned and shrugged. "Your legends are told and retold, and I had been tasked on many occasions to copy retellings of your deeds."

He shook his head. "Oh, no. You will not dismiss it as easily as that."

I frowned over at him, irritated at whatever game he was playing. "What are you *wanting* me to say?"

"Do you remember getting up on stage and correcting them?" His eyes glittered when he turned to face me.

It was impossible to hide my blush of embarrassment. "No," I snapped. "I clearly had too much to drink."

He laughed. "You are an *admirer*!" he declared, proudly. "You know my ballads, my legends, and you care enough to see it's done right!"

I glared out at the trees. "What does that matter," I snapped. "They're only stories, right? Men take heart in stories of heroism and hope. I assume most of them are exaggerations."

He nodded, still laughing. "I suppose that is why you are so angry. Not the hero you thought, then?"

I sighed and shook my head. "No," then quickly amended. "Not that." I shrugged. "I suppose I'm... I don't know, frustrated." I looked over at him, managing to suffer his smug grin without rising to anger. "I'm very accomplished, very skilled at what I set myself to. I take pride in it. Never mind that no one seems to notice or care; *I* care." My shoulders slumped at the admission. "Since failing as a wizard, this is the first task I've really not performed well."

He nodded, and I tried not to be irritated by his agreement. "You've never been a hero or a quester, before," he observed. "You're a babe in this world, and in your first few days you've seen pestilence, death, and a vengeful god." He smirked over at me. "I think you're doing fine."

This time my flush was from the unexpected and genuine praise of a long-esteemed idol. I looked down and swallowed back another lump.

"So, you've questions?"

I looked up. "What?"

"Admirers always have questions."

And with that smug statement, the afterglow of his praise snuffed out. "No."

He laughed again and shook his head. "Out with it. You've questions." He fixed me with an expectant stare, awaiting my response.

I sighed and relented with a nod. "All right, the sword." I nodded to the two-handed haft rising from the scabbard that was presently secured to the saddle. "I've heard a dozen stories about how you came by it, and I've heard a dozen names for the blade, itself."

He nodded. "Yes, the Talon of Butev," he responded.

"Is that its true name?"

He smirked. "It is one of them," he agreed. "What have you heard?"

"Predominantly two legends. The first is that your father was a blacksmith. He created many fine swords, but his gift was underappreciated. The gods had decided to create a great hero to defend men from the dark creatures and deeds that no normal quester could vanquish. Butev saw this blacksmith's skill and filled him with the inspiration to create her Talon. He worked for five days without sleep, laboring over the crafting, possessed by the power of the gods. The task nearly killed him, and he collapsed right there in his forge, sleeping for days. Word had gotten around town of the masterpiece he was creating, and that night, several men snuck into the forge to steal the completed sword, only to find his young son bent over his body, trying to wake him. The child, afraid for his father, took up the sword that rested upon the anvil nearby, though he had no training and could barely lift it. Inspired by his bravery and willingness to defend the helpless, Butev gifted him with the skill and strength to wield the sword and defeat the thieves. From that day on, he became The Chosen One, wielder of the sword of the gods and bearer of their gifts."

He chuckled. "I like that one."

I smirked and looked over at him. "So it's not true?"

"What do you think?"

I eyed him for a long moment. "I think you look like you could be a blacksmith's son. You've the strength for it."

He pursed his lips and nodded. "What was the other legend?"

"Hm? Oh, yes." I paused to regain the path of my thoughts. "Skalah saw the suffering and need of men to be protected from great evils such as those birthed from the dark pairing of magic and malice. He drew together many of the other gods and created blessings to bestow upon one hero. Once they were done, the gods all began to argue about which human should wield the great powers they had collected, each having their own favorites and wanting to be represented by their own worshiper. Through it all Butev offered to create a great sword in which to pour all of this energy and wrap it in a working that would prevent only but the most heroic of souls to claim it. Each god chose a gift the hero would need to possess to own the sword, and Butev herself created it. When it was done, it was cast down into a great city in the center of the world, commonly accepted to be what is now Krichev, Opolchia.

"It struck deep into the earth, only the haft showing above the cobblestones of the main road. Every manner of man, woman, and child tried to free it, but to no avail. There it rested for nearly a hundred years, a curious mystery that soon fell out of memory for most alive. One day, a merchant cart ran afoul of the haft, breaking a wheel clean from the cart, which fell down upon a small boy from the village. A dozen men could not lift the cart free of the boy, and the child was doomed, perishing before his own parents. A stablehand rushed forward to join the men. Though he was not strong, he believed that if enough people with enough will joined together, they could accomplish even this seemingly impossible task. It is said after straining, lifting, and pulling with all the others, his hand came to rest upon the hilt of the sword. In that instant, he had the strength to lift the cart with his other hand.

"In him, a simple young man, was everything the gods deemed should dwell within a hero, and all of their gifts poured into him. In that moment, The Chosen One was born."

He smirked and nodded. "In all the stories I always start out as some young, weak, common boy."

I considered all of the legends I had read and smiled. "Yes, I suppose that's true." I looked over to him. "So how did it really happen? How were you chosen by the gods to wield their power and their sword?"

He laughed. "It depends on where you are. The second story is told mostly here, in Opolchia. The first is told where you come from. In Piolmaa, I dove to the bottom of the frozen sea to save the king and found the sword in a shipwreck. In Tergo, I caught lightning and it became a sword. In Voki I sacrificed myself to the volcano to save a village and the sword found my hand while I burned in the lava."

I nodded. "Yes, but how did you really come to have it?"

He sighed. "You're not listening, Tiberius," he snapped.

I held back my retort and considered what he was saying. "So... wherever we go—"

"We honor the legends of that land," he finished. "It is not Tiberius' job to tell my stories or to correct them to another version." He fixed me with a gaze so sincere it seemed completely unlike him. "It is your job to *know* them and honor them." He looked ahead to the road. "You need to study, to learn me. To learn what the people believe wherever I go, so I can live up to their expectations. A legendary hero needs to be believed in to accomplish the impossible." He fixed me with another stare. "You saw it yesterday."

I considered that for a long moment. "Okay. I understand that, and I'll certainly do my best." I glanced over at him. "But will you not tell me what really happened? Because of my binding, I can't share it unless it's common knowledge."

He pursed his lips. "Maybe. Someday."

I sighed and shook my head. "What's the point of asking questions if you have no intention of answering them?"

He smirked. "Ask another."

"Okay," I watched the road while I thought. "The dragon and the princess."

"Yes," his face broke out into a grin. "One of my greatest deeds. You do seem enamored with that one!"

"Was there really a princess?"

He nodded. "Oh, yes. Several. The dragon had been collecting them and keeping them in a cave high above the ocean, in a cliffside. No man could reach them lest he dangle a hundred feet from a rope only to be eaten like bait by the dragon."

"Huh," I tried to imagine The Chosen One dangling from that great height, clothed in full armor, one hand brandishing his greatsword. Surprisingly, I could actually picture it. "What did you do?"

"Dangled like bait," he admitted.

"Did he try to eat you?"

"*She* certainly did."

"*She?* Okay, so how did you not get eaten?"

He laughed. "I called down lightning and she fell into the sea."

I thought about that for a moment. "Wouldn't the rope burn?"

"It did, but I managed to make the cave."

"I thought the dragon burned you, or was that another one?"

He looked over at me and raised a brow. "You must not know what a dragon is that you think they are so common."

I let out a frustrated huff at his condescending tone. "Would you educate me, then?"

"I suppose," he drawled. "A dragon is the offspring of a mortal and an immortal, usually a god or another dragon."

I stared in horror at him. "How could... a human and a dragon—"

His laughter cut through my bafflement. "Dragons can take human form, as can most other immortal creatures."

"Oh," I sighed. "I should have known that, I think."

He nodded emphatically, and I glowered at him.

"So, the dragon returned as I was freeing the maidens," he continued. "And we fought."

"How were the princesses not burned?"

"Because I am The Chosen One," he declared proudly. "With enough will, I can accomplish any task. The only sacrifices need made are mine and what I deem necessary."

I had a hard time accepting that at face value. "The gods cannot really leave the choice up to you as to what sacrifice is required."

"I doubt they do," he replied. "I simply believe they gave me these blessings to use them as I have been, or they would not allow me to continue. I believe they would not give me a task that could not be done, nor point me in a direction I was not intended to go. If I need to understand something, I do. I trust what my gut tells me, and it's what hears them the most often."

That did not sound entirely implausible, but it was still strange to hear him speak humbly when he was the most arrogant, prideful man I'd ever met. Of course, believing the gods spoke directly to his gut was also arrogant in its own right. "So, you knew they would be protected?"

"As long as I fought with all that I was, and was willing to suffer on their behalf."

My stomach churned a little, thinking again of the extent of the burns he described. They must have been unimaginably painful, but he was willing to suffer them to keep the princesses safe and willing to fight in spite of his grave injuries. "Did you know, then, that it would be so...?"

"Of course," he replied somberly. "The foe was the greatest I had ever fought, the terrain among the most difficult I had ever seen, and the prize among the most worthy I had ever sought to reclaim." He nodded to himself. "The price needed to be the greatest I had ever paid. That is how these deeds are won."

I was once again struck mute by his potential for true heroism, true devotion and sacrifice. Though I had time and again been disappointed in him as a man, I had yet to find him any less of a hero than all of his legends proclaimed. There was no doubt that—though he was a brute and a jerk—he deserved to wield the Talon. "Did you know it would cost your hair?"

He shot me a fierce glare. "No!" he spat at the ground in disgust.

I smirked. Horribly burned and killed in the battle of his life, and his true regret of it all was the loss of his hair. "If the dragon was the offspring of a human and an immortal, who were her parents?" Perhaps now I would learn why the legend had somehow always seemed incomplete.

"*That* is the first good question you've asked all day," he praised. "The Warrior Queen of Castre, Her Majesty Queen Baltesa... and Trion, himself."

I nearly fell from the saddle, I spun so quickly to face him. He glanced at me, clearly satisfied with my mortification. I clutched at my chest, sure my heart would shrivel and be devoured by my suddenly very acidic stomach, so fierce was the pang of fear that shot through me. "You..." I choked. "You..."

He let out a long sigh and nodded. "I killed Trion's daughter." He stared ahead again, his expression drawn. "Now you see why I do not bear his favor."

"By the gods," I whispered, bowing over the horn to keep my balance as my head swam and my blood pounded in my ears. "By the gods."

The Chosen took my reins and pulled our mounts to a stop. "Do get a hold of yourself, Tiberius," he snapped.

I glared at him. "You killed the *child of a god*. And not just *any* god, the god of strife!" I could hear my voice becoming increasingly shrill, but I couldn't reign in the sudden horror this discovery churned in me.

He nodded. "Yes."

"How... ? Don't you *work* for them? They just allow you to kill one of theirs?"

He nodded. "She had been consumed by her jealousy. She'd lost her ability to take on her human form and had gone mad with a need to murder and destroy." His expression turned darkly somber. "She'd consumed hundreds of men and women, laid waste to many towns, and was kidnapping the children of the kingdoms' rulers to watch them wither and starve in that cave. To watch them fall as she had to the weaknesses of her human half."

"Still, how could you do it?" Somehow his unshakable calm was helping ease the pounding of my heart. "How could you kill the child of a god, knowing he would forever despise you?" I shook my head in disbelief. "Knowing that he would ever loom over you, threatening anything you love until the end of your days?"

He nodded. "I thought about that," he said, chewing his cheek for a moment.

"*And*," I insisted. "How do you dangle from a rope for that mad half-god to devour you knowing even if you survived, Trion would shadow you *forever more*?"

He sighed and shook his head. "It needed done, and I was the one called to do it." He looked over at me. "It matters not if I am afraid, nor does the price I must pay. I was called to do a deed."

"I just... at any point did you think you would rather lay down the sword? You *must* have thought about walking away."

"That wouldn't be very heroic of me," he chided.

"Tell me you at least *considered* it?"

He sighed and looked away for a long moment. When he spoke up, his voice was oddly quiet, even subdued. "Tell me something about you, Tiberius."

I blinked at the change in conversation. "Um, okay."

"What is your most embarrassing moment?"

I blinked again and sat back in the saddle. "Are you serious?"

He met my gaze. "What are you most ashamed of?"

I frowned. "Those are not the same thing. Embarrassment is not the same as shame."

"Then tell me both, and then tell me what you are most afraid of."

I choked out a mirthless laugh. "Um, I don't know." I shrugged and looked away, turning red at the memory of the many shames I tried very hard not to think about. "We've only known one another for six days."

"Exactly," he said, kicking his mount into an easy walk.

Topher fell in with him out of habit, and the beasts pulling the wagon started forward to keep from being left behind. Silence fell upon us again as the weight of the discussion hung heavy in the air. The plodding of the horses and the sounds of the forest around us seemed unimaginably pedestrian after the great events we had been discussing, but they were strangely comforting in their monotony. After a time,

I couldn't hear the roaring of my own heartbeat in my ears, and I thought perhaps I might come to reconcile with the idea that I traveled with and worked for the man who had killed Trion's daughter. Neither of us seemed inclined to speak again, so we rode on without another word for the remainder of the day.

    On and off throughout the day I tried to read the tome I had on hand, but my mind kept traveling back to the cave high above the sea where a hero had sacrificed his body and any hope at peace for the rest of his life to kill the insane offspring of a dark god. I kept thinking of the lightning-eyed man and his dogged fury and grief. I felt an icy chill settle in my gut knowing what that could mean for me, that I had gone from a nobody huddled in the shadows of an alley to the possible target of a sinister god's ire.

    When we came to the next clearing intended for rest, The Chosen One marched into the trees to take care of himself and left the camp duties to me. Luckily, one of the entries I had read earlier detailed the basics of bedding down for the night on the road. One of the trunks contained only a tent, and the instructions for how to pitch it were neatly scrawled in Ethan's elegant hand on a note just inside the lid. I once again thanked him for his aid, but then thought to curse him for the strife he'd passed on to me. I had never pitched a tent before, and by the time I had done, The Chosen One was watching me in the gathering gloom with mingled amusement and disapproval. He walked up to one of the main posts and pushed on it, causing the entire structure to collapse.

"What are you doing!" I shrieked. "I just—"

"Do it again, and do it right," he snapped. "The wind could knock that over. Use some sense." He went to his horse and began speaking sweetly to it, leaving me to sputter in impotent frustration. I suffered a momentary pang of jealousy that the horse warranted better treatment than me, but remembered it had to carry his sour ass around and decided it could keep the saccharine praise of the warrior.

I pitched the tent a second time, finding I had not placed the stakes properly. I watched with crossed arms and narrowed eyes as the hero tested its stability. When it remained upright, I rushed around camp to gather the supplies and wood needed for the fire. I grumbled under my breath that he might have at least gathered wood while I worked, and he ignored my griping, going through several more rounds of practice with his sword. I wondered with a smirk if he'd had a mirror to watch himself flex that morning.

I was pleased to find the innkeep had stowed a healthy portion of meaty pottage and several loaves of crusty bread in the parcel he'd added to our cart, and I quickly rinsed out the masonry bowl and transferred a hero's portion of the pottage into it. I transferred embers from the fire to a patch of dirt and laid the large bowl on it, having learned from that afternoon to not simply put the pot in the fire.

By the time I'd opened the trunk with the bedrolls and bedding in it and transferred what we needed to the tent, the pottage was steaming. I poked one of the loaves into it, and brought the meal to the hero who awaited it by the fire. He watched me work as I laid out our beds, selected his next day's clothes, and hung a lantern from the highest peak of the two-man tent. When I finally sat down, he was cleaning the inside of the bowl with the remainder of his bread, a content smile on his face.

It was I who broke the silence. "Why did you not wear armor today?"

He looked up, genuine surprise on his face. "All day of brooding and *that* is what you ask?"

I nodded. "You had to ride into town with fanfare to live up to your legend and remind them you were a great hero." He glowered a little at my unflattering recounting. "But you ride out in fine but rather common garb. No armor, no swooning maidens, no rose petals."

"Firstly," he stated setting his bowl in the dirt for me to clean. "Plenty of women swooned this morning."

I rolled my eyes and retrieved the masonry to scour with dirt.

"Secondly, it is *your* job to arrange fanfare and rose petals."

I grumbled under my breath at that pointed declaration.

"Finally," he intoned. "They needed a man."

I frowned up at him. "What? The women?"

"No. Rshavin."

I sat back on my heels. "I don't understand."

He sighed as if I were an imbecile and spoke slowly to facilitate my impaired comprehension. "When I came to town they needed a hero. They needed someone bigger then themselves to defeat something beyond their means."

"And they didn't need that when you left?"

He shook his head. "No, they needed to see a man. They needed to know that they have in them what they need to keep their town safe."

"Huh." I had to admit that it was surprisingly intuitive and thoughtful for him to think of what might inspire the recovering souls of Rshavin to face the upcoming days of hardship. The pestilence was gone, but the grief and loss it had brought with it wouldn't go away overnight. They had to recover and rebuild, the work of normal, mortal men. I slid back on my rump and watched him pick food from his teeth with a twig. Before I had fully comprehended where my thoughts had brought me, I spoke. "My mother left us when I was a young boy."

He frowned over at me. "What's this?"

"My greatest shame," I replied sincerely. "When I was five or so, my mother decided she didn't want me and didn't want her life. I was not reason enough, worthy enough to warrant her attention a moment longer. She simply left."

He nodded slowly, and I felt for the first time he was actually listening to me, considering me as one man does another. Finally he let out a deep breath. "About a hundred years ago, I was tasked to do something big, something that would cost me too much." He looked toward the fire, picking at his teeth again. "I considered laying aside the sword, passing on the legacy to another man."

I stared in shock at his admission. "I can see you did not. What made up your mind?"

"Tiberius," he answered simply.

I looked at the fire and wondered what that version of me could have done to spurn the hero to act. "What did he say?"

He shook his head. "He didn't. He just believed in me." He chucked the twig into the fire and rose. "I'm bedding down. Don't make too much noise when you settle the horses in." I listened to the sounds of him disrobing and dropping down into his bedroll. I was not surprised that he left the lantern burning.

I thought about his quiet, somber words for a long while. Tiberius a hundred years ago had been enough to sway the hand of The Chosen One. I wondered what had changed since then, that the hero didn't even trust me with his name. Had it been the possibly fifty Tiberiuses since then? Would anything I ever said or did be enough to sway him now, and did I want that kind of power if I had it? At length I pushed the thoughts back to mull over when I was less weary.

I did not have an extensive amount of experience caring for horses on the road, but was grateful it wasn't none. When apprenticed under the wizard as a white-sash and later as a simple servant, we'd traveled more often than we had stayed in his cold manor. He'd had duties and great deeds to perform on his own as well as spell components to acquire in distant and rare markets. As a white-sash, I had watched the servants care for the horses. Later, when it was apparent that I would never contain color in my sash, the wizard relegated me to servant duties most days, though he didn't strip me of the apprentice title. I had been in the process of learning how a quester travels when my master had literally flown the coop. I had assisted the more experienced servants a few times, more as an observer than anything else, but I was surprised at how easily the distant memories came back as I stripped the horses down and led them to the picket line I'd strung up at some point without even thinking about it.

I took time to brush them down, and gave some extra care with the temperamental destrier. He tolerated my attention with surprising patience and only attempted to bite me a few times when I was brushing down his chest and front legs. Still, I got the impression the nips were his way of reminding me that I was beast fodder if I ever underestimated his power and magnificence. It was so reminiscent of the Chosen's arrogance, I found myself chuckling at his antics. It was very well dark when I was ready to bed down myself and slid quietly into the tent.

To my surprise, The Chosen One was laying on his back, his eyes open, staring at the top of the tent rippling in the night wind. I was grateful he'd pulled the blanket up to his chest, concealing his nudity, and I dropped down onto my own bedroll. I was sore and exhausted from the day's travels and duties. When I was settled, I looked back at his unmoving profile. His blond curls cascaded around his strong-featured face, the very image of a brooding hero. "Are you not tired?" I asked as the silence grew uncomfortable. He grunted, the only indication that he'd heard me. After several long moments, the sounds of the forest and the subtle whisper of the tent's canvas lulled me into a light doze.

"Tell me a story," he said, his deep baritone filling the entire tent and instantly pulling me free from sleep.

I blinked a few times, stared at his unmoved profile, and wondered how long I'd been asleep while he'd lain there. I cleared my throat and tried to prod my exhausted brain into order. "Um... what kind of story?"

"A happy one," he quietly replied.

"Hm," I thought. "What about The Chosen and the Mermaid?"

He frowned and shook his head. "Someone else."

"Okay," I sat up and rubbed my eyes. "Um, The Giant and the Lord's Goats?"

"No," he grumbled, his eyes finally shifting to me to show his disapproval. "*About* someone else."

"Oh!" I blinked in surprise. He didn't want to hear one of his own legends? I had thought he would never tire of talking about himself. "Okay." After a moment of me riffling through tales of my youth, he turned his gaze away from me. "Ah!" I nodded, happy with my choice. "One of my favorites as a boy. My moth—uh, it was often told to me at bedtime when I was very young."

He nodded his approval and closed his eyes as I told the story of a clumsy wizard trying to save a town from a mystical curse that rained increasingly larger animals on them every three days. It was often told comically, and though the wizard in the end lost a toe, it had a very satisfying ending for the town and the hapless quester. Long before I finished, the hero was snoring, but nostalgia was upon me, and I finished the story before sleep claimed me as well.

12. All Children, Except One, Grow Up

"Tiberius!"

I jerked awake at the resonating bellow and tangled frantically in my blankets, still in the throes of a nightmare full of raging storms, rotting and ravenous wolves, and the lightning-eyed man riding me down upon the corpse of Braknik. The tent flap jerked open, and sunlight poured into my eyes. I cried out and curled away from it.

"Gods' mercy, man!" The Chosen One shouted. "I've been about for an hour! Get up and feed me."

I rolled onto my back as reality settled in and panted up at the tent ceiling. The Chosen departed with as much haste as he had come and left me there to calm my pounding heart. I found myself wondering if I would endure nightmares of Trion until the end of my days. Perhaps I could entreat Jaya to soothe my night terrors, but legend often revealed she enjoyed cruel and unforeseeably disastrous bargains. "I've spent too much time with The Chosen if I passively imagine myself bartering with gods," I grumbled.

Sluggishly, I dragged myself from bed and forced my wooden muscles to limber enough to make my way to the fire. By the time I'd coaxed the embers to flame, I was fully awake, and The Chosen One was vaulting around the clear spaces of camp battling invisible villains with his sword and mystical shield. His private war raged over the stump seat, around the picket line, and over the cart. I numbly acknowledged how impressive leaping backwards across the cart really was before I started riffling around in our supplies for a small box I knew contained eggs carefully packed in straw. I heated up the last of the pottage in the masonware bowl and scrambled half a dozen eggs in an iron pan. The Chosen, clearly victorious, stabbed his sword into the dirt and dropped his sweaty personage down onto the stump to accept the meal with a grunt of approval. I nibbled on a small crusty loaf of bread as I broke down our camp, holding the parcel in my teeth whenever a task required two hands.

I was proud of how quickly I packed the tent away, the previous day's experience lending to my efficiency. I scoured the hero's bowl, tended to the horses, and packed everything away in the cart. The sun had well risen before the fire was doused and we were prepped for departure. The Chosen One occasionally cast me disapproving frowns at the late hour, but somehow managed to keep his teeth together.

"The innkeeper said the journey to Vevesk would be four days, and I believe every stop thus far has been in a designated resting area," I offered as I checked the horses' tack one last time. "If we make good time, we should only be sleeping on the ground two more nights before we find an inn."

The Chosen One grunted his agreement. He watched me from his stump, sipping from the mug of warm ale I'd provided to keep him busy while I finished the morning's duties.

"Do I need to ride ahead when we make Vevesk to prepare them for your arrival?"

"What do you think?" It was the first thing he'd said to me all morning, and I was a little surprised to get any response at all, even a non-committal one.

I bit back my irritated response, took a long breath, and rolled back on my heels to genuinely consider our options. Vevesk had a relatively small population, any advanced fanfare prep would be hard to keep discreet, and rumors of his self-aggrandizing might hurt his reputation in the small town of hard working farmers. For what I'd paid all the women, performers, and shopkeepers in Rshavin, a few handfuls of Gold Chosen tossed into the crowd might serve the same purpose of enrapturing the public, but at a discount. "I think it would less serve and more harm your arrival," I admitted at last. "Full armor, Braknik, and best dress should do it."

He nodded, finished his ale, and tossed the tankard to me for stowing in the cart. I couldn't tell if he was agreeing with me or simply had no opinion on the matter. At any rate, there wasn't any mocking or shouting, so I had to wonder if he was either under the weather or secretly planning some other way to foul my somewhat decent mood.

He rose, stretched, and headed to the already saddled Fellowyn. No sooner had he walked two steps than he suddenly let out a yelp of startlingly un-masculine pain and crumpled to the ground. I vaulted to his side as he was curling on himself hugging his knee to his chest, whimpering and writing.

"What?!" My eyes darted around looking for a snake, blood, an arrow, anything to explain his sudden display of weakness and pain. "What is it? What's happened?"

He rocked from side to side, hugging his knee. "My foot! I can't reach it," he whimpered.

Without hesitation, I jerked his boot from his foot and peeled back the knitted sock. I was expecting some sort of swelling, perhaps a bone protruding from the flesh. After a panicked moment of searching, I realized what I was looking at. One of his toes stood straight out, ridged and locked in place while the others wiggled and clenched.

"Oh, gods!" The Chosen cried. "Fix it! Fix it, Tiberius!"

With all his thrashing and writhing, I could barely get ahold of the afflicted foot, and in the end kneeled on his calf to hold him steady. "It's just a cramp," I growled. "Nut up, man."

"Fix it!" he shrieked in response.

My mind quickly went through the inventory in the cart, trying to remember if there was a tonic stowed to help with muscle spasms and pain. The Chosen One jerked and bucked me off, rolling to his other side, kicking at the air and intensifying his crying and writhing.

I growled and straddled his leg at the knee, pinning it to the ground again. No time for tonics or books, I grabbed his foot and started working my thumbs into the meat of the footpad between his toes. The smell was not good, and his frequent kicks to my side with every deep probe of my thumb was even less pleasant. After a few minutes, the ridged toe relaxed somewhat, and The Chosen One slumped to the ground, panting. I kept massaging until I felt the hard knot in the muscle relent more.

"No more battles today," I grumbled. "Stay off this foot as much as possible."

He growled and shoved me away with his free foot. "Get off," he snapped. "I'll do as I please!"

I sighed and rose to my feet, brushing dirt from my knees and rump. "You're welcome," I growled.

"It's your job!" he snarled, his face red from the morning's excitement. Only after a moment did I realize he was being especially belligerent because he was embarrassed. I just wasn't sure if it was because of his unmanly display or because the mighty Chosen

One was apparently susceptible to something as common as a toe cramp.

I let out the angry breath I'd been holding and walked away. If he didn't have to put on a heroic face for me, maybe he could regain his composure and stop being an ass. He strode around camp a few times, undoubtedly demonstrating to the forest that he had not been felled by the near-fatal injury to his foot. I pulled the Tome of Tiberius from my saddle bag, stowed it in my trunk, and withdrew the research materials I'd gathered in Noblan. I had a clear enough head this day to read the clumsy scribbles of the assistants through the rocking motion of Topher. By the time I'd arranged the scrolls and loose parchment in a way that would ease retrieval, the hero was codling Braknik and clearly ready to travel.

We rode in silence for a time, and I was quietly grateful for the cessation of my constant duties to The Chosen One. I remembered Ethan walking behind the great hero that first day, content in his book and the moment of peace stolen while the grandmaster hero was parading about town and playing to the crowd. I wondered how long it would take for me to become so accustomed to the adoration of the masses that I could retreat into my own mind and read through the parade.

I had never been fond of scrutiny or crowds, and was very uncomfortable with any type of performance. When I was attempting magic, my intent upon the lesson was what enabled me to endure the attention of my fellow apprentices and the master mage. Even then, I usually threw up afterwards. But then, I had managed the parade with enough grace not to vomit on the onlookers. Was it because The Chosen One held their eyes? Perhaps the Tiberius Blessing had something built into it to keep my stomach from overturning whenever I was needed to perform as part of my duties. Another strange and somewhat comforting thought crept into the back of my mind. Perhaps it was because a part of me felt as though I was better suited for what I was doing now than anything I'd ever attempted before.

Startled by the idea, I lifted my eyes from the scroll I hadn't been reading for some time. I had tried to work my way into several guilds, always feeling I was destined for great deeds though I had neither the stomach nor the natural talent for it. I had always had a more dedicated interest in The Chosen One than anyone else I'd met. The array of skills I'd acquired were unlikely to all be used or even learned if I'd stayed at any one of my life's ambitions, yet all would come into service while as a hero's assistant. What were the odds that I would be at my most desperate the day I saw The Chosen One for the first time, or the day Ethan began posting "trades needed" posters? Was it possible that I was fated to be in that alley, to have walked the difficult path I had through life?

I looked over at the Chosen, and marveled at how quickly I had fallen into the rigid demands of his assistant. Though I'd argued, lamented, and bucked against his stubbornness, I had also felt more at ease with what I was learning and doing than with any other school or apprenticeship I'd ever entered. The more I considered the idea, the more certain I was that all of my trials and lessons in life had lent themselves to the school of The Chosen One's assistant.

"What?" he snapped, glowering over at me when my gaze had held for too long. "Is there something in my hair?"

I wasn't able to stifle the snorting laugh before it bubbled out, and he glared harder. "No," I quickly said. "No, nothing like that." I sighed and looked ahead to the path. "I was just thinking about the road that collided our paths."

He harrumphed and looked away as well. "What does it matter? We're here now."

I nodded. "Sure. It's just... I'm honestly not a likely companion for you in any other circumstance. We aren't very much alike."

"You know nothing about me," he grumbled. "You have no idea what company I would keep."

I nodded. "Fair. One week of hard travel is not enough time to learn someone. But I can assume you likely wouldn't keep the company of a book-obsessed coward with very little talent or ambition of his own."

He frowned over at me. "Is that how you see yourself?"

I shrugged. "I suppose. Do you not think so? Perhaps it is because you've not seen me swoon from excitement in a library."

This time he snorted at me. "Have you ever taken up a sword?"

I shook my head. "Scarcely ever even held one."

"Have you ever had to physically fight another man?"

I smirked. "No. Though, the day before you met me, I'd received the worst beating of my life."

He glanced over at me. "Have you ever seen a man die?"

"No," I sighed. "You see? Not a very good companion for a Grandmaster Hero."

He grunted. "But you swam to a barge full of dead men, kept your feet when the god of pestilence stared you down, and navigated the politics of a last-minute hero's welcome to a dying town."

I felt my brow climb nearly into my hairline. Was The Chosen One actually *praising* me? "Um..."

"I have had assistants who fainted at the sight of blood, assistants who could barely give directions, who cried whenever confronted with danger. I've traveled with cowards, with lazy and useless men, with prideful and arrogant men, with the weak and the stupid and the undriven." He sneered in memory. "I've had dozens of assistants, and with many of them it was as much a trial for me as it was for them to work out their two years of contract."

I considered that for a long moment. I suppose I did exceed those disappointments. "Was Ethan a trial to endure?"

"Who?"

I laughed and shook my head. "Of course, he didn't have a name to you, did he? The Tiberius before me."

He narrowed his eyes at my barely veiled disapproval at his dismissal of all of his assistants' individuality. After only a brief brood, though, he looked away with a weary sigh. "No. I thought he was rather good at it."

I glanced down at the scroll and remembered Ethan's eagerness to be free of his contract, of his clear distaste for The Chosen One and his duties. Had the hero known the depth of his assistant's unhappiness, or had it been a jarring shock to lose a good servant to a barely competent one right before this great campaign? "He should have said goodbye," I conceded.

The Chosen growled. "Keep your sympathy," he snapped. "It is the way of things. Two years is all you have to endure, and you can keep a fair share of your blessing and enough wealth to be comfortable." He glanced over at me. "This life is not for the weak or lazy. It is for true heroes, and no one expects Tiberius to be one." He shrugged. "So no one is going to expect you to fight or act like a hero. You just have to keep *my* sword sharp."

I nodded and let out a breath. Just like that, he was back to his arrogance and dismissal. I opened the scroll and continued my reading about undead and animated dead. Apparently there was a significant difference between the two.

When we reached the midday turn-off, I quickly started the fire while The Chosen One relieved himself in the woods. By the time he'd returned, I'd assembled sandwiches of thick-sliced bread, salted meats, and hard cheese. When the coals were warm enough to use, I laid the sandwiches on the pan to toast and soften the meat and cheese. I poured some cider into the masonware and threw in a dash of rum. I served the meal on a wooden plate and took care of my own needs while the hero ate. Neither one of us spoke, and the routine of making midday camp felt as familiar as if I'd been doing it for years. Perhaps the hero's expectations and acceptance of my duties born of years of having a Tiberius made it feel like something I'd done dozens of times rather than three.

I sat to eat my own sandwich and glanced over at the hero. He actually seemed to be enjoying his meal, and I felt an inexplicable twinge of pride. "I've been reading about necromancy," I said. He just gave a dismissive nod and took a long draught of the liquored cider. "More than once, I've seen Triton referenced as the deity worshiped by infamous necromancers."

"Of course," he replied, joining the conversation only when he could make me look like an idiot by confirming what he clearly believed to be common knowledge.

I let my immediate temper pass. "Is it because of the pestilence unclean necromancy can inflict on the living things around it?"

He snorted in clear mockery of my guess. "No. It's his domain."

I blinked in surprise and stared for a long moment before I realized he wasn't going to elaborate. "What do you mean, *his domain*?"

He shrugged. "Animating the dead, necromancy, they're some of his gifts."

"But..." I shook my head. "Resurrection belongs to Skalah."

"Sure, but those aren't the same thing."

I frowned. "Animating the dead... requires the constant will of the wizard to direct the body?"

He nodded. "And true resurrection restores a man's soul. Completely different, like night and day. Trust me, I've been resurrected a few times."

I stared down at my half-eaten sandwich, my appetite gone at both the knowledge that The Chosen One had given his life more than once and at the thought of a hollow, rotting corpse of some poor man being puppeted by a servant of Trion. A sharp jolt of realization shot up my spine, and a bone-deep shiver followed. "Gods," I whispered as the mortifying thought fully cemented in my mind.

The hero blinked up at me, frowned, traced my line of sight to the empty trees, then back. "What is it, man?" he grumbled.

I shook myself clear of the terrified paralysis that had halted my hand in mid-gesture to lift the meal to my mouth. I took a steadying breath and met

The Chosen One's eyes, afraid of what I was certain his answer would be. "Tr—the god of strife. He's here because what's happening in Rshavin and Vevesk has to do with him. It's a follower of his, that has *his* blessing, who is causing all of this sickness and death."

The hero let out a deep-chested sigh and nodded. "I suspect as much," he admitted. "Normally, I would advise you not to use his name so much, but I think he may already be watching us. He is undoubtedly aware that I am here and why, given he's shown himself twice now."

I hugged my arms to my chest and scooted close to the fire, suddenly too cold to think clearly. "We've pitted ourselves directly against him." The hero grunted and downed the last of his cider, not seeming overly concerned with my numbing terror. "What if he should..."

The Chosen One shook his head. "The gods don't usually work like that," he muttered, pouting into the empty stein. "They have champions."

I gaped at him. "How can you be so calm about this!" I shouted, realizing after a moment that I had lurched to my feet, perhaps in a justifiable desire to physically flee the fear smothering me. "The dark god is here to set himself against us!"

The Chosen raised his brows at my outburst. "Because," he said, rising to look down at me. "*I* am a champion of the gods." He pounded a fist against his barrel of a chest. "And I respect and trust the gods that sponsor me a hell of a lot more than I do the god of criminals and murderers." His eyes glowed with such pride and faith, my fear rolled back like the fog when the sun burns across the land. "And *you*, Tiberius, are sheltered by those same gods. *You* are a champion in your own right." He leaned down, meeting my eyes with intensity that caused me to squirm beneath it. "And they protect you only as far as you trust them to," he warned darkly. "It's time you mustered your faith. Fear is one thing, but doubting the gods whose blessings you carry is a sin so disgraceful, it turns even *my* stomach."

He shoved his stein and plate into my ribs and brushed roughly past me. I fumbled to keep hold of my sandwich with the sudden addition of the new items as he strode to Braknik to pour some praise upon the beast. I stared at his broad back for a long moment, shame burning my cheeks at his scorn. He had insulted me countless times before, but it had never felt so personal or so genuinely sincere. Without his pride and steadfast courage, I felt the fear return to settle in the pit of my stomach. Why should I feel ashamed of being afraid of the most terrifying being in the world? It wasn't as though I'd had a hundred years to accustom myself to the god's malice. And yet, I did share some of The Chosen One's disgust at my own weakness. Just a few minutes ago, he had called me "not a coward," so what had changed?

The hero was feeding Braknik some oats poured from a feedbag into his hand when I approached them. Neither concerned themselves with me, so I stood for a moment, watching the fierce beast contentedly lap at the treat with his long, pink tongue. "I..." I sighed. "I have knelt at a dozen temples in my time," I admitted. "In the service of half a dozen gods."

The Chosen glanced over at me, his brow turning down in a frown, but he didn't voice whatever disapproval he might have felt.

"I have plied my faith to whatever deity seemed the best fit for what I was trying to accomplish. Whatever was expected of me from my peers and superiors in whatever station I was at the time." His silent regard was both unnerving and somehow comforting at the same time. At least he seemed to actually be giving me his genuine attention. "I have never considered myself pious or religious. I've never considered myself tied, indebted, or loyal to any god or goddess. I was just doing what was acceptable."

The Chosen One grunted and looked back to the horse, stroking the animal's long snout. "Faithless," he growled.

"In a way, but probably not like you think." My face burned with his continued scorn, but I lifted my chin to meet his gaze. "It's not that I don't believe in the gods or what they can do, quite the opposite." I gestured all around us. "There is too much evidence in this world and in the records of history to think otherwise." I sighed and shrugged. "But what am I?" I looked down at my too long, slightly too snug tunic borrowed from Ethan's discarded wardrobe. "I am a beggar, an opportunist, a failure at everything I've ever set my mind to accomplish." I laughed mirthlessly. "Of so little consequence, the Scriveners' Guild didn't think me enough of a threat to cleave my hand when they had a right to." I looked down at my fingers, still quivering in fear. "Why would any god think I was worth a moment of their attention, the tiniest sliver of their power?" When I looked back up, the hero was quietly regarding me once more. "So I went through the motions and spoke the words, because it was expected of me. But never once did I have any delusion that a god would have use of me."

"Well," he replied in his gruff way, dismissing my confession of hopelessness and humility with a quick shake of his head. "The gods have a use for you *now*." He fixed me with a pointed stare. "So it's time to say the words with a little more heart." He turned and stepped into Fellowyn's stirrup, swinging into the saddle. He didn't wait for me to stow the dishes before he kicked her into a walk.

I tossed the stein and plates into a crevice in the cart and hauled myself onto Topher's saddle, squashing what remained of my sandwich against the saddle horn. I was irritated at his ambivalence after I had shared something intensely personal. Of course, what had I expected? When I came abreast of Fellowyn, I glowered over at the hero. "You said not so very long ago that I was doing well, all things considered. With what this new life has thrown at me, I think that I am *still* riding forward should be merit enough."

"Should I ride ahead and prepare your fanfare?" he snarked without bothering to glance my way.

I gave Topher a quick kick to cut off Fellowyn's stride, and The Chosen One's eyes flashed in quick anger. "Don't—"

"No!" I shot back. "I'm doing my best; I truly am. I have been in the questing business for a *week!* So maybe I'm taking an extra day or two to acclimate! Maybe I'm—"

The hero's hand flashed out so quickly, I had no hope of evading as he snatched the lead to Topher's bridle and jerked the mount's head across Fellowyn's shoulders, pulling us nose to nose. "We go to face an adversary likely the equal to the most dangerous and savage that I have ever encountered!" He snarled. "We don't have a few more days for you to *acclimate*! You need to find your courage and find your faith. We *both* need to be ready to face what is to come. I don't have time for you to quaver. Tiberius *will* be needed. There is no other way of it." Spittle sprayed my face with every snarled word, but I barely noticed. A pit had opened in my stomach at his words.

"But... they're *weasels*."

He scoffed at me and shoved on Topher's snout till the horse danced back and snorted in derision at the rough treatment. "Have sense, man. Surely you cannot believe that is all that awaits us in Vevesk." With that curt statement, he kicked Fellowyn forward, leaving me behind several lengths to guide the labor horses.

I thought about his words and remembered his confession by the campfire, that he had once been asked to do something that made him want to abandon the sword. My very first quest with the great hero was to be among the most frightening even The Chosen One had ever braved. I didn't know how to do all the things I'd skimmed in the first Tome of Tiberius, all the tasks that made him stronger, helped him heal. I scarcely knew how to ride, let alone charge into battle. I couldn't wield a sword, was of little use with magic, and didn't know how most of his or my blessings worked. If he was in need of me, it was indeed a dark and uncertain challenge ahead.

Then I remembered. It had been *Tiberius* to remind him of the hero he was. What if The Chosen One was struggling now with walking away, with leaving behind his many long years of heroism? The gods knew he deserved to take a rest after so many years giving of himself for the needs of the weaker folk of the world. Not a soul would be right to begrudge him for walking away after over a hundred years and countless souls rescued. But then, what would become of Rshavin, of Vevesk? What would become of all the cities along the Gorod River?

The thought that turned my stomach the most, however, was what if more than anything, what The Chosen One needed was Tiberius to believe in him? What if it wasn't my lack in faith of the gods' protection that had pricked him so? Perhaps it was because I did not trust *him* to keep me safe. If Tiberius lost faith in him, could the hero face the terrible foe that awaited us in the foothills ahead? It was not as though I could just turn off my fear, as if I could simply *choose* to be willing to risk terrible injury and death. My life had not been stable, but until this point, it had at least been safe.

"A very long time ago, there was a simple blacksmith's son," I said, raising my voice so he could hear me. I saw his head turn slightly, though his jaw was still in an angry set. "He was not so different from any other boy, loving to chase a stick with his dog or steal sweetcakes from the baker's window." The Chosen turned to look at me, his eyes narrowing in quiet suspicion at the unexpected tale telling. "His father, however, was of such great skill, that though they lived far from the renowned forges of the capitol city, Butev had taken a fondness of his creations." The hero allowed the caravan to catch up with him, and he silently listened as I wove the first story I had ever heard of how the grandmaster hero had earned the sword of the gods.

When the telling was done, he rode in placid silence, content it seemed for the time. He did not comment on whether he liked my telling of this version, but his lack of a sneer told me he was not displeased. After a moment of consideration, I began the story of The Chosen One defeating an army of dog-men. It was one that was more humorous than heroic, but had been a favorite of mine when I was a boy. More than once I heard him snicker, and by the time we began looking for the turn-off for the night, we were riding in amiable spirits once more.

I finished another story of the hero as we found the encampment, and the Chosen dismounted to leave me to care for the beasts. I immediately set the fire before readying the horses for the night. By the time I was done, there were enough coals to cook by, and the hero had relieved himself of his boots and cloak to recline on a plush patch of grass and watch the blaze. I filled a large cooking pot with water, scraped out a decent pile of hot embers, and settled it on them. I cut vegetables, tossing them in as I did, and threw in some of our dried meats and cheese to make the soup thick and hearty.

"Why do you do it," I asked as I worked.

"Hm? Do what?" His distant eyes never left the dancing flames.

"Be The Chosen One."

He gave a half-hearted snort. "Asked and answered," he replied. "Because it is needed."

"Sure, but why *you*?"

This time his eyes did shift to me, narrowing. "Because I was *chosen*."

I nodded and stirred the pot with a wooden spoon. "But you also need to choose it, am I right? If you can choose to lay down the sword, then keeping it is also in your hands."

He shook his head, dismissing the question as if it were too absurd to consider.

"I really want to know," I insisted. "Why day after day, year after year, do you answer the call?"

He frowned at me again, this time irritation flashing in his eyes. "Because *I* was chosen to do it," he snapped. "*Listen* for the answer, foolish man."

I sighed and sat back on my heels regarding him. "And if you lay the sword aside, another would be chosen. Yet you answer the call. Simply doing what is expected is not enough, if what you said before has any merit. So then, why do *you* choose to keep answering the call rather than let another hero do so?"

He shrugged. "What else am I to do? Farm?" He sneered at the idea. "Innkeeps keep, fishers fish, and I am The Chosen One. You should ask why the rain falls and the wind blows. It is as it should be, as the gods choose."

I wasn't sure why I expected a deeper answer than the one he gave, but in a way it was a little comforting to know that the great Hero of Men was as steadfast as the mountains, like a force of nature. "Before you were chosen, did you imagine you would do anything else? Maybe be a blacksmith?"

He chuckled and shook his head. "It was so long ago, why should I remember the life and duty of a child? That will not slay a dragon or win a maiden's affections. You spend so much time asking *why* and *how* things are. Do you not get tired?"

I contemplated his question for a long moment before I conceded with a nod. "Sometimes, yes. I suppose I do. I wish I could simply accept the will of the gods as you do. Perhaps it would be less jarring to be thrust from one life to another as I have been this past week. Perhaps I could find the faith you say I so desperately need before we face the foe that awaits."

He nodded. "Then do what I do."

"What?"

"Drink, be merry!" He flashed me that broad grin, his eyes glittering for the first time that day. "Enjoy a good drink, enjoy a good *woman*, and thank the gods you've another day to do it."

I sighed. "I don't think I could live like that, at least not for a hundred years."

He plucked a twig from the ground and picked at his teeth with it, eyeing the stew that was beginning to release a very appealing aroma. "So aim for two years." He chuckled and flashed me a challenging smirk. "If we survive the next two days."

I glowered at him through the steam as I tossed various herbs into our dinner. "Now you are taunting me."

"Fear is not shameful," he said. "Bowing to it, is. At least, when you have the gods on your side, as we do."

I let out a slow breath, resisting the urge to rise to the barb. "It is hard for me, I admit, to think a god may wish to spare a moment of his time on a mortal such as myself. Do you think it would be acceptable to you if I believe in something a little more tangible?"

"Like what? A shield? A wall?"

I smiled across the fire at him. "How about a hero?"

He leaned back on his elbows and regarded me with an approving smirk. "If that is all you can muster, it should be enough."

I nodded. "Especially if that hero bears the blessing of *most* of the gods?"

He laughed, a merry sound after the weary day of traveling and bickering. "Indeed, and the better of them, as well."

I dished out the soup, giving him the hero's portion in the large mason bowl. I left mine in the pot to eat when it had cooled and went about pitching the tent. The Chosen One ate, placated by my compromise, and I found myself smiling at his acceptance. In the very least, if I couldn't wield a sword, I could stand beside the hero who did. Or more likely, a little behind him.

13. I Have Never Begun a Day with More Misgiving

I wrested myself from sleep as the sound that had roused me came again. An odd, unsettling rustling stirred in the night not far from the fabric of the tent. I rolled toward The Chosen One to find him staring up at the lit lantern above our heads, his eyes distant as he, too, listened for the eerily abnormal disturbance. I heard a grunt, then a gurgling growl, and a shiver slithered up my spine. It sounded *wrong*, off in some inexplicable and intensely unnerving way. I swallowed hard and whispered, "What is it?"

His gaze tracked to me, then distant again as he listened. In form of answer, he sat up and reached for the sword by his side. A volley of excited, raspy snuffling erupted very near to my head, and a yelp of alarm clawed out of my throat as I tangled helplessly with the blanket. The sword scraped from its scabbard, and before I had freed myself from the bed, a glinting arc of silver flashed over my head, plunging through the canvas and out of sight into the night. When The Chosen One jerked the blade clear, a spray of dark, foul-smelling blood spurted across my chest and the side of my face. I turned away from the sudden violence, too terrified to register my disgust. Still entangled, I wormed and crawled away from the unseen creature and toward the armed hero who now stood naked, befouled sword held at the ready, his eyes bright with the excitement of battle.

"Silence," he snapped, and I realized I was gasping for air like a drowning man.

I clamped my teeth together, and slapped a hand over my mouth, smearing slick ichor. It was then that the smell registered, like the rotting scraps behind the butcher shop, or a bloated animal corpse baking in the sun. I tried to turn away from the noxious odor, only to realized I was covered in it and had accidentally rubbed it across my lips and under my nose. The back of my mind screamed at me to be quiet, even as I rolled to my knees to vomit violently into the dirt toward the edge of the tent.

"Gods, man," The Chosen One complained with a sneer. He seized the lantern from the hook dangling above our heads, and pushed through the tent flap, armed with only a sword and light.

I was instantly plunged into terrible darkness, alone with my fear, bound by my own blankets, and covered in gore. By sheer will, I managed not to be sick again. I held my breath and listened to the hero's feet crunch around in the grass and dirt of the clearing. Whatever had disturbed the night was silent. I nearly jumped out of my skin when the hero called out to me.

"Tiberius! Bring my scabbard and blanket, and ready this fire."

No part of me wanted to go out into the dark forest, but I shoved it down and extracted myself from the blankets. I had to grope around for the items he requested, and steel myself to step out into the night. The air was cool and fresh, and I gulped at it with relief. The Chosen One sheathed the now-clean sword and threw the blanket around his shoulders, his eyes not leaving the trees.

"Is it dead?" I asked as I fumbled with the still-warm embers.

"It already was," he replied. "But the sword purged it of necromancy, so it no longer moves."

My hands shook so violently, I was grateful there was enough heat in the coals to reignite the flame without my need to resort to flint. "It was..."

"It looked like a weasel," he affirmed.

So we had finally encountered what The Chosen One had been called to confront, a vampire stoat. "Where—"

"Over by the tent. It appears to have been alone." His eyes constantly scanned the trees and brush, a steadfast and stolidly protective presence that eased my fear of what lay beyond the modest circle of light the lantern produced. "When you're done, go and clean up our tent. Might as well break it down, the sun will be up before you're done."

I let out a slow, steadying breath, taking shameless comfort in his iron-firm confidence. I spent several moments scrubbing my face, chest and arms with fresh grass and rinsing with canteen water. After three passes of the crude baiting routine, the smell was bearable.

I dragged everything out from the tent and busied myself separating the clean items from the befouled, packing the first and setting the latter aside. I was grateful to find my blankets had protected my bedroll, but my pillow was likely ruined. The tidy incision in the tent was only revealed by the growing glow of the approaching sunrise. I alternated scrubbing with soap and rinsing with water until the inside was clean. It was only when I had completed everything I could within the tent that I realized I was avoiding walking around to the side of the canvas wall that concealed the re-dead creature.

"Come, now, Tiberius," The Chosen One chided from beside the fire. He'd folded the blanket and wrapped it around his waist, tucking it in to his off side. "You will see a good number of foul things in the next few days, let alone the next few years." His eyes sought mine, and I realized this was as close to comforting as he could likely come. He'd clearly recognized my hesitation before I had.

  I sighed and forced my feet to carry me around the tent to the forest-facing wall that had been where my bed was located. On the ground next to the fabric was a soiled, stinking pile of limp flesh and white fur. I swallowed hard and clenched my jaw, refusing to look away until my heart had calmed. He was right. This was *my* job. His was to kill the things that skulk in the night, mine was to shed light upon them. This thought propelled me toward the corpse.

  I drew my dagger and carefully prodded the mass into a prone position. It matched the description of a stoat to the letter, and as I looked at its milky eyes and mangy patches of soiled fur, something unexpected came over me. I didn't fear it anymore; I pitied it. This creature had probably died a painful death and had dragged its rotting carcass around the forest until it found release at the point of the hero's blade.

  I hooked the tip of my dagger under its chin and lifted it from the grass to carry into the morning glow of the clearing. I spent several minutes examining it, looking for injuries, markings, or anything else that might later prove to be useful information. After several moments, The Chosen One let out an impatient huff, and I shook my head. "It appears to have died from the necromancy that animated it," I concluded. "The only injury to it is from your sword and my dagger."

  He nodded. "Like the fish."

  I raised my brows. "You asked about the fish."

  I saw him resist a sneer and was both irritated and relieved at the gesture. "*Someone* had to."

I huffed a mirthless chuckle. He was right. My job was to investigate, his was to attack and defend. I had been remiss in the town. Who knew how much information I had missed, because I was too absorbed with my preparations and my disgust with the whole process? "Well, I'll do better at the next town." I ignored his emphatic nod. "Something that concerns me is its pelt."

"Yeah?"

"Yeah. It's white." I looked up at his blank, uncomprehending expression. "It's late summer, early fall. His coat shouldn't be white."

He frowned down at it. "How do you know that? Just a week ago, you didn't even know what a stoat was."

I sighed and sat back on my heels, looking down at the poor, foul creature. "I've been reading about them. Ermine comes from the winter coat of the stoat. This has either changed into his winter coat early—"

"Or he's been dead since winter," he finished. He nodded and paced away. I watched him make a thoughtful circuit of the camp before I surmised that our conversation was over.

I made my way to where the creature had died for the last time and scrubbed the other side of the canvas, pushing down a gag every few minutes at the smell of the death stain in the dirt. I pulled out the sewing kit I'd kept out from my pack and quickly lashed the opening closed. It wasn't pretty, but I could have it professionally repaired at the next town. By the time I'd pulled down the frame and began folding the tent, the foul spot was already drying.

As I worked, the sun crested the trees, and warmth spread across my shoulders. I thought of the earlier discussion about faith and wondered if Skalah's eye was upon us at that very moment. Perhaps this sunlight was meant to chase away the fear and cloying chill of the night and bring the courage and the comfort of a god's support to my heart. "Or," my cynical-self muttered. "Maybe it's just a sunrise, like any other." I had worked up a light sweat by the time I'd packed the tent in the cart.

"Ahem," The Chosen One barked out, snapping me from my well-deserved brooding. He impatiently gestured to his blanket skirt. "Forget something?"

I let out an impatient huff. "You are a grown man. Can you not dress yourself?" I snapped.

His eyebrows shot up, and I saw the expected flash of anger in his gaze. "*Tiberius* prepares my garb an—"

"I've read that part of the tomes!" I shot back. "I prepare your garb for special occasions, needs outside of your daily routines such as disguises, and battle." I jabbed a hand toward his garment chest. "Every-day wear and travel... that's *your* job. Think you a hundred-year-old man can figure out how to select a pair of trousers and put them on his own body?"

Somehow his eyebrows rose even higher as we stood, facing off through several heated breaths. Finally, he let out a growl and stripped off the blanket. I looked away, and he thrust the blanket at me as he reached up to the chest. Without any time wasted on selection, he jerked out the first set of clothing he could find and quickly dressed. "Think you can manage breakfast?" he snarled.

I let out a calming breath, folded the blanket, stowed it in the appropriate chest, and climbed into the cart to find the items I would need to prepare food.

I decided to burn the corpse after we had finished eating. The smell of the smoke was rank and made the horses dance nervously, but I was concerned if left to rot it might poison anything that came upon it. We set out in rigid silence, and went the entire morning without talking. The unresolved anger and my own thoughts of what lay ahead made me hyper-vigilant and jumpy. Every rustle in the bush or loud bang from the cart made me jerk and set my heart racing. By the time we stopped for lunch, I was exhausted from the unending anxiety.

The Chosen One made a circuit of the camp before heading into the trees to relieve himself, and I was grateful that I was not the only one who was being cautious. It made me feel less foolish for being on edge all day. The scores of rotting fish and the corpses on the barge were entirely different from what we went to face: undead creatures that could actually pursue you.

I'd tried to occupy my mind with the menial tasks of Tiberius during the ride in a vain effort to distract from the gnawing fear that churned in my guts. As a result, I had already decided grilled bread with salted meats was the best—and fastest—choice. I was nearly done preparing our lunch when The Chosen One returned. He took the plate and stein I offered, uttered a near-inaudible grunt, and lowered himself to a fallen log I had left vacant for him. It was the only thing resembling a seat at this rest stop. After several long moments filled with the unnervingly loud rustle and creaking of the trees, I could bear the tension no longer.

"Tell me what you're thinking," I broached.

His gaze lifted to mine, and I could see he was still smoldering from my rebuke that morning. "That I suppose I'm glad you have *some* courage, though it is gravely misplaced."

I chuffed. His comment surprisingly softened some of my own anger in spite of the bite it had been intended to carry. That he could acknowledge the courage my challenge of his tyranny required was actually encouraging. "It amazes me that the Tiberiuses before tolerated being treated like slaves."

His anger flashed again, and I saw his muscles tense as if he were about to stand.

I put up a hand, and his lip curled into a sneer. "Listen," I said, as surprised by the calm in my voice as he apparently was. "I want us to be able to work together, to find a rhythm where what you do and what I do mesh seamlessly and work off of each other." His response was a grunt. Though I couldn't tell if it was acquiescence or distain, he settled and took another bite of his sandwich. "I think being thrown into this situation with no time to adapt—"

"There's never time to *adapt*," he grumbled.

I nodded, more to myself than him. "Regardless, it means I have to learn on the road, and you have to learn how to let a new Tiberius into your routines without any kind of grace period. We are *going to* butt heads." I looked down at my own sandwich and wondered if he was even understanding what I was trying to say. "It seems as though we keep having this discussion, and I am beginning to suspect previous Tiberiuses rolled over and didn't bother to have it at all." I sighed and looked up to find him staring at me. "I think they were just putting in the time until they could shrug their responsibilities onto the next Tiberius, and I don't want it to be like that."

He pursed his lips and turned his gaze to the smoldering embers of the fire.

After a moment, when he didn't say anything, I continued. "I can't be the only one to give ground. We have to find someplace in the middle if you want me to work *with* you instead of *for* you." When his reaction was more silence, I sighed. "What I'm trying to say is that I think I can be a *lot* more useful to you as a partner of sorts than as a servant."

He glowered and set his jaw.

"Let us face the fact that *anyone* can pick out your clothes and cook food for you." Another grunt, but I thought maybe I could see some reflection in his downcast eyes. "But, the gods chose to give you an assistant with some really incredible blessings of his own."

This time he did meet my gaze. "Then you *do* accept the hand of the gods in your status," he jabbed.

"I never denied I felt the gods' power in the Blessings of Tiberius." I wondered if this was the right time to try and come to terms, given that he was so set upon arguing, but at any moment we might face the terrible enemy we both knew lay ahead. "We need to find a way to work better together if this foe is as great as you have alluded you believe he is."

He snorted. "Just stand back and let me work," he snapped. "Have supplies ready to heal or purify. That's what Tiberius is good for."

I shook my head. "You see? That is not *all* I can be good for." A brow rose at that, and I pushed on. "You are not alone," I insisted. "I'm not just here to patch the tent and rub salve on your toes. I'm here to stand with you."

He barked out a laugh. "Oh? Truly? You wish to carry the sword, too?"

I sighed. "Okay, stand *behind* you," I conceded. "But..." I struggled to find the right words. "Look..." At his impatient gesture, a flare of anger bolstered me to put voice to my thoughts. "Even after all of our bickering, I still... I'm still in *awe* of what you do. Of what you *are*."

He seemed a little mollified by my flattery and accepted the comments with a smirking nod of arrogance.

"I think about what you battle, about the people you protect and save, and it sickens me to imagine you going into untold danger with no one to look after you but a jaded body-man who is so busy counting down his days to retirement, he has little time for anything else."

I could have imagined it, but for a moment his bravado seemed to falter, and his gaze flicked away, perhaps wistfully. There was so much more I wanted to say, but I thought it might be a good idea to give him time to think over my offer and the intentions behind it. I had no way of knowing if he would believe I was sincere, or if he understood what I was struggling to convey. Only after several minutes passed and he neither spoke nor ate did I start to truly regret saying what I had. If I had upset him enough to affect his appetite, something that had proven mightier than the legend of The Gods' Chosen himself, I had clearly crossed a line.

I watched him stare into the trees, his gaze distant and shadowed. From the moment I had first seen him, he'd always exuded pristine strength, a fierce and stolid presence that inspired devotion and awe in everyone around him. He was just a step away from the gods, a light almost as bright as the sun.

Now, beside the dying embers of the cook fire, he looked tired, old, and filled with unfathomable solitude. In spite of thinking better of it, I felt irresistibly compelled to break the glass-fragile stillness of his contemplation. My voice was hushed, as if the ground had become hallowed, and only the truest words of the heart could be uttered.

"When you spoke of your battle with the dragon," I muttered. "How you hung before the maw of a monstrous beast choosing fang and flame, pain and death over risking even the chance one of the women in its captivity could be harmed... all I could think was: *where was Tiberius?*"

His gaze lifted to mine, and I saw a crack in his bravado, a sincere attentiveness so rare, it startled me. "I am no good at the sword or much of anything else, for that matter," I said. "But I *can be* good at being Tiberius. I can be a shield of sorts, an anchor, a bolster... whatever you need a simple man to be to help you do what you do. I can also be a partner, and perhaps if it is something you also desire, a friend." Amazingly, I felt as though he was looking at me and actually seeing me: a man who truly wished to make a difference, to do genuine good, to have a fraction of the honor and courage The Chosen One possessed. I had no idea how, and I was shocked to find the desire within myself, but it was there nonetheless. "I can be, and I *want to* be."

He let out a deep breath, and looked away. Neither of us spoke for a time, and I thought he was likely dismissing my impromptu monologue. After a painfully long stillness, I stood to go about the business of smothering the fire and preparing for the road.

"He died," he said, his eyes still fixed on the trees.

I paused, crouched next to the smoldering fire. "Who?"

"Tiberius. That's where he was," he quietly replied. "The dragon killed him and threw his remains into the sea. We never recovered him. He couldn't be resurrected."

I sat back onto my heels and looked up at him, my mind connecting pieces of information into the full story. "He was the one," I deduced. "He 'reminded you' of what you are and what you do when you went to face your greatest enemy."

His gaze didn't leave the trees, but his back went a little rigid and his jaw tightened.

"Is that why you keep the Tiberiuses that follow at so far a distance?"

His eyes flashed to me, and I saw them harden. Without warning, he rose and strode to the horse. "We're wasting daylight," he grumbled. "We have a lot of preparation before we reach the village, and I would like a chance to fortify the tent before we sleep."

I let out a breath and shook my head. "Well," I muttered. "I tried."

14. The Cold Passed Reluctantly from the Earth, and the Retiring Fogs Revealed a Frightened Town

The rest of the ride that day was quiet, uneventful in spite of the sharp anxiety of what monsters potentially lurked in the trees. I was not surprised The Chosen One had decided not to comment on our deep discussion that afternoon, and after a while the intensity of that interaction softened into an almost surreal memory that seemed more distant than it was.

He kept us at a hard pace. When we came to the stop, we had more daylight than we had the prior days, but the sumpters were exhausted. I reminded myself to trade out the lead horses in the morning, and quickly set up the tent. I wasn't sure what The Chosen One had meant by "fortify," but it was clear he wanted daylight to do it in. While I worked, he circled the camp, looking intently into the trees, his hand resting on the hilt of his sword. It was then that I noticed the set of his shoulders. In my own arrogance, I had thought his quiet had been a result of my words, but he was clearly at attention and may have been all afternoon.

I paused from fire making to watch him. Had he sensed something I had not, or was it merely a result of the stoat we'd encountered before? I realized my heart was thumping in response to his not-subtle attentiveness, and I took a few calming breaths. "The gods are with you," I whispered under my breath. "The Chosen is with you. Stop being a coward."

"Smart words," the hero responded, though he was quite a distance away. It actually wasn't a barb, and his quiet affirmation had accomplished what I could not. My heart calmed.

"Do you... is there something out there?"

"Of course," he replied, his usual arrogance setting my jaw. "We are here to fight undead creatures, after all."

I huffed and shook my head. I coaxed the flame to light in the stone firepit as he finished his slow, thorough circuit.

He came to stand over the fire as I fed increasingly larger sticks into it. "Why don't you use a spell to light it?" he asked after length. "This is so much more effort."

I sat back on my heels and looked up at him through the distortion of the growing heat. He was genuinely asking, not mocking. "Well, I did see the working in the tome that previous Tiberiuses used," I conceded. "I don't have a limitless store of magic to expend, and I am certain I will need all I have to be of use to you. I'm conserving it."

He pursed his lips and strode over to the cart. "There are tonics," he said. "Green fluid the last man would drink before and sometimes during times of casting."

"What?" I shot to my feet. "I have heard of such workings, but using magic to create magic is... well, it's *rare*. I've never seen one."

He glanced at the trunks and pointed to the one I had already determined was dedicated to consumable workings such as poultices and tonics. It was where I would have looked first, but that he could recognize it and was actually trying to be helpful spoke volumes of how far we had come.

I climbed into the cart and flipped the lid open, pulling out the corresponding burgundy tome. I skimmed the contents. "Did he ever happen to mention what it was called?"

He shook his head. "He never bothered to explain any of this to me."

I smirked. "Would you have cared to listen? Isn't this *Tiberius work*?" I didn't realize what I had said until he stiffened and wordlessly walked away. "I'm sorry," I said at his back. "This is quite helpful. Thank you. If there are any of those tonics here, they could really help us during this upcoming endeavor."

He just nodded stiffly and began a more relaxed but somehow no less vigilant circuit of the clearing.

I found the tonic working in the contents and flipped to the indicated page. The Chosen One had said it was green, but I did not remember any of the vials being that color during my cursory inventory. As I read the description of the potion, I realized why. It was pale and inert until it had been activated, then it emitted a chartreus glow. Apparently it had a slightly bitter, sour apple flavor... and hurt like hell. I sighed and shook my head. A sudden, lingering pain could interrupt a casting. I would have to be careful to maintain my concentration if I needed to use it while directly expending magic. Few things were as volatile or unpredictable as undirected magic. The roving undead and living, rotting fish of the harbor were indication of that.

I skimmed the contents of the box until I found what I sought: three precious vials of the incredibly rare tonic. They were far beyond my ability to create, so they must have been purchased at a major city with a stronghold for the Wizards' Guild. They were undoubtedly very expensive. I returned my attention to the tome. There were not even instructions for the potion's construction, just how to activate the working. No doubt the secret was closely guarded. Tonics like this often had rare and powerful ingredients, and the creation of them was sometimes dark and immoral, something that would cast a poor light on the grandmaster wizards that ruled the guild. If that were the case, there was no chance I would ever learn to make them. "Not that it matters," I muttered. It would still be beyond me.

"What?" The Chosen One's voice sounded from near the tent. He was crouched beside the first stake, sword in hand.

My heart immediately leapt into my chest, and I involuntarily slammed the chest closed, protecting the important cargo. "What is it?" My voice came out embarrassingly shrill, and I cleared my throat. "Is it another stoat?"

His demeanor had apparently been relaxed, because he transformed as he stood into an indomitable warrior both hands taking the hilt as he spun on his heel to scan the trees behind him. "Where?" he barked. "Where did you see it?"

I let out a nervous laugh and deflated. "Oh, no," I muttered, securing the chest. "It was a misunderstanding."

He glowered at me, his shoulders still tight. "What? You saw a squirrel and panicked?"

I sighed and swung down from the cart. "No. I saw the sword and thought—"

He rolled his eyes and crouched next to the tent again. "I forget how ignorant you are," he grumbled.

I bristled at the remark, but pushed through my chagrin. "What are you doing?"

"Fortifying the tent, so no undead can pass the threshold," he muttered.

As I approached, I noticed the subtle glow of the sword. I couldn't see it from across the clearing, but it was definitely reflecting more light than the darkening overcast would allow. "How does it work?"

He glowered at me. "Would you be silent?" he snapped.

I clenched my teeth and resisted the urge to call him an ass. As instructed, I stayed a few feet back and kept my mouth shut.

After one final glance of rebuke, he bowed his head and began to pray. "Great Skalah, king of the gods, lord of the sky, reach out with the light of your protecting embrace." The glow in the sword redoubled and cast an unmistakable light onto the fabric. "May your favor shine upon us through the dark of night and see us safely to your glowing visage come morn." His voice was quiet, humble, and reverent in a way I had never heard from him before save perhaps when he was singing his ballads. He moved the sword up and down from the peak of the tent to the ground, standing and crouching over and over. As he worked, the glow of the sword appeared to seep into the very weave of the fabric.

I contemplated his actions since we'd stopped. He must have needed to do this blessing while the sun still hung in the sky. He must have needed to complete the process or start over again, thus the thorough search of the perimeter. That led me to the conclusion that he was vulnerable while he was concentrating at this level. I was actually a little surprised that he could dedicate so much attention to anything but food, drink, or women. I chastised myself immediately after having the thought and drew my dagger. The Chosen One glanced to me, but he didn't stop repeating the prayer.

Before I entirely realized what I was doing, I walked between him and the trees. My stomach dropped out as I looked into the thick brush, knowing what could be out there. If there were stoats, there could be larger animals. Boars, wolves, or worse. I shuddered and opened all of my senses to what may lie hidden in the growing darkness. Though every rustle made me jump and the blade shuddered in my fingers, I was determined to stand my ground. I would not leave the great hero with his back to the woods while he was unable to defend against a sudden attack. I had no hope that I might prove a worthy adversary, but I could be a target. I could raise an alarm or delay a strike.

The moments stretched into what felt like hours, and with the fading of the light, the darkness of the trees reached toward me with malicious, smothering fingers. Every twig became a claw, every glint a glowing eye, every shrub a crouching beast.

A hand took my shoulder, and I let out an exceptionally un-masculine yelp of surprise, swinging wide with my dagger. The Chosen One caught my wrist, his brow quirking as he firmly took the blade from my fingers. "You're really that afraid?"

I shivered but jerked fully upright to glare up at him. I opened my mouth to say something biting, but held back when I registered the unfamiliar cast to his features. He wasn't mocking me, he actually looked... impressed? I snatched my dagger from him and jabbed it back into its sheath so quickly I pinched my finger. "So?" I grumbled. "I told you I was a coward."

He shrugged one shoulder. "A coward would have hidden in the tent," he remarked, turning back toward the dying fire. "I'm done. You will have to set up our beds after you've made dinner," he instructed. "I'm hungry."

I retreated from the trees with wobbly legs, too quickly to appear casual. "Blessings appear to be hungry work," I remarked as I rummaged for the supplies needed to prepare dinner.

He grunted an agreement and stood beside the fire. He kept the light to his back as he watched the trees, arms crossed with one hand on the pommel of his sword. His relaxed but vigilant posture helped steady my fear-weakened limbs. I was grateful that he was turned away, so I wouldn't have to endure the often judgmental and arrogant scrutiny of my labors. We only had a small portion of the salted meats left, not enough for two, so I sliced it thin and seared it with the remaining pearl onions for his entree. We had quite a few potatoes, and I tossed three into the coals near the edge of the flame. I would eat the smaller two with the last, stale-hardened heel of bread. I would supplement with trail rations if needs be, but I suspected my appetite would suffer after the excitement of the day.

When I began distributing the fare onto wooden plates, The Chosen One moved to crouch beside the fire with the cart to his back. I broke open his charred potato and quickly scooped out the steaming flesh onto his plate, and his lips curled up into a smirk at the few quiet hisses of pain that escaped me when I was not careful enough with the coal-hot tuber. I gave him a flat look of rebuke, which he ignored with no effort whatsoever. Though he ate ravenously, his eyes rarely left the trees that were now almost entirely engulfed in darkness. Only the faintest hint of deep blue lingered in the sky, and rather than define our surroundings, it backlit the trees and made it more difficult to see into them.

The Chosen One finished his meal with gusto before either of my potatoes had cooled enough for me to brave eating them. He glanced around, as if to see if there was more, and I quickly broke open the remaining tubers and scraped their flesh onto his plate. He furrowed a brow at me, but took my portion without comment. *And without thanks*, I thought to myself.

He sat back and sucked at his teeth, his gaze distant and—perhaps I imagined it—sated. "If you're going to put yourself in harm's way, you will need to learn to fight," he said.

I'd had no way of knowing what was going on in his mind before he spoke, but I would never have guessed his thoughts were of *me*. After a long pause of shock, I cleared my throat and gave a conciliatory nod. "Um, sure. I can try."

His eyes flicked to me and stayed for a long time while he worked food out of his teeth with his tongue. Finally, he said. "You swung a blade at me today."

A hollow place opened in my stomach at his words. I had been so worked up at the time, and The Chosen One so dismissive, the seriousness of the incident had completely passed over me. I stared down at the fire, my jaw dropping a little at the realization. I could have cut him, even seriously hurt him. What had I been thinking? And why hadn't the blessing punished me? Perhaps without intent to harm him, it was lenient. When I looked back up at him, he was still watching me, his expression undecipherable.

I nodded again. "Yes. Of course. I'll learn. I'm so sorry—"

He put up a hand to silence me. "Just pay more attention. If you're going to guard me, you have to guard yourself, as well. You can't be so focused on one direction that you don't know what's happening behind you." He rose and began pacing around the fire, peering into the trees. "A sentry can't look in just one direction; he must be attentive of all of his surroundings."

I nodded. "Do you think we should start my training tonight?"

His eyes shot to me, and his lips twisted into a barely restrained sneer. "I didn't mean *I* would teach you," he remarked. "Find another instructor."

My mouth dropped open. "What? Why?" I sputtered. "Who?"

"Not my problem," he grumbled, turning his attention back to the trees. "You figure it out."

I shook my head and again resisted calling him an ass.

I quickly scoured the plates and set up our beds and camp needs. The Chosen One made quiet circles of the camp, though he retreated halfway between the fire and the trees when true darkness set in. I was amazed at how comforting the tent felt, finding as many excuses as I could to linger inside while prepping for the night. I was surprised the hero kept guard until I was done bedding down the horses. Previous nights, he'd laid down the moment his roll was ready. I found myself wondering again if he sensed something I did not. The moment I seemed essentially done, he cast me an impatient frown and ducked through the tent flap.

Alone in the night, I shivered and looked around, trying to discern what might have inspired his vigilance. I rested my back against the cart, swallowed hard, and closed my eyes. I tried to stretch out my awareness, but nothing felt "wrong" as the undead stoat had. The only sound in the night was the creak and whisper of the trees in the breeze. No animals stirred or called, no crickets chirped, no wings buzzed around the horses or our food stores. My stomach twisted as the wrongness I had been seeking alarmed in my head. No living thing could be heard around us save the animals we'd brought with us... only the forest holding its breath and waiting for death to come.

I sprinted to the tent and dove into the light of the lantern, my breaths coming out in choked gasps.

The Chosen One stiffened where he stood, his shirt half pulled up his torso, and his brows rose in condescending judgement. "Did you encounter something dangerous, or were you just frightened by your own shadow again?"

The tone of his voice bespoke of his belief it was the latter, so I didn't bother to respond to the mockery. Instead, I secured the flap and crawled to my own bedroll. "If you insist on keeping the lantern lit all night, we will need to procure more lamp oil." His movements paused again, and I knew my biting remark had not gone undetected. We had not spoken of the night we'd shared a cot, and the reminder that I'd figured out his fear of true darkness doused the air of the small space with bitter ice. I swallowed and kept my eyes downcast as I gathered the notes garnered from Noblan's scholarly guilds. "I'm sorry," I muttered.

I kept my eyes fixed intently on the hastily-scrawled text while The Chosen One stripped down and slid under his covers. I wasn't able to truly relax until his rumbling snores filled the night. I dared a glance over at his bare back and contemplated how we could possibly build a rapport if we were always at each other's throats. My tendency to fire back with insult when I was barbed, though deserved, was working against that end. I had butted against his arrogance and condescension, because I thought he needed to learn a different way to treat Tiberius. But, perhaps I was becoming part of the problem when I talked back.

I let out a slow breath and nodded to myself. I would have to resolve to keep my temper in check. I could challenge his misconduct without rising to his barbs. In truth, he was probably resisting a kinship out of habit, and his mockery and criticism were just tools he was using to that end. I reminded myself that it had only been nine days, and change took time. I had already seen a few glimmers of hope where he treated me with consideration and deference. If I could keep the barb out of my tongue, maybe I could nurture that growth. In the very least, I could stop setting us back. I would need to swallow my pride a little more and let the arrogant ass be himself. Hopefully, in time we would find enough common ground to not be miserable in each other's company. "Lead by example," I muttered.

Horrific visions of being overrun and mauled to the bone by a pack of rotting weasels followed me into the real world, and I awoke with a cry of blind panic as groping hands rolled me about. I was smothering, my body aching from straining against my bonds. I could still see the gnashing teeth, feel my own blood flowing over my torn flesh, soaking through useless armor.

"Gods, man!" The Chosen One bellowed. Ice cold water crashed over me, and I wheezed through the shock. "Stop that girlish screaming and come out of it!" Giant hands shook me until my teeth clacked together, and my eyes focused finally on the grandmaster hero who kneeled over me.

I gasped and wriggled as much as I could, helplessly bound in my own blankets, and looked over my body for the gore I expected to see. After a few panting breaths, I realized I was soaked with sweat and water, not blood. I sagged against my bedroll, all strength seeping out of my body, and looked up at the hero. He still held my shoulders, his eyes searching my face. After a moment, his painfully tight grip lessened, and he lifted a hand to my forehead. His frown deepened and he sat back on his heels. I realized too late that he was still naked, and didn't manage to look away before I saw more than I wanted.

"You're fever delirious," he observed. "The sun has just risen." He stood and found his clothes, beginning to dress as I squeezed my eyes shut and tried to compose myself. "Your blessing must not be entirely protecting you," he deduced. "Don't worry about breakfast. We'll eat rations. Just pack up as quickly as you're able. We need to make Vevesk before the sun has reached its zenith."

He strode from the tent, leaving me alone with my own shallow breaths and pounding heart. He was right; I did feel feverish. I felt the flush in my cheeks and a clammy sweat from brow to toes. I grumbled miserably and wrestled with my sodden blankets until I was free of them. With shaking hands, I quickly changed into my clothes for the day and packed up our supplies. I didn't roll my bed or blankets. I would strap them across the trunks in the hopes that they might dry while we rode.

I loaded up my arms and headed out of the tent. I came to an abrupt halt when I stepped into what seemed like a solid wall of thick mist. Personally, I was fond of fog; it covered the land with an inspiring shroud of mystery. This blinding white murk felt alive with malice. I imagined it crawling down my throat choking the air from my lungs. Suddenly, I couldn't breathe. I gasped, dropping my load to claw at my throat. I tried to suck in air, but the white murk filled me instead. Panic flashed quick and fierce through my brain. I was drowning, suffocating in the weightless water.

A hand sprung from the darkness, striking my chest, and I staggered backwards into the tent... and out of the wall of mist. I gagged and gasped, taking in deep lungfuls of cool, unthreatening air. I had never been so grateful to fill my nostrils with the smell of sweat, mud, and unwashed linens. The Chosen One followed me into the space and stood over me, his expression intense and searching. After a few moments of watching me intermittently suck in air and cough out tendrils of mist that dissipated instantly, the solid knot of his shoulders relaxed.

We watched each other for another long moment. When I finally regained my voice, it came out as a barely legible rasp. "What is happening?"

"You need to discover your faith," he grated, his eyes hard and unyielding.

"What's that supposed to mean?" I snapped. "It's my fault that—*whatever that is*—was choking me?" I shot to my feet, and though I waivered, stood my ground. To my surprise, he didn't respond with anger, just with that same hard intensity.

"You've let him in," he quietly rebuked. "That's why your blessing isn't working."

"Let who—"

"*Trion*, you fool!" He shoved me aside, and shouldered his trunk before tucking his bedroll under his arm.

"I have not!" I shrieked, mortified and enraged that he would even *suggest* that I had entered any kind of allegiance with the god of pestilence. "I'm pretty sure the blessing would strike me down if I were in league with Trion, given that he's openly your enemy!"

He brushed past me, my words chasing after him as he disappeared into the white wall. I opened my mouth to continue arguing when it dawned on me what had just happened. The Chosen One was *helping* pack the cart? The shock of it shook me loose of my fury, and I realized my response had been a gross overreaction born of fever and fear.

It seemed like an eternity before the hero returned. This time he quietly loaded up *my* trunk and turned to face me, his glower set in stone. "You fear him more than you trust Skalah," he quietly replied to my argument from several minutes before. "He cannot protect you if you do not give him your faith." He strode out, his succinct and surprisingly wise words heavy in the air.

I stared down at my bed and chewed my lip. I was terrified of Trion, and rightly so. But, had my fear given him a way in? A way through the Blessings of Tiberius? I wiped at the fever sweat on my brow. Had he been giving me these night visions to breed more fear, to pave his way into my waking mind? I dropped to my knees in the wet grass and mud, barely noticing the slick damp that soaked through my pants. "What do I do?" I pleaded to the air. "What *can* I do?" I bowed my head, my shoulders shaking from shame and fear. I had spoken such brave words yesterday, promising in my arrogance to stand beside the great hero, but I had been too petrified of an empty forest to be useful. Now, instead of helping The Chosen One prepare to face the horrors that had undoubtedly befallen Vevesk, I was huddled inside a canvas shield, drinking in the precious air of its protection.

A coward would have hidden in the tent.

The Chosen's words the night before echoed in my mind so clear, my head snapped up, and I involuntarily glanced around for him. The words came again, a mirror in my own voice, reverberating in my mind. I swallowed hard. I could not help him if I was too afraid to step out of the tent. I let out a slow breath, a shudder passing through me as I realized what I was resolving myself to do. "The sun has risen," I reminded myself. "Skalah shines upon his chosen and the man who stands with him." When I rose and faced the tent flap, my knees shook and threatened to buckle. "In the least, The Chosen One won't let me die." I closed my eyes, took one last breath, and sprinted out of the tent.

I felt the cool damp of the mist against my face, but I didn't stop running until my toe caught a lump in the grass, and I nearly fell. I stood hunched, hugging myself, willing my lungs to breathe out. Skalah would protect me. The Chosen One would protect me. I just had to be brave enough to breathe out and back in. In spite of my self-encouraging thoughts, I held my breath until it burned, then until I could bear it no longer, as one does when they're submerged. Air exploded from my lungs, and I sucked in choking breaths with a shuddering whimper of fear. I had no way of knowing where the tent was, and I was certainly more afraid of suffocating than I was confident of protection. When the cold moisture poured into me, I jerked and tried to force it out, but my suffocation reflex kicked in, and I panted in and out hysterically.

It took several breaths for me to realize I wasn't dying. In fact, the cool felt good against my flushed face. I opened my eyes to find the grandmaster hero standing directly in front of me, still nearly concealed by the thick mist. He was grinning wide, his arms crossed and feet planted like a triumphant warrior. He slapped my shoulder with enough force to stagger me half a step to the side. "Now, break down the tent," he said. "We should have been on the road by now."

I woodenly turned until I recognized the dark shape of the tent. My hands went through the practiced motions while my mind rolled around what the morning had entailed. At some point, it all sank in and my senses cleared. I sat back on my heels, my fingers in the process of bundling the stakes. My eye tracked up to the glow that had just crested the shadow of the tree line. Skalah *had* protected me. I hadn't cast a spell. I hadn't even really prayed. I had simply asked what to do and the answer had come to me. Tears stung at the corner of my eyes, and I thought about The Chosen One's grin. I could not remember a time in my life when anyone had believed in me, was proud of me as he seemed to be at that moment. I swallowed hard and nodded to myself. These rare moments of clarity could sustain me, no matter how much of a jerk he could be. This glimmer of faith could see me through the battle to come. "I pray it does," I whispered, continuing my work.

To my surprise, The Chosen One had drawn out his light armor and had already fastened the straps he could easily reach. He'd even saddled and prepared Braknik, though he seemed content to ride Fellowyn until such time as trouble sought us out. Throughout all the preparations, it seemed as though I were swimming through milk, barely able to make out my own hands at arms-length. Whenever a task took me close to the treeline, I found myself shuddering, my imagination providing a myriad of terrifying ideas about what might jump out at me amidst such thorough cover.

After securing the load and preparing the horses, my tasks quickened by fear and the desire to be nearer to the land's greatest hero, The Chosen One shoved Braknik's reins into my hands. I fumbled to catch them and quickly dodged a nip from the prideful beast. "What am I—"

"I need my hands and flanks free," he grumbled as if I should simply understand his intentions.

The warhorse nipped at me again, its teeth snapping closed just a hair from my shoulder, and my subsequent gasp and jerk earned a smirk from the hero. I mounted Topher and secured the warhorse's reins to my pommel.

"He rides between us," The Chosen One corrected with a naked burr of frustration.

I let his ill-tempered tone roll over me and unsecured the reins to guide the beast to my other side. Though I was sorry to lose the comfort of Braknik on one side and a hero on the other, it made sense. If he needed to mount the destrier, he would need easy access. With that thought, I gave the warhorse as much rein as I could and bound the leather straps to my saddle in a way that would make them easier to free.

We set off at a speed I considered dangerous considering our impaired view of the road, but The Chosen One seemed confident, so I let him take the lead by half a length. Braknik rode alongside him at the limit of his reins, and he snorted regularly, his head turning this way and that at every rustle in the brush as the occasional white flashed in his eyes.

The mist held all morning, and the vigilant, rigid seat of the hero both comforted and unnerved me. I couldn't help but think about the Tiberius who had been eaten by a dragon and thrown into the sea. The last assistant who had earned the hero's regard enough to inspire him to act in spite of fear had met a horrible end. Perhaps I was being ridiculously foolish and arrogant, thinking I should be anything more than a body man. If The Chosen One had maintained an unsentimental, working relationship with every Tiberius that followed and had kept them alive, maybe that was how the gods had intended it. Perhaps two years was the length of the contract, because any longer would form too strong a bond between the great hero and his *replaceable* assistant.

The minutes stretched into exceptionally long, monotonous hours. In spite of the persistent, gnawing fear, my eyes began to droop at the unending white wash and rhythmic plodding of the horses. I had drifted half-asleep for a long while before Topher jerked to a stop. I came awake with such a start, I nearly pitched from the saddle. The Chosen One caught a fist full of my tunic and yanked me upright, simultaneously saving and choking me.

"Idiot," he grumbled, giving my shoulder a shove when he released me.

I gagged out an unintelligible apology and thanks, but the hero was ignoring me. We had come to stop at a rise in the road, and from the vantage of our position, we could make out a shallow valley below. A fairly large village could be seen in the distance, curved in a tight crescent around the lip of a massive lake. The body of water was so large, it stretched infinitely into the dissipating mist of the morning. The whole depressing tableau huddled beneath a persistent, mute-gray overcast.

"Vevesk?" I asked, still trying to clear my throat. His answer was a grunt, and he kept watching the sleepy town as if it were a riddle to be deciphered. I followed his gaze, frowning, trying to read the landscape as he seemed to be. "What am I missing?"

He looked at me then, his lips turning down disapprovingly. After a pointed moment of judgment he gestured to the torn and cleared earth to the east of the town.

I looked from his point of reference and back, awaiting explanation. I felt my temper bristle, but pushed it back. Instead, I calmly asked, "You'll have to explain it to me. I'm new, remember?"

He growled out a deep-chested sigh. "Shallow digging for stones and mud, cleared trees, and a fresh fence line around the entire town."

I looked back to the landscape, taking in all of his observations with a slow nod of comprehension. "They've recently fortified. The fence looks too tight to be intended to keep horses in, and too short to thwart an accomplished man."

He grunted again.

"So what they're keeping out is small but persistent enough to require the measures in the first place." I leaned forward, peering harder. "And sentries every sixty feet or so?"

He nodded and shifted smoothly from Fellowyn to Braknik, thrusting the reins of the sumpter to me.

Without looking away from the view, he felt for his weapons and checked the buckles on his armor.

My stomach churned. "You think something will attack?"

He pursed his lips and looked around at the trees, then down at the horses. "They seem to think we're in no more danger than we were this morning." He reached forward to stroke the long neck of the warhorse. "I like to be prepared."

I nodded and led Fellowyn back to secure to the cart. I wanted my hands free in case riding became difficult. I didn't trust my limited skill to keep me seated if the sumpters didn't step together. "Why aren't the sentries affected by the mist?"

He snorted. "That curse was meant for you." He kicked Braknik into a quick walk, ignoring me as I gaped in horror at his back. Trion had sent a curse *just for me?* I swallowed hard, remembering the choking tendrils. For a moment, I felt my chest tighten, but Topher took up a fast pace to match Braknik and shook me from my thoughts. I took heavy, steadying breaths, and forced the imaginings back. "No. Stay out," I growled. "You can't come in."

I kept my eyes on the trees as we descended down into the valley and Vevesk fell out of view. I noticed changes in the trees that didn't bespeak of the approaching fall. Withered leaves, limp, shadowed underbrush, and a boggy smell that came from everywhere though the ground was dry and firm. "This forest is suffering," I mumbled.

"Now he notices," The Chosen One grumbled in reply, earning a glare at his back.

"Sorry I've been a little preoccupied looking for monsters."

"Being afraid, you mean." The hero cast a disapproving look over his shoulder.

"I'm doing my best," I retorted, managing to pull back my anger for the most part. "I'm not used to being terrified all day and night. We are opposed by the *god of strife*; I think it's justified."

He snorted. "And you were never afraid before?" He shook his head. "I would wager you felt fear every day of your life. Afraid of failure, afraid of disappointing your betters... afraid of being booted out of *yet another* guild."

I stiffened, my jaw going tight. Had Ethan told him? "What makes you think I'd—"

He gave a quick bark of laughter. "You know enough of magic, you *must have* been in the Wizards' Guild. Your writing is fine enough, you were certainly trained as a scribe." He fixed me with a pointed look over his shoulder. "Yet, you never speak of either without a *lot* of bitterness." He shrugged. "There's shame there. And anger. You've clearly never been in the Questers' or Heroes' Guilds." He chuckled. "Plus, you're *very* annoying. And a fuck up."

"Hey!"

He checked Braknik to fall back beside me, and cast a smirk at me. "So, this is guild three, then?"

My cheeks burned with impotent anger at his surprisingly perceptive remarks, and my eyes cast down in shame. "Clearly, I'm not good at this either."

He pursed his lips, taking my comment as the admission it more or less was. "So, answer the question. Wasn't your life before full of fear every day?"

I glowered at the ground. "A different kind."

I could see his nod out of the corner of my eye. "Sure. If you fuck up now, people die."

I cast a half-hearted glare at him, but was shocked to find he was being sincere.

He shrugged one shoulder at me. "Fear for yourself all starts to feel the same after a while, be it shame or bodily harm," he admitted. "The edge will come off of it, and you'll ride it through the danger."

I huffed out a deflating sigh. "Riding it out will not make me better at this kind of work. I mean, I've only been doing this for a little over a week, and I can already tell I'm no quester."

"Have you accomplished nothing?"

I frowned, staring down again. "Well... I suppose saving Marlo... healing Rshavin. Even just *helping* you do those things was more meaningful and impactful than everything I've ever done the whole rest of my life." Amazingly, a tiny flower of pride bloomed in my chest, remembering the river man's gratitude and the merriment of the plague-free city.

"And that was all in your first week," he pointed out.

"Sure," I said. "But a better equipped Tiberius—"

"Stop there," he cut in. "I'm going to help you help yourself."

I looked up in surprise at his interruption. He generally didn't care if I berated myself; in fact, he usually joined in.

"I think what you're really worried about is not being enough, not *helping* enough." He raised a brow, and I conceded with a reluctant nod. "Here is a revelation that made my work a *lot* easier."

I sat up, attentive, excited to learn the rare jewel of advice from The Chose One.

"All you can do... is all you can do." He gave me a pointed look, and I gaped at him.

"That's it?" I asked, incredulous. "That tired adage is your best advice?"

He laughed and nodded. "It's tired, because it's accurate." His gaze swept away from me, over the trees. "We do our best, and sometimes people die, it's true." He shrugged. "The ugly truth is: those people most certainly would've died if we'd never shown up in the first place. So what if we only save some, or even just *one*. Every life we save is one that would have been lost. And every life could be a dozen down the road."

I contemplated the simple but deep meaning of the concept. "One becomes many? How?"

He chuckled. "Do you know how many thousands yet live because I'd saved their parent or grandparent?" He smirked over at me. "You keep saying you're a coward... but you're here. You showed up." He nodded back the way we came. "And you might be terrified of your own shadow, but you don't run and hide." He shrugged. "That's what matters. The rest you'll learn."

I looked down at the reins in my hands and contemplated his words, both the sincere deference in them and the genuine merit they contained. I was not good at fighting, but *much* to my surprise, I had been willing to stand my ground. Perhaps he was right; perhaps I would acclimate to the fear and use it to hone my senses and reflexes as he had. "I suppose... everyone has to begin at the beginning."

He clapped me hard on the back, sending my teeth rattling. "There you are! Exactly right! You're a babe!" He chortled merrily at my expense, but at least it wasn't mean spirited. "You'll grow into it so long as you don't quit and run away."

I gritted my teeth, but I'd become so accustomed to his insults and brashness that the compliment came through and took the bite out of my anger. "In retrospect," I grumbled. "I haven't quit *anything* yet, just failed out."

He nodded. "Which is why you've a fair shot at this in spite of being terrible at it."

I didn't even bother to glare, turning my attention to the sickly vegetation around us. "Such a large area," I commented.

He nodded. "And as you pointed out, this has been creeping out of the foothills since at least last fall."

I shuddered. "How are the people not ill?"

"Likely," his somber gaze caught mine. "They are."

I listened, but still could detect no living sound save the clomping and snorting of the mounts. "Have they no game, no crops?"

He lifted a shoulder. "We will have to ask them when we arrive. Likely, they've been surviving on what comes north for trade."

"One of the merchants I spoke to in Rshavin said he'd stopped making this run." I immediately regretted not asking more questions to determine when the trade to Vevesk from the south had dried up.

"I heard the same."

I thought about the fishermen to the south and the villagers falling ill to poisoned meat. "They can't be hauling fish from the lake, likely for longer than Rshavin, being closer to the source of the poison."

He nodded. "T'will be a miserable place, to be sure. Men in this state will be quick to fear and temper. Be wary."

I absorbed the wise advice and found myself checking the hilt of the dagger at my waist.

The rest of the ride was relatively uneventful, save for the continual decline of the forest. We were able to see the break in the trees long before we reached it, the branches and brush were so decayed. We became accustomed to the boggy smell, but it never went fully away. It was like a living thing that permeated every thread of fabric, every inch of skin. I was thankful when it ceased turning my stomach, but appalled at the thought of sleeping and eating while immersed in the stench.

The tree line was a sudden break, a thick row of dead sticks reaching into a bleak sky. The land loping down into the small valley was churned from digging and peppered with fresh stumps. Where the land leveled out, there were no crops. Though I could clearly make out plot divisions and tilled soil, not even a persistent sprig of weed poked up from the dark, dry land. All around the lake, bare earth stretched into the trees, and no animal sign or sound could be detected.

When we passed the farmhouses, neatly fenced by dead trees, they looked deserted. No smoke rose from the chimneys, and no movement shifted the sun-bleached curtains.

"No one has lived here in some time," I pointed out, indicating where one roof had begun to sag from neglect.

He nodded. "Even if one could coax a farmable crop from this tainted soil, it would sicken anyone who ate it."

My stomach knotted in sympathy for the townsfolk. How had they endured amid such difficulties? "They must be starving."

He shook his head. "If there are people here, they are not so desperate yet as to flee. I think perhaps so many have died from pestilence, it left enough stores for the others to survive for a time, even after the merchants stopped coming."

His words descended upon me like a heavy weight, and I couldn't help but suffer a touch of the despair these poor villagers had undoubtedly come to feel. How could we hope to help them? In Rshavin, we had cured the river and the fish, but *everything* was sickened here. The earth, water, and air were all poisoned, and there was only a fraction of the population the bloated port-city boasted. Was the clustered, terrified handful of townsfolk remaining in this cursed town enough to help The Chosen One heal the land? "What can we do," I found myself muttering.

The hero glanced over at me, his expression as grave as my hopes. He huffed out a deep breath and lifted his face to the sky. "Skalah has led me here; there must be a path to follow."

I shook my head. "I will have to let my faith in you lead me to faith that Skalah will show us the way."

He flashed me a broad grin. "There is hope for you, yet!"

15. He Was a Portly Man Who Stood Alone on a Well in Vevesk

Despite the vacant outskirts that made the village seem deserted, the moment we were within range, we could hear a cacophony of mingled voices carried on the wind from the center of town. We could see a pack of agitated people on the main street long before we, ourselves, were noticed pacing along the thoroughfare.

"What are they doing," I mumbled to myself.

"Town meeting," The Chosen One responded quickly. "If they are wise, they're discussing fleeing the pestilence here."

I frowned over at him. Just a moment ago, he'd said Skalah had sent us. "Do you really think that is their only recourse?"

He shook his head and set his shoulders proudly. "It was until *I* rode into town."

As we neared, we were able to make out voices in the din. There were countless pleas for guidance and demands of action directed at one haggard, portly man standing on a chair next to the town's central well. He had one hand raised in a desperate and ineffectual attempt to calm the crowd that was growing increasingly animated. His fine clothes hung from his frame as if he had once been even larger and had not had them re-fitted. All the same, he seemed significantly healthier than the several hundred lean, gaunt townsfolk who had packed in close to him.

Genuine fear was starting to drain the blood from his face when he looked up and locked eyes with the stern and indomitable hero beside me. A flash of hope washed over his features so drastic and palpable that more than a dozen faces turned to follow his gaze. Voices died down and an eerie, suspicious stillness fell over the harrowed crowd. For a moment, the motionless tableau seemed surreal, like the illustrations that accompanied articles about pestilence in the books I'd been reading.

The Chosen One squared his shoulders. "We must be careful," he quietly advised. "It will not take long for them to realize our cart contains food."

I grimaced, and a tremor ran through me. It had not occurred to me until just then that we were riding directly into a throng of starving, desperate citizens. Our horses were likely the only healthy animals they had seen in many months, and our many rich-looking boxes undoubtedly contained the very things they needed most. Eyes were starting to track toward the sumpter horses behind us, and the crates beyond.

The Chosen One moved with such speed and efficiency, all eyes were drawn instantly to him as he vaulted onto his saddle. With expert agility, he stood upon Braknik's back, the warhorse keeping steady pace without guidance. "People of Vevesk!" he boomed, rattling my teeth. The crowd almost fell over themselves to break way before him, and a wide path formed clear to the well and hapless ruler clutching one of the support beams of the watering-hole's canopy. "Know you my name?"

Only the sound of scuffing and rustling as the townsfolk repositioned themselves greeted his—frankly terrifying—inquiry. "I say again!" He thrust his arms out in a grand gesture to welcome adulation, and his eyes fixed on the doughy ruler, whom I quickly assumed must be the mayor. "Know you my name?"

The man stood up taller, his fear melting away beneath the hero's unfailingly comforting confidence. "T-the Chosen One," he replied, his voice growing louder with each syllable. "My good people! The Gods' Chosen is among us!" Heads swiveled back and forth, the silence breaking first into incredulous muttering, then excited cries of praise and hope.

The Chosen's grin could have lit a cavern, and he let out a masculine bellow that sent my heart thumping with awe in spite of myself. The crowd responded with a deafening cheer and descended upon us like a hoard. Hands reached out to touch his legs, his horse, his cart. My internal shift from the inspiration he commanded to horror of being crushed was nauseatingly swift as the pack of people pressed against my outside leg and pushed Topher into Braknik's flank. Topher tossed his head, his eyes wide, and his white teeth flashing. The warhorse beside us showed remarkable restraint and neither bit nor danced, keeping his feet and head with significantly more dignity than I kept mine.

"Hold!" The Chosen One commanded. That single, deafening syllable somehow struck the crowd mute, and Braknik shouldered one scrawny fool into a pair of onlookers. "Make way for my man and me!" The dumbfounded townsfolk parted again, this time forming a much narrower channel. Hands still reached out to touch us—mostly him—but the hysteria had been expertly culled.

I marveled at the grandmaster hero's control of the crowd and cast a glance over my shoulder at the horses and cart behind us. We'd picked up a handful of young travelers, wide-eyed boys and girls who didn't seem to blink as they drank in the glistening armor and waving blond locks of the great hero. They didn't appear to be riffling through the cart, so I let the sumpters bear them forward with our rich haul.

We reached the well and the waiting mayor without further overt molestation. With one mighty step, The Chosen One climbed onto the canopy of the rickety structure, lifting himself even higher above the crowd. The canopy swayed and creaked, and I sucked in my breath, praying to Skalah that it held the staggering weight of the hero in his armor for as long as this performance required. Falling on his ass would not instill the much-needed awe and support of the townsfolk.

Unaware of his own peril, the great hero lifted his arms again. This time a cheer instantly rose up. "Good people of Vevesk!" He called again. "Know you my name?"

They roared, his many titles ringing out with overwhelming enthusiasm.

He held himself tall, grinning, and nodded his approval. "Know you why I'm here?"

Another deafening volley of replies filled the air. I made out a few exclamations of "heal us," "help us," "save us," and "gods' sent." All of which he took in with a deep, prideful breath and an all-encompassing nod.

"I have been called by your noble ruler," he announced, motioning to the chubby man on the chair. "The gods have deemed your need great, and I have come to answer your prayers!" Another cheer filled the street, and The Chosen One outstretched his arms to soak it in. I tried to remind myself he wasn't just being an arrogant ass, though I was certain that was no small part of this display. "I have much to discuss with your leader, but prepare yourselves, for tonight, we will *feast*!"

My stomach immediately knotted at the declaration, and my head swiveled back to the cart so quickly, my neck cracked in protest. Screams of desperate hope and anticipation pounded against me as the crowd became an undulating sea of bodies in motion. Some leapt, some danced, some scurried off to presumably spread the word to what few citizens were not gathered there.

The Chosen One stepped back to Braknik, and dropped down into the saddle. He motioned to Fellowyn and swept his hand toward the wide-eyed town ruler with a frown of impatience directed at me, clearly expressing his expectation that I should somehow have read his mind and have already been in motion. I pushed forward, letting the sweaty breast of Topher part the people enough for me to pull the vacant palfrey alongside the mayor. The portly man awkwardly climbed from the chair into the saddle, gushing a hurried thanks. When he seemed stable, though he was quite a far ways from reaching the stirrups, I looked to the hero for instructions.

He glared with obvious irritation, and nodded to the mayor. "Ask him!" Though there was no possible way I could have heard the town's ruler over the din.

I leaned the other way and shouted. "Where to?"

The mayor gestured a quick, shaking hand forward, and The Chosen One kicked Braknik into a surprisingly quick walk given the pack of the crowd. Those that didn't make way were brushed aside by the large warhorse. Though the monstrous animal snapped and shrieked his indignation at countless people, he shockingly refrained from biting anyone. I wondered if he was actually behaving himself, or if he sensed the townsfolk were likely also tainted by the necromancy poisoning the land.

We did not have to ride far before I could make out the mayor's house, the only two-story building on the west side of the street, nestled close to the bay on the backend of a modest estate. Though it was not much to my eye, having passed through many large and opulent cities, it was the nicest building on the main strip. I glanced back to make sure our cart still followed, and noticed quite a few more had climbed aboard. The sumpters were not struggling to pull the load, and the stowaways weren't looting, so I let them be. There were even a few eager youths ineffectually pushing the load from behind, and nearly the whole town followed in our wake.

The Chosen One followed my gaze, and his face broke into a wild grin. He twisted in the saddle, lifted an arm into the air, and bellowed out the first few words of one of his most energetic ballads. I recognized it as one that was very well known and joined in. By the time we'd reached our destination, the crowd had taken over. They sang and hummed through the verses with gusto, and the hero laughed like a child at every bawdy expression.

We rode into the carriage house, followed by our caravan, and half a dozen servants came out to take charge of the horses. I was shocked to see such a large staff, given the state of the town, but didn't complain as they took over the task of guiding the beasts and ushering out the interlopers.

When the carriage house doors closed, I spun to the hero, my frustration boiling over. "What were you thinking?" I quietly snapped. "Feeding this town will exhaust the last of our supplies! We've no hope to recoup them, and have a long journey back." I took a breath to go on, but his hard eyes stuck the words in my throat. Anger I expected, confronting him in front of others, but his palpable disappointment stabbed straight through me.

To my surprise, he didn't say a word, but merely slid from the saddle and strode to the cart where three young faces poked up from the crates and trunks. They'd evaded the notice of the servants by hiding, and now watched the great hero with shining eyes. He reached up and plucked a young girl from her perch, drawing her across his shoulders, and she giggled with hysterical glee. The two boys wriggled down to follow The Chosen One into the house, and I sat dumbfounded atop Topher.

The children were sickly and rail thin, their cheeks sunken and their eyes dark. I felt disgusted with myself for saying we should keep the food when both The Chosen One and I were well fed and enjoyed the health of the gods' blessings. I huffed out a quick, shamed breath, and let a servant help me down. "I will need two men to help me unload some of these supplies."

I spent the next hour directing what could go and what needed to stay, keeping only the sparest of rations for me and The Chosen One. Somehow, though I knew the hero would complain of hunger and the lean meals, he wouldn't cast a single word of blame to me.

A servant directed me to a small entertaining room when I was finished, and I found the hero and the mayor sharing wine from one of our casks, the children sprawled around on the floor listening to their conversation. The Chosen One cast me a dark look, and I bowed my head in supplication. "I apologize," I immediately offered. "I was out of line, and *of course* we should share our bounty with these poor people." His look of surprise gave me the tiniest jolt of satisfaction, and I turned my attention to the mayor. "I've directed your people to the supplies we can spare. Do you have sufficient staff to prepare the feast?"

The portly man blinked, and his eyes rimmed with moisture. "Truly?" He turned to The Chosen One. "Oh, thank you! You've no idea what this means to us!"

The hero planted a huge hand on the man's shoulder and nodded magnanimously. "Of course. My man will see to the details."

I opened my mouth to protest. After all, I needed to hear what news the mayor was sharing about the state of the town, but the hero cast me a curt look and jerked his head toward the door. I sighed and headed out. I would have to garner as much news as I was able from the staff while we worked.

"First the animals started acting strange, coming out of the woods at odd hours and attacking people, unprovoked," I supplied as The Chosen One stripped unceremoniously out of his clothing. Per usual, he didn't seem particularly embarrassed by his own nudity, so I just gathered up his road-soiled garments and turned away. "They looked sick, smelled foul, and were afflicted with horrific sores and eerie white eyes."

"Undead," he supplied, and I nodded my agreement. "Like the beavers and the rat-things."

I nodded again. "Stoats. Yes. Apparently, however, *West* Vevesk reported the animal attacks many months before they noticed anything amiss here, and long before the water and river became tainted enough to begin affecting the fish."

"West Vevesk?" he asked, sliding into a steel basin of steaming water with an obscenely loud moan of pleasure.

I sighed and sifted through his trunk for a set of fine clothes that would suit the impending repast in the modest manor. "Yes, it is nearly three times the size of Vevesk, and is the center of trade for the mountains to the north and the farmlands to the west. Apparently, when most people refer to Vevesk, they actually mean *west*. It's on the far side of the lake, north and west of here, and accessible by ferry or barge." I glanced over to assess the progress of his bathing and frowned. He'd not even started soaping yet, and we were running short on time. "There is a road around, but it would take two days and the ferry is only a few hours."

He grunted and slid further down into the water, closing his eyes. "They have a temple?"

"Several, and a few of the major guilds. Scrivener and wizard at least." I walked around, scooped the forgotten bar of soap up from a nearby table, and held it under his nose until he opened his eyes. He scowled, but took the soap from me and began lathering. I returned to his things and inspected his finer boots to be certain they did not require polishing.

"Tiberius, bring the tweezers," the hero ordered. "This hair is driving me insane."

"They stopped sending the ferry across the lake when the other town began reporting pestilence, but West Vevesk continued to send the occasional ferry and road merchant for a time." I located his grooming kit and held it out, keeping my eyes averted.

"No," he snapped. "I can't see it, you'll have to."

"Have to what?" I had a sinking feeling that I would hate what he was going to require of me, and I wasn't disappointed. When I dared a glance, he was peering at his reflection in the water, flaring his nostrils at himself. "Absolutely not," I quickly countered. "There's a hand-mirror on the—"

"No." He looked up sharply, his expression a confusing mixture of anger and something considerably less flattering on him. Was it embarrassment? "You'll have to do it."

I glared. "You can't be serious. Certainly you are capable..." His eyes tracked away from mine, and his face fell into a sulking expression of shame and frustration. I growled and stalked several feet away. "Why?"

He crossed his arms and glared at the wall. "Just do it."

"Tell me why, and I will," I insisted. "Tell me why you can't pluck your own hair, why you would need another man to do it for you."

His glare hardened, and he turned even further away from me. "I just..." His eyes closed, and he chuffed out a breath. "I just can't do it."

For a long minute, we each held our ground. The chime of a clock in the hall broke the silence, and I sighed. "We're running out of time." I opened the kit and located the tweezers. "To be clear, I feel this is beyond the border of absurd."

He gave a sulking grunt and tilted his head back, closing his eyes. He pointed to his right nostril and crossed his arms again. There was, indeed, and exceptionally long, dark hair curling around to the front of his nose. I reminded myself that I'd cleaned up rotting blood and dealt with foul-soiled garments; there was no reason for me to feel nauseated at this simple grooming task. My mind in the right, focused state, I plucked the hair, shuddered, and dipped the blades into the water to clean them.

The Chosen turned away to sneeze, and then began lathering in subdued silence.

I cleared my throat and quickly picked out my own garments for the night. I did not have time to bathe and help the hero prepare, so I stripped down to my trousers and wetted a towel with the bathwater. I held my hand out for the soap, and The Chosen One looked at me for the first time since admitting he couldn't groom himself. He stared at me for a long, uncomfortable moment, looking over my bare skin as if assessing something.

"What?" I snapped, gesturing impatiently for the soap. "I need to clean up, and it's the only bar they provided."

He handed the soap over and started rinsing his arms in the now, blissfully, murky water. "You're really different than my last man," he said. "He was a rail."

I snorted. "Just now realized that? Ethan's clothes were fairly uncomfortable until I lost some weight on the road. Now they're just too long and tight in the, um, tight in a few places."

"Ethan?"

"Your last assistant."

He grunted and went back to rinsing, apparently finished with the conversation. I let out a slighted breath, lathered the soap against the towel, and scrubbed the worst of the road-dust from my skin. "Think you can dry yourself, so I might finish cleaning up?" He shot a glare at me, and I lifted a hand. "Sorry for the tone. But the question was in earnest. Can you dry yourself?"

He rose up out of the water without warning, and I quickly looked away. I grabbed the towel left for him on the table and held it out until he took it from me. I used the water from the tub to finish my own ministrations while the hero toweled off. I was happy to see he'd put on his own underpinnings when I was ready to see to him.

"What else did the cooks say?" He held his arms out for me to begin dressing him.

"Oh, yes." I'd gotten distracted by his neediness. "They also said people started getting sick, but not in the same way as the animals. Fever, rashes, delirium."

He paused and raised a bemused brow. "Pestilence," he mumbled. "Strange."

"Yes," I agreed. "But this plague is resistant to wizard healing."

He turned abruptly toward me, and the button I was trying to secure slipped out of my fingers. "A *magic* plague?"

I readjusted his shirt and started anew. "I had already begun to tell you: they stopped sending the ferry across the lake for fear of spreading the plague when the pestilence showed up, and thus far have had no signs of the terrible illness here."

He frowned and scratched his chin. "If it were catching, it would already be here."

"I agree. That makes me think it's either based on something specific to West Vevesk, or perhaps it has a range that does not reach across the lake."

I took his subsequent grunt as one of agreement.

"From what the servants here have heard, those who did not take sick sheltered in inns, temples, and the guildhall, and barred the doors. Those who did take sick cloistered in their homes." I retrieved his trousers and held them out. "Apparently there are a great many still living, but a frightening number died almost immediately."

He grunted again and took the pants. "You need to find out as much as you can about West Vevesk."

"I've already made some arrangements. I've sent a messenger to call upon a previous resident of the town to give me an idea of the city plan. They don't have a guildhall here, but all the town's records are kept here in the mayor's house. I have been granted permission to seek out whatever I need. They asked that I return what I take, which is good, because I do not have the time to copy the documents I might require."

"That is certainly true. We leave after the feast, tonight," he replied.

I stared in shock, his vest suspended in my fingers. "What?" I cried. "*Tonight?*"

"Yes." He met my gaze as if what he said was perfectly reasonable. "The mayor's nephew owns the only barge left in town. He has offered to take us."

"That's not enough time!" I shoved his vest into his hands, not caring if he caught it or not. I rushed to my trunk and hurriedly pulled out quills, ink, and scrolls. "This is impossible!"

He stood and watched me, clearly not comprehending my panic. "What are you doing? We have to be at the feast in a matter of moments, and you are not even wearing your tunic."

I cast him a scathing glare. "I won't be going to the feast," I snapped. "I will be in the basement with as many literate servants as I can find, trying desperately to locate a map of the region and anything pertinent to the plague and undead infested town we're heading into *tonight!*"

His brows shot up at my tone, but he didn't seem particularly offended. Not that it mattered to me at that moment in time if he was. I jerked the too-tight tunic over my head, gathered up my supplies, and rushed out. He just watched in stunned silence, the vest still hanging from one of his wrists.

The mayor's records were blissfully well organized, and the middle-aged messenger was actually the man who was responsible for their keeping and knew how to find what I sought. When he returned with the elderly gentleman who was a previous resident of West Vevesk, I was able to send him to find what I needed while I interviewed the elder. I had nearly completed a rough sketch of the city streets and landmark buildings when a heaping plate of food arrived, complete with utensils, buttered bread in a basket, and a glass of wine. I stared at the rich repast in shock, and looked up to the lovely girl who had delivered it. "Um, thank you."

She smiled and bowed her head. "I was instructed to ask if you require anything else."

"Oh, um, would you be able to secure a quantity of safe water for us to take with us? Or perhaps something fermented, like wine or beer, any grade?"

Her dark eyes glittered when she bobbed her head, surprised by the request but eager to help.

"Oh! And thank the mayor for the food. It was kind of him to think of me."

She smiled again. "I shall, but it was The Chosen One who asked that I bring you a plate and see to your needs."

My mouth dropped open before I could think about how inappropriate it might be for me to show shock that he would think of me at all. "Oh, yes, of course," I quickly corrected. "I intend to thank him, myself. I only meant to thank the mayor for being so gracious a host."

Her smirk told me I had not recovered quickly enough, and she bobbed her head once more before she departed.

The records keeper and old man were watching me when I turned back to my work. "Oh! I am keeping you men from the feast—"

"My grandchildren are very weak," the elder cut in. "I am too old to venture south, and my children and wife have all been taken by illness." He shook his head wearily. "The great hero and you are our last hope. I will gladly stay and help as much as I can."

I smiled at him. "But no need to go hungry, Hamon." I looked toward the messenger. "Forgive me. Would you see to getting a share of the feast for you and this good man." I nodded to the elder. "And your grandchildren? Were they able to come?"

Hamon shook his head. "They are with a kind neighbor."

I glanced at the messenger again. "I think The Chosen One and your mayor have already seen to it, but could you remind my master that we intended to be certain food from this celebration was taken to those too ill to travel to the mayor's house?"

"I shall!" He grinned and stood. "All of the records you requested are on the table over there, in order of the list you provided."

16. They Say When Trouble Comes Close Ranks, and So the Villagers Did

The sun had set long before we could clearly see the far shore, which had only ever been just a distant promise of land across the great expanse of lake. The flat-bottom barge, fueled by a limp breeze, drifted steadily forward. Its uninspired progress was an ominous portent to what we expected to find in the sister-town Vevesk had not had dealings with for several months. The Chosen One stood at the prow, his intent gaze fixed on the water and his hand well seated on the pommel of his gods-given sword. Though I tried to ignore his vigilance while I hurriedly read what little I'd learned about the cursed town, his motionless attention made all of us tense. His unyielding focus commanded silence from the already anxious crew. It made the stillness of the water and the long, dark minutes stretch into almost unbearable eons.

Braknik snorted, his head on a swivel, and the sumpters hitched to our much lightened cart danced often, balking at nothing I could see. I heard one man muttering about ghosts upon the lake and another whisper a prayer for a friend on the approaching shore whom he suspected was already dead. No one wanted to be there, but they were desperate for the relief the great hero promised with his very presence.

Though I was taut as a bowstring, nothing worthy of my imaginings happened during the long hours on the boat. My jaw ached, and I realized I'd been clenching it for a majority of the night. As we neared the dock, it became apparent there were no lights anywhere near the water, and the dock had been long abandoned. The captain began giving quiet orders for how to unload their cargo, and us, as quickly as possible, already eager to be away from the cursed shore. He caught me listening and cast an apologetic look in my direction, but didn't cease his anxious preparations.

I glanced over my shoulder to the wagon, confirming visually that the trunks were secure and the horses still hitched properly. The journey across the lake had not been taxing, but the horses had been far from still. All looked well enough, and I let the deckhands take charge of the beasts. The animals seemed skittish and far too eager to get onto dry land, and I didn't relish the idea of being bitten, kicked, or dragged.

The moment I stepped out onto the dock, I noticed the stench. I quickly determined it was rotten animal flesh from both land and lake, baked in the sun for a day or more. The Chosen One observed the motionless buildings and streets from the boat, his shoulders going rigid. I nearly vomited. The deckhands made gestures to their gods and muttered prayers as they hurriedly unloaded the supplies Vevesk and the Chosen had pooled together to relieve the quarantined town. Next came the animals, and without coaxing, the coursers and spare sumpters surged forward until their feet touched solid ground. The other horses were led next, carefully held steady by many hands to keep them from rocking our cart off of the gang plank.

The fierce destrier, who had not been unsaddled in case of need, would allow no one but the Chosen to touch him. Even when the hero took his reins, he snorted and stamped his feet against the deck, flashing his teeth at the air. Then his eyes suddenly went wide with alarm, and The Chosen One instinctually pulled himself onto the horse's back. He let out a battle roar, and rode the beast from the ship. Braknik vaulted clear over the plank, landing on the dock with a cacophonous clatter of hooves, and made for land at a gallop. The Chosen One, his entire posture intense and focused, heaved on the reins. The horse slid and half-spun to a halt on the dirt dockside road, coming to an impatient and nervous stop. "Something is amiss," the hero called to the captain. "Have your men ready."

A breeze blew in from the city, bringing a much stronger wave of rot, and my stomach churned violently. I dropped to my knees and leaned over the side of the dock barely in time to direct my mostly digested remains of the mayor's feast into the water. When my tear-blurred vision cleared, I shifted my eyes away from the foul that was drifting away.

A face looked up at me from beneath the water.

I screamed, threw myself backwards, and vomited again, this time all over the weathered pier. Behind me, The Chosen One barked at the destrier, and its hooves pounded back up the dock. In one swift movement, he leaned down, seized the back of my tunic, and pulled me across the saddle. Without pause, he turned the fierce beast and returned at a full gallop to shore. We were on dry ground before I realized what he had done, his reflexes and immediacy to action further stunning me.

"There are dead in the water!" a deckhand screamed.

"Take your crew out into the deep of the lake," The Chosen One ordered, his eyes never resting as he scanned the shore, buildings, and water. "Drop anchor there for the night." He glared at the crew who were still craning to look into the water. "Go! Now! Watch over the sides. If someone tries to climb in, cut the anchor loose and row to save your souls!" The deckhands ran back to the boat, even before the captain had time to voice the command. They shoved off the dock with frantic haste. "Leave at highest sun if you do not receive message from us by then," the hero shouted after them. "Take no one into the boat but me or Tiberius. Understand?"

"Aye," the captain called back. "Gods be with you!"

"What is happening?" I managed to choke out through the jarring of the nervously-prancing horse, a saddle horn in my ribs, and my acid-hoarse throat.

"Don't move," he ordered when I tried to slither down off the saddle to relieve my side. "Pray to me," he muttered, his head swiveling this way and that, watching the darkness around us.

"What?"

"Pray *to* me, like a god," he repeated impatiently. "Pray for me to save you." His tone was different. Intent, focused, and sharp like a naked blade.

I craned to look awkwardly up at him, sudden fear threatening to choke me. Certainly he *would* save me? "You're not going to leave me *here*!" I blurted out. "You could have left me on the boat; it would've been safe—"

"No!" He glared down at me. "Just do it! Use magic."

I shook my head, not comprehending through the swell of my terror. All the same, I bowed my head, called upon my power... and hesitated. I wasn't sure what to say. I had never spoken in a common tongue with magic before. I had no idea what would happen if I did. "Oh... great and powerful Chosen One. I pray you spare this humble soul." Once started, the words poured out of me, fear lending truth to my plea. I *was* terrified, and The Chosen One was the only thing that could protect me in that horrible place. "I pray your sword is swift, your fury biting, that you may save this simple man. I pray your gods' blessings keep you safe, that you may protect this town and fight back the evil that has come to these waters!"

I realized light was shining through my eyelids, and I looked out over the landscape. It was lit as if we held a dozen torches, and I squinted up at The Chosen One, who shone brilliant against the night sky. "What... ?"

"Light of Blessing," he answered, his eyes flowing over the town around us and then down at the water. "Sometimes, when creatures of darkness are nearby, I can call upon it to fight them. It takes a prayer of power, and I have none."

"Creatures of darkness... nearby?"

He nodded, lowering me to the ground. I started to protest in spite of my discomfort, but he shushed me. "I need my sword arm free."

I did as he bade, though I was shaking so violently my teeth chattered when I closed them. "What do we do now," I asked, my eyes fixed on the eerily quiet road ahead of us.

"We stable the team, and hopefully wait out the night at an inn."

I looked up at him. "But you said..."

"There is mystical pestilence here, and there are creatures of darkness nearby. We need daylight; I *need* the sun." His eyes flicked to me. "Do you know where the inn is?"

I nodded, numbly.

"Climb onto the cart and lead us there. Prepare to take cover between the trunks if there is trouble."

Though every noise and shifting of light made me jerk in the seat of the wagon, miraculously, nothing attacked us. The reek of the city was terrible, but I soon became accustomed to it, and only a strong breeze would churn my guts. The Chosen One didn't seem bothered by the smell, and I wondered if he was somehow immune to it. Perhaps the Blessing of Rosy Nostrils. When I rode the team into the carriage house, no one came out to take it. I threw the reins over a picket rail and slid from the saddle at The Chosen One's instruction.

"Leave them. We'll care for the team come morning. I need my heavy armor, and you need your trunk," he said, looking over his shoulder at me. "Put my armor in a sack. I can carry it."

I quickly did as he instructed, my hands shaking. He slid from Braknik, led the warhorse to a stall, and threw the sack of armor I'd gathered over his shoulder. I quickly stowed what I thought I might need into the top of Tiberius' trunk. The Chosen watched over my progress, and then took one handle while I took the other. Though he was able to lift his side with one hand, it took both of mine and all my effort to keep pace with him. We paused only to allow me to secure the carriage house doors. When we reached the inn, the door was closed and barred. I shifted to free a hand, since The Chosen One had none, and banged on the door. "Open up!"

The viewer door slid open, and a brute of a man peered out at us, his eyes full of fear and nervous violence. Then his gaze tracked to The Chosen One's glowing visage, and after a dumbfounded moment, he jerked open the door. "Come in! Come in, please!"

The great room was filled wall to wall with dirty, frightened villagers. They were quiet, sullen, and packed in so tightly, there was no room for anyone to lie down. They all leaned against each other and the walls, huddled in fear, waiting out the night. Their demeanor suggested this was a common occurrence, and I wondered how many nights the entire town had huddled together in cramped spaces such as this. Was every gathering place, guildhall, and temple swollen with these refugees of their own city?

Whispering immediately started, frightened at first, then hopeful and excited. At long last, The Chosen One had come to save them. After somberly looking over the crowd of desperate souls, the great hero shifted to set the trunk down. "Tiberius," he said. "Help me with my armor. I will sleep while you question the villagers."

Exhausted from travel, lack of sleep, and unspent fear, I started to protest; then I realized the plan had genuine merit. He needed rest in order to fight whatever this was, and we needed answers as soon as we could get them. With so many already there, it was a perfect opportunity to interview many people in a very short span of time. I wearily nodded, and together we armored him. He made his way to the back of the room, nodding assurances as he passed, unbothered by the many hands that reached out to touch him. A chair was quickly offered, and he set it in the corner, dozing sitting up while I asked the innkeeper and townsfolk what evil had befallen their town.

Several hours later, The Chosen One clapped my shoulder, waking me from the unplanned nap I had apparently been taking on the bar. My head jerked up, and his grip tightened to keep me from toppling from the stool. I expected him to berate me for sleeping, but he merely took the stool next to me, which had been vacated in his honor. The innkeeper was by the door, muttering tired well-wishes to the departing people as the barest hint of light shone through the front windows.

With a flush of embarrassment, I wiped up a puddle of drool and tidied up my notes, which had been scattered by my abrupt wakening. The innkeeper had apparently set out a few mugs of watery ale and an even more watery porridge for us. The hero's contained a small cut of hard cheese and a few pieces of dried meat propped up on the rim of the bowl. He stared at it for a moment, his lips pursed in thought. I cringed at the impending complaint and demand for better fare, but it never came. Instead he ate with his usual gusto, looking up at the occasional villager who whispered "gods bless you" to him, and nodded his responses.

I drank my breakfast, ignoring the spoon that had been set beside the bowl, and skimmed what information I'd gathered the night before. The recountings were all much the same, but I might have forgotten a detail in my weariness. The innkeeper ushered the lingerers out, bidding them to go home and insisting the grandmaster hero and his servant needed the space to prepare. He closed but didn't bar the door behind the last man, and returned to refresh our ale.

I shook my head, but The Chosen One quickly spoke up. "Of course he'll take it, Wald." He gave me a hard look. "The water isn't safe here. Drink it."

I sighed and conceded. "Yes," I offered to the innkeeper, "thank you, Wald."

The barkeep filled our glasses and leaned against the bar, looking down at the tidy script on my papers. "Never thought so far out here I would ever live to meet The Chosen One," he confessed. "Though I've been praying day and night for the past year to do just that."

I cast him a sympathetic glance, and then turned to the hero. "The trouble started north of here, so far as anyone knows. Some hunters took down a deer around the foot of the mountain, and when they retrieved their arrows, it was '*alive and not alive.*'"

The Chosen One wrinkled his nose, nodded his acceptance to a second bowl of porridge, and drank it while I continued.

"They did their best to dispatch the diseased animal, but it resisted death, though it looked and smelled as though it were already long dead," I continued.

"I thought it started with vampire stoats," he argued.

I sighed at his impatience. "The hunters were far to the north and hunting large game at the end of last season, before the snows came down from the mountain and made travel more difficult. Since it was their last opportunity to stock up before the winter, they did not return to town immediately after the incident with the deer and encountered no other anomalies on their expedition. It was the first event *chronologically*, but they didn't arrive back in town to share their stories until after an entire wave of cursed stoats passed through West Vevesk and then Vevesk."

He grunted, though I suspected I would need to explain it again. Unencumbered by questions, I continued. "These stoats attacked people, biting anything that moved, but not eating. The townsfolk thought them vampires because their mouths were covered with blood, and their eyes and fur were white."

"Undead," The Chosen One supplied, and I nodded my agreement.

"Those who were bitten developed severe infections, and several died. That is when the Wizards' Guild sent word down the road to garner assistance."

"Why didn't they deal with it, themselves?" the hero asked, nodding to a third bowl of porridge.

"There *is* a guildhall here with a decent number of wizards, but most of them had never encountered anything like this. It is a simple country town that also happens to be on a healthy trade route. Most of the wizards here were specifically trained to aid crops, eliminate pests, heal, and the like. They sent for aid from the Heroes' Guild in Rshaven, and a handful of heroes responded."

The Chosen One pursed his lips. "And?"

I sighed. "The winter held them back, and they arrived after the thaw. By that time, the animals were all acting strange or sick, and even the livestock had become sickly. They slaughtered all of their herds, keeping the meat of only the healthiest and burning the rest. New crops wouldn't take, and what the forest was producing proved to be foul and toxic to consume. Many had taken ill and died from eating tainted food, and their bodies were burned out of fear."

"But what about the *heroes*," he insisted, impatiently.

"I'm getting there," I snapped. "With spring came the new pestilence, and the heroes arrived shortly after the first few dozen had died from this second illness. Only a few days after crossing the lake to West Vevesk, they also took ill and died."

The Chosen One stared at me, then at the innkeeper, who nodded gravely. "That was more than six months ago," the hero said.

"Aye," the innkeeper agreed.

"Why are there fresh dead in the lake?"

Wald scratched the back of his neck. "A lot die in their homes, and people are afraid to go in to deal with them. Some go mad and wander wherever a madman does, in all directions. Now, the dead pollute the lake as well," the innkeeper said. "So many died so quickly, and keep dying. We're afraid to touch them. We're afraid to go into the water."

The Chosen One glared down at his ale. "We are certain, then: undead *and* mystical plague?" He fixed me with an intent stare. "What manner of necromancer is this?" he demanded.

"I believe it is a wizard," I answered. "These things cannot have happened coincidentally at the same time in the same place. From all I've read, the pestilence caused by necromancy taint presents as what we've seen in Vevesk and downstream: loss of appetite, sickly appearance, low body temperature, significant malaise, skin lesions, infections or necrotic flesh, and finally death. The second wave, consisting of pustules, high fever, and sudden death without any of the former symptoms, is definitely a different malady. Someone is creating both great works of necromancy *and* a mortal pestilence." An impatient gesture of the hero's hand encouraged me to expedite my findings. "There have even been several sightings of what can only be undead or animated dead *humans*. The plague *might* have been created to better prepare already tainted victims to be animated by necromancy, and a specialized disease such as this would require more nuance that I would expect from any manner of spell caster below master wizard."

He grunted, pursing his lips in disgust. "Wizards can be killed," he said. He looked at the innkeeper. "Where are your wizards? Is there one of the guild nearby, or must we go to their hall?"

"All dead," I answered. "They were the first to die from the second pestilence."

The innkeeper nodded. "When we went to them, we found their offices full of dead, their homes as well. Dead for days. Men, children, women alike. Every last one."

I nodded. "Whoever is behind this expertly eliminated the only threat to them in West Vevesk with a very specialized plague. I think the city becoming ill, just as the animals becoming undead, was a sloppy consequence of excessive and inefficient magic." I could tell from the hero's expression that he wasn't following me, so I opened my notepad to a blank page and drew a small circle. "The wizard *intended* to kill the members of the Wizards' Guild," I drew arrows outward from the circle and a sloppy outline around those. "But they killed their families and released a plague in the wake of it." I drew another small circle. "They rose undead, for whatever purpose," I drew arrows and an outline. "And the animals nearby were affected as well."

"I'm familiar with necromancy tainting life. But is it possible to *accidentally* infect an entire town with a disease?" The Chosen One asked. "How does *one wizard* do this much harm?"

"With a lot of power and a good deal of help," I replied somberly. "How does *one hero* do so much good?"

He glowered. "So it is as we have suspected, the god of strife and misery," The Chosen One confirmed with unwavering confidence. "I have dealt with him before; I can do it again. *He* is why my

Blessing of Light waned so quickly last night. He is why the sun struggles to shine today."

"The god of darkness," I whispered, and glanced to the windows. "It is only just morning, perhaps the—"

He shook his head. "The sun is well up, I can tell, but my god is far away."

A cold, sick fear settled in my gut. "How can we fight a wizard with the strength of a *god* on his side when yours is away?"

"Butev sent me a dream last night," he answered. "I am *meant* to be here. My sword was created in a forge blessed by her fire. It is the only weapon in the world that can cut through a god's curse. I would not have been sent if there was not a path to follow."

I looked at the great sword on his hip. "Forged by the goddess of forges," I muttered.

His fierce blue eyes fixed on me. "When an evil wizard calls upon Trion to raise an undead army and poison an entire town with deadly pestilence, The Chosen One is called to cleave his skull in two."

"You know the layout of this town," The Chosen One said after his fourth and final bowl of porridge-water. "Where is there a temple of Skalah?"

I frowned. "You wish to pray?"

"I require prayer," he answered. "To fight undead if we encounter them. Stronger than you can give."

"Down the main road," Wald supplied. "Head north, and it will be on the left. Large building; you will not miss it."

"Thank you," I supplied. "For everything." I placed a bag containing a Gold Crown on the bar and headed for the door.

"Lead the way," The Chosen One instructed. "Find me a priest to bless my sword and helm."

Though not thirty minutes before, I'd seen a packed common room empty through the inn's doors, the street was vacant. "Huh," I muttered.

"What?" the hero asked, sounding only partly interested in my thoughts as he scanned the street through the thick fog that had risen. As we walked, his armor creaked and banged, but even that noise was muted by the foul-smelling damp in the air.

"I thought people would be clamoring to see you, that they might be crowded around the inn to cheer."

He paused, and his face twisted in thought, an unfamiliar and decidedly constipated look for him. I had to choke back a chuckle at the obvious effort it required. "You're right," he muttered, looking around with what could only be an expression of disappointment. "They should be."

I mulled over it for a moment. "Perhaps it means the streets are unsafe even during the day."

He shook his head. "I bet it's the fog."

I raised my brows. "Because it's ominous?"

"Many reasons," he replied, heading toward the carriage house. "It conceals the enemy, so you cannot be sure from what direction danger may come. It also conceals sounds."

"So if an undead is wandering around, you can't hear it." I nodded my agreement.

"Many people don't realize the god of strife uses it to confound, but they can sense the ill will in it."

My frown deepened, remembering the choking mist that had nearly killed me the morning before. "Is this meant for me? Another attempt—"

The Chosen One snorted. "Not everything is about *you*, Tiberius."

I snorted in return. "You're one to talk."

He turned to glare at me. "What do you intend to mean by th—"

A body speared out of the mist-shrouded shadows of the carriage house at a full sprint, bowling the hero to the ground and out of sight into a thick patch of white. I heard the air explode out of the hero's lungs even over the crash and clatter of his armor, and a moment later, his roar of anger and frustration practically shook the earth. I started toward the sound of his voice, but froze when I heard his sword scrape from its scabbard. I didn't want to be cleaved, and he likely wouldn't be able to distinguish me from his attacker. "It might be a villager," I warned.

"It was, once!" he snarled back.

The sword whistled through the air and impacted with a meaty, wet sound. Cold, foul liquid sprayed across my face and chest, and a disembodied head rolled awkwardly to a stop on the toe of my boot. Pale, vacant eyes stared up at me as the gelatinized remains of badly decomposed brain-matter oozed out of the neck hole and down my foot.

I threw up so hard and so violently, it shot out my nose. I choked and puked again, sobbing in disgusted, befouled, sinus-burning misery. It took a full minute before I'd recovered enough to begin clearing my nose and throat from a more rational approach. When my watering eyes finally cleared enough to see, The Chosen One stood over me, his lip curled in dumbfounded disappointment. "Gods, man," he growled. "Try not to puke yourself to death while I'm saving your life."

I nodded at the well-deserved rebuke and mockery. My throat was in no condition to offer a verbal response, so I gestured lamely at the shadow nearby that was undoubtedly a corpse.

"Animated," he supplied, pursing his lips at it. "It had to run past you to find me. It was sent. Our arrival has not gone unnoticed." He started walking again as if someone hadn't just tried to murder him with a dead man, and I mutely followed.

When we were in the shelter of the carriage house, I was able to choke out a garbled inquiry about his wellbeing.

"It's well, just a scratch." He pulled his arm to his chest so I could see a crimson streak running down his armor from an unseen gash in the hard-to-reach gap between his right arm and torso, beneath the pauldron. There could have been only one approach to find the opening, and only when his arm was raised.

"Do you think it was aiming?"

He barked out a laugh. "No chance! Lucky strike. A jagged finger bone caught me when he bore me down."

I looked away and swallowed back a sudden wave of queasiness. The Chosen One gave me a reproachful look, and I threw up my hands in supplication. "Hey! At least I care enough that my stomach turns at the thought of you receiving an injury."

Apparently mollified, he just nodded and went about scanning the stalls for more walking corpses.

"You will need to stitch it. Get your tools from the chest."

My feet locked in place, and I stared at his retreating frame. Only when he disappeared into the farthest stall and I was alone with my back to the doors did I rush to join him. "I... I can't do that! I've *never* done that before. I don't think—"

He narrowed his eyes at me. "If I can take a decomposed finger in the armpit, *you* can stitch it up!"

I was too busy choking back another gag to argue. It took me a few breaths to recover. "Gods help me," I whispered under my breath.

"I second that," he replied without looking over at me.

Quite a lot of grunting—and the hero frequently pretending to have "something in his eye"—later, we were able to strip his armor down to the hauberk and slide him out of the chainmail shirt. His padding was soaked from the armpit to the waist with blood, and I swallowed hard. I had no idea how I was going to stomach piercing his skin with a needle. "This was just reaching the carriage house," I muttered. "What happens when we go to face a greater quantity?"

He glared over at me. "Skalah will *protect me*, as always, from the cursed and undead," he snapped. "We go to his temple that his priests may aid in that protection as best they can."

I let out a breath at his confident and condescending reproach. "I'm sorry," I conceded. "Of course you will have the strength when it is needed."

"*We* will," he snapped. "You also carry the blessings of the gods. You'll need to start showing it soon, or I won't be able to protect you."

I grimaced and turned toward the cart to keep from responding. I suspected the tools I would need were in the inn with my trunk, but I riffled through the remaining containers none-the-less. After a fruitless search, I glanced over to the hero. "I... I think the doctoring supplies are in my trunk."

He glowered. "Then go get them."

I halted with one leg dangling off the edge of the cart. "You... you're coming with me, right?"

He shook his head grimly. "What confidence do you think it will inspire should one of the few remaining villagers see me like this? Stripped and bloody?"

My heart started pounding, and I slid the rest of the way to the ground. My mouth hung open to argue, but the sour taste on my tongue spoke of my mind's unconscious acknowledgment of the decision to go... alone. My feet carried me to the door while I considered what it meant of me that I had accepted this task before I'd had time to really weigh the risk. Was I becoming brave? Or was I developing a reckless death-wish?

A whisper issued from the back of my mind: *Or is it faith?* I abruptly stood straight, my chest swelling with something akin to awe. Was I growing to believe I might be worthy of the gods' attention? Was I really beginning to have *faith* that they would see me through, as the great hero believed? After all, how many times had Tiberius followed The Chosen One onto the battlefield and come out unscathed? "Many," I whispered. "Countless."

I took a deep breath. "All the same, I could help myself a *little*." I sprinted with all my strength for the door of the inn. I crashed into the wood, fumbled with the latch, and practically fell through. I slammed the door shut and collapsed against it, chest heaving.

"What has happened?" The Innkeeper rushed around the bar, his voice pitched in fear. "Is The Chosen One all right?"

I looked at him and let out a semi-hysterical laugh at his lack of concern for *me*. "Yes, yes," I quickly answered. "All is well. I just need to get some things from my chest, and I felt a little vulnerable without the Hero of Men at my side."

He nodded knowingly. "Yes, I understand that. I do not dare these streets when the mist rises. You must be very brave." He gestured to the hall leading off the main room. "I had your things taken to the finest room. It will be his for as long as needed." He cast me a bolstering smile. "Last door on the right."

I quickly went to find my trunk, hoping he didn't notice my flush at having been mistakenly called "brave." Rather than riffle around, I pulled out the most recent of the Tomes of Tiberius and skimmed for a recounting of a battle. It took me a few minutes to find one in which the hero had been harmed. Ethan's tidy script gave a detailed description of the hero's minor wounds, and even commented that battles often took place at some distance from town. He wrote of his distaste for stitching human flesh, and detailed which tools he'd used. Apparently, there existed a small doctoring kit for just such an occasion.

I found the leather bag tucked into the side of my trunk and nodded to myself at its portability. It had loops to run a belt through as well as a strap that could be attached to throw over my shoulder. I did the latter, and quickly scanned the box for anything else I might wish to carry into battle should we be attacked again. Then I drew my dagger a few times to remind myself that I had it and how to reach it.

I returned to the carriage house at a run, shocking myself with how readily I threw myself into the mist with minimal mental preparation. I burst through the doors, and blinked in surprise. The air was perfectly clear, as if the fog had been held back by a pane of glass. It must have receded when I was inside the inn. Rather than dwell on it, I found The Chosen One where he loitered in Braknik's stable. He'd worked off his padding and stood shirtless, his side a smear of blood. I noticed with a sigh of relief that none of it looked particularly fresh. Accelerated healing was apparently part of his blessing, and the blood flow had stopped on its own.

He glowered at me. "That took a while."

"Yes, sorry." Though I didn't feel particularly regretful at the time I'd taken, it seemed easier than getting angry.

The Chosen One looked away and focused on petting the horse's muzzle, his jaw clenched as I quickly cleaned the wound with a sterilizing agent. I noticed with a stomach-churning jolt that something protruded slightly from the injury, and my mind worked out it had to be a splintered fragment of finger bone. I quickly focused my eyes on the kit I'd hung from the stable wall, and took deep gulps of breath as I located the large tweezers. I had to not think about the fact that the finger had belonged to a rotting corpse... and it was stuck into a man's living flesh. I reminded myself I *could* do this; I just had to pretend it was a wooden skewer in a morsel of rare beast. Without giving myself time to think further, I turned, gripped the shard with the tool, and pulled it free.

The Chosen One roared in pain and threw his elbow back, catching my jaw. I spiraled to the floor, and the fragment of bloody bone skittered into the hay. "Damnit, Tiberius!" the hero bellowed. "That hurt!"

I clapped my hand over my jaw, smearing fresh blood across my cheek. The whole side of my face instantly erupted in pain, and my vision blurred. I blinked and shook my head in a vain attempt to clear it, my quick anger even more quickly gone. In all honesty, I had been careless and paid for it. "I'll work on my bedside manner later," I grumbled. Though stars still spun in my vision, I set about cleaning the wound again. I pressed the bandage to the puncture for a moment, earning another growl of pain and barely dodging a second blow of the same elbow. "Hold still!" I snapped. "This is hard enough without you bucking like an unbroken stag!"

He glared over his shoulder at me, tears glistening in his eyes. "Isn't there something you can put on it? Some kind of tonic?"

"Yes, but the object had to be removed first." I met his gaze until he looked away. I actually suffered a pang of guilt at his pain and reminded myself he'd received this injury ridding the world of an undead creature. If the abomination had been permitted to roam, it undoubtedly would have killed or infected an innocent villager. "Sorry," I finally said, and my anger at my throbbing jaw waned entirely. "I will try to get better at this."

"Good! See that you do," he snapped, awakening my irritation once more. "I don't want another two years of the Tiberius before the last one."

I could see his muscles visibly shudder at the memory, and a strange thought struck me. No matter how bad I was at something, at least one of my predecessors had been worse at it. It was a strangely comforting idea, and I found myself smiling. "Don't refer to me in the third person." He grunted, and I caught a smirk before he buried his face in the warhorse's neck as I finished the grisly job. I pretended I was mending a water skin, tied off the two ends, and stood back to scrutinize my mediocre work.

At some point in the coming months there would undoubtedly be times when The Chosen One took a day or so off. I would visit local infirmaries and universities to get some hands-on experience with cadavers or more appreciative patients. For the time being, I would have to remind myself that as horrible as treating wounds was, having them treated was definitely worse. I would find a way to suck it up and be strong for the Chosen's sake.

17. The Towers of Skalah Aspired Above the Morning Mist

    The Chosen One rode his destrier in full armor, Braknik wearing all of his barding, and the two creaked ceaselessly against the silence of the ill-fated day. I rode close behind on Topher, leading Fellowyn, the two coursers in case a quick escape was needed, and a pack-laden sumpter. We'd decided since the temple was near the north end of town, we would set out for the mountains from there.

    Long before we were in reach of the temple, we could see the tall spires even through the thick fog, brilliant against a backdrop of dark, overcast sky. I smiled in spite of the horrific ride through corpse-town, inspired to hope by the bright beauty of the temple steeples, apparently untouched by the darkness that had befallen West Vevesk. When we approached the palace of worship, we could see a cluster of townsfolk milling about just in front of the impressive stone structure.

    "Why don't they go in?" I asked, unease settling into my stomach as I watched the shadow figures drift through the mist. "Surely they could have easily gathered *inside* the temple to greet you." My stomach knotted, and I realized why the scene set my hair on edge. Nothing about their shuffling steps spoke of the bone-chilling fear that gripped every living person we'd seen since descending into the valley.

    "They can't," The Chosen One answered as his sword hissed free of its scabbard. Braknik's eyes rounded with excitement as he snorted and chewed at his bit. "Creatures of darkness cannot enter the temple." With a bark of sound from the hero, the ferocious warhorse exploded into movement. They charged into the small crowd, a plume of upset mist billowing after them.

My stomach leapt into my throat, and I jerked the reins of the four horses I guided, as much to steady myself as them. The fog ahead of me boiled with movement. Braknik's clattering hooves and both the hero's and horse's armor were almost deafening as they clanged and echoed back at me from all directions. Only then did I realize I was trapped inside a stone courtyard with at least half a dozen undead and no hero in sight. What had once been a man rushed out of the endless white, his dead eyes fixed on nothing as he changed directions and reached for me.

I screamed like a frightened child, and all five horses joined in the chorus. I was nearly pulled from the saddle by the reins of the other mounts, and only my terror-strengthened grip on my own saddle horn kept me astride. I hauled on the reins of the spare horses and looped them around the pommel, wriggling and kicking with my heels in an attempt to get Topher to turn. He did in time to snap his teeth closed just short of the corpse's fingers.

"Topher! No!" I jerked his reins to discourage a second attempt, mortified the beast might become poisoned by the necromancy that animated the dead man. I kicked at the foul creature, and it made no effort to elude me. My foot, stirrup and all, sank into its chest cavity with a sickening crack of shattered ribs and a spatter of rotten organs and ichor. My terror escalated to unimaginable heights in the span of one heart beat when I tried to jerk my foot free and only succeeded in pulling the undead into the flank of the horse. Topher bucked, I kicked, and the undead reached around my trapped leg toward me... though all he could reach were my ass and my groin.

My manhood in danger, the dagger flew into my fingers before I realized what was happening. Screaming, I stabbed with all my strength down into the top of the corpse's head. The blade slammed home with such force, the guard punched a groove into the half-exposed dome of skull bone. The creature let out a noxious belch and collapsed, dragging my leg downward with it. My foot popped free just before I could be unseated, and I jerked my hips to direct Topher away from the fallen foe. Shuddering, panting, and my ears ringing with fear and battle fury, I looked around for the next charging shadow in the mist. That was when I realized all I could hear was the frantic hooves of the horses in my charge.

The Chosen One, sword in hand not two horse strides away, stared at me with a grin that split his blood-spattered face ear-to-ear. He let out a deafening battle cry that ended in a bark of laughter that could have cracked the sky. "Well done, Tiberius!" With a twitch of his knees, Braknik trotted toward me, and the hero bent down to jerk my dagger free of the undead man's skull. He handed it back, handle first, still belly-laughing.

I flushed an even brighter scarlet than the battle heat had risen in me, and stuttered out a rush of words born of fear and unspent need to act. It took a moment to realize I wasn't making any sense, and fell silent, looking to the ground. Dismembered and decapitated bodies in all states of decay lay in a swath between us and the temple doors. A chill passed through me, and I felt the blood drain from my face. One of them was a young girl, no older than thirteen.

The hero's eyes followed mine, and all of his mirth dissipated.

"Clean and sheath your blade," he muttered. He turned Braknik toward the temple doors. "Inside," he ordered.

I numbly did as he directed. I followed, and thanked the gods the horses knew to step around the bodies.

The Chosen One rode straight up to the massive doors and banged on them with his armor-clad foot. "In the name of Skalah and the gods' chosen warrior, open these doors!" His voice boomed in the now-empty courtyard, every resounding word sending my heart skittering anew. After a pause, he kicked and shouted again. Finally, a clang and the sound of a wooden bar sliding away could be heard. A frail old man and a young boy peered out in fear. "Are you the head priest here," The Chosen One demanded.

"The *only* priest that yet lives," the old man answered. He drew the door back and The Chosen One rode directly into the temple.

Not knowing what else to do, and not wishing to be left alone in the courtyard that had become a graveyard, I rode in leading the four spare horses with me.

As the young boy barred the doors behind us, I could hear The Chosen One's voice ring out in the cavernous space. "Bless me, Priest, with all of your power! I go to fight the darkness that has fallen upon your town!"

While I waited for the priest to levy every prayer and blessing he knew upon The Chosen One, I knelt at the altar and prayed. I prayed till tears of fear and desperation coursed down my face. I had never been so frightened before in my life, and I had never felt such rage and need to do violence. In those shaky moments of quiet after the horror that had preceded, I was lost like I had never been before. I was woefully out of my league and terrified that I would fail The Chosen One and these desperate people. Two men went to face a wizard and a god? I thought about the bloated face in the water, of the bodies in the streets as we rode past, slumped and rotting where they fell. Some were babes cast out of kitchen windows, some were old women. I wept harder.

"Please, great god of joy and light," I begged. "Please save us. Please bless your Chosen One with the strength to defeat this terrible foe. Please protect us as we go into the darkness to find the *disgusting reptile* that has done these terrible deeds."

After a long span of time, the old priest laid a hand upon my shoulder. I looked up at him, unashamed for once of my tears.

"He is not just the god of light and valor; he is also the god of misery," he reminded me. "He is both sides of the coin."

My gaze tracked to the starburst windows above the altar, now dim with little sun filtering through the heavy overcast. "There should be misery enough in this place to please him, then," I replied bitterly.

The priest shook his head. "No, no. He neither brings nor celebrates misery. He *is* misery. And he is joy... he is *life*. He is all the passions that give life its meaning." He smiled kindly down at me. "You honor him with your tears, your compassion, and your courage. He will bless you this day, I am certain."

"I hope so. We need all the help we can muster."

"Then you do not hope in vain." He squeezed my shoulder before releasing it. "The Chosen One is prepared, and he has asked all of us to meet in my office to talk."

I followed the priest down a narrow hall to where the hero and the acolyte sat in front a modest wooden writing desk. The Chosen glowed as if a brilliant beam of light shone upon him, and his expression was set in a stern frown.

"I'm sorry," the boy was saying. "I do not know of any wizards who survived."

"Nor I," the priest offered as we entered. He took the seat behind the desk, and I took the chair the boy vacated for me.

"I was afraid of that," I answered. "Perhaps we can find him another way. Raising the dead requires grave soil, a lot of it." I looked between them. "Any defiled graves?"

Both shook their heads, and the priest answered. "Just a few whom we buried who did not stay that way. No dirt was taken."

"Caves," I asked. "Dirt that has never seen the light of day can sometimes be used."

"Yes!" the boy exclaimed. "There are some caves! Over near the marshes to the north. I went there once as a boy with some friends."

"Does a wizard live there?" The Chosen One asked.

"Perhaps," the boy said. "I didn't think of him before. A lord lives there. Not *our* lord, but *a* lord, by the look of his manor. I believe he does practice magic, that I am aware."

"So he *is* a wizard?" demanded The Chosen One.

"I am in the Scriveners' Guild," the boy supplied. "I helped organize the records for the Wizards' Guild when they moved their library a few years ago."

"And that is how you know this man is a wizard," I asked.

"I did not say wizard," he quickly responded. "I didn't have access to their member roster, but I *did* deliver some records to him at that time at the behest of a master wizard." He pursed his lips. "Records and items of a sort I imagine only a wizard might find use for."

"Workings," I asked.

"Yes, and more... spells and cryptic things. I did not read them. I only observed as they were gathered and from where in the library they came."

The Chosen One leaned forward. "I don't know that I care for your hesitancy to tell us of this lord in the first place."

The boy frowned and quickly shook his head. "Until now, I assumed if he was a wizard, he was dead like the others," he replied, his voice squeaking in alarm. "I knew *many* wizards. It wasn't until you mentioned the caves that I thought of the one man I knew who lived near them. I only met him the once, several years ago."

The Chosen One leaned away from him, but still seemed suspicious. "Where does this lord live?"

No amount of talk or promise of rewards could convince the young man to join us, but he did draw a crude map with landmarks to show the way. It didn't take long comparing his map to one acquired in Vevesk to estimate where the manor might be. It was already late morning when we set out. The reek in the town was strong, and the dense fog summoned by a lack of sun made the odor heavy and thick in the air. With the exception of the clomping of hooves and the ceaseless creaking of armor, the day was quiet as death. We could barely make out the houses, and only when the road transitioned from cobblestone to dirt did we know we had left the city.

"How long will the priest's blessings last," I asked when I could bear the silence no longer.

"As long as needed. Why?" The Chosen One grumbled, his eyes constantly scanning, his hand resting on the pommel of his sword.

"If I read the map correctly, we will need to make camp at least once before we reach the manor."

He grunted, and fell quiet again. I thought about the undead that had attacked the hero in town when we were arguing, and I decided to suffer the silence rather than distract him. I also tried to keep watch, looking frequently behind and to my side of the caravan. Everything looked murky and washed out, and my eyes quickly tired. I didn't become drowsy as had happened before Vevesk; the road was narrower, and every branch that reached out of the mist made me jerk and reach for my dagger. It was a strenuous waste of anxious energy. I almost wished something would jump out at us, so I could release some of the tension in my shoulders.

"Noon," the Chosen announced abruptly, and I nearly jumped out of my skin.

"Oh!" I let out a tense breath and dropped back alongside the pack animal. "Lunch time, then."

"Not hungry," he mumbled, his pace not changing in the least.

I paused from my awkward rummaging through the sumpter's pack and frowned up at him. He had slurped down four bowls of porridge, presumably to keep his strength up for battle. The Chosen One did *not* skip meals. "Are you sick?"

"No," he grumbled. "Just not hungry."

I mulled over his words and contemplated the implications. He *had* gotten an undead finger in the armpit. "How does the injury feel?"

"Fine."

I nodded. One word answers. Fantastic. I sighed and gathered sufficient dried meat from what remained of our mostly depleted rations and filled a small sack with oats. I rode up beside the hero and held them out. "Here."

He glared at me. "Not. Hungry," he snapped.

"Too. Bad," I snapped back and pushed them into his chest. "You made me drink that ale to stay hydrated. You *will* eat this meal to keep your strength up."

He glowered back at me for a long moment. I thought he might yell, but he took the food, instead, and began eating while watching the trees.

I thought about what could have caused his loss of appetite and surlier-than-normal attitude. I remembered the face of the young girl in the courtyard, the one the hero had nearly cut in two and mostly decapitated. It took two attempts to swallow the food around the lump that rose in my throat. Maybe he was remembering that battle. It couldn't be easy for him to cut down all those villagers, even if they were already dead. I had been carefully not thinking about the man I'd stabbed in the head, because imagining him as anything but a creature made me want to sob or vomit. Or both.

The Chosen One tossed the empty sack at my chest, breaking my reverie. He forgot to glare at me when our eyes met, and I offered him a supportive smile. With a snort, he returned to watching the trees.

"I will start looking for a place to camp."

"It's too early."

"It will be dark quickly with this overcast, and this road is not traveled enough for regular rest stops," I reminded him. "We will need to find an opening large enough to pitch the tent before dark to give you time to bless it. It's our only hope of decent sleep tonight."

He grunted, but didn't argue further. I let out a breath and decided not to take his anti-social attitude personally. After all, *I* wasn't the one who went to fight a terrifying necromancer who wielded the power of Trion. To him, I was just there to carry his stuff and deal with the aftermath. I didn't blame him for not seeing me as an ally in the upcoming battle. In the past week, I had done nothing but prove how unworthy I was of the Questers' and Heroes' Guilds. I remembered the incident outside the carriage house and flushed with embarrassment. How could he rely on me when I was too busy being a coward to help him during the fray?

Over the following few hours, anytime I could not make out the trees or underbrush through the fog, I asked The Chosen One to slow enough for me to check it for suitability. Nearly every time, one step off the road revealed the patch of bare earth to be too small for the tent. A few might have fit the tent, but had dead trees leaning dangerously toward the road or clearing. Daylight was already fading by the time I found a suitable area. It looked as though it might have been used for camping some time ago, and only the sickness in the land had kept it from becoming too overgrown.

"Perhaps it was where the hunters stopped on their way back to town from the north," I suggested, quickly setting myself to start a fire in the crude stone circle someone had created.

The hero grunted, dismounted, and stepped just inside the trees to relieve himself. The fire had taken when he returned, and I braved the woods next, rushing back the moment I was done. "Tent, then food," I said. "I want to give you time to work."

The Chosen One stroked Braknik's muzzle and watched the trees, not even bothering to respond. I could tell from the set of his shoulders that he was tired, likely even more worn than I was from the vigilance the day had demanded. Plus, he had also carried full armor and fought two skirmishes.

I pitched the tent in record time, even though going between the sheet and the nearby trees terrified me. When I was done, I saw the hero had relieved Braknik of much of his barding, and was hand-feeding him oats from a pouch. I cleared my throat to alert him that the tent was prepared, and went to ready the other horses for the night. None of the fare with us would benefit from cooking, so I was less concerned about its preparation than I was about getting the picket-line set for the horses before dark.

I ran back and forth from the pack horse to the tent to bring our supplies inside, and had the horses ready for the night before The Chosen One disappeared behind the far side of the tent. I rushed to his back, drawing my dagger and watching the trees. His gaze flicked to me between muttering of prayers, and I saw a glimmer of genuine appreciation before his attention returned to his task.

The blade quivered only a little in my hand, and I was able to watch the trees, listen to the wind, and track the hero's progress without losing my head. When the tent's blessing was done, I slid inside with a sigh of relief and set up our beds. I allowed myself the slightest moment of personal pride that I'd not done anything too embarrassing in several hours, and that I had kept watch over The Chosen One's back without becoming a blubbering coward.

I had our beds set up and our necessary supplies laid out before the hero joined me. I expected him to snap about the tardiness of his meal or the fact that I couldn't be bothered to cook it. Instead he just began undoing the straps of his armor. I didn't even try to hide my surprise as I rose to help him. "I'll have something ready to eat in a moment," I assured him.

He grunted and saddled out of the breast plate that could have easily contained two of me.

I frowned and helped him with the hauberk. "You've been quiet all day. Are you sure you're—"

"I'm fine," he snapped, glaring at me when his head popped out of the still-bloodied gambeson padding.

I allowed my fingers to linger on his skin longer than necessary, and decided he didn't feel feverish. He also looked hale, if visibly tired. "An undead did pierce—"

"For gods' sake!" He bellowed. "I've been blessed a dozen times over. I am *well*, you stupid man!"

The return of his rudeness in the face of my concern actually brought a relieved smile to my lips, and I turned away to hide it. "I'm afraid dinner will be much the same as lunch."

He grunted and dropped down onto his bedroll, stripping out of his shirt. He flopped back on his blankets without removing his trousers, and my concern awakened once more. He usually wasted no time stripping off his clothes and parading around the tight quarters of the tent in the buff.

I put together his meal and set it beside him. When he didn't move to take it, I cleared my throat, drawing his glare. "Eat it or I'll start annoying you with questions again."

That got the slightest hint of a smirk from him, and he sat up to glower at me while he quickly ate the meager repast. He half-heartedly chucked the sack at my head, and flopped back again. This time he wriggled out of the last of his clothes and slid under the covers.

"I should check your bandage."

"It's fine," he grumbled. "Doesn't even hurt."

I pursed my lips, considering how much effort I was willing to expend to force the issue. "Okay. But, I *am* checking it in the morning."

"Fine," he grumbled, crossing his arms behind his head and staring up at the lantern.

He didn't say anything else the rest of the time it took me to prepare for bed and tidy up his clothes and armor. I cast one last concerned look in his direction, which he expertly ignored. With an impotent shrug, I laid down. I felt safest with my back to the hero and my face to the tent's blessed canvas, and knowing he lay awake and vigilant gave me the courage to fall asleep.

I awoke with a start, my heart thumping hard against my ribs. It took me a few terrifying moments to realize the horrors that had roused me were trapped on the other side of sleep. I stared at the rippling canvas of the tent, and took long, deep breaths.

"Hear something?" The Chosen One asked, and I nearly jumped out of my skin.

"Gods!" I gasped, rolling onto my back. I clutched my chest and closed my eyes for a moment. "No. You scared me."

"Mm," he responded apathetically.

I glanced over at him. He hadn't moved in the least, though I felt as though I must have slept for hours. "Did I wake you?"

"No."

I nodded and rolled toward him. "Then you haven't slept, yet."

Another noncommittal grunt.

"Are you keeping watch?"

"No."

"So... then you can't sleep?"

He shifted for the first time to sneer at me. "*Obviously.*"

I sighed and rocked away onto my back. With the night terror chased away by a wakeful hero and a steady lantern, my eyelids grew heavy again. I was just starting to doze off when a thought jarred me alert. The Chosen One *needed* to sleep if he was to be effective against the foe we went to face. Earlier in our journey, he'd expressed concern this may be among the most difficult challenges he'd ever been tasked with, and that knowledge had never been far from my mind. Perhaps it wasn't far from his, either.

I glanced over to find him staring at the lamp once more, his eyelids drooping but not closed. If he didn't sleep, he would be weary going to face a truly dangerous adversary. I watched him for an obnoxiously long time, but he refused to acknowledge my blatant attention. I took a breath to ask him again if he was all right, but something else came out instead. "Once in the great, cold kingdom of Tersunia, there was a town so small it had no name." I surprised myself by voicing the inspiration before I'd fully committed myself to it.

He looked over at me, his brow quirked in matching confusion. After a moment, he pursed his lips and looked back to the ceiling. "I don't often hear tales from the north kingdoms."

I smiled at the unspoken encouragement to continue. "The villagers, whom every last one shared blood within two generations of the others, all simply called it 'Home.'" I gazed at the lamp, my eyes unfocusing as I concentrated on recalling the legend. It was a meandering sort of story that was more ridiculous than frightening. "Since they were all family, whenever a man or woman came of age to marry, they were sent into the world to quest for a spouse. Such was the case of Mary, the plainest girl, of the plainest family, of the smallest village in Tersunia."

When I looked at The Chosen One, his was smiling faintly, and his eyes were slowly drifting shut. His part in this ridiculous tale, was a little unflattering, but his character did get bedded quite often, so he likely thought it fitting.

"But she had great plans, for she sought a hero to be her mate. The only trouble was, Home had no troubles. So she went into the world with one thought in mind: find trouble so a hero would need rescue her. Unfortunately, Mary had three protective brothers, all of whom insisted on accompanying her to ensure her safety and an acceptable pairing. Thus, our story begins with Mary's quest to rid herself of her three brothers."

A snore cracked the air, and I smiled to myself, letting my eyes drift shut as well. I continued the story until the hero had been snoring rhythmically for some time. Only then did I let sleep claim me once more.

18. Somewhere in Opolchia, in a Place Whose Name I Don't Care to Remember

  The morning was as dreary as the two before. I was awake before The Chosen One, so I let him sleep as I studied the map and contemplated how best to carry the supplies previous Tiberiuses had brought into battle. It was not lost on me that my first quest with the great hero was to be among one of his greatest deeds. Other assistants had had time to familiarize themselves with the hero's needs and their own place in his routines. I'd had only eleven days, much of which had been spent in difficult travel with little opportunity to study outside of researching the challenges we'd faced along the way.

  I'd only brought the most recent tome with me on this last leg of our quest, and I used it to read up on how Ethan had assisted the hero in battle. I clearly possessed a greater magical gift than he'd had—amazingly—so he was limited to using objects and potions that only required activation. He was barely able to summon the light I'd maintained all night while on the boat, and he'd used bespelled items and workings whenever possible or else his own two hands. He heavily favored expensive workings, and was not shy about spending the hero's money whenever the opportunity arose, since all but the simplest and weakest spells were beyond him. Luckily, his small stockpile would surely prove to be a great help to me in the upcoming fight.

  I emptied all unnecessary items from my shoulder bag, hip bag, and component belt, and I gathered every tonic, working, and bespelled item I even imagined might be useful into one pile. I organized them in a way I thought I could remember, keeping the most important in the easiest to reach pockets, and stowed the rest of the precious items all over my person.

I was just finishing with my preparations when the Chosen opened one bleary eye and stared sleepily up at me. "Still here?" he grumbled. "I half expected you to flee back to the village."

I glowered obligingly, though I was strangely in a fair mood, as if I was somehow numb to the nightmare the upcoming day was bound to be. "It's yet dark. I'm waiting for daybreak before I tuck my tail and run yelping back to the city plagued by undead. *Alone.*"

He chuffed at me, and I thought I caught a glint of amusement. He aggressively rubbed his face and let out a series of disgruntled animal noises. I paused to watch him, my frown becoming more genuine. I was certain in the past weeks, I'd seen the great hero in every state of his "worst" that I possibly could. What I struggled to do, even after everything I'd witnessed, was see him as human, as just a man. Today was different.

In that moment, something about his demeanor, his lack of arrogant demands, brought to mind the vulnerable conversation beside the fire. I remembered the sadness in his eyes when he spoke of the Tiberius who had helped him face his most terrible foe. The Chosen eluded that he'd hesitated, had considered setting his sword aside, and it was his assistant who had reminded the hero who and what he was. "Are you scared?"

The Chosen One abruptly stopped, and parted his fingers to glare at me between thick digits. "Scared?" he hissed. "Did you truly just ask me that?"

My first inclination was to balk at his sudden anger, but I stood up straighter instead. "So much is expected of you, even from yourself." I pushed. "It's human to be scared when you are confronted with true horror and evil."

Quick as I'd ever seen him move, he sat up and hurled his pillow at my head. I was so shocked, I didn't have time to react, let alone evade. I was thrown onto my back, and it took more than a second to recover my wits as he bellowed at me.

"I'm The Chosen One!" he hollered. "I'm not some second-rate hero! One accursed necromancer doesn't merit a *second* of concern from me!"

I shook my head to clear it and pushed myself back into a seated position. I watched his face turn scarlet as he launched to his feet, and I quietly let him rant. I was somehow neither fearful nor surprised by his rage.

"Who are *you* to even *suggest* that I, the gods' chosen hero, would doubt my strength or their support in this quest? *I* am not the coward in this tent! Just because *you're* afraid doesn't mean—"

"I *am* afraid!" I blurted out, the truth of those words peeling back the strange calm I'd been in all morning to reveal the raw, wild storm beneath. My face must have looked truly insane, because The Chosen One stood there in seething nudity without interrupting. "In fact, I'm so *terrified*, I can't even register my brain." I let out a shrill, hysterical laugh. "You said the gods choose champions... and this horrible *nightmare* of a creature was clearly chosen by *Trion!*" I gestured to my bulging pockets and bags. "I have *no idea* how to help you, what I could *possibly* do to make any kind of difference—except maybe try really hard not to puke in terror the *moment* we get within view of the manor."

I laughed again, though it came out more like a sob. "Is it really so impossible to imagine that you might be maybe a *tiny* bit nervous, great hero not withstanding? When I am one faulty buckle away from *completely unravelling*?" My vision blurred, and I let out a shuddering breath. "I'm more afraid of the animal you ride into battle that I've been of anything. Now we're going to face... what? A—a man? A monster? We don't really know. Just that he is capable of *unimaginable* evil on an unbelievable scale!"

I let out the sob that had been choking me, and shook my head in shame. "I'm *scared*," I whispered and let my hair fall into my face to save myself from tying to make out his expression through the blur of my tears. "I'm terrified I'll fuck up, terrified I'll be eaten... or worse, mutilated into some ungodly monster to shamble around hurting innocent people." I huffed out a breath, and my spent passion poured out, leaving me feeling small and pathetic. "And terrified that you'll need me to do something or know something... and I'll fail *you*."

The Chosen One crouched in front of me, drawing my gaze. I quickly looked away from his nudity, but he unabashedly put a hand on my shoulder. I was so shocked by the gesture of comfort in spite of my unmanly display, I looked up at him, and was instantly awed by the expression of quiet calm on his features.

"You can stay in the tent if you need to," he said. "It's blessed. It should—"

I shook off his hand and glared up at him. "I most certainly will *not* stay behind while you go to fight Trion's champion! I might be a fuckup, but I'm still going to *try*," I snapped. "Weren't you the one who said showing up was what really mattered?"

A broad grin split his features, and I realized too late that he'd intentionally baited me. "It is." He stood up and began dressing himself. "One Tiberius never came within an hour's ride of danger. He always waited in the tent or the inn."

A thick swell of anger at the hero standing alone against unknown horrors squashed the last of my emotional outburst, and I clenched my jaw. How had such a despicable man been allowed to accept the blessing? After a long moment, I cleared my throat. "Don't use my name in the third person."

He grinned over at me, his eyes shining. I rose to help armor him, and we were quite for a long while, both engrossed in our own thoughts. I was grateful for the time to finish recovering, and even more grateful the hero chose not to mock my tears. After a moment I realized I hadn't checked the wound.

"Wait! Your side—"

"Healed," he quietly assured me. "I took the bandage off already."

I let out a breath and nodded. "The stitches were designed to dissolve when—"

"They did." He smirked over at me. "This is not my first time being sewn up by you."

I opened my mouth to argue that it actually was, then realized he'd meant previous assistants, and we both chuckled.

I tidied up the tent as The Chosen One looked out the flap at the dreary drizzle that had begun. "Leave everything. We'll come back here tonight."

"I was going to suggest that," I agreed. "We are very near the manor. If it's not the location of our necromancer, we can come back here and decide where to go next."

He nodded. I finished making our beds and looked up at the hero. I frowned at his somber stare into the rain. I wanted to ask him again if he was worried, but held my tongue. I simply waited until he was ready.

After a long time, he nodded slowly. "I was," he mumbled. "A little." He smirked and shook his head. "You reminded me why I'm here." He looked over at me. "Annoying as you are, you're no different than the villagers by the lake."

"What?"

"You're just a simple, frightened, sad little man."

"Hey—!"

"I'm here to protect *you*, as well." He smirked at me, his expression surprisingly candid.

I let out a measured breath and eventually returned the smile, though he was already looking away once more. With the return of his infallible arrogance, I noticed a firmer set to his shoulders. I realized then what I'd not been able to define earlier about the unease that had settled in my gut: his posture had changed. It had happened over a few days, slowly and subtly, and I hadn't consciously noticed. Unconsciously, though, I'd sensed a shift in his bravado from genuine to rehearsed. He'd been unsure, scared even, about our enemy and his ability to best it. The confidence he normally oozed had lessened, and the intensity of his assuredness hadn't comforted me in days.

He looked out into the bleak weather as if he could dissipate it with his mere will, and I once again felt the stirrings of awe that had given me the strength to face the horrors we'd encountered along the way. I had once promised him if I could not take comfort in the protection of the gods, I could find faith that the strength of The Chosen One would keep me safe. I hadn't realized he was faltering, but I had felt the loss of the living shield that stood between me and Trion. Now that the hero had apparently rediscovered his worthiness, I was bolstered by his very presence, as I had been many times along the way.

"Should we bring the horses inside the tent for protection?"

He snorted. "So they can piss and shit all over our beds?" He gave me a look normally reserved for adults ridiculing an ignorant child. "The priest didn't just bless my arm and my helm, he also blessed the horses. They should be safe from molestation while we are away." He looked me up and down as if deciding something. "We will leave the coursers here."

"But, if we need to flee—"

"You are only familiar with riding Topher, and Braknik is already faster than him, so neither of us would benefit." He nodded to the picket line. "Have them saddled and ready. If we must commit a strategic retreat to camp, we can have them ready as backup should either of ours go lame."

I nodded at the uncommon wisdom of The Chosen One. In many ways, he was such a simpleton; I sometimes forgot he had more than a hundred years of experience battling villains.

"Ready?" he asked, surprising me again with a lack of impatience in his voice, which I felt denoted some actual concern for my mental preparedness.

"Almost." I withdrew Tiberius' tabard from where it was neatly folded in one of the saddle bags.

"Why are you wearing that?" he grumbled, clear disapproval on his face. I had not yet read of a single battle where Tiberius had worn his tabard, and it had always seemed a strange omission to me.

I thought about it for a long moment, trying to find the words for how I felt. "Well, you go to hazard yourself, and granted in a best-case-scenario your foe won't live to recount what he saw—"

"He won't."

"Yes. But *I* and you will remember."

He snorted. "So?"

"So," I countered, irritated. "If I'm going to stand beside a great hero—"

"*Behind*," he corrected, and I growled.

"If I'm going to stand *behind* a great hero... I want to show how honored and proud I am to do so. Every time you draw your sword to defend the innocent and to destroy evil, I want to be wearing your banner. If anything should happen to me..." I swallowed hard at the idea. "I can think of no worthier symbol to perish beneath."

He cocked his head to the side and pursed his lips at me in thought. "Is this some sort of attempt to inspire me or... I don't know?"

I laughed and shook my head. "Surprisingly, no." I pulled the tabard over my head and secured it with the component belt. "We may have butted heads, and I still think you're an arrogant ass most of the time."

He growled at me.

"But you are, and likely will ever be, the greatest hero of men. Your deeds and character inspire others to be brave, present company included, and regardless of whatever words we banter, I will always respect that."

He huffed, still looking perturbed, but he gave a placated nod of approval. "Fine."

I chuckled at his overwhelming show of appreciation for the gesture, and pulled back the flap of the tent to look out into the steady, gray drizzle. My stomach churned at the idea of being saturated with rain from this poisoned land and born of the ill will of the god of strife. "Today will be remarkable," I muttered. "I hope I keep my breakfast down."

We trudged through a muddied trail that was long-overgrown from little use until we arrived on the almost-equally-overgrown road that would lead to the manor. The closer we got to our destination, the thicker the air became with the smell of rot and decay. The land was becoming increasingly boggy, but even that did not account for the stench. A heavy rock settled in my gut along with the certainty that this manor was indeed the location of our foe. As long as we had been uncertain, there was a sliver of hope that we wouldn't encounter horrible evil that day. With each passing moment, as the forest became more rotten and the stench became almost unbearable, we knew the necromancer's poison was leaching into the world from somewhere up ahead.

The Chosen One rode rigid, his eyes hard and searching. His hand never left the hilt of the gods-given sword, and every rustle drew his undivided attention. Ever mounting fear lent me a hyper-awareness that sent my heart skittering every time the wind rustled a decaying twig. I was actually grateful there were no animals; my chest might have exploded if I was startled by a bird fleeing the horses' hooves. My jaw throbbed from how tightly my teeth were clenched, and I was physically weary from tension less than an hour into our ride.

The drizzling rain gave way to a thick mist of choking stench that lifted into the air, obscuring the road and limiting visibility to a dozen feet. Luckily, landmarks provided by the novice priest proved accurate, and I was able to direct The Chosen One off the road onto a footpath just before the manor would be in sight. I imagined the narrow trail was likely carved by decades of staff traveling from a servants' door to the main road. It clearly had not been trodden in some time, but the hard-packed earth had resisted regrowth enough to allow our horses to pass single-file.

"Here," I muttered. "I think it's just ahead. We should stop here."

"Why?" he grumbled, his tone quieted to match mine in spite of his obvious irritation at the interruption to his progress. "Don't tell me you're too scared to—"

"Not now," I snapped. His eyes flashed in anger, and I sighed. "Just give me a moment."

His glare hardened and his every muscle oozed affronted impatience, but he waited for my direction. I got the distinct impression Tiberius did not often tell him what to do when preparing for battle.

I withdrew one of the precious tonics for bolstering magical strength and broke the seal, activating it. I drank it and almost immediately doubled over in pain, grinding my teeth as my guts twisted in protest. I had expected the painful side effect, as many workings designed to alter the body or magic often did, but this was almost blinding in its intensity. Somehow, I managed to keep from issuing much more noise than a groan. After an excruciating moment, it receded, and I was able to breathe again. As the effects dissipated, the working left behind a feeling of raw power unlike any I had ever felt before.

My magical gift was small, made only slightly notable by the Blessing of Tiberius, and I had never known how it felt to contain such energy within me. I knew it was not an amount that would impress a true wizard, but for my experience, I almost felt like a god.

Still drunk on the meager power of the tonic, I saddled Topher forward and placed one of my hands on the hero's sword arm and the other on Braknik's neck. Both man and beast bared their teeth and shifted as if contemplating biting me. The Chosen One gave a quick jerk at the reins to steady the irritable warhorse, and fixed me with a warning glare. I let out a breath, forced my irritation at his impatience out of my body, and closed my eyes.

I called on the power within me and breathed out, imbuing as much magic into my prayer as I could. "Great hero of men, chosen of the gods: may your arm be strong, may your sword be quick, and may your mighty steed carry you to victory. May you have an abundance of courage, strength, and cunning." I felt the energy leeching out of me, and I could see light gathering on the other side of my eyelids. I poured every ounce of my overwhelming fear and hope into each word. "I pray you vanquish this foe. Protect this humble, frightened servant, and save this land from the poisonous taint of evil."

When I leaned away, I felt light-headed from the drain of energy and clutched at the saddle horn to stay astride. The Chosen One quickly gripped my shoulder to steady me, and I glanced over, muttering a quiet thanks. He and Braknik both shone brilliant against the gray backdrop of a fog-swaddled swamp. His eyes were a little wide, and I thought I discerned approval and perhaps appreciation in his gaze.

"I just thought... I'm not much good at anything you might find helpful. I thought I might summon a light for you; this way I don't need to maintain it, and if I'm distracted or incapacitated, you can still see." I smiled faintly, thinking about his great dislike for dark places. "I held back enough to do several activations, so if we need a potion or a tonic, I can still be useful."

He squeezed my shoulder, and a genuine smile turned his lips. For a moment, I thought he might even say something appreciative or encouraging. Such things were apparently against his nature, because he simply nodded and turned Braknik away to continue down the path. The next several moments, though horribly tense with the expectation of violence, were somehow lightened by a lingering sense of comradery.

The manor was closer than I thought it would be. We came upon it suddenly, nearly riding straight into the stone outer wall as it loomed out of the mist. I looked down the stone face one way, then the other. "There is probably a servants' entrance near where this path ends. It must be somewhere around the side here."

"I still don't understand why we're not taking the front," he grumbled.

"You could demand they open up, but would you?" I smirked. "Dumb question: of course you would. But I doubt they would just open the door, and they would then have the advantage. This way, maybe we can catch them off guard."

He frowned but followed my lead. "I am not fond of The Chosen One *sneaking* into battle."

Thankfully, the building was not as fortified as a keep, and the outer wall looked more like it belonged to a sturdy, stone house than a fortress. I was grateful it did not seem designed to repel or out-siege an enemy. We followed the wall away from the main road and found a servants' entrance and a gate for a small cart on the back wall. I stared at the closed door. "I wonder if it's locked."

The Chosen One's destrier bombarded it with its hooves until the gate crashed inward. My heart almost stopped.

"Good," The Chosen One declared. "It's unlocked."

I clutched my chest, staring agape at him as I gasped for breath. "Clearly subtlety is not your strong suit!" I hissed, though being quiet at that juncture was pointless.

He laughed. "Please tell me you are not just now learning this."

I growled, following him as Braknik plodded into the dark hallway over the debris. "Remember, this lord could be innocent," I muttered, trying to see through the gloom after the meager light of day we'd been traveling through.

"Not likely. And if he is, he's certainly already dead," The Chosen One countered.

The hall turned into an empty courtyard with a well, laundry station, and empty chicken coop. It was obviously intended for servants' work. We crossed the enclosed clearing of overgrown vegetation, and the destrier kicked in another door on the other side, leading us into what appeared to be the main house. Though decrepit and ill-kept like an abandoned building, all the architecture, decorations, and furniture were of a fine quality, intended to impress. Soon we found ourselves trotting through empty halls and looking past ajar doors into dark rooms.

"Maybe it's abandoned," The Chosen One suggested.

"The floors have been traveled," I answered.

He looked down and noticed the clean path through the dust on the floor from passing feet. He let out a grunt and nodded.

We traveled the distance of the structure from back to front, through a stately, over-wintered great hall, and paused in the anteroom. Light poured in through the cracks around a set of double doors, and the destrier kicked them open into a large, enclosed courtyard. The reek of rotting bodies rushed in with a gust of air... and a hoard of undead men and women quickly followed.

I gagged at the stench, then seeing the charging mob of corpses, screamed like a frightened child. I jerked on the reins, and Topher, eyes rolling in terror, emphatically whinnied and backed away.

The Chosen One shouted back at me. "Stay close, you fool!" His destrier kicked and chomped at the foul creatures while the hero slashed and hacked until the air was filled with the disgusting shrapnel of putrid flesh and bone.

I screamed again, but managed to keep enough of my wits to kick Topher into advancing instead of retreating. I fumbled for my dagger, but had managed to knot myself up in the reins. The brief moment of immobility was perfectly timed to when one of the foul creatures wriggled past The Chosen One. My terror peaked at an unprecedented level, and a sound not unlike a dying cat wrenched from my throat. The destrier kicked backwards, and the undead's head nearly detached from a badly rotted neck, twisting and flopping forward. It advanced a few more steps, its skull dangling and bouncing from strings of black flesh.

I finally got fingers wrapped around my dagger when the monstrosity crumpled to the floor. The room was suddenly distressingly quiet, except for my embarrassingly loud gasping. I promptly twisted in the saddle and vomited, not entirely missing poor Topher's flank.

All around us and in front of The Chosen One, people in all stages of decay had been hacked and stomped into pieces. Both hero and horse were covered with putrid flesh that sizzled from the blessings laid upon them. The hero turned to grin back at me. "I counted twenty-eight," he declared, triumphantly.

I swallowed hard, and nodded. "Me too," I lied. I looked at the mounded body parts to my left and right and marveled that the hero had dispatched all of them before they could reach me. It was a good thing we had not been set upon from behind and that the hero was able to defend the small entry chamber. If we had come in through the wide, entry gates without confining walls... I shuddered at the thought and freed my dagger for use should more surprises await us.

The Chosen led the way out into a partially paved courtyard. In the center of an overgrown field, the ground had been dug up, dirt mounded all around it like a dark lip. A tunnel deep and wide enough for a mounted man struck downward at an angle until the floor of a natural cave was revealed.

"Do you... suppose this necromancer knew the cave was here when he made the manor," The Chosen One asked.

"Perhaps. Or perhaps what was inside came up and corrupted the lord and his servants."

"Do you think?" The hero scratched his head, looking as dubious about the suggestion as I felt.

"No," I admitted. "I think all of this was intentional. This whole manor was built for channeling power. I believe this man held the charade of an ordinary lord for only as long as he needed to. I think an army of undead creatures was always his goal, and I think he's just getting started."

"How's that?" He twisted his face at me in an expression I could only assume was bemusement. It would have seemed comical if his features weren't spattered with off-color blood.

I shuddered. "Because I have been paying attention to the layout and the hallways," I explained grimly. "There is intention in this structure's design, a diagram built into the stone, runes set periodically in the tilework." A wave of foul, unnatural energy belched up from the hole and parted around us like water breaking around the hull of a boat. I shuddered again. "This cave is the apex."

19. In a Hole in the Ground There Lived a Monster

The Chosen One's face was grim as he scrutinized the dark opening of the necromancer's lair. "You recognized a pattern in the building of the manor?"

"Yes," I muttered.

"What can you tell me?"

I was so surprised by his genuine request for my opinion that it mostly shook me out of the well-deserved, mind-numbing terror of the darkness emanating from the hole. "Oh, uh..."

"*Now*, man," he barked, earning my glare and successfully wresting my brain the rest of the way free.

"I'm trying to remember," I snapped. "I was only a white-sash. They didn't let me read the good books; I had to 'borrow' them without permission." I looked away from his bloody visage and concentrated on my late-night studies those handful of long, hard years ago. "They're like a conduit," I mumbled, picturing the layout of the manor in my mind. "Like tributaries to a river."

He grunted, but didn't share what thought had wriggled up from the echoing cavern of his strained understanding of complex magic.

"The runes we passed over seemed to have intent, to evolve the energy as it flows through the hallways, changing it into something... well, something more useful to whoever would want to inflict pestilence, pain, and death." I shrugged one shoulder. "I don't know enough to tell you more except that basic guess, which is mostly based on my understanding of magic channeling from my early years of training."

He huffed. "Not very helpful."

"Actually, that might not necessarily be true," I said excitedly as an idea came to me. "He is using this building to gather energy from the world around him, pulling it from the sun, the wind, and especially the earth. Sucking it out of the living things that were once here." I turned Topher back toward the manor's facade. "We could potentially disrupt that flow by destroying a key character. That might weaken or even hurt him." I closed my eyes and tried to picture the progression of runes and imagined how they might interact. With a sudden flash of clarity, I pointed to a large rune in the center of the front steps. "That one," I insisted. "I think all of the converted energy channels through it, and probably down a path that leads into the cave. It's like the neck of a bottle. We could cut off his constant source of energy."

He turned Braknik around and stared down at it, twisting his face in thought. "Sounds dangerous," he grumbled. "Will it explode?"

"Um... well, maybe," I admitted. The hero would be disrupting a powerful channel of magic. I wasn't entirely sure what would happen when it was no longer controlled and pouring down into the cave. "I guess, yeah. Good chance."

He glared at me and pointed his sword at a large, naked, oak tree not far away. "Then go over there."

I opened my mouth, but stopped when I realized my argument wasn't that I wished to help him so much as I didn't wish to be separated from him. I bowed my head in shame at the fear that so easily transformed my muscles to quivering jelly. "Skalah is protecting us," I muttered, grudgingly directing Topher to the other side of the tree.

"That's right," the hero agreed behind my back. "Among others, but he is enough." He dismounted and knelt on the steps. He turned his sword downward, pressing the tip against the rune while he held the hilt with both hands. I had seen an illustration once of him praying in such a manner, and I was momentarily swept away by the romanticism of the pose. He bowed his head and closed his eyes. "God of light and life. God of good death and righteous resurrection. Upon these stones are markings that defy your law and poison the living with a vile and unnatural taint." I was once more moved to awe by the true devotion in his voice and the humility of his pose. Whenever he spoke to the gods, respect, honor, and purest faith uncommon to his normal personality shone through. "Give to me the power to destroy this stone and stop this river of evil from flowing into the earth and poisoning the land and creatures in your domain."

All the light that had been glowing warmly from his skin and armor from the blessing flowed over his body and down the sword, concentrating into a brilliant glare upon the tip of the blade. It quickly became too intense to look into, and I turned my gaze away... just in time to see a trio of animated undead clamoring out of the cave and up the ramp, headed straight for the hero's turned back.

"Chosen!" I screamed, digging my heels into Topher's flanks. The horse screamed protest and fear, but charged forward. The beast responded so quickly, I was almost thrown from the saddle. I nearly cut my own wrist trying to wrangle saddle horn, reins, and dagger. I managed to keep hold of my sad little blade as I charged forward to battle three monsters with no sign of the hero turning to aid me.

    I leaned into the gallop, but couldn't manipulate the reins and hold the saddle horn with one hand. As I had witness The Chosen One do, I twisted my hips in an attempt to direct Topher. The beast turned toward the leader of the trio, and I let out a breathless "whoop!" of success. I had planned to cut them off and put myself between them and the occupied hero, but Topher crashed into the head monster. The horse came to a jarring halt, bounced, and frantically stamped his hooves. The man's head exploded beneath the bombardment, and the courtyard was filled with the sound of crunching bones and squelching flesh. I didn't have time to respond to the mounts dramatic and gruesome overkill as the two remaining corpses, a man and a woman, collided into my leg and the horse's flank.

    I slashed ineffectually at them, too busy wriggling and trying to keep them away from me with a stirrup-hindered foot to make sure strikes at any vital targets. The woman let out a shriek that stopped my heart cold, and reached for me with skinless fingers, the distal bones sharpened to putrid talons. She raked down my leg from hip to knee, shredding the fabric of my tunic and pants, and laying open the pale flesh beneath. I screamed before I even felt the pain, and hot blood instantly poured down my leg. Topher cried out as the man clawed with similar results at the beast's hind quarters.

    My brain, unable to process the horror of the pain and danger I was in, took over with raw, animal instinct. I stabbed hard at the woman's face, and the dagger ricocheted off of cheek bone to bury hilt-deep into her right eye socket. Topher danced away from the attack of the man, kicking awkwardly back and to the side, almost throwing me from the saddle. I was hauled around, and the hilt of my only weapon, now covered in slick ichor, slipped out of my fingers. One of the horse's hooves struck true, crushing the man's chest and shattering the half-decayed vertebrae in his neck with a sickening chorus of wet cracks and pops. The abomination crumpled down, landing on top of its own head.

The woman had apparently only been momentarily disorientated by the maiming of her eye and whatever brain matter still existed behind it, and she recovered more quickly that I did. She charged again, her shriek gargled as the foul blood from her injury poured out her nose and mouth.

"No!" I screamed, lashing at her with the only thing left in my hands: the reins. The leather struck with a loud crack, and her head snapped to the side, sending her careening against Topher's already injured hide. The horse hopped, kicked, side-stepped, and took the woman down with a horse-shriek of pain and fury. He stomped and danced long after she and the second man had stopped attempting to move.

I clung to the pommel, letting the horse take his time crushing the foe as I frantically looked around for more attackers. A brilliant flash of light flooded the entire courtyard, and the earth beneath our feet rumbled. Behind me, a rending sound tore through the air, and Topher bolted forward, away from the manor. I hauled on the reins before the horse could take me down into the pit, and managed to turn his head. He slid to a halt and bucked, but banked enough for me to see The Chosen One.

The hero was radiant, a beam of light pouring down from the heavens directly upon him. The stone at the tip of his sword had shattered into a spider web of cracked earth. The manor bucked and rolled, the structure collapsing like a house of cards upon a rippling tablecloth. Everything undulated with unnatural and disorientating movement, and Topher danced anxiously, unsure of his footing on the shifting terrain. With a violent crescendo, the entire manor crashed in on itself, belching out a plume of disgusting, gray dust.

Then everything was eerily silent except the occasional skitter of a piece of rubble coming to rest. My whole body was shaking from the raw display of power, and I whispered, "Great gods."

"Indeed," the hero agreed, rising to his feet. It was then that I noticed everything around us seemed cracked or overturned, everything except a triangle of undisturbed earth that began at the broken rune and encapsulated The Chosen One, Braknik, Topher, and me. "That they are."

I was still deeply shaken, both by the frightening skirmish with the undead and the raw display of unimaginable power from the gods. My leg throbbed with a fiery pain that clamped my teeth together and soured my guts, all my muscles felt like quivering noodles, and every nerve was buzzing from a hundred kinds of overstimulation. I was overwhelmed to the point of mute immobility, paralyzed by an inability to process everything that had happened in the previous few minutes. I had never been so miserable in my entire life, but I couldn't even seem to comprehend the possibility of taking action to remedy any of my pains or discomforts. I simply sat astride a nervously shifting Topher and stared numbly at the hero.

The Chosen One's gaze fixed on the mangled remains of the three corpses, one hand stretching reflexively out for Braknik as he sheathed his sword. The warhorse stepped up beside him, offering his head, and the hero swung astride without shifting his focus. "You did that?" he muttered, clearly dumbfounded. "Three undead all on your own? Most would have no chance against even one. The gods must have been guiding your hand."

"M-more like T-Topher's hooves," I replied. My voice seemed very far away, and I frowned at how terrified I sounded. I hoped the hero would not call me a coward again. I was, after all, trying my very best to show up for this challenge. Even if I was no good at it, I was still *here*.

The Chosen One's eyes snapped to me as if he sensed danger, and he stared hard at my face. "You're white as a ghost," he observed, and his attention flashed down to my leg. "Gods, man." He clicked and Braknik carried him over to my injured side, his frown deepening as he drew near. "That is an unhealthy amount of blood. We'd best stop that before we head down, or you'll be no good to me."

I smirked dryly. "I would hate to be no good to you." Again, my voice sounded odd. It was like listening to a stranger. Without warning, the hero slapped me across the face, and I gasped, reeling backwards and almost falling. He caught my arm and pulled me back into the saddle, and the pain in my leg and hip came roaring into the front of my brain. I made a decidedly un-masculine sound and doubled over, only barely keeping myself from gripping the torn flesh and making it worse. Tears blurred my vision, and I only barely choked back a sob.

"There's the Tiberius I know," the hero commented with a grim smirk. "Hold on to Topher, and I'll get you straightened out."

I wheezed and twisted forward, whimpering when the movement sent daggers of agony up my hip and all the way to my heart. I wrapped both hands around the pommel and saddle horn, panted, and silently prayed for all I was worth that the gods see me through the day. The hero pressed one of his giant hands to the gashes, and I cried out and spun before I realized what I was doing, jabbing an elbow toward his temple. He batted my arm away with an unfazed chuckle. All I could do was hiss through my teeth, clutch the saddle, and mutter every rude and unkind thing that had ever entered my vocabulary. It took several moments for the high-pitched ringing in my ears to subside, and I realized he was praying.

"...this man who has fought bravely and honored his duty by shielding your servant with his own body. I ask that you heal him and his noble steed of this injury that we may better serve you and Skalah in the upcoming battle against an agent of death, decay, and violence against the natural laws."

My breath stopped at the reverence in his tone, the genuine sincerity when speaking of my bravery and honor. Tears blurred my vision again, this time born of an unexpected and potent pang of gratification at the hero's regard. Maybe his arrogant and dismissive behavior was a facade, crafted to keep from becoming too attached to a servant who would be gone in a few short years. Perhaps he really did appreciate me. I was genuinely shocked at how much I cared that he took stock of my deeds and recognized the danger I had stupidly risked to protect his back.

I was also dismayed that I had done it in the first place. I could have died. I truly could have died, and I hadn't hesitated even one second. I swallowed the lump in my throat. Maybe I wasn't a coward, after all.

"Gods," The Chosen One griped. "You're not going to cry are you? I'd rather you puked." He checked Braknik so quickly, I barely had a chance to register his words or the sudden lack of pain, let alone respond to his rudeness. "Man up. It's just a scratch."

My jaw dropped open, anger following so closely on the heels of reverence, I couldn't get my mouth to work. I fumed in stunned indignation while the hero trotted over to the undead mush and dismounted. He jerked my dagger free from the skewed head of the woman's corpse and held it up toward me.

I clenched my teeth and nudged Topher forward to reclaim the lost weapon. "Thanks," I grumbled.

"Don't lose it again," he snapped.

My jaw ached, and one of my teeth might have cracked under pressure. I was only able to manage a grunt of acknowledgement. The blade dripped clumps of dark, horrendous-smelling goo, and I quickly looked away to choke back a gag. It took a moment to steel myself enough to clean the blade on the ankle of my—Ethan's —pants and replace it on my hip. I ignored the hero's look of disgust at my stomach's weakness with every bit as much stubborn fortitude as he'd ignored me over the past week.

The Chosen One's face became grim, and he silently rode to the mouth of the cave. Braknik pranced slightly when his hooves touched the disturbed soil. A foul, inhuman stench belched up from the depths with a gust of disturbing, damp heat. Nothing I had ever encountered before sent shivers through me like that unsettling odor. I didn't know how I understood it was not natural, but all of my senses screamed at the wrongness that existed in the darkness below.

A huge noise split the air, a horrible, shrieking roar. It was full of fury and anguish, and had I not been astride, my legs would certainly have failed me. I hunched in the saddle, gripping the pommel with all my strength, fighting a sudden, near-overwhelming need to flee. My hands shook so violently, I almost lost the reins. My brain summoned up the lightning-eyed man and the terror his gaze had brought me.

"This is not a mere necromancer, or even a wizard," The Chosen One whispered. "I've fought a creature like this before." He twitched, and Braknik started carefully forward, down the steep incline.

My heart thumped against my ribs, and I choked on a whimper. It took more than one kick of my heels for Topher to heed and follow the hero. "Y-you have?" I swallowed hard. "Creature?"

"This smell, the great magic," he mumbled as if he were merely speaking to himself. "The sloppy and careless spells... I should have remembered. It was a long time ago."

"*What is it,*" I hissed, my voice shrill with mounting anxiety.

"Feel the heat in the walls?" The Chosen One said, holding a hand out to hover over the passing dirt. "It's a dragon." His voice took a dangerous, ominous edge. "A dragon of darkness and pain."

My stomach fell, and I'm certain my heart skipped a dozen beats. A dragon. "A half-god? A b-bastard child... of Trion?" My brain instantly assembled all of the events and clues into a clear picture of what lay in the darkness below. A demi-god. We went to face a creature equal in strength to the one that had nearly turned the grandmaster hero away from his path a century before... A quest that had ended in the death of Tiberius. I almost began crying again.

He nodded, and though I couldn't see his face, I heard the starkly bleak tone in his quieted voice. "Start praying to me, Tiberius. And don't stop."

My vision blurred, and my body began to shudder beyond any hope of usefulness. I looped the reins around the pommel to keep from losing them, and I lowered my head, pouring as much power into my voice as I could. If this was all I could do to help him defeat this monster, I would give him everything I had. The words rushed out of me, tumbling out in an unending, frantic stream of breathy prayers. I prayed to every god I'd ever heard supported The Chosen One, to every deity that might listen or take pity on a hopelessly outclassed servant of the greatest of men. At some point, I realized I hadn't once asked for protection for myself, even though I could not have been more frightened.

All I could think about were the three poor souls Topher had trampled in the courtyard. The bloated faces in the lake, and the sick babies left in the street to rot. Tears coursed down my face, remembering the gaunt men, emaciated old women, and terrified eyes staring up at The Chosen One in desperate hope as he made his grand promises. "Oh, gods of all things, protect him," my voice cracked. "Keep him safe, make him strong. Help him strike down this terrible foe. Please, I beg you, let him end this nightmare today. Bring peace and relief to those poor people." I shook my head. "I know I've not done right by you before, and I've only ever bent a knee when it suited me. I've no right to ask anything of you. But please, you trusted me with this task. Help me help him."

"Shhh," The Chosen whispered.

I opened my eyes, and quickly lifted a hand against the bright light that shone from the great hero and his steed. I'd given so much energy to the prayer, darkness was creeping in around my thoughts. I drifted through a surreal moment of imagining I was following the sun down into the ground, beyond where it set on the horizon.

"Beyond the map," I whispered. "*Here there be monsters.*"

"Shut up, stupid," The Chosen One snapped under his breath.

I pulled Topher up short just before he ran into Braknik's halted hindquarters. The cave had opened abruptly into a cavern piled high with all manner of objects and foul things. There were ploughs, cannons, chairs, statues... rich and poor goods alike. Treasures of both paupers and kings were hoarded into every corner of the enormous cave, separated by winding footpaths of heavily compressed dirt. Gold and gems glittered from every direction in the mounds, sprinkled heavily with slimy piles of unrecognizable filth. The path was lined with human and animal carcasses and bones, and the stench was more palpable and potent than my mind could register.

"Child of Trion," The Chosen One suddenly shouted into the cave.

I nearly fell from the saddle. I clutched at my chest, certain my heart would explode.

"Chosen of Skalah," a man replied. But it wasn't a man. The voice wasn't human. The very sound of it struck me mute with terror, as the terrible eyes of lightning had done. Somehow, the sound of his voice alone spoke clearly of his lineage. Something like a man strode around a tight bend in the path ahead some distance away. It had eerily angular features, and its dark, oily skin glistened like snake scale in The Chosen One's glow. It wore no clothes on its tall, sinewy body, and a long tail slithered along the ground behind it.

"I remember your stink," it said. "From the cave by the sea."

"And I remember yours," The Chosen One replied. "I spared your life those years past. I regret my mercy. You have murdered hundreds, *thousands* these past few years."

"You murdered my sister," the thing hissed, and its black, forked tongue licked out at the air.

"I was sent to stop her evil, and now I have come to put an end to yours." The Chosen One's posture changed, readying I realized for battle.

The foul creature's black eyes widened into perfect spheres, and a fiery red glow gathered in them. "I was young when last we met. You will not leave my lair alive this time," it hissed.

With speed as if they'd been released from a catapult, The Chosen One and mount surged forward.

Suddenly horrified that he might be defeated and leave me alone with the monster, I gathered the very last of my strength and threw all of my power into one final prayer. I don't know where the words came from, they just felt right. "May the sun live within you this day, Chosen One!" The last of my magic poured out of me, and I dropped numbly from the saddle. I landed hard on a pile of treasure and offal, unable to move, helpless to do anything more than watch.

The Chosen One blazed so bright, the beast twisted its head away, throwing its hands over his bulbous eyes. Braknik pounded into the creature, but it was somehow able to spin away and avoid the bulk of the horse's weight. The hero's glimmering blade swept down and cleaved clean through the tail of the beast. Black blood sprayed, hissing and smoking with a foul miasma wherever it landed.

The monster shrieked a terrible, inhuman wail. It leapt, higher than hero and mount combined, onto a great mound of filth-covered hoard. It jerked a massive sword free of the rubble and spun to face its foe, wielding the greatsword one-handed with mortifying ease. Its great wound had already stopped bleeding, and it dove at the hero with unnatural speed. Even fast as I knew The Chosen One could be, the hero was barely able to turn Braknik in time to deflect the pouncing man-beast. The two crashed into a heap of bones with a terrible clamor. Braknik bucked, striking the creature in the hip and spinning it enough to force the next swipe of its sword just wide of the Chosen's head.

The monster twisted around from the new injury and screamed again, raking a hand at the horse's flank with talon-like claws I hadn't noticed. Braknik bucked and pranced away, whinnying in pain as scarlet blood spattered the monster and the hero. Though the reaction had taken a second at most, it afforded The Chosen One an opportunity to strike. He was too close to stab with the blessed sword, but was able to sweep a tight circle and cleave the monster's attacking arm at the elbow.

The creature leapt backwards, away from another swing of the hero's blade, and black wings exploded from his back. The new limbs snapped open, flicking foul fluid in an arc behind it, and instantly began to beat furiously, lifting the half-god higher. It continued flying backwards as the hero rushed after, swinging when his sword had hope of making contact. A few times, the tip of the blade grazed a heel or a toe, throwing small spatters of flesh or blood in his wake. I realized that I recognized the movements from the hero's morning practice, and a smirk turned my lips. I sometimes forgot how his entire life was dedicated to his duty.

In only a matter of seconds, the creature was higher than the hero could reach, and it turned to cling onto a stone formation hanging from the ceiling. It opened its mouth and released another deafening, soul-shattering scream. I slumped backwards, unable to resist the terror that rolled through me, so potent my brain stopped functioning.

The Chosen One shuddered, but shook off whatever magic the beast was using. "Come at me, bastard half-breed!" he hollered.

The creature screamed in fury and launched from the ceiling. As it dove, it shimmered and changed. I thought it was exploding, but when it landed where the hero had been standing, the magic dissipated with a plume of iridescent residue, revealing a massive lizard-like creature. The ground shuddered and glittering bobbles rained down the hoarded stacks, filling the air with their discordant music.

The Chosen One had barely sprinted out from under the beast's attack, aided by the monster's momentary blindness from the shift. He spun as he was sliding to a halt and slashed at the restored and much larger tail. Though the sword was not long enough to strike through the limb, a blade of light burst from the tip and cut like solid steel. The tail came free with a gush of blood that instantly covered the ground and the hero from chest to toe.

The monster shrieked, more with rage than pain, and kicked backwards. It solidly struck, its talons raking across the hero's armor with showers of sparks as the hero was thrown several dozen feet away, sailing past me and into a mound of hoard. The breath exploded out of him at the impact, and objects shattered in all directions from the hero-sized dent his body created. The creature spun, unhindered by a tail, and lurched toward the unmoving hero with a gaping maw full of glistening, yellow bone-knives.

"No!" I screamed. With an unexplainable surge of frantic strength, I fumbled for the most damaging object in my possession, an incendiary working. I shouted the activation with magic I didn't possess and hurtled the object at the monster's eyes as it pounded past me. The small, round vial flashed red as it struck the bridge of the creature's nose. It burst into a shower of flaming embers, and the dragon's momentum carried its face right into the explosion. It jerked its head to the side in a vain attempt to avoid the fire and crashed into the rubble just a few feet wide of the hero's unmoving body.

I fumbled for another working with shuddering fingers, anything to keep the thing distracted. I was terrified The Chosen One was too hurt to fight... or worse. I couldn't imagine anyone surviving what I had just witnessed. "G-get away from him!" I screamed. "F-fight me!" My voice turned a pitch I didn't realize I could reach. I lifted my pathetic dagger, though I hadn't remembered I still held it, and shakily pulled myself upright. My legs were barely strong enough to hold me, and I had no hope of running, let alone moving faster than the creature. I simply stood my ground, a sad little dagger in one hand and a working I was certain I didn't have the strength to activate in the other.

With a cold and oddly calming thought, I realized this was where I ended. I felt a twinge of regret at all my silly dreams that would never come true, followed by a surge of hope that my sacrifice would enamor the gods enough to give The Chosen One the strength to kill this monster and save the poor, suffering people we'd promised to protect.

The beast turned toward me, the hero momentarily forgotten, its eyes blazing with brilliant red fury as smoke wreathed its face from a dozen burning embers. It circled slowly, its muscles tightening as it stalked toward me. "Tiny human," it rumbled. "You will suff—"

The Chosen One drove his blade deep into the mass of the creature's hindquarters, hilt deep through the hip and into its belly. The monster kicked with the impaled leg, screaming and writhing in pain from the injury and the movement. The hero was thrown back again, this time with much less force, and he sprang forward without hesitation.

Relief washed over me, and I dropped to my knees, all of my strength concentrated upon keeping hold of the miniscule weapons with which I'd armed myself.

The dragon spun to face his adversary, swiping a claw tipped with daggers at the hero. The Chosen One danced to the side, sparks flying as talons grazed his glowing breastplate. His gods-given sword swept in a radiant arc and clipped three of the massive fingers from the claw. The dragon shrieked and raked with its other hand, shifting its weight quicker than I would have thought possible. The claw caught the hero below his left arm and threw him into the pile of hoard I was occupying, the resulting impact pelting me with shattered corpse fragments and glittering gems.

I flinched, but quickly scurried backwards as the beast rounded in my direction. Something like the sound of a strident tea kettle burst from my throat, as I hopelessly lifted my dagger toward the attacking dragon. Its eyes flashed to me, its head turning slightly at the loud, unmasculine sounds I was making. The Chosen One surged forward and struck high, launching himself into the air to sink his blade deep into the soft flesh under the monster's jaw, up until the hilt met bone. A beam of light shot out through the top of the charging monster's head.

    The beast crashed bonelessly down onto the hero, sliding for an endless moment to the base of the hoard just inches from my frantically kicking feet. Stones and rubble showered me, and I curled around myself in gut reaction to the hulking, descending mass. The cave was instantly filled with silence and darkness, the hero's light snuffed by the dragon's enormous body. It took less than a second for panic to set in at the engulfment of the near-total darkness. I was alone with untold horrors, and The Chosen One was buried beneath a mountain of a carcass.

20. This Is the Saddest Prayer I Have Ever Heard

"No!" I emptied my hands and clambered forward, reaching toward the dead beast. Its stench and heat found me as my palms came down on hard scales. "Chosen! Chosen," I screamed. I fumbled my hands under the creature's enormous jaw, but had no hope of lifting its head. I realized with horror, there was a good chance the creature's momentum had carried it past where The Chosen One made his final stand, and The Chosen One was trapped under the dragon's huge chest. I grunted, heaved, shoved, and prayed that any god listening would grant me the strength to free the great hero from the crushing weight of the massive corpse.

"Chosen! Gods! I don't know what to do!" I turned my back, planted my heels, and shoved, but the head only slightly shifted. I slid to the ground, my head light and spinning from the day's exertions. I tried desperately to get my exhaustion-addled brain to think of any working on my person that might be useful.

Then the head shifted against my back. I shrieked in panic and scrabbled away. A confused mix of horror that the creature could now devour me unencumbered by a hero and sheer joy that it might lift itself off of said hero coursed through me like a drug, giving me the strength to scurry halfway up a mountain of be-fouled treasure. I told myself I wasn't fleeing, but rather was drawing the monster away from The Chosen One. My foot slipped, and I slid on my face back down to the ground with a shower of sludge, remains, and gold coins. A whimper clawed out of me as I spun and pressed my back to the hoard, preparing to be savaged by the dragon.

The creature was slowly opening its enormous maw, horrifically sharp, yellow teeth separating as light poured out of its mouth. "Gods' sake!" The thing growled... in *The Chosen One's voice*. "Tiberius! Stop that girlish shrieking and get something to prop his mouth open!"

My jaw nearly fell from my skull. It took another second of the hero grunting and painstakingly slowly opening the jaw for reality to come back into focus. "Oh my gods!" I gushed, rushing forward, too overjoyed with relief for a moment to realize I was useless to him barehanded.

"Damnit! Tiberius!" the hero hollered, and the jaw closed a little before jerking back up another few inches. I could now see the hero's legs, though every inch of his armor was covered with hissing, bubbling gore. He must have cleaved clean through the soft flesh of the jaw and been shielded by the hollow of the monster's mouth and throat.

I bolted down the path, looking for anything long and sturdy. "I'm trying!" I skidded to a halt, landing on my ass, when I saw an entire stand of spears. "Yes!" I clawed up the few feet to where the stand was awkwardly protruding from the legs of a table. I hastily threw each spear toward the trapped hero, and they stuck or clattered short of the dragon by several feet. I was a terrible aim, but I got all of them close enough to be useful. I slid down the pile, no longer caring what slime rubbed off on me, and dashed back.

One after another, I retrieved the spears, butted them up against the roof of the mouth, and pushed the tips down into the dirt. When I was done, the monster's head looked like a gruesome canopy. I collapsed against what was undoubtedly the rotting corpse of a deer, and stared at the abomination. I couldn't move, could barely think, and it took an increasingly untenable level of effort to keep my eyes open.

The Chosen let out a groan and relaxed down onto his knees. When the teeth didn't clamp down, he carefully crawled out through the treacherous daggers of bone. His glow had diminished considerably, and I could see red blood mixed in with the foul, black slime that had come from the monster. He stood for a moment, clearly getting his bearings, before he turned to look at the fallen beast. He dragged his sword out of the maw and dropped to a knee beside the dragon with a painful grunt. Though I did not think it possible for him to further surprise me, he assumed the same prayer position as he had in front of the manor.

"Great god of strife and darkness," he said with true humility. "It is with a heavy heart that I completed my duty this day. You have my sympathy on the loss of your son, and though I do not expect your forgiveness, I pray for your understanding. I will see to it that his body is not desecrated, and that he is given a proper burial as befitting one who possessed the blood of a god."

Somewhere not far away, thunder boomed and a tree crashed to the ground. Light flickered around the cave, and back out where we had entered the hole. There a man stood. Except he wasn't a man. He was tall, his skin the color of tanned leather and his hair a shock of coppery red that flowed around a lean, mostly naked frame. He wore a blue sash that held up an exotic animal pelt the like I had never seen before, and his eyes shone with an eerie brightness that cut straight through me to the frightened child within. He was beautiful in a way no human could be, and terrible beyond my brain's comprehension.

He stared at the monster with such gut-wrenching sorrow, tears actually pricked my eyes. "Chosen," he whispered, and quiet as his voice was, it never seemed to stop echoing through the cavern. "You've taken them both from me."

The hero lifted his gaze to the god, his face one of true pity that was somehow devoid of regret. "I have," he answered quietly. "My deepest sympathies, god of thieves. Though my quest was necessary, I regret the pain I've caused you."

Lightning flashed, pouring radiance through the opening of the cave with a heart-stopping boom, and the god's eyes lit as if the sky-fire lived within him. "Keep your pity!" he roared, sending another shock of terror through me. "*I* command pity, and you are not worthy to wear it!" He threw his hand forward, and though the hero didn't flinch, I curled into a tight ball of helpless terror.

A rush of air whipped around me, followed by silence.

The Chosen One sighed, and the creak of his armor encouraged me to peer out through the cage of my arms. He'd risen to his feet, and both the god and the body of the beast were gone. Only a semi-circle of half-rotted spears remained, and an immense black stain upon the earth.

I choked back a sob of relief, and sagged against the deer corpse.

The Chosen frowned over at me. "Pull yourself together. You've got work to do."

I gave a mirthless bark of laughter. "That's going to take a minute. I think I might pass out."

He snorted and walked over to drop down on a less-disgusting section of the pile I inhabited. "If you must," he muttered with as much weariness as I felt.

"Do you need healing?"

He looked down at the scarlet tracks on his body that spoke of claws, teeth, and shattered rubble that had somehow circumvented his undamaged and subtly glowing armor. "Your efforts worked better than nearly every man who came before," he commented. "Even after this, the blessing of light lingers." He raised what could actually be described as an impressed eyebrow at me. "His talons and fangs will leave scars, but only the ladies will know them." His face broke into a wide grin, and I let out a light-headed laugh. "If you can manage it, I could use one of those vials that smoke." His strange politeness triggered an inexplicable alarm in me, and I realized his face was quickly taking on a white pallor. His shoulders slumped abruptly, and I jerked, immediately enlivened with deep concern.

I knew which tonic he meant and shoved myself into a seated position. There was no way I could cast the healing activation in my current state, so I withdrew one more of the insanely expensive magic bolstering tonics. The activation on these required almost no energy, but I nearly swooned into unconsciousness nonetheless. The hero's hand caught mine to keep me from spilling the vial, and he growled in frustration as if I was simply being careless. Jerk.

I downed the magical shot, my face twisting up at the exceedingly-sour flavor and waited. It took only a moment for the working to take hold, and I doubled over as pain stabbed through my gut and radiated out to every nerve in my body. It took longer to subside then it had before, and I realized I likely had used them too closely together. Tonic workings did not like to be mixed, even with others of their own kind. Pain lanced through me again, and breath wheezed out through my teeth as I tried with all my might to keep from putting on too much of a display for The Chosen One to mock.

"When you're done," the hero grumbled. Though I wanted to snap back, the faintest slur to his words sent another shock of alarm through me.

I forced my eyes open, squinting through the pain. His face was ghost pale, and he'd reclined back onto his elbow to watch me. His blood covered several objects beneath him, and a small stream of red was starting to flow out from the hoard and onto the dirt path at his feet.

"Damnit," I hissed, ordering my cramped stomach and protesting body to move. The healing vials were among the easiest to reach, in anticipation of a scenario like this. I closed my eyes and forced my own body's misery to the back of my brain, trying to recall the activation incantation. It had not been complex, but it was a verbal component that could not vary in the least from its proper pronunciation. I practiced a few times without power, then popped the cork and activated the working. Pushing energy through my body and out with my breath felt like issuing fire through my mouth. I managed the activation, but the last syllable was followed by an uncontrollable sob of agony.

I gritted my teeth, choked back further complaint, and slid toward him. His eyes were drooping, and his head lolled onto the pauldron of his armor. I could see the greatest source of blood was coming from the side closest to me. His hand reached weakly for the vial, but I grabbed his wrist instead. I pulled him into a seated position and propped him against me as I unfastened his belt. He grunted, though if it was one of protest or acquiescence, I couldn't tell. Once the belt was free, I wrangled open the buckles on his breastplate and hauled on his hauberk to pull both it and the breastplate away from his torso. I awkwardly slipped my hand holding the vial under them and let the mist pour up into the pocket I'd made. I prayed the working would function even through the layers of his padding and clothing. His head drooped until it was resting against mine, and I pushed back against it to hold him up.

"I can't tell," I muttered. "Is it working?" The pain was finally starting to fade, and my mind was clearing. I was filled with the same strange, overfull sensation as the last time I'd taken the tonic, and it pulled me free from the exhaustion the fading adrenaline had left me in. "Chosen," I said louder. "Is it working?"

He grunted again, and I pushed him back against the hoard. His eyes rolled partially opened, then closed, and he muttered a few unintelligible words.

"Shit!" I hauled on the padding with my free hand and shoved the arm holding the vial deep as I could, holding all the garments up with my bicep as I reached into his clothes to feel along his skin with my other hand. Inside his padding, all his flesh was wet and slick with blood. I found the gash under the arm where a talon must have pierced, and thrust with my whole body until I was awkwardly holding his clothing aloft with one entire arm while the other held the vial under the wound.

After a moment, I felt around for the gash and found the skin unbroken. "Oh, thank the gods," I muttered. I quickly felt along under the armor and found another gash on the other side in much the same place. It was clearly a weakness in the armor's design, and I wondered if the dragon had known this and aimed accordingly. Its strikes had seemed random, reflexive even, but the success of its few blows had been too great for them to have been purely luck. I had to shove my head under the lip of the awful-smelling padding to hold it up and shift the vial to my other hand to reach the second wound.

When that gash had closed, I pulled back and tried to ascertain were his other injuries might be. There was so much ichor, blood, and worse, I couldn't tell where much of the scarlet was coming from. I could see a particularly bloody cut on the back of his skull and healed it with the fading tendrils of the working. I shook the hero and called to him, but he didn't wake. I tossed the vial way and hastily stripped his armor. It was difficult without him shifting to aid my progress, but I was able to get the plate off. The hauberk I got off by moving side to side, rolling the hero back and forth to work it up and over his arms. It caught in his hair and almost pulled off the blond wig. Knowing how angry and embarrassed he would be if he awoke bald, I took extra care to untangle the rings of mail before lifting it free of his body.

The padding was buckled in the front, so it was much easier to remove, and once all that remained was a layer of clothing, I cut it free to see the flesh beneath. I sucked in a breath at the mess of blood and bruises that covered the hero's chest and arms. The blow that had thrown him into the hoard must have been terrible, and the armor had clearly not absorbed all of it. He'd had to have been in great pain when the beast fell on him, and still he'd managed to lift its skull and jaw to free himself. I blinked, and my vision blurred as a pang of shame at having not been faster or more helpful choked me.

"Stop it," I muttered. "Regret your uselessness later. Get to work." I had several more of the healing vials, and I used all but one of them, going over his belly and torso first with the entire contents of one of the workings. I stripped the rest of his armor and padding, cutting his clothes until he was only modestly covered, and labored to heal his head, arms, and legs. Everywhere I exposed skin, I was mortified at the abuse he'd taken. When I was done, I used my skin of water to clean a majority of the blood and gore from his chest to look for signs that I had missed anything.

He'd been right, there were ugly, gray scars anywhere the skin had been broken by the beast's talons or fangs. More than half a dozen in all, including a gash along his forehead and down the right side of his jaw. I actually felt a twinge of pity for how his pride would suffer every time he looked into a mirror. At least twice he had battled a dragon, and both times he'd been grievously injured. When we had been swarmed by more than two dozen undead victims, he had dispatched them with a wild grin. When battling this scion of strife, he'd actually seemed outmatched in speed, strength, and power. As before, when he'd inflicted the killing blow, he himself had already been mortally wounded. Were it not for the healing power of the tonics Ethan had stowed, The Chosen One would not have survived this encounter. I remembered the hero mentioning the *several* times he'd given his life and been revived, and I shuddered. It would have been horrible to have to convey his corpse to the nearest town with a major temple of Skalah to be resurrected.

I looked down at the pool of scarlet blood that had formed on the ground at his feet and swallowed hard. I'd barely had time to inspect his wounds, but I was certain he'd suffered many broken bones, ruptured organs, and a significant loss of blood. I had no way of knowing if the beast's fangs and claws contained venom as dragons purportedly did, but the gashes must have hurt immensely regardless. Through all that pain and injury, he'd fought without regard to personal risk. So often, he'd discussed his duty with unwavering resolve, spoken of the innocent he protected and the great beings he served without question. He might be one of the most offensive and insensitive brutes I'd ever met, but The Chosen One was a hero in the truest and fullest definition of the word.

I looked toward the oily, black stain were the beast had fallen, and I thought about the price of the last dragon slaying. I had not been there for the defeat of the daughter of Trion, but I imagined the hero got off a little lighter this time, with fewer scars and no need for resurrection. I smiled slightly at that thought, and hoped my meager effort had given some contribution to that outcome.

"Did you have to undress me?" The Chosen One griped, sitting up to examine his torn and bloodied clothing with a sneer of disgust. "I prefer to wake up in this state beside a buxom maiden, not the likes of you."

I smirked, still in a high born of narrowly escaping death and the lingering effects of the tonic. "Well, a buxom maiden likely wouldn't have thought to stow an extra set of clothes in her saddle bag, as I have done."

He glared at me. "Well, I wouldn't *need* clothes, would I?"

Though he was doing his best to be an ass, I simply smiled at his back when he sauntered to Braknik to shower the beast with praise for his performance. I wasn't even jealous that he ignored my contribution while he doted on the destrier. Mostly. Besides, the horse had suffered injury, while I remained relatively unharmed. He healed the horse, stripped, and quickly washed with a rag and what remained in his skin of water. He glared over his shoulder at me. "When you're done admiring my ass, you could fetch my clothes!"

"Oh!" My bubble of glad-to-be-alive contentment popped, and I pushed to my feet to retrieve his garments. Clearly he was immune to the introspection aspect of the healing tonics, or perhaps he was just incapable of deep thought. As I made my way to Topher, my eyes cast out at the dead people and animals, tucked in among the rubble like wattle. My stomach twisted with pity and numb horror. "Why did he do this?" I asked when I returned and held out his underpinnings. "Why did he kill these people? Why did he make that sickness and poison the land?"

He gave a solemn nod to the black stain where the beast had fallen. "He was mad."

"Mad? As in, insane?" I handed him the garments one at a time, and he began dressing.

He sighed and took the clothing, without looking away from the death stain. "It happens sometimes with half-gods. I've seen it before."

"Why? They have all of this power. I'm certain they never have to worry about aging or disease. He probably could have been a great man, like a hero or a king."

"Do you remember how you felt when Trion was in your presence?"

I shuddered. "I could never forget."

"That was your human-self recognizing a god... what he was, what his *power* was. Trion is the shadow that defines the light. He is the purest and most powerful form of those things he represents."

I frowned at that thought. "Like the personification of fear, strife, and pestilence?"

"Whatever that means," he grumbled. "Now imagine living with that energy looming over you, coursing through you, through your *human* half, through your human mind." He fixed me with an emphatic stare. "For *eternity*."

I shuddered again and looked down at the darkened earth, a new understanding awakening pity for the man who had died that day. "I can't imagine anyone would remain sane." I sighed. "He was probably always at odds, part of him like you and me, full of hope, love, and compassion."

"And the other determined to define the best things of life by destroying everything he could," the hero finished.

I shook my head. "So the god half won out in the end?"

He sighed. "No. I think even in the end, he was grateful I was here to stop him. I think he could have fought harder. I think he could have better evaded the final blow."

I tried to imagine what the human trapped in the beast was thinking in his final moments as he fell upon the Chosen's sword. "How do you do it?" I asked. "To know these things, to know he was a man probably full of pain and desperate to undo the evil he couldn't help but bring about... and choose to kill him?"

He gestured to the mutilated and badly decomposed corpse of a woman nearby. "Not so long ago, she was full of hope, love, and compassion."

A long silence followed, where we both looked around the cave, witnessing the horrors that had taken place there over the past few years. I shuddered again and tried to push my dark thoughts away. I couldn't function if I let myself imagine what the villagers who died down there must have endured. And I couldn't continue to think about the nightmare inside the dragon's mind. "Did he have a name?"

The Chosen grunted. "The scion?"

I nodded.

"Probably," he admitted. "But he never told it to me. It's best that way, when you know one day you will try to kill each other. It's easier."

The wisdom and reality of that statement filled me with sorrow. "So, when you met him over a hundred years ago..."

"He was a child of Trion. Of course he would eventually go mad, and I would have to kill him."

I frowned and gestured around the cave. "Why not do it then?"

He stopped and fixed me with a reproachful glare. "Because he wasn't a monster *then*."

"But so many could have been—"

He jabbed a finger into my chest so hard my rib instantly throbbed in protest. "We are *not* gods! We do *not* judge a man on what he *might* do. That is not why we have been given these blessings." I backed a few steps away at the intensity of his response. "At the time, he was both a man and a god. It was *not* my place to judge him by actions he had not committed, and might *never* commit. Understand?"

I lifted my hands in surrender. "Yes! Yes. Sorry."

He nodded once, a stern finality in the gesture. His voice calmed to one of arrogant instruction rather than affronted reprimand. "When I met him all those years ago, he was still a creature who it was my duty to *protect*. I warned him of what his future might hold should he let revenge fester, and I advised him to seek the company of those who would help him keep his humanity."

I blinked in surprise that he had shown such empathy and forethought, and had acted upon it even for a creature he knew he would need to someday kill. "Did you think he would?"

He nodded. "Of course. He witnessed the demise of his sister. He was afraid."

I frowned. "But he still went mad," I observed.

"He *tried*. But we both knew we would someday battle to the death."

"Why didn't you mention this earlier when you were talking about the battle in the cave by the sea?"

He rubbed his chin. "I usually don't, or *didn't*, because I was worried I would jinx it." He shrugged. "At least he was able to keep his humanity for a hundred years. That's better than most humans."

I snorted a cold laugh at the bad joke, then let out a breath, changing the sad subject. "I'm concerned about our remaining water."

"Don't be."

"...okay." I sighed and looked away. "We're also out of food, though we have some feed for the horses."

"So we go hungry until the next town."

I frowned. "You mean West Vevesk?"

"No, idiot," he snapped. "We need to travel on and send help back to the villages. The supply line is dead, and only a promise from The Chosen One that the threat has been eliminated will remedy that." He shook his head at my apparent stupidity, and only my acknowledgment that he was right took the sting off the insult.

"So, we travel on to Mardit to the southwest." I nodded. "It's a little farther than Vevesk, but nearer than Rshaven. It might well be outside the range of this necromantic taint." I let out a long breath. "Thank the gods this is finally over."

He grunted. "The dragon may be dead, but this is far from over."

A tremor of fear shot through me at his words, awakened by an errant thought of hungry young dragons or mindless hordes of undead waiting just around the next bend in the path. "What? Why? What else is there?"

"Well," he gestured around the cave. "If you'd been reading that confounded book of yours," he said as a smile crept up his lips. "You would know your job is to clean all the dragon shit off this treasure and have it appraised." He laughed heartily at my dumbfounded expression. "After all, *Tiberius*, one percent of this is yours!"

Though I was relieved he'd not been referring to danger, my stomach fell as I looked around the cavern mounded high with corpses, trash, treasure, and offal. It was a hopelessly huge task that would be a major undertaking, even after employing men and wagons from Mardit. "Fine," I conceded, though I wanted to scream in frustration at the unending nature of my duties. "But please, I beg of you, can you grant me *one* favor."

He crossed his arms and narrowed his eyes at me. "I just saved you and thousands of strangers from pestilence, horrific death, undead, and a *dragon*. What more do you want?"

"Please, just this one time while we're alone in this abandoned place... call me Perry."

He sneered. "Perry? Why?"

"Because," I sighed. "That's my *name*."

END

A Note from the Author

Thank you for reading *The Chosen One's Assistant!* If you enjoyed this book, please help other readers find it by leaving a review wherever you acquire books.

If you want to learn more about what I'm working on (and when you can expect to see Tiberius again), please visit: **KimberGrey.com**
and/or
Patreon.com/KimberGrey

If you would love to get free short stories, updates, and a lot more, please sign up for my mailing list on my website or reach out to me at
author.kimber.grey@gmail.com
You can expect semi-monthly mailers with free stock photos, my latest forays into bushcraft, free fiction and poetry, & tons of behind-the-scenes snapshots!

If you're a big fan and would love to be a Beta or an ARC reader on my street team and receive ebooks pre-publication, reach out to the email address above and request to be added to *Kimber's Kindred*.

Lastly: if you are 18 or over & love romance, please visit:
Patreon.com/HarleeJordan

Kingdoms Lost

By: Kimber Grey

Rise of Faiden, Book 1: Kingdoms Lost

Chapter 1: An Enslaved King
Northern Mountains, Autumn, 802 FF

Red light spilled across the dark lord's gaunt features as he watched the setting sun to the southwest. He felt the change in the world before the whispers in his mind began. He knew a shift of powers was coming; he'd been feeling the ebb of this era for the past nine years. He'd felt the subtle manipulations of the Oracle seven years before, when fall had come early to Faiden, and two years before that, when Faiden had stirred beneath a blanket of winter. The mighty prophetess was making her move. She was slow, careful, and forever patient. What he couldn't understand was why she had let him rule eight centuries unchallenged. There had been rebellions, of course. He'd had to crush the blood-elven Kingdom of Arylas to keep its sister Kingdom of Ceradon under his thumb. Since that brutal war six years past, all the kingdoms and territories within the High Kingdom of Faiden had been still.

"How is it that you can sense the Oracle moving, but not tell me where she is?" he asked the whispers in his mind. "You want her power, but you will not help me capture her. What game is it that you play?" There were never answers for his questions. The Power whispered, manipulated, and sometimes demanded, but it never gave answers. "When we took Faiden eight hundred years ago, I always thought you were looking for something," he mused, his expression as vacant as his heart. "What were you looking for in the bloodied and broken ruins of my father's castle?" He waited, but no reply came.

The large, circular balcony on the other side of the glass doors was collecting a dusting of murky gray snow. The sun had disappeared behind the foreboding black spires of the Northern Mountains, throwing his obsidian tower into darkness. The dark lord turned away from the ash and ink clouds and strode to his fireplace on the western wall. It blazed to life with a slight gesture and a miniscule amount of effort on his part. The firebox glowed, slowly filling his chilly chamber with warmth. The dark lord didn't require its heat, only its light. He turned back toward the glass doors, but his gaze shifted quickly to the only color in his ebony chambers. A large, amethyst stone caught the light of the fire and threw faint reflections onto the walls around it. Inside its glass shield, it stood solitary on its tall pedestal, the only decoration in the center of the southern floor.

He didn't go to it. He didn't speak to it as he once had, when he'd first banished himself to the bleak and lifeless mountains north of Faiden. He no longer ached for the woman who had worn that crystal until the day he murdered her. It was a reminder now, a standard for what he had destroyed and left behind, for the price of resisting the Power. The black crack striking to the heart of the fist-sized gem was a symbol. It was a dividing line of his life *before* and his existence *after*.

"No," he said to the whispers of the Power. "I no longer miss her. I no longer feel regret or sorrow. You have succeeded in taking even *that* from me." This time, it didn't punish him for his quiet words. He wasn't being sarcastic; he wasn't speaking with bitterness or rebellion. "I have felt nothing for a good many centuries." It was pleased with the resignation in his mind.

A knock sounded on the outer door of his suite, down the hall and beyond the entry room. He lifted his hand absently, his gaze still fixed on the violet fragment of the life he had once had. The entry door opened, as did every door leading to his bedroom. The clink and creak of steel and leather armor preceded his visitor, a young sorceress who had recently attained the rank of captain. He didn't watch her but was aware of her hesitation. Her gaze lingered for a moment on the large, four-poster, canopy bed in the northwest corner of the room, directly across from the door she'd entered through. After only a moment of awkwardness, she strode forward and knelt to the ground beside him, a task made difficult by her partial-plate armor. "You called for me, High Lord."

He looked to her then, taking in the tight knot of her black hair on the nape of her neck and the pallor of her skin. All of the sorcerers he commanded bore those traits. Skin the color of death, everything else stained black. "What is your first name, captain?"

"Vesakan, High Lord." She didn't stir, her head bowed deep. Her voice was pleasant, but held a tremor of trepidation . . . or was it anticipation?

"Rise."

She stood and lifted her chin, bravely meeting his gaze. Her armor was shaped and flattered her fit frame in spite of its bulk. Her features were stunning, her eyes wide and bright. He watched her for a long moment before speaking. "I have heard of you, Vesakan. You are ambitious, unwavering, and sharp. You have accomplished much in the last few years. A captain at what age?"

"Seventeen, High Lord," she responded quickly.

He nodded, circling her. She was slight, but sure of herself. He frowned, discerning a shudder across her shoulders. "You're shaking."

"Yes."

He crossed in front of her again, meeting her eyes. "You do not seem afraid."

She shook her head, her stern expression softening. "No, High Lord."

"Then . . . ?"

"I am . . . overwhelmed. I could not have hoped to be in your presence so early in my training. I am very proud to make your notice, High Lord."

He watched her as she stiffly delivered what was an undoubtedly passionate reply. "What is it you are hoping to accomplish?" he asked at length.

Her gaze met his, though he'd begun to circle her again. "I do not understand your question, High Lord. I only wish to please you."

He smirked emptily at her programmed response. "You are rising in rank quickly and with notable vigor and ambition. What are you seeking?"

She turned to face him, knelt quickly, and pressed her forehead to the tip of his boot, stopping his pacing. "Please, High Lord. *All* I wish is to please you. *All* I do is for you. If I seem ambitious it is only because I am devoted, completely, to being everything and doing everything I can to make you that much stronger. However insignificant my addition to your mighty empire, I remain forever devoted to giving everything I am to you."

The dark lord raised a brow at her gush of emotion. He watched her bent shoulders for a moment in silence, considering her appropriateness for the task he needed filled. He had questioned dozens of sorcerer lords but had dismissed all of them, uncertain of their loyalty. Now, low in the ranks, he might have found exactly what he sought. How could he be sure? "A few days ago, I ordered for you to be delivered a series of tasks, then tests. I was told that you performed at the level of a sorcerer lord, though you are only in your fifth year of studies."

"I study late, High Lord. I use my cousin's books. I am ahead of my classes. I did not think this would displease anyone, and I had hoped it would create in me a better tool for your army."

He nodded. "How many years ahead are you?" She hesitated, and he cut off her reply. "Do not humble your training; I want an honest reply."

She nodded, her forehead brushing against the black leather of his boot. "I have finished with the training for novice, intermediate, and advanced sorcery. Lacking the ability to train at a higher level because of my age, I have been borrowing books from the library to practice after class and weapons training. I have been doing this for over a year now, but I do not believe I am at the level of a master or a sorcerer lord." She sat back on her heels to look up at him, her hands still on the floor. "I did not hesitate because I intended to humble my training, High Lord, but because I do not know at what level I would be graded."

His smirk deepened; she had skill near-equal to what he had shown in his youth. He had risen to the rank of Master Sorcerer to the High Kingdom of Faiden by the age of seventeen. In many ways, he could see the same spark in her that had driven him. "Tell me the nature of your devotion to me. Is it out of fear, resignation, lust for power?"

She lowered her head to his boot once more. "You ask me again and I reply with the same simple and true answer, High Lord. I *only* wish to please you.

Whatever you do with all that I offer, I will gladly accept."

"What if the task I have for you is uncomfortable, dangerous, and potentially painful and fatal?"

She looked up, her eyes filling with hope. "You would assign me a task? You would personally address my duties? No matter what the danger, pain, or discomfort involved, I am overjoyed to hear you would take a moment of your time to—"

He waved off her hurried speech, but she merely took his hand and pressed his knuckles to her forehead, her voice thickening and her tone inviting. "Please, High Lord. Command me. I am not afraid. No task is too menial, too dangerous. Ask it of me." Her eyes lifted to his, and she rose to her knees, pulling his knuckles to the breastplate of her armor. Her neck craned, her eyes darkening with a woman's allure. "Ask of me whatever you wish. I am *yours*. I am *anything* you wish me to be."

He slid his hand from her grasp. "I hear something in your voice, captain. An eagerness that is unsettling. I am not capable of what you expect of me." Finally, he was beginning to understand her.

She threw herself down again. "Forgive me, High Lord! I expect nothing of you. I *only*—"

"Wish to please me," he finished for her. He strode away from her and faced the glow of the fire. This time, she remained where she knelt, not daring to lift her face again. "You cannot help it. I should try to remember that." He reminded himself that she, like every sorcerer and sorceress born since the fall of Faiden, was under the thrall of the Orb of Power that hung from a steel chain around his neck. The sentient, black globe hidden under his robes was whispering to him again. She was the one to send.

She was the one to trust. She was *the one*. "You made her for me, didn't you?" he quietly asked the Power. "I do not want her."

Though she undoubtedly heard his words, Vesakan did not stir from her prostrate posture. The dark lord faced her again. "I have a task for you, Commander Vesakan." She looked up, her gaze filling with hope. She had been forgiven of her presumptive offer. What's more, he had elevated her title. "I am placing you under High Commander Jellen. You are to report to him in the human territories of North Faiden."

She bowed again. "I shall do as you please, High Lord."

He nodded, satisfied with the somber acceptance of her new office. "Your task is quite simple. Be completely devoted to *all* of his wishes."

She slowly looked up, the impact of his orders not lost on her. Just a moment before, she had offered herself to him, and he was ordering her to shift her devotion to another. Though her eyes were shadowed with disappointment, she did not seem disgusted or offended. "I am yours to command, High Lord. I am eager to do your bidding."

"Good. Every night that you are able, you are to write a full report of what transpires around you. You are not to raise suspicion, but gain the trust of as many as you can. Jellen will never trust you, since you are appointed by me, but you are to garner as much information as to his actions and intentions as you can. Be wise. Separate suspicion from fact. You are to send me this report immediately upon completion."

Her lips turned up in a pleased smile. "I am to be your eyes and ears in the human territories. I am overjoyed, High Lord." She bowed to the floor. "I will *not* disappoint you."

Kimber Grey

End of Chapter 1

If you enjoyed this excerpt, *Kingdoms Lost* is only $0.99 no matter where you shop for ebooks!

About the Author

Kimber Grey was born in the arid and alien land known as southern California. She began consuming fiction at an early age, and has ever been eager to emulate the works that dramatically shaped her heart and mind as a child. She began creating short fiction and poetry in grade school, and she published her first stand-alone novel, *Seeking Destiny*, in 2012.

Her epic fantasy universe *Defying Chaos*, was introduced in 2017 with the first book of *Rise of Faiden: Kingdoms Lost*. There are now four books and two novellas that take place in that universe, with several more slated to come out in 2023 and 2024.

Her short fiction has appeared in anthologies such as: *Missing Pieces IV* (2013), *VI* (2014), and *VI* (2015); *The Hapless Cenloryan: The Troubadour's Inn, 2nd Edition* (2017); *Itty Bitty Writing Space* (2019); and *On Wings of Steam: Ears and Gears* (2023).

About the Bard

The Chosen One's Assistant was heavily inspired by Mikey Mason's Song: *(Not Quite)The Chosen One* from his album: *Dangerous Gifts*. Mikey is a brilliant wordsmith. I have been a big fan of his geek-rock music for many years, and this song is one of my all-time favorites. I am very grateful that he was kind enough to emphatically give his blessing when I said I wished to write this book.

You can listen to the song and/or album for free (or you could generously donate) on his BandCamp site:
MikeyMason.BandCamp.com

You can also visit his page and support his genius:
MikeyMason.com

Made in the USA
Monee, IL
23 July 2024